A RELIC
OF MAGIC &
FRANKINCENSE

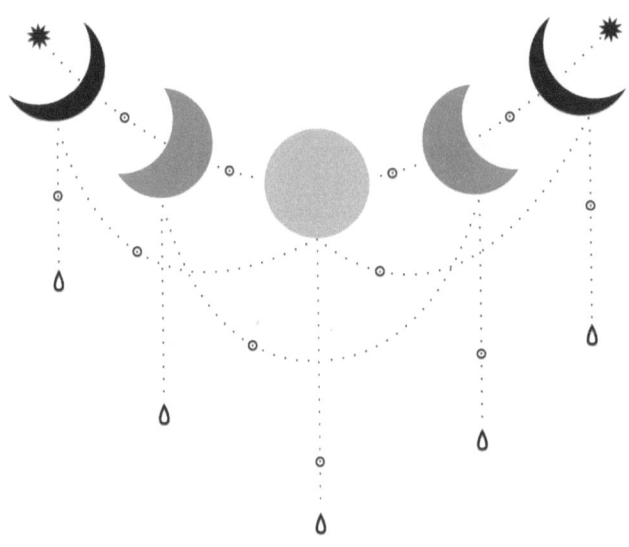

A RELIC OF MAGIC AND FRANKINCENSE

THREE GIFTS TRILOGY

RELICS AND LEGENDS
BOOK 3

HM HODGSON

Ebook ISBN: 978-0-6454516-5-8

Print ISBN: 978-0-6454516-6-5

Edited by Sarah Proulx Calfee, Three Little Words Editing https://threelittlewordsediting.com

Proofread by Jo Speirs, Nurturing Words

https://www.nurturingwords.com.au

Front cover design by Amanda Pillar from Smoking Hot Covers

https://www.smokinghotcovers.com

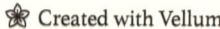 Created with Vellum

PROLOGUE

Three years ago

CYNANE ENTERED The National Archives building, gave her name and designation as a Templar Knight to the reception staff, and within minutes, a representative ushered her into a private reading room with soundproof walls, a round table and one chair. A pair of white gloves and a locked box with the key inserted sat in the middle of the table.

"Everything's set?" Cynane asked.

"Exactly as you requested."

"Excellent. Thank you for your help. I'll take it from here." She unbuttoned her suit jacket and sat down. Years and years of searching for R-104C had all led to this little box of documents. Hands steady, Cynane turned the key, donned the white gloves and lifted a vellum-bound book from the box.

The HMS *Vincere*'s capture log.

Her heart wanted to race, but she took an even breath and forced herself to remain calm as she opened the ledger to the date she was after.

These documents weren't on the archive website and had to be viewed in person after permission had been granted, which, of course, had occurred as soon as Cynane confirmed her Templar status.

So this was the moment of truth.

Please, let this be where she found the relic of frankincense. Where two hundred years of her family's shame at losing the relic ended. Where Cynane proved herself a Templar Knight, not a half-blood daemon.

Her stomach clenched, and she pressed her lips together to hold back the tremble that wanted to shake through her as anticipation warred with resolve.

She turned the browned, torn page. There in the corner: *Seventh day of May 1814.* The capture log for the French ship *Prospérité* and a record of everything confiscated.

Crew. Two civilian passengers. Food. Valuables. Non-valuables.

And ... one ceramic receptacle, symbols carved into the clay at four points, containing a small volume of fragrant resin.

"Mother of the gods," Cyn whispered. Her heart pumped this time—but how could it not? Finally, she had a lead worth tracing.

Six months ago

Fathom LA had to be the hottest new club for humans and otherworlders in the city's nightlife scene, and this close to Christmas, the queue to get in wrapped around the block.

But all Cyn cared about was that her three hired muscles were waiting where she'd instructed by the main entrance. They were an essential part of her undercover identity as a high priestess, helping perpetuate the mystique and rep she'd worked her ass off for months and months to build, not that they had a clue who Cyn really was.

She pulled her Rapid Red Metallic Mustang Shelby GT500 over to the curb, swung her leather-clad legs out of the low door, then rose to her feet in one long move.

She gestured for the valet and stared at him as she held her keys out. "Do you know what I am?" His gaze flicked to her forehead, and he nodded. "Good, then know this—treat my baby like the most precious thing in your life, and you'll be well rewarded. Hurt her, and you'll have my nastiest curse to deal with."

The valet swallowed hard and nodded fast. Perfect.

But before Cyn had even turned around, several people milling around the door rushed at her, and she threw her hands up and stared them all in the eye. "Back up." She jerked her chin at the hired muscle, and they slipped into place. This was another reason why she paid their asses a decent wage when she was out in public—especially when she was here for actual business and didn't have time to fight off continuous requests for her services.

Either they knew her rep, or they'd overheard her warning to the valet, but the security at the entry had the front doors open before she could break her stride—just as well, since she had multiple places to be tonight, and this stop hadn't been on the original schedule.

Something in the air, a low-level electric hum on the threshold of being audible, made her belly warm and had her stop. Turn around.

A sea of dancing bodies stretched across the ground

floor, and the hum seemed to come from right in the center. She headed up several steps for a better view. Across the dark club, lights pulsed to the beat of the music, and in one strobe of neon blue, a figure stood out on the other side of the dance floor. Women surrounded him, though he seemed ... detached from them.

Well over six foot, black pants and shirt, a powerful build, and a stance that screamed those muscles would be used to deadly effect.

A firm jaw that shouted he'd be stubborn-assed. A straight, high-bridged imperial nose. Shoulder-length reddish-brown hair, the top half tied back into a knot at the back of his head, much like her own. A devilish pair of eyes —not that she could make out their color—but filled with a gleam that screamed of all the delicious things he'd do to you. With you. And finally, a sinfully curved mouth that backed up that promise.

Focus on the job, Cyn. There was only one reason she was even at the club tonight—and that didn't include hot-as-Hades males.

But tension continued to gather in her belly, and those knots only tightened further as she made her way around the club—refusing to look back at the unknown male—until finally, she spied Grayson at the back of the ground floor.

Then the crowd shifted, revealing two others at his table. A stunning young woman and the male she'd spotted when she'd entered. She had to fight herself just to keep her gaze on Grayson and not the sexy AF ... daemon. Holy shit. *He was a daemon.*

She almost froze; only her training had her fake a calm expression. Was that why she'd reacted to him so strongly before?

Grayson introduced her to the female, Isadora.

And then the daemon introduced himself. "Rohan."

His cognac voice sent a shiver up her neck, made her nipples pebble. His green eyes—brilliant like peridots—traveled over her from head to toe, screaming *you and me: a fucking feast.*

Now that was someone she'd like to get to know more. But damn it, this level of attraction—distraction—had zero place on the cards for Cyn tonight or any other. She shot him her most scathing look and made sure he knew this high priestess was off the menu.

Cyn was on the job, and that was all that mattered.

1

Today

RAIN STRIKING the cobbled streets muffled Rohan's steps as he trailed his prey through the night all the way to the Tenth Gate. Not that the chinterra's growling-snorting-howling made the hellbeast hard to follow.

With the ease of too much practice in the last six months, Rohan slid his hellblades free from their leather scabbards.

The chinterra clawed its way up the stone steps, razor-studded tails lashing the columns lining the walkway.

Rohan paused in the shadows. Where the gods damned hell was Lord Deimus? Shit. No time to wait for the gate lord to make an appearance. "Stop, chinterra." Rohan stepped into the moonlight. "You know the rules."

The hellbeast spun and roared. Vile acidic spittle flew and splattered down Rohan's shirt.

"Really? You had to slime me?"

The beast clicked and smashed its tail into the ground.

"Don't frigging laugh. And damn but that stings. Last

warning. If you pass through, you know the outcome—which neither of us wants. So come on back like a good hellbeast and go find your dinner Hellside."

More snarls and spits.

"Well, fuck you right back." Rohan spun the blades. *Don't pass. Don't pass ...*

The chinterra lunged beneath the arched column. Disappeared.

Oh hell.

Rohan ran up the steps and lunged through the hellgate, landing on his feet in the sparse grass of North America. Dry, crisp night air infused his lungs. Stars lit up the sky as they did back home. An animal cry echoed into the night, followed by crunching and snarling. Rohan's night vision kicked in and he ran for the sound.

Fly swiftly, blade. He sent one weapon spinning through the air.

The next sound to echo through the scrub was a grunt. A sigh. Then nothing.

By the time Rohan reached the body, the chinterra had perished—one nick from the hellblade equaled instant death.

Rohan said a fast blessing for the creature's soul, then hefted the chinterra around his shoulders and strode back through the gate—and ran into Lord Deimus.

"Rohan the Red," he yelped as Rohan placed the chinterra at his feet. "What are you—?"

"Stopping a hellbeast venturing into downtown LA." He rose to his feet. "Where the gods were you?"

"Raising the alarm. I tried to stop it, but an upper beast got past me and through the gate—"

"Wait." Rohan grabbed the lord's arm. "You're not talking about the chinterra?"

"That lowlands beast? Nay. The beast that crossed was a trichorn—full battle armor."

Rohan's gut clenched. An upper hellbeast in LA. How fucking bad could this get?

-(((●)))-

Summer fireworks lit up the city skyline far off in the distance, and the partygoers filling the sweeping pool deck of the LA Hills mansion chugged back batshit-ass expensive bubbly wine as they oohed and aahed.

Except one. Cyn had eyes only for her target: Simion Seros—aka the Love Whisperer—currently holding court from a daybed covered in huge sorbet-colored cushions.

Cyn forced a smile for the millionth sycophant to leave with a kiss on Simion's feet. Ugh. Really? This lead better pan out. No way was she hanging out with a throng of love-obsessed fools for any other reason.

"Priestess," Simion cooed after the fireworks had ended. "Join me. The view of the city from here is truly breathtaking."

"It's some place you have," she murmured as she sank down as smoothly as her skintight leather pants would allow. "Thanks for tonight's invitation."

"How could I not have our city's most powerful high priestess grace my little soiree?" Simion clinked his crystal flute against her highball. "And I have to say, I'm intrigued. I'm familiar with finding love for those seeking the genuine attachment that marks two souls as being entwined on a cosmic plane that no force in the world or other can tear apart. However, your reputation had me thinking surely you could find love ... even by magic ... yourself?"

"Ah, but that wouldn't be, how did you put it? A 'soul marked as entwined with mine that no force—not even one of my potions, presumably—can rip apart.'"

"True, my dear. Very true." Simion reclined on the daybed and sighed. "I should warn you, I'm awfully select with my clients. Finding your soul mate is not a simple matter. I take it you've never been in love before?"

"Love?" Cyn barely kept her lip from curling. "No. Never."

"Well, what about desire?"

A face flashed through her mind. Reddish-brown hair half pulled back into a man bun. A square, hard jaw. Aquamarine eyes. Lips tilted in a promise of fun, heat, and danger —no. No, no, no.

Not. Him.

She shoved the image away.

"Ah, I saw that look. So, lust, then?"

"Of course. I'm a living, breathing human." Half, anyway. And physical attraction was far more manageable—safe— than any emotional ties.

"Well, desire is an important element of your love match."

"Really?" She forced the dryness out of her voice.

"Of course, I find you extremely desirable. But then ... I find all my clients utterly delicious."

"And they you, by the look of it." Cyn glanced around the curved pool deck. Not even the breathtaking view held the attention of the partygoers—they continually cast glances back at Simion. Not surprising given the sexy, lush, bohemian vibe the male gave off.

"Well, there's no harm in enjoying ourselves while we look for love, is there?"

Cyn laughed and raised her glass again. "I like your style, Love Whisperer."

"Please, call me Simion."

"Simion."

"Might I inquire to what we should call you? Is it by your title—High Priestess?"

"For you, I'll allow my name. Call me Cynane, or Cyn."

"Sin-ane?" Simion blinked, as most people did when she gave them her name. "Cyn?"

"Spelt with a C. Although I have to say I'm okay with the latter too."

"Oh, me too. Me too," Simion said with a laugh.

She peered at the likable love whisperer over the rim of her drink. But she was here on a mission, not to make friends.

"Now, dearest one," Simion said, "may I introduce you to my assistants? You would've heard from them by email, I imagine, for the party invite. This is Aleesha and Sonja." Two stunning women with gorgeous dark skin emerged from the partygoers. "They are the most wonderfully efficient assistants and run pretty much everything for me; however, they don't speak, so be prepared to be bombarded by emails. Now, Aleesha, Sonja, meet Cynane; she'll be our newest client, I daresay."

The women's gazes locked on Cyn, and for a moment, the hairs on the back of her neck prickled; then, they nodded in unison at Simion and melted back into the party.

What had that been about? And wow, they really didn't speak? "Well, have to say I wasn't expecting your assistants to be so stunning. But if they want to correspond by email, fine by me." Cyn raised her glass in a mock toast. "So—"

A crash thundered from behind the house. Cyn stilled. That hadn't sounded good. Another crash. Steel screeching ... Someone screamed. Oh shit. Definitely not good.

"Think someone's at your front door." Cyn stood up and pressed her weight onto the balls of her feet, ready to move in any direction.

"Party crashers?" Simion frowned, and as he turned, his assistants again stepped through the crowd to his side. "Are we expecting more guests?"

Another scream echoed through the mansion, and partygoers ran out onto the pool deck shrieking, some already cut, bleeding and holding injured limbs.

"Don't think that's a guest." Cyn hauled Simion to his feet as she mentally reviewed the building and property plans from her research. "Get everyone down to your basement—the concrete bunker you use as a wine cellar. Now."

"Wait—what are you doing?"

"I'm a high priestess, remember. I'm going to explain the party's over to whoever—whatever—is smashing through your mansion right now." Simion blinked at her, and his mouth dropped open, but then more of his guests came out screaming and crying. "Go. They'll follow you. Get them to safety, and yourself."

Cyn shoved Simion and his assistants toward the end of the deck. She hadn't spent years working on this invitation, only to lose the lead on her relic if Simion got killed.

As soon as the pool deck was empty, Cyn took out the pin holding her hair up and raced into the mansion.

More crashing and smashing ... and ... cussing?

Cyn rounded the corner into the central living area, where a huge crystal chandelier hung from the soaring ceiling, and skidded to a stop.

What. The. Hell?

She saw a giant creature, easily eight feet tall, with three eyes and three rows of tusks running from its T. rex-like mouth. It had four legs and a huge rounded back covered in some kind of armor ... like a dinosaur, a warthog and the biggest frigging armadillo imaginable had all somehow genetically combined to make the scariest motherfucking thing Cyn had ever seen.

Who needed action movies when you had this?

Then a bare-chested figure leaped onto its back and struck two double-ended blades into its armor.

Cyn's breath stalled. Those were hellblades. *Two* hell-blades. Right here in LA Hills.

"Just die already!" the figure yelled. He drew the blades back and shoved them in again. "Fucking armor-plated bastard."

Holy mother of the gods. That cognac voice. Not even six months had erased just how delicious he sounded.

Rohan.

Warmth pooled low in Cyn's belly, and her heart went kerchunk in her chest.

Then the creature threw its massive head up and those batshit-ass tusks tangled in the chandelier. Glass shattered. Marble smashed. It thrashed, and the entire light fixture and a massive chunk of ceiling crashed down on Rohan, making him disappear beneath the rubble. "Bloody hell!"

Oh shit.

Cyn pricked the point of the hairpin into her thumb until blood welled, then closed her fist and yelled a stun spell.

She ran for the creature and unleashed the magic directly into its face. But at the last moment, it swiveled on its hind legs, way faster than such an enormous animal should be able to move, and her spell hit its armored shoulder.

Come on, work, baby, work ... She held her breath.

But the damn thing kept thrashing, its tusks still tangled in the remnants of the chandelier. More glass shattered beneath its massive feet.

Then its middle eye locked on her, and it screamed a high-pitched bellow. Cyn jammed her hands over her ears. What the hell was this animal? And where was Rohan? Had he been pancaked? Her stomach tightened, and an unwelcome icy jolt of emotion struck her chest, but she shoved that aside.

Crap, *now* she wished she had her Templar weapons. Seriously, being undercover was a bitch when you couldn't bring your firearms—except what would even work on this thing? It wasn't like she could carry an RPG in her purse.

But no, Cyn didn't need her tech. She had her magic. Stronger stun spell time.

And then Rohan erupted from the pile of rubble. Blood smeared over his forehead and down his chest, but he had all his limbs, and the light of battle was visible in his eyes, so guess he was okay.

And that was *not* relief unclenching the knots in her belly.

He took off for the creature; then, as if he sensed her, Rohan's gaze swiveled from the beast to Cyn. His eyes widened; his mouth dropped open.

The thing bellowed again and stamped its front feet, looking for all the world like it was going to charge her.

Adrenaline slicked through Cyn, and she steadied her feet. This time she *would* land her stun spell.

"Get back," Rohan yelled. "You don't know what you're dealing with."

"No, you get back, motherfucker," Cyn yelled just as loud. "I know exactly what the fuck I'm doing."

"Think you can dial back the fucks there, Priestess."

"It's *High* Priestess. And why? I'm totally cool with my profanity, fuck you very much. Now don't get in my way. I'm going to stun this motherfucker."

But Rohan took off, and then, with another of those batshit-ass leaps, he jumped onto the creature's back and once more tried to penetrate the armor with his blade.

Crap. The way the thing bucked and swiveled, she was just as likely to stun Rohan from this distance.

"How's the bareback bronco thing going for you?" Cyn called out as she darted behind the beast. At least it seemed more focused on getting rid of Rohan than worrying about her.

"It. Would be. Easier," Rohan said between buckings and swivels, "if this damned armored tank didn't. Fucking. Move so much. And hello, by the way. Always knew I'd run into you again."

"Personally, I'd prefer we hadn't, not if these were going to be the circumstances."

"Come on, you don't mean that." The thing reared up on its hind legs. "Seriously? Just frigging stop moving."

"Ooh, does that mean you'd like my help?" Cyn took up position close to the creature's back. And her nose watered. Ugh. Stinky thing.

"What, like you can take it on?"

"I could do a damn better job than you right now."

"One last ... try. Going to climb its neck. Need to get. Skin."

Cyn rolled her eyes but readied her spell. *Come on, you armadillo-rex-hog, just stay the fuck still.*

On its back, Rohan jammed a blade into one of the

armored plates and used it to draw himself up the neck. Then it gave a colossal shake of its head. The rest of the chandelier flew free, smashing into the far wall. Glass and marble smashed. And Rohan went flying at Cyn, one blade still stuck in the armor, the other in his hand.

Oh shit. Deadly hellblade—as in the only blade in the universe that could sever body and soul with a single cut to anywhere on the body—flying through the air.

Cyn tensed, readied herself to jump, but somehow Rohan kept the blade in his grip while he did a flip midair and landed on his feet in a way-too-graceful move.

"Fine. Let's give your way a go," he said as if they weren't facing the asshole of the scariest thing Cyn had ever seen. "What spells have you got?"

"Gee, thanks. Crap, the thing—whatever the hell it is—is going outside." No way was she letting it anywhere near where her best lead in over a year was currently hiding out in the wine-cellar-slash-bunker.

"Trichorn. Upper hellbeast. And my blades can't pierce its armor."

"The armor must be protecting it against my spells too. Where is it vulnerable?"

"Eyes, mouth and nostrils if you can get past the tusks. It's deaf, but its other senses are super heightened."

"Got it. I can knock it out if I can get close enough." She flicked the clasp of the ruby ring on her middle finger open and twisted the band so the inside compartment faced her palm, then she splayed her hand wide and held it away from the daemon. "Can you dispatch it, then?"

"Work together?"

"Don't make me take you down too." She waggled her hand.

"Like you could. Won't your knockout juice take you down as well, though?"

"I created it—I'm immune, but you can't get close; otherwise, you'll be out flat. And I don't fancy dealing with your stunned ass."

"Wow, I'm touched."

"By yourself, undoubtedly." Cyn eyed Rohan's massive chest, sweat gleaming along the ridged muscles. Her mouth went dry.

"Wouldn't you like to know?" Rohan smirked.

"No, no, I wouldn't." *Liar. Shit, stop!* She shut her inner voice up with a mental slap and took off, calling over her shoulder, "Are you coming or not?"

Cyn sensed rather than saw Rohan as he tracked her around the trichorn. And there was no question when it saw them—the trichorn did another of those squealing bellows.

"We'll do it together. It's searching for food, so if it thinks you're injured, it'll come straight at you. Let's get its attention. Let's both act wounded, and then you can have a go at it when it comes for us."

"All right, you son of a bitch, this way now." Cyn backtracked into the mansion. "Are you hungry, hellbeast?"

"It's deaf, remember?"

"Why are you grinning like that?"

"Because I like your scowl. I haven't felt this alive in forever."

"Then welcome to the land of the living because it's time to stop your hellbeast. Ready?"

"Ready." Rohan twirled the hell-blade in his grip. "And whatever happens, do not touch this blade. Or the other one when I get it out of the tricorn's back."

"You're freaking batshit to have one—two—of those

things here. But we'll deal with that later. Right now, let's get its attention."

Cyn ran for the hellbeast, then pretended to fall over and let out a loud cry. Rohan joined her and did the crappiest job ever of falling over and groaning too.

"You're overexaggerating," Cyn said.

"Don't knock it. The trichorn's taken the bait. Keep it up."

"Where are you going?"

"I'm going to flank it—just in case. Keep pretending to be injured—or better yet, dead. She'll love an easy meal."

"I told you I've got this." But Cyn went with his idea and played dead as the hellbeast came at her. And sure enough, it stopped its run and instead, nudged her leg with its tusks.

Mother of the gods, please don't be too hungry.

With her heart thudding so hard, surely even a deaf hellbeast could hear the beats, Cyn took a deep breath and forced back the urge to leap up and jab a knife or a gun into its side. Come on ... come on ... just a little closer—

Yes!

She slapped the thing in the mouth with her open hand.

2

Amid the wrecked once-luxe living room of the love whisperer's mansion, the stunned hellbeast made one hell of a party guest. Exhilaration bubbled through Cyn's veins—more intoxicating than the finest champagne.

Now that had been magic! For all her high priestess spell work, she'd never stunned such a massive living being before. How much further could she push her power? Except no. No, no, no. She wasn't here to test her power. She was a Templar Knight, vowed to protect dangerous supernatural objects and keep them from falling into the hands of anyone wishing to harm in the human world—embracing her daemon and witchcraft heritage *only* so she could find R-104C.

Cyn snapped the ruby back into place on top of her ring, resecured her hair with the hairpin, and smirked at Rohan. "Told you I had it. Now, dispatch the hellbeast, and we can get rid of the body."

"You're a bloodthirsty one, aren't you? And I don't want to kill her unless I absolutely have to."

"Her? And hold on. It—she—was going to chomp me."

"Not her fault. She's just doing what trichorns do. Whoever—"

"Whoever let the hellbeast through the Tenth Gate? Surely the Lord of the Tenth Gate wouldn't have done that knowingly."

"Uh, yeah. That too." Rohan scratched his ear and then turned back to the hellbeast.

Cyn stilled. Something was not on the up and up here. But what?

"I just have to get her back to the hellgate."

"Let me make a call," she finally said. "I know someone who might help."

"Is it the Templar from six months ago? Grayson, right? Do you see him often?"

"Yes, it's him. And no, I don't see him often."

"So I never found out how you know the Templar and Isadora?" Rohan said.

"I'm a high priestess." Cyn gave a cool shrug. "I know people. Now, how about you go make sure there aren't any more ... hellbeasts ... heading our way while I make this call?"

"Of course, Your Majesty. I'll check the grounds." Rohan sketched a mock bow.

"*High Priestess.*"

As soon as the daemon disappeared, Cyn grabbed her cell. Time to organize a priority pickup for a freaking hellbeast.

"Hey," she said as soon as Marcella, the US ops 2IC, picked up. Cyn gave a concise report of the situation, then added, "Make sure no one connects me to the Templars coming up, though. I'm getting closer, I can feel it, and I don't want to blow my cover now."

"Will do. And heads up—the council are getting angsty

about the frankincense. They're calling like every other day for updates."

"The council or my mother?"

"Both, chica. And man, she scares me. She said something about visiting for an in-person progress report."

Great. All Cyn needed. "Just don't let her bully you. You can confirm I've gotten close to the love whisperer, remain confident this lead is worth pursuing, and there is no need to come here and blow my cover."

She'd barely hung up her cell when Simion appeared at the end of the pool deck. His eyes widened.

"What's that?" He gazed at her with awe. "Did you—did you take that down?"

"She had some help," Rohan's voice slid out from the night just before he appeared from the shadows at the other end of the deck. All those delicious chest and ab muscles gleaming with sweat and blood. Huh. How had he got there so fast?

"Oh really?" Cyn rolled her eyes, which helped break her gaze from the magnificence of the daemon's chest. How could a man covered in blood be so freaking hot? She darted another glance at him. Yep. Abso-fucking-delicious.

Her body warmed, and she almost squirmed in her leather pants. Clearly she hadn't banged anyone in too long if she was getting turned on at a time like this.

Rohan's nostrils flared, then his pupils dilated before he smiled and threw an arm around her shoulders.

"Oh, gross. You're covered in ... guck. Get away from me," Cyn said.

"Don't be like that. I thought we made a good team. You acting all 'oh no, I'm going to die, hellbeast.'"

"And then I took it down. Which is better than I can say for you and your 'me tough guy, me jump on back and get pancaked' attempts." Cyn gave Rohan her most scathing look.

"Well, hello," Simion purred. "Cyn, dearest one, aren't you going to introduce me to your friend?"

"He's not my friend." She turned to find Simion looking Rohan up and down. Appreciation gleamed in Simion's expression, and Cyn didn't bother to hide her eye roll. So what if the guy—daemon—had a hot body? And face. And sinful lips. And gorgeous eyes she wanted to bask in. Or that he made her blood boil and her core drench?

Oh hell. What if he did that to everyone? Just who, by the mother of the gods, was Rohan?

Cyn said, "Simion Seros, Rohan. Rohan, meet Simion, the love whisperer. Now, as fun as this party has been—"

"Hi. Great place you've got." Rohan smiled at Simion for one second before turning back to Cyn. "Listen, I have to get this thing—" He whirled back to Simion. "Do I know you?"

"Not yet—I think, anyway. But I'm more than happy to change that. And please, call me Simion."

Cyn sighed and stepped between the two men. "Okay, okay, let's focus on the giant"—shit, what had Rohan called it?—"*animal* currently knocked out on the pool deck. Simion, you're remarkably chilled about this, so I'm guessing you have some experience with things out of the ordinary—way out of the ordinary. But your guests may not. Keep them from coming up here. And if anyone asks, say a bear wandered in—"

"A bear?" Rohan choked on a laugh. "No one's going to believe that."

"After the alcohol everyone's had here tonight, no one'll bat an eyelid. Now, Simion, please see to your guests. No one is to come up here. I repeat—no one."

"You're rather bossy for a high priestess," Rohan interjected.

"And you're rather annoying for a—oh wait, what are you exactly?"

"Right now," Simion said, "he's a rather wonderfully bare-chested hero who's come to save us all." He cocked one eyebrow while clearly still enjoying the view of Rohan's chest.

"Thank you, Simion," Cyn said, "very helpful. Now—your guests?" She made a firm shooing gesture and couldn't stop shaking her head as he left with another glance at Rohan.

"Do they even have bears in LA?" Rohan scratched his jaw. "Coyotes, maybe the rare mountain lion, but—"

"Technically, yes, though they live in the Angeles National Forest, and fine, they're black bears and not grizzlies, but that's all I've got unless you have a better idea?"

"I take it the truth is out of the question?" Rohan asked.

"Get real." She didn't even bother rolling her eyes at him. "Now, I've got a pickup crew coming, but my knockout juice will wear off in"—she checked the time—"thirty minutes, max. And that's a true guess since I've never knocked out a—what did you call it again?"

"Trichorn."

"There you go, never even heard of them."

Rohan scowled, all humor vanishing from his expression. "What? But you're a daemon. How have you never heard—?"

"Half. I haven't crossed."

"Still, your parents should've ensured you had some Hellside knowledge."

"Nope." Thanks, Dad. But no—that wasn't even right. All of Cyn's focus had been in one direction. The blame for her poor daemon knowledge wasn't one-sided. "Anyhow, I'm going to see if I can help any of the injured downstairs. You wait here for the pickup crew. They won't be far away."

"I'll have to go with them and arrange my end of transporting the trichorn across."

"Fine. You do that." And that was not disappointment curdling in her belly.

"Hey, Priestess?"

"What?" She whirled back around.

"Snappy. I like it. Come here—you've got something—"

Rohan reached out and, with his thumb, wiped something back from her forehead. This close, his warm scent made her belly hum, and when his eyes dipped to her mouth and his nostrils flared, that hum dropped lower still.

And for all the night's drama, even the fact she had close to zero energy left for any more magic, one part of her was wide awake and zinging.

He stepped closer, his body heat washed over her. She could step back, except she didn't retreat for anyone. And more than that, she didn't want to.

Cyn shifted forward, and the hot appreciation in his gaze sent a thrill through her.

"High Priestess," he murmured in that cognac voice. "You're out of this world. Want to finish the night off with a real bang?"

After a night like tonight? Yes. Yes, she did.

She lifted onto her toes—damn, he was tall—and snaked one arm around his neck. "As long as you're not a dud."

A devilish smile spread over his lips. "Let's see." He fitted her to his frame—miles of hot, hard muscle met her body, and then his mouth was on hers.

He devoured her. Heat and spice and an exotic energy

punched through her as his tongue surged into her mouth. Her nipples tightened. Her belly heated.

Fuck, she needed to get closer. She wrapped one leg around his hip, pinned him to her and got the hard length of his dick right where she needed him. A growl vibrated through his chest, and he grabbed her ass, pulling her even tighter as he continued that assault on her mouth.

Shaping, owning, consuming.

And as *right* as a key sliding home in a lock.

She wanted more. Right now. She fumbled for his pants—

Shit. Shit, shit, *shit*. That was too hot for a kiss. Too hot for anything. Cyn dropped her leg and wrenched herself out of his hold.

Even in the night, his eyes glowed, and his chest rose sharply with each breath as he stared at her.

"You taste like ambrosia," Rohan whispered.

"And you taste of blood and sweat. Icky, you know," she lied through her teeth. "I've changed my mind about that bang—think I've had enough crashes for one night."

"Tell yourself that all you want, High Priestess." Rohan's lips quirked and something too knowing, followed by the deepest longing she'd ever seen, entered his eyes. Her chest constricted, and she almost swayed into him—but *he* backed away. "See you round."

"Not if I see you first." Cyn didn't need that kind of distraction now—or ever. She strode across the pool deck. This time she didn't look back.

-‹‹‹●›››-

The skyline above LA was turning indigo when the last ambulance pulled away from Simion's mansion, and Cyn dropped onto the daybed. The sorbet scatter cushions were long gone, but her legs were so tired she needed to sit or risked falling.

"High Priestess." Simion shuffled to stand in front of her.

"You look as tired as I feel," Cyn muttered. "Here." She slid over to make room for him.

"Thank you for providing medical assistance to my guests tonight. Your spells have done wonders."

"They worked well to help make people more comfortable and at least stabilize the worst of the injured until the paramedics got here."

"And how are you after everything?" Simion asked.

"Well, the adrenaline has well and truly worn off now."

"You do look ... tired."

"Not surprising. Making magic takes energy. And that many spells, over and over, has me depleted. Do you know how high priestesses create their power?"

"I know it's different to other witches."

"Because I'm half daemon *and* a witch, I extract power from sacrifice—mine or others." She watched for how he'd react—but like with the hellbeasts, Simion barely blinked.

"Well, I'm indebted to you. In fact, I'm going to take on your case for love as a priority."

Yes! She was in. But she kept up her cool expression. "And I would love to take you up on your offer." Anticipation zinged through her. Finally, the last eighteen months of work was paying off.

"Excellent," Simion said. "Now, you never said if you were looking for a man or a woman for your love match."

"I don't have a preference either way—love is love."

"Well, we agree there. However, I should tell you I think I've already found them—your soul mate."

"What?" Maybe Cyn was more tired than she realized. "Say that again? You've already found them?"

"Perhaps, perhaps not. I'm very good at my job, and I've had a fair bit of experience with love, and something tells me that your bare-chested hero might be the soul mate you're searching for."

Cyn choked on a cough, then waved Simion's hands away when he tried to help. "I'm okay. I'm okay. Uh, no, Simion, think you've got that one wrong."

"Well, I did only just meet you both, so that's a possibility. But there was something between you two ..."

"Contempt? Distaste? Antipathy?" *Liar,* her inner voice piped up.

"Desire. Attraction. Connection," Simion added.

"Anyway, he's not from around here. So, I think we should look in another direction."

"Oh? Didn't you say love is love? What challenge can distance be against two souls where—"

"Let's just say I like my lovers less rash and cocky."

"Well, we shall certainly find out. However, I have another client I'm working with right now, and as I promise to give each client my entire attention, I'll take you on once my current love mission is complete."

Love mission? Cyn restrained an eye roll—she needed to convince Simion she was here for love, so showing any contempt for the freaking useless emotion was out of the question.

"Perfect. I'll be here when you're ready." She forced her lips into a smile. Damn it, Simion better be good at finding love fast—she was close. She could feel it.

3

THE FOLLOWING MORNING, Rohan stood on the agate steps of the Tenth Gate of Hell and withdrew his blades from the natcha attempting to pass humanside. Yet another hellbeast dead on the steps of a hellgate.

Frigging hell. How many more had to perish like this? Anger revved through him, and when scrapes echoed on the steps, he regripped his weapons and whirled around—

"Rohan the Red, you're injured." Lord Deimus staggered up the steps, followed by three of his soldiers—blood trailing in his wake.

"Just a scratch. You, too." He nodded at the lord's leg. "Nasty. Hopefully, it heals before the next attack."

"Hell. How many more are there?"

"Well, one less now the natcha's dead."

"Don't sound so sad. If you keep returning them to their lands, they'll keep coming back."

"I know. But they're not responsible. They're acting on instinct and following the scent of easy prey."

"Are humans really that easy to kill?"

"Yes." Most, anyway. A vision of a certain high

priestess flashed through his mind. And even though exhaustion dragged at his blood-covered limbs, a surge of energy followed, like it did every time he thought of Cyn, which had been way too often in the past six hours. Hell, since he'd first met her at the club in LA all those months ago.

The air within the gate shimmered, and Rohan stiffened —what now?—before a familiar figure stepped through. His uncle, the High Lord of Hell, stood before him. He was perfect and ageless.

"Uncle." Rohan dropped to one knee.

"High Lord." Lord Deimus did the same.

His uncle nodded at them before staring at the natcha. "I'm sorry you had to kill it, Rohan."

"Same here. And for the hundred other hellbeasts that have tried to pass in the last six months. Did you hear about the trichorn last night?"

"Yes." His uncle sighed. "Did it cause any fatalities humanside?"

"No—luckily, a smooth operator of a high priestess wrangled it."

His uncle looked thoughtful for a moment. "That's some high priestess."

Tell him about it. But Rohan just nodded and addressed the actual issue. "I need to find that hellgate key, but I'm too busy here fending off hellbeasts to have time to search humanside."

"That's why I'm here. We have an ... additional issue."

"What now?"

"The scholars in Hell City have advised that if the key isn't returned by the close of the next solstice humanside, then the Tenth Gate will be forever open. Nothing will reengage the lock on this gate."

Rohan's gut sank. "An endless array of hellbeasts drawn to the humanside. And solstice is in ..."

"Eleven days."

"If I go, Lord Deimus will have to hold the gate alone."

His uncle turned to Lord Deimus. "How many guards have you lost in the last six months?"

"Easily two score. It'd be a lot more if Rohan hadn't been here with his hellblades."

"That's what I thought. So I'm sending you one other who has the honor of dual hellblades."

"Wait, you're talking about your Master of the Magic? But that means his role will be unattended ..."

"I'll take over his duties while he stays here. This must be done, Rohan. He'll arrive within the next three days—he's on a ... mission for me right now. As soon as he returns, he'll help guard the gate. Lord Deimus, I need a moment with Rohan."

Once Lord Deimus had bowed and joined his men at the bottom of the steps, Uncle gestured for Rohan to come closer.

"You *must* find the key. However, I have a starting place for your search. Your cousin Nicasia has divined for the key's location multiple times, but while she cannot find the key, she sees a high priestess who wears her mark—"

Rohan's gut tightened. "Let me guess. In the middle of her forehead?"

"The one who helped with the trichorn, then?"

"Yes."

"Then you're already on the right path to find the key," Uncle said. "It's nice to get good news."

"But if the key isn't visible when divined for, does that mean it's shrouded?"

"Perhaps. The truth is, we don't know. But if your cousin

can't divine the key's location, then it's taken someone with a lot of power to hide it."

"Shit. Why would someone risk opening a permanent gate from Hell to Earth?" Rohan said.

"Good question."

"Do you think it's Lord Forneous?"

"I don't know. It could be, but while one open gate is bad for the humans, we both know your sire has a thirst for power greater than that."

"That's a worry. Okay, I'll find the high priestess and stick with her until I find the key. And thank you for the opportunity to do something worthwhile instead of sitting behind the thirteenth gates."

"Well, with your sire ... occupied by other matters, the time was right to provide you with a purpose before he could say no. I would do more than that if I could."

"You've already made a difference. Believe me. Giving me the role with the hellgates, getting Forneous to cede control over me to you, I don't have words to describe how grateful I am."

"I'm sorry I could not get you away from him sooner." His uncle's jaw tightened, and the fires of hell blazed in his gaze momentarily. "Good luck, Rohan the Red. I think you —and we all—are going to need it."

As his uncle departed, Rohan stared at the gates until the air no longer shimmered. He might not know everything that was coming—and that was one gift he was grateful he didn't have—but the immediate future was clear. Rohan was going to find the high priestess who'd made his heart slam in his chest from the moment he'd first seen her six months ago and then set him on fire with her kiss only hours ago.

Anticipation zinged through him.

But wariness dampened the sensation. Attraction was

one thing—and hell, he'd have to be dead not to be
attracted to the high priestess—but emotional attachment
was a no-go. At least the high priestess was the total opposite of the halfling he'd fallen for in his youth, so there was
zero chance that would ever happen again.

-‹‹●››-

Three evenings later, Rohan once more passed through the
Tenth Gate of Hell into the human world and hefted his
satchel over his shoulder.

LA was into full night mode with humans, witches and
otherworlders roaming the streets. Restaurants full. Bars
crowded. Traffic everywhere.

Not too unlike Hellside. Except the transport and buildings—mostly—in that realm were straight out of the human
Middle Ages or earlier.

Rohan rolled the sleeve on his right arm high enough to
show the intricately scrolled, interlinked chevron tattoos of
his gate markers inked into the skin from his wrist to his
shoulder.

Several groups of humans tried to get him to join their
revelry, but he bypassed each offer. One goal. One focus.
The hellgate key.

And it wasn't long before an otherworlder spotted his
gate marker tattoos, and he had an address for the high
priestess.

Thirty minutes later, he'd made his way to a red door
halfway down an alleyway similar to other little avenues
he'd passed in the city—bars, people, trash here and there
—except for the pavement right here.

His heart picked up. This had to be it. Although there was no buzzer. No intercom. No window. No obvious sign of surveillance. So Rohan knocked, and a low-level electric buzz raced up the back of his neck. Magic.

And then the door clicked like an internal lock had released. Guess someone knew he was here. With his heart beating faster and faster, he entered a pitch-black corridor that led on forever, so dark only his enhanced vision let him make out the walls and floor, except for the frigging neon-red glowing cow skull at the end. That he could see just fine.

As Rohan eased toward the end of the corridor, more buzzing passed over his skin. Just how many magic wards were in place here? Although none were set to stun, given he was still walking.

"Well, hello," the high priestess purred from beside the skull. Goosebumps raced up Rohan's arms and neck, and his damned loco cock decided to pay attention. Really? At her voice? Why did he respond like this around her every single time?

"Hello to you, too." Thank fuck for small wins; his voice hadn't cracked—just as frigging well, because acting like a lovesick youth wasn't the playbook here. In fact, scratch any link of love and this warrior of a woman from the outset.

And then she stepped forward, and the red glow of the skull picked up her face.

His breath stuck in his chest. Exquisite. No other word for it. Not conventionally beautiful by human standards—her chin was strong. Her cheekbones angular. Her direct eyes tipping up at the end, framed by ridiculously long lashes. Wickedly arched brows. And every bit as stunning as she'd been every time he'd seen her.

Hell, stunning wasn't even right.

The high priestess was a star blazing, and he was a planet trapped in her orbit.

And he didn't even know her name.

"Interesting entry," he murmured. *Get it together, Rohan. Get it together. Eight days till solstice.*

"I like it dramatic."

"It suits you."

"Well, now that you've flattered me," she said, "to what do I owe the honor of your presence? And how did you find me?"

"Well, we did have a rather nice visit last time we met." *Nice? That kiss had rocked his world.*

"Visit? As in almost getting flattened by your hellbeast?"

"That part was fun too," Rohan said. "But no, I was talking about how it ended. That part."

"Ah." *Did her eyes deepen, or was that wishful thinking?* He took a deep breath and inhaled a creamy, woodsy scent, with a hint of something sweet at the end ... her arousal. His mouth watered. *Oh, yeah, she remembered all right.* "And so that's why you're here? You want to pick up however we left off?"

Gods, yes. "Well, it would be a great way to celebrate the upcoming solstice. But I thought I'd do the chivalrous thing and not bring that up."

"Chivalry? From you?"

"Don't judge a book by its cover."

"Oh, I'm not. I'm going solely by experience. I've seen you in action twice now, remember? The first time, that night at the club—you had women dripping off you."

"Wow," Rohan said, "you did see me."

"Hard to ignore an orgy right in front of you."

"That was all them—I promise, I was just an innocent bystander. And I got rid of them the moment work called."

"Because you needed something," the high priestess said dryly. "Don't try to con me."

"You know, as lovely as verbally sparring with you is—and I mean that—is this where you do all your high priestessing? The skull has a certain ambience but not even a chair?"

"You want a seat?"

"It's been a long night. A seat would be frigging heaven."

The high priestess regarded him for a long moment, and ... his mouth watered.

"This way," she finally murmured. Then she pressed something on the wall behind the skull, and a door behind her soundlessly opened.

4

CYN TOOK a deep breath and stepped back to let Rohan pass. As he did, she got a hint of his spicy cologne, tinted with a delicious, warm leathery scent that screamed straight up *fuck me now*. And her inner daemon reacted to that aroma; she had to stifle the instant urge to run her fingernails down his marks, to add her own art to the tattoos she'd already seen. To show the rest of the world that this male was hers.

Down, girl.

"So, this is it." Cyn hit the button to close the door, strode into the middle of her windowless shop and tried to see it through his eyes.

A good friend had described it to her once as a cross between an arcane witchy shop and a dominatrix boudoir. Which wasn't far off the mark.

A red velvet chaise and a table and chairs were her client furniture, both comfortable and practical. And everything she needed for those spell casting—crystals, bowls, candles, jars of herbs and resins, censors and bells and pendulums and her tarot decks—plus a few items for atmosphere, like her whip and chains, lined the walls and filled the shelves around the rest of the room.

All creating, in her mind anyway, a dark, moody space filled with potential and possibilities ... and not a little danger—which gave Cyn a sense of comfort and belonging.

Her lips curved before she could stop herself.

Her place.

"What's through there?" Rohan nodded at the doorway on the far wall. "Some kind of inner sanctum?"

"Just a storeroom," she lied. No way could he see her personal space—where she slept, ate and worked as a Templar. Although, she supposed that was the truth of her these days—high priestess out here, tech and weapons expert Templar Knight behind closed doors. A complete reverse of what she used to be.

"Amazing," he murmured. And when she followed to see what he was talking about—she met his gaze, locked on her.

The look in Rohan's eyes made it clear she was the most interesting thing he saw.

Mother of the gods, but this man was fine on so many levels. Which was bad. She was on the clock here.

"All right, you've come by my business; now, what can I do for you?" Cyn asked. "I've got a client on their way here, then I need to pack for a flight first thing in the morning."

"You're leaving town?"

"That's what I just said. So come on, Red, spit it out."

"A spell. I'm looking for something important from my world. I started looking six months ago but had to ... pause my search. Now I'm back, and rumor is you're the best around, so I've come to you."

Was this still about the hellgate key? Grayson had mentioned the Templars had agreed to help Rohan with a search for something. Or was this something else? But

Rohan couldn't know *she* knew about the key, so Cyn had to be cautious here. Although ... this was an excellent opportunity to observe his behavior if he lied.

"Is this about what you were working with the Templars last year?" she said.

"Yep. But I got ... called Hellside before they could find anything." Rohan held her gaze.

Okay, that was the truth. "And you think I'll be able to?"

"I'm willing to pay you a shit ton of money to find out."

"Ever heard the saying a fool and his money are easily parted? You want me to divine the location of something ... important ... to you. That's one of the hardest branches of magic around. There are a few witches, though, who might help you out. I've heard of someone over on the East Coast —Seattle—that's pretty good."

"You won't do the spell?"

"It would take time—and like I said, I'm out of here tonight. So sorry and all that." And damn it, she really was. Divining for him would have meant spending more time together. "But seriously, try the witch in Seattle. Or you can go to the Watchers; they seem more open to dealing with daemons and otherworlders these days."

"Yeah, I'd heard about that. Maybe. But this is important. I don't have long here either."

Cyn stopped and rocked back on her heels.

Something hot and ... desperate entered Rohan's gaze. But what was that desperation about? Was the missing hellgate key really that bad? It had been missing for over six months, and so far, there had been no talk of dangerous ...

Holy mother of the gods.

The hellbeast at Simion's. She almost whacked herself in the head. But if that attack was related to Rohan's missing key, was it a one-off or had there been other incursions from Hellside she wasn't aware of?

Ugh. Being undercover right now sucked. She'd much rather be straight up with Rohan about the hellgate key.

"What about us—about that kiss?" Rohan asked.

She couldn't hold back a frown. "What about it?" The fact it had been one of the hottest experiences of her life? That for the last three nights she'd dreamed of that kiss? And those dreams hadn't stopped at just their lips meeting.

"Priestess—"

"High Priestess."

"Fine. *High* Priestess, I have no doubt you've kissed others. As have I." Rohan's voice lowered, and he stepped toward her with that lethal grace of his. The temperature in the room rose. Cyn's nipples pebbled. "But that kiss ... our kiss ... that was unlike anything I've tasted. And I think you felt it too. That wasn't a kiss. That was a fucking explosion. And I know I want more. Yes, I need a spell to find a hellgate key. But I also want to get to know you. To see if that explosion was a one-off, and if it wasn't—then to see what might come next."

Oh shit. She was a puddle. Totally freaking drenched. From his words alone.

Cyn clenched her thighs, and as she did, a growl rumbled through Rohan and his pupils blew wide open.

"Woah," she whispered. "What the fuck—are you okay?" She forced herself not to give in to the urge to step back. She backed away for nobody. Certainly not a daemon, even as delicious as this one.

His nostrils flared, and he prowled another step closer before halting in front of her. Something hot and almost ... craving glittered in his eyes.

And damn if the heat simmering low in her belly didn't

turn to molten lava.

"Listen, yes," Cyn said. "That kiss was good. Okay—wait, not good. Out of this world, even. But I still have a job to do. And the fact your kiss was so explosive—that's why you have to go. Because when I have a job, I need to be focused."

For a heartbeat, he stared at her, then his gaze cut away to the shop wall, and with an abrupt move, he changed direction and stalked over to the shelves. When he looked back, the glittering heat in his eyes was contained.

Something heavy weighed in her gut. Damn. If he'd stayed in front of her, there'd be no question she'd be discovering exactly where that predatory interest would've led to.

"What kind of job does a high priestess do that's so important?" Rohan tapped one jar of resin.

"Can't say." Understatement of the century. "So—"

The magic warning spell, an electric buzz to her wrist tattoo, from her front door triggered. Shit. Cyn stalked over to Rohan and grabbed his arm.

"What?" He scowled at her. "I just tapped the jar—"

"My client is here early. You need to sit on the chaise. Do not say a word and try to look as ... unintimidating as possible." Rohan complied and Cyn let Jaz in. "Welcome back. How's it going?"

"He found me again. He might even have followed me here. Damn it. I don't know what to do—"

"Calm down. We're going to complete the ritual now, and then he won't be able to find you again unless you allow it. He'll never see you—you could even stand right in front of him. Now, did you bring what we need?"

"Sure—" Jaz's face paled as she looked over Cyn's shoulder.

"Ignore him. He's ... an acquaintance."

"Oh. Am I interrupting? I'm early, sorry, let me go out—"

"No, you did the right thing to come here if you're worried. The faster we get you protected, the better. But I promise Rohan isn't here for you. He doesn't know you. And I won't say your name. In fact, he's the one interrupting. You trust me, don't you? Good. Now, let's complete this potion, okay?"

Cyn took her time leading Jaz through the spell steps and, when she was done, handed over one glass jug filled with oil.

"Now, dab one drop onto your forehead at the same time every morning, and this will hide you from your ex's sight. But when you're ready to do more than hide—to face him and take him down, come back and see me. I know some people who can help."

After Jaz had left, Cyn returned to her shop. And to her next issue.

"You were good there," Rohan said.

"She needed the reassurance. And thanks for getting the tea."

"Personally, I'd have had the coffee."

"Me too." Cyn traded smiles with him. Without warning, the heat that had been simmering while Jaz had been there leaped back to life.

And then her door warning spell triggered again. "I think she's back. Wait here."

Cyn went back to the corridor, and her gut sank. Nope. Not Jaz.

Her mother.

"You kept me waiting long enough," Katherine Mont-bard bit out.

"And hello to you, too." Shit. Shit. *Shit.* Rohan was in the shop—he couldn't overhear this. Cyn yanked out a strand of hair—ouch—and whispered a spell to conceal their conversation.

"Why did you call a concealing spell, Cynane?" She pronounced it 'kee-nah-nay,' of course.

"It's Sin-ane, while I'm undercover, remember? And I have someone in my shop, *Mother*, so without the spell, we can't talk privately. Now, I didn't know the council were in LA."

"We're not. I'm here for a personal visit." She looked at the skull and displeasure creased her face. "Did you really need a shop? Isn't that taking your role too far?"

"Do we have to do this again? If I want this undercover assignment to be realistic, then yes, I need a shop."

"So this person—are they a client?"

"No, someone I'm trying to get rid of, actually."

"Well, I can help there. I'll tell—"

"Mother. I'm undercover, remember? I can't be seen just talking to a Templar Councilor."

"Why not? I could need a high priestess."

"Mother, I'm working. Right now. I have to leave in an hour to follow up on the best lead we've had in decades on R-104C."

"You can pack while we talk. This matter cannot wait."

"Let me guess—there's another promotion?"

"This is serious, Cynane," her mother said. "Every Montbard for three hundred years has taken a leadership role within the organization. It is time you considered your future."

"And let me guess, there just happens to be a role somewhere you want me to apply for."

"Grayson is occupied with other matters, and this is the perfect opportunity to place you in a high enough role for a future council seat."

"And what about the undercover mission that I've been working on for years? Should I just give up tracking R-104C?"

"We have a diviner on the books now; they should be working this case. You should be working as a leader."

"Even the diviner—you can call her Isadora, you know—has tried but can't see it. Which only reinforces my belief the relic is being purposely shrouded."

"Regardless of that, we need to talk. I'll get rid of your nonclient. Now, let me in."

-((●))-

Rohan didn't have to move to hear the conversation in the corridor. A female voice—modulated and crisp—was speaking with the high priestess.

The high priestess—and hell, he still didn't know her name—whispered something, but he struggled to make out the words, and then everything went silent. As in, the conversation completely stopped. He went to the door and pressed an ear close. Nope. Nothing. Not even breathing.

So, either both women had disappeared, suddenly dropped dead, or someone had called a concealing spell.

But why?

Rohan returned to his seat just as the door opened, and the high priestess stalked through, lips pursed, eyes glittering—clearly steamed about something.

And it seemed to do with the woman walking through after her. Tall also, with silver hair in a stylish cut and eyes almost the same color as the high priestess. And hell. He knew this woman …

"Councilor Montbard." Rohan forced a calm expression. "How lovely to see you again." Now it made sense. The Templars must be paying the high priestess to work a job for them. No wonder she'd concealed their conversation.

Frigging Templars—always getting others to do their dirty work.

"Delegate." Montbard inclined her head coolly.

"You need a high priestess, too?" He forced himself to keep his tone polite.

"Yes, as a matter of fact."

"Templar business?"

"While we, the council, agreed to work together on one occasion, that does not mean I'm at liberty to discuss any other aspects of our business."

"Of course, of course." What the fuck was going on here? By the look on their faces, they wanted him gone, but that he couldn't do.

"And what brings you to ... a high priestess?" Montbard asked.

"What? I show mine, but you don't show yours?"

"We're the Templars; we're in charge of everything to do with otherworlders—"

"Oh really? And who put the Templars in charge?"

Montbard's lips tightened. "The who doesn't matter."

"Kind of does given you think you're in charge of me, of *us*. And guess what? Otherworlders don't subscribe to you having any say over us. At all. But you wouldn't know that because the Templars don't actually talk to us. And to be clear, I don't have any issues you don't already know. I'm searching for something, the same something you *Templars* promised—and failed—to help me with six months ago. Thought I'd try my luck with another option. And I have to say, the option is rather attractive—"

"Well, as lovely as this has been," the high priestess interjected. "Councilor, thank you for your inquiry. But as you can see, I already have a full client list. And you." She turned to Rohan. "I'm also denying your request. So, it's time for you both to leave and let me pack for my actual client."

"What about if I go with you?" Rohan put on his most winning smile. "I can pay for my travel."

"No, that really wouldn't be wise," the councilor said. Her lips thinned so much they almost disappeared. Was she looking down her nose at him?

"And you don't get to decide who I take—or don't take—on as a client," the high priestess said through her teeth. Rohan stilled and looked closer at the women. Yep, undercurrent going on here for days. "So I really think you should go, and I'll contact you about the matter when I'm back."

"You'd better. That matter won't wait forever." The councilor glanced around the shop, her nose wrinkling like she'd smelled something bad, and then strode out of the room—her purposeful strides not unlike someone else he knew.

"So is that a yes? I can go with you?" Rohan said.

"You know you sound like a plaintive puppy, right?"

"If it does the trick—"

The high priestess jumped and scowled at her wrist. "Who now?"

Rohan eyed her wrist, too. A Celtic knot was inked into the skin there. She looked like something had stung her. But there was nothing around. Unless ... she must have a spell tied to that tattoo. Ah. So that's how she knew someone was at the door. Clever priestess.

"Wait here. Again," she ground out.

Gladly.

Once again, Rohan's daemon hearing didn't leave him any doubt about the next visitor.

"Simion," the high priestess's voice dropped. "What a surprise. Didn't expect to see you until tomorrow morning at the airfield."

"Change of plans. My last client wrapped up early—yes, I really am that good—and since I abhor the vacuum of unfulfilled love, I moved you up to immediate help. So I've changed the flight plan and we're leaving tonight. But I really wanted to see your shop for myself—you have no idea the hype around your business, dearest heart."

"Of course you can look around." There was a pause. "But I'll need to leave soon to pack if we're flying out—"

"Never mind that. We can get everything you need where we're going."

"You want to go now? I guess, at least my spell book is here, and I can pack a few crystals and tarot decks. And exactly where *are* we going? You just said the beach when we last spoke."

"We're going to the beach in Australia. A delightful place called Byron Bay."

"What? You have a beach right here—?"

"Not like this one. Now, I'm dying to see your shop. You really are the talk of the city. Can we go in?"

"Fine. But I have a visitor. And don't get any ideas."

Ideas? Rohan had a mind full of those, but he just slipped his hands in his pockets and waited for Simion and the high priestess to return to the room.

"Rohan! How delightful." Simion's face lit up. "I was going to find you, so this is serendipitous indeed."

"Why?" The high priestess planted her hands on her hips. Her chin raised, and a dangerous air settled around her. Dangerously sexy. His pulse picked up. Hell, why did he respond to her so easily? "What do you want with him?"

"Hey," Rohan said. "You say that like I'm a bad penny."

One of those slashes of brows rose. And damn if he didn't want to laugh. Ah, but he liked her sass.

"Anyhow," the high priestess said, turning away from him. "Seriously, why do you want Rohan?"

"For you, of course." Simion's smile widened. "I've been reviewing your case, and so far, he's your best option."

Rohan straightened. Now this was interesting. "Care to share, Priestess?"

"*High* Priestess. And no." She pulled Simion over to the side of her shop and lowered her voice to a whisper. A furious whisper at that—and he loved he could hear her just fine. "Surely you can find another—better—option than him?"

"I'm wounded, Priestess." Rohan rocked back on his heels and couldn't stop himself from laughing.

"Shush. This is a conversation about you—not with you."

"I'm still looking, of course," Simion said in a soothing tone. "But so far ... he's it. Now, you came to me, remember? You need to trust the process. If you won't trust me in this—how can I expect you to trust me at all?"

"Shit." She glowered at Rohan. And something in that look made his chest tighten—something hot and fast and brutal in its intensity.

Heat licked through him, but he forced it away.

The hellgate key was his focus here. And this woman ... this high priestess ... was his path to success.

Bloody hell, was Fate rolling over in fits of devious laughter or what right now?

"Fine." The high priestess glared at him. "You're coming with us. But we're leaving now apparently, so hope you have whatever you need handy."

5

SIMION'S private jet had two cabins, a bed and bath in the rear section, and a long couch opposite a fully stocked bar and two sets of comfy chairs in the front.

"You look like you're ready for a party here, Simion." Cyn took a window seat facing the rest of the jet and withdrew a tarot deck from her purse.

"It's a fourteen-hour flight—we need something to entertain us," Simion said.

She forced a laugh as Rohan ducked his head to enter the cabin.

"Where can I stow this?" Rohan held up his satchel.

"The crew can take it—" Simion nodded at a crew member holding a tray of sparkling water.

"Thanks, but I prefer to know where the bag is."

Simion had the crew member open a locker at the front of the plane.

Cyn eyed the bag as Rohan stowed it, and when Rohan sat opposite her, she checked on Simion, Aleesha and Sonja —all sitting on the lounge at the rear of the cabin—then leaned across the table. "Are your you-know-whats in there?"

He copied her movement. "Of course."

"True or false that one nick from a hellblade, even the tiniest of scratches, and it's ..." She swiped her finger across her neck.

"Truth."

"Shit." She sat back in her seat. "What if someone accidentally—?"

"Calm down. They're sheathed in their scabbards, which are spelled to only respond to my touch. No one is going to get near the scabbards, let alone the blades."

Cyn held his gaze for a beat, but his stayed steady, so she eventually sat back.

As they took off, Cyn stared through the window, watching her baby get smaller and smaller in the lights of the airfield before the jet banked and they headed west over the Pacific Ocean.

"They better look after her," she'd murmured before she could stop herself.

"The car?" Rohan frowned.

"She's not just a car. She's my baby."

"That's why you were shooting daggers at me when I bumped the dash?"

"Yes! She's a work of art—you don't hit a Mustang."

"Hey, you were driving like you were being chased by another trichorn. I was holding on for dear life."

She smirked at him. "I noticed."

"You know you have a mean streak, right?"

She did laugh then. "Yes, yes I do."

Rohan laughed, and damn if their exchange didn't make power tingle in her palms. Shit, shit. Shit. Why did she react this way to him? And was it dangerous? What if she reacted too much—what if she got too attracted, so much so that she lost sight of her purpose?

Her stomach went rock-hard. She turned away from Rohan, back to the view of the ocean.

No, she had this covered. Keeping Rohan close was going to support her cover, keep Simion unsuspicious, and help Cyn achieve her goal—that was all. And she was stronger than her hormones, no question.

Thankfully, distraction arrived in the form of Simion, holding two glasses filled with something pale gold and bubbling.

"Champagne, dearest ones?" He held them out a glass each and then sank into the seat beside Cyn.

"So why Byron Bay?" Rohan asked Simion.

"It's a stunning part of the world—have you been there?"

"Nope."

"Well, think long, golden sand beaches where the subtropical rainforest meets the ocean. A small eclectic community where it doesn't matter who you are, and you can walk around the streets with no one going cray cray— well, unless you want them to, of course—with delicious food and weather."

"And you've been going there for how long?" Cyn interjected as casually as she could.

"About a dozen years all up, although at first, I only stayed as a guest. A famous actor built the compound initially—you'll know him, but I'm not allowed to say— hush hush and all that. I'd helped him with his love situation years earlier, and he and his beautiful heartmate invited me to visit a few times. As you'll see, it's just the most perfect place for love ever. Recently, he was looking to offload the property, but we kept the transfer quiet to protect his privacy. His family still comes and stays every now and again."

Holy mother of the gods. No wonder the Templars hadn't found a record of any property linking Simion to Australia. Cyn's radar pinged. Maybe she was finally onto something.

She needed schematics. Which meant locating who had built the property so the Templars could get the building plans. "Sounds amazing. And I bet some famous architect designed it, right?"

"Oh, I don't worry about those things."

"And is it big?"

"Vast, dearest heart. Absolutely vast. But enough about my house. Let's talk about you two. Now, Rohan, tell me all about yourself. Do you work, or do you just run around with that fantastic bare chest saving the day like an ancient hero? Achilles. Perseus—"

Cyn choked on a laugh.

"What?" Rohan swiveled to her.

"Nothing. Ah, just keep going." And actually, this would be interesting. What would Rohan the Red, representative of the Daemon Congress, say to a human?

"I'm here in the human world to manage the hellgates in this realm."

"I thought the gates had a Lord or something in charge who did that?" Simion gave a vague wave of his hand.

"The Lords of the Gates handle who pass through from Hellside; I'm looking after the gates humanside."

"Ah, well, how lovely. And thought I detected an accent. British?" Simion said.

"From much earlier in my life. These days I spend a bit

of time in the States and a bit of time overseas. Very little from where I grew up, which is a shame. I liked it there."

"Ah, a person who appreciates their childhood. I like that. So do you enjoy your job?"

"I enjoy having a purpose. That's satisfying."

Simion nodded as if Rohan had said something deep and immensely meaningful. Cyn resisted rolling her eyes.

"And what about love?" Simion asked.

"What about it?" Rohan said.

"Are you open to that moment where your soul takes flight and that finest, purest of emotions casts your entire being in a rainbow of unending warmth?"

"Ah ..." Rohan looked at Cyn, and she couldn't help but smirk. *Your turn, Red.*

He narrowed his eyes as if to say, help me out here.

Cyn leaned back in her seat and gave him her sweetest smile before taking another sip.

He sighed and shoveled a hand through that outrageously ... beautiful hair. Seriously, what males had hair that good?

And Simion continued, "Are you open to the rapturous embrace—?"

"If I say yes, will you stop?" Rohan said.

Cyn laughed out loud, and Simion turned to look at her and gave her such a smug smile she almost groaned. Damn. Rohan had walked right into that—and he didn't even know that Simion was setting the two of them up.

"Hold up." Rohan lifted a hand. "Why do I get the feeling you're sizing me up for something?"

"Don't you know why you're here?"

"Because Her High Priestessness here is on a job for me."

"That might be why you're here for *you*," Simion replied, "but for our dearest one, you're here for me to determine if you're her soul mate. Her forever love. The yin to her yang. The—"

"Stop. Stop, I get it."

"Excellent. Now, I really need to refresh myself—there's a full bathroom at the back of the cabin—and I might even have a little nap. The couch extends into a delightful bed, and I know Aleesha and Sonja are going to have a nap too, so we'll leave you two to get better acquainted."

As soon as Simion disappeared into the back of the plane, Cyn stood up.

If Simion had R-104C, and he knew what it was, what were the odds he'd leave it in a secure location versus taking it with him? Unlikely he'd move it, but still ... she needed to check the plane.

Cyn forced a relaxed smile and turned to Rohan. "So these chairs extend in both directions to make pretty comfortable beds. Why don't you have a sleep? You must be tired after all that ... bare-chested heroism." She didn't bother to hide the smirk in her voice.

"Thanks, but I'm wide awake. Different time zones, you know?"

Actually, she didn't know. What were the time zone differences from Hell to the human world? Huh. Did they have full days and night cycles there too? Damn it. More questions. That was something she hadn't found in her research books—apparently, no one thought to include relevant information like that in texts about Hell. The urge to demand Rohan tell her everything about that world—his world—itched at the back of her throat.

"Something you want to say?" Rohan asked and stood

up too. And suddenly the cabin became way too small, even though it was just the two of them.

"No. Nope. All good." Cyn hammed up an enormous yawn. "I'm going to walk a little, feeling stiff." Damn. How was she meant to check the plane with him right there?

"Aren't we meant to be 'getting acquainted'?"

"Seriously? Judging by that look, I guess yes. All right, all right, here you go. I like coffee—no milk or sugar. I love reading and libraries. And my favorite color is black. There. You know me."

"Actually, apart from 'dearest one,' as Simion calls you, and High Priestess, I don't even know your name."

"Fine." She didn't bother restraining a sigh. "Call me Cyn."

"Sin?"

"It's a soft C. C-Y-N."

"Not a name I've heard before. Is it short for something?"

"You're really focused on this knowing each other stuff, aren't you? It's short for Cynane. Spelled C-Y-N-A- N-E."

"Now that's a name I know. Alexander the Great's sister, leader of an army, and the daughter of an Illyrian princess. Pronounced 'kee-nah-nay,' I thought. Any relation?"

"Of course, you know." She bit back the urge to grind her teeth. Three years ago, Kee-nah-nay had been exactly the pronunciation she'd have used to introduce herself, but the new pronunciation had been the perfect disguise—and surprisingly, she liked it. "Apparently, there's a link there," she said lightly. "Although I'm not so certain. And yes, that's one way to say my name. But growing up, no one at any of my schools ever said Kee-nah-nay,"—not a lie, although the next part was—"and by the time I was a teenager, everyone just called me Sin-ane."

And fun fact, the new pronunciation horrified Cyn's mother. Which only made Cyn love it even more.

"Cyn ... ane," Rohan said slowly, teasing her name out. Almost savoring it. She shivered. His cognac voice made her want to hear him whisper into her ear ... and other places. "Blood relative of an Illyrian princess. Suits you."

Cyn said, "Okay, so that's enough of getting-to-know-you time."

"No, not really. I have loads of questions. Like how much do you know about Hellside and daemons in general? For a half daemon—"

"Half human."

He rolled his eyes. "Either way, you don't seem to know too much about one *half* of your life. You can ask me anything if you want, and I'll tell you."

Shit. She didn't have time for this. Except ... this might be too good an opportunity to miss.

"Go on," Rohan said. "Ask me anything. Even just one thing."

"Fine. How do the gates of Hell work?"

"Starting with the complicated questions, I see. Well, to start, each gate is a set of arches carved from a different crystal or stone. So the first gate is made from lapis lazuli—"

"I know that. I also know that's why daemons have such an affinity for crystals."

"Okay. So what do you want to know?"

"How do they work? Like—you just step through and wham, you're in another world?"

"Pretty much. Although the gates of Hell are invisible and inaccessible unless you're a daemon, so they'd be hard to find. Think of the gates like this: humanside, the doors are static, so if I pass through the Tenth Gate into the human world, I'll always emerge outside of LA. Although, we can change the location of the gates humanside, but that hasn't happened in decades."

"Which is why you daemons can't just pop up wherever you want in the human world," Cyn said.

"*We* daemons, but yes. Precisely."

"So how do the gates work in Hell?"

"Each realm of Hell has its own gate—and only one. When you step through a gate, you hit Limbo, basically a land of nothing but charcoal mist. But from Limbo, you can access all the hellgates, depending on what realm you come from. You know how that works, right?"

"Yep. The hierarchy of gates. Whichever realm a daemon 'comes from,' they can travel through gates to a lower realm. So my ... sire ... is from the Seventh Gate, meaning he can travel from gates one through six."

"Exactly. And before you ask, I'm from the thirteenth, and yes, Isadora and I are related. Anything else you want to ask?"

If it meant listening to his smooth voice, hell yes. But no. Time to get this mission back on track—and get some space from the too-sexy daemon. "I'm good. Although you know how I like my coffee, so what about you?"

"No milk," Rohan said, "and as strong as it can get."

Warmth tingled through Cyn's belly. She knew something she'd bet was long and strong ... Shit, there she went again.

"Be right back."

Holy mother of the gods—Rohan was dangerous if he could distract her that much.

Cyn escaped into the galley of the plane—surprised the cabin crew there—and generally made a pain of herself until she was no longer fantasizing about strong, long bits of Rohan and insisted on taking his coffee out.

"Here you go." She slid into the seat beside him.

"Thanks." Rohan's eyes narrowed. "Why are you being nice? And sitting close?"

"Don't know what you're talking about." Cyn forced a casual shrug. "We're getting to know each other, aren't we? Well, now you know I can order you a coffee. And I'm looking for love, after all." Phew, she hadn't stumbled over the words this time. "So we're in this plane for another thirteen hours, might as well use the time ... wisely, don't you think?"

"Really?" His glance dropped to her lips, and she felt his gaze like a physical touch.

"Well," she purred, "Simion and his assistants are asleep, so it's just you and me ..."

Rohan shifted in his seat. Leaned into her until their shoulders brushed. "And ..."

She pretended to yawn and stretched her arms—one of them just happening to land around Rohan's shoulder, and that devilish grin of his tilted his lips.

He turned. She turned. Their breaths sighed against each other.

Then Cyn pressed her palm, ring already in position, into his neck, and his eyes drifted shut.

"And it's time for you to sleep," she whispered against his mouth and caught his head just in time.

With a bit of maneuvering, Cyn snagged the plane pillow from the opposite chair, jammed it between Rohan's neck and the window, and turned his head so it was a little cushioned.

Twenty minutes later, after a search of the plane, she flopped back into her chair. Damn. Nothing but some extra pillows and luggage. Well, there was always the baggage

storage, but it wasn't like she was checking in there any time
soon.

At least she knew R-104C wasn't out here.

An hour later, Simion rejoined Cyn in the main cabin,
and then his gaze widened as he took in Rohan.

"What's he doing?"

"Oh, he was tired." Cyn smiled and made a shushing
gesture against her lips. "He's having a nap. Let's let him
sleep."

The sun had just begun to tint the night sky over the most
spectacular human-world coastline Rohan had seen as
Simion drove him, Cyn, Aleesha and Sonja in an all-terrain
vehicle from a private airfield to the town of Byron Bay.

Rohan had woken up midway through the fight to
Australia to find Cyn sound asleep in the chair opposite
him, her face unguarded for the first time, although a level
of tension had still hummed about her body as if she was
ready to spring to wakefulness in a second.

He'd instantly known the high priestess had drugged
him. But why? She was attracted to him—that was unmis-
takable. The scent of her desire drove him mad; it was so
strong. So maybe she didn't want that attraction? Possible.
Look at his own unwilling reaction to her.

Or ... was there another reason?

Simion had been awake, though, and invited Rohan to
join him on the couch at the back of the cabin where they'd
sat and talked about Simion's love of love. That's when it

had pinged where Rohan had seen Simion before—a fancy party in England, well over a century ago. And just what was the minor deity doing living among humans?

But Rohan hadn't said anything to Simion. Whatever the hell was going on here, Rohan was keeping all cards close to his chest until he understood the bigger picture.

His mission to locate the hellgate key had to work. And right now, Simion, or whoever the hell he was calling himself these days—and even Cynane and her mightier-than-frigging-thou clients—didn't matter.

Although one thing did have to be acted on—Cynane couldn't knock him out again.

"What a spectacular sunrise," Cyn said to Simion from where she sat in the front seat of the ATV. The wind whipped her hair back from her face, the sun gilding her profile in a way that made Rohan's chest ache.

Fuck, but she was spectacular. And sneaky. Which only made him like her even more.

Damn, damn, *damn*. Why had he had to find such an amazing creature?

"Rohan, did you hear me? I asked what you think?" Simion's voice made Rohan blink and turn his attention to the other male. "The sunrise?" Simion asked, looking a bit smug.

"Yeah," Rohan said, "spectacular."

Simion's brows rose in a way that suggested he knew exactly what Rohan found spectacular, and he bit back a groan. Do not encourage the love whisperer any further.

Although, at least it was keeping Rohan close to Cynane. And right now, that was the key. He just had to keep a lid on any emotional stuff while he was with her.

"So this is the town. Simple, but gorgeous. You'll love it."

Simion waved to various buildings as they drove down what was apparently the main road. "We're up on the hill over-looking the township and the beach."

Simion turned the ATV onto a steep road, and they steadily climbed to a plateau with a driveway sealed off by two huge gates.

"Full security, of course," Simion continued, "but as my guests, you can come and go as you like. Now, for my would-be lovebirds, I've got you in side-by-side suites. And there's a spectacular surprise—which I know you're going to just love. But I won't hold you up any further. You two go explore, and breakfast will be served by the pool in about an hour, where you can meet Maurice, my personal chef. I nabbed him from a superyacht just this year.

"He makes the most divine creations, and I send him ahead to wherever I'm going. Also, I've had some clothes left out for you since you joined us on such short notice. Not that there's much difference between LA in early summer to this beautiful part of the world in winter. Still, we want you to feel comfortable here with the locals."

Rohan glanced at Cyn. What did she make of all this setting them up? Well, if she had a problem with it, she didn't say so because she kissed Simion on the cheek and told him she couldn't wait to explore.

But when she looked back at Rohan, her cool expression had the hairs on the back of his neck prickling. Exactly what was the high priestess's game here?

He let her lead the way to the guest wing, and sure enough, their doors were side by side.

"Well, see you at breakfast." Cyn entered her room, and the door swung shut behind her with a cold, sharp swoosh. Huh, nothing remotely lover-ish in that.

Rohan entered his room—no lock on the handle, just great—and pulled up short. "Well, damn."

He placed his satchel on the enormous bed, wide enough to easily fit him and five others—Simion had guests who enjoyed that kind of stay, no doubt. And then he checked out the rest of the room. An ensuite with a shower big enough to accommodate everyone from the bed. A door between his and Cyn's room—of course. Sliding glass doors lead to a deck beyond. And the view ... lush green foliage dropping to the township below, followed by endless ocean meeting the almost same-hue blue sky in a glorious living artwork.

Did humans realize how lucky they were to live among such magnificence?

And something else outside ... Rohan wandered onto the deck and shook his head. A hot tub. Well, it would be a spectacular place to take in the view. And you wouldn't be alone, even if you didn't have anyone in that giant bed with you, because the deck was shared with the suite next door.

And then the other sliding glass door leading to the balcony opened, and footsteps echoed on the deck. No need to turn around to know who stood behind him.

"Some view," Rohan murmured.

"Yep. He's looking after us." She joined him at the railing.

He eyed the tub and then Cyn. Would she ...?

"So, I'm hungry. Time to eat." She spun and headed back for her sliding glass doors.

Guess that was a no.

Without a doubt, whatever Cyn wanted from Rohan, it wasn't a romance. So why was she pretending to Simion that she did?

Rohan took a fast shower and washed off the plane

grime, then pulled on cargo shorts and a tee from the wardrobe of clothes Simion had provided.

Time to ferret out what the hell the high priestess was up to and figure out her connection to his hellgate key.

Anticipation surged through him. Something told him he was going to enjoy this day.

6

AFTER A DAY OF LOUNGING, eating and chatting by the pool—which could only be described as a secret grotto meets subtropical oasis—the inaction and constant food caught up with Cyn and she had to move.

She finally escaped Simion and his love talk and changed into loose-fitting pants and a tee, and made her way to her bedroom deck.

Over the ocean, the horizon was a homage to blues and purples, from pale lilac to deep indigo. And thank fuck, she was on her own. Finally.

Cyn squared her shoulders, then let her body settle into the familiar rhythm of a tai chi workout.

Twenty minutes later, her mind was clear and her body felt one hundred percent better than it had all day.

"That was beautiful," Rohan said.

She stiffened but didn't turn around. "How long were you standing there?"

"Ten minutes. Simion sent me to check on you. He's ... invested in your love match."

"So he should be. I'm his client, after all."

"Really? You don't seem nearly as invested in finding your love match as Simion."

"Don't know what you're talking about." Damn it. What more did she have to do? She'd freaking *lounged* all day with Rohan and Simion. Seriously—was this how people found love for real?

"Tell you what," Rohan said, "that hot tub looks good. Want to take a dip to say goodbye to the sun and welcome the moon?"

At that, she did turn around. "That was really lovely. What makes you say that?"

"It's something my mother's people used to say, apparently. I never knew her—she died in childbirth, but I've met a few beings from her lands over the years, and that was a common thing they'd say at moonrise. I like it."

"And just who are your mother's people?" Cyn asked.

"She came from a long line of Norse gods."

Holy shit, Rohan's mother was a god? And she'd died?

"She was only a minor deity," Rohan murmured.

"Reading my mind now?"

"No, just your expression." His jaw tightened. "When my ... sire ... denied her the healing magic she needed, she was vulnerable, and she lost her life."

Cyn's heart tugged, and she'd taken a step toward him before she could stop herself.

Shit. No—not feeling softly toward this male. "I'll take a pass on the hot tub. Maybe another time."

Rohan slipped his hands into his pockets. "Now, if I was looking for love, and a possible match was out here with that view and hot tub, I'd be in there in the split of a second."

"Split second."

"Whatever—you know what I mean."

Cyn resisted the urge to grind her teeth. She'd just gotten away from him and now this? "Fine." She stripped down to her sports bra and boyleg undies and settled into the hot tub without another word.

Damn, that was actually good. She sighed and sank back into the headrest.

And *that* was even better.

Rohan pulled his shirt up and off. Her mouth went dry —oh yeah, there were those abs ... that chest she remembered from his ride on the hellbeast.

A hint of freckles smattered over his shoulders, tempted her to run her tongue over them—join them up in a long, delicious lick ...

And then he unzipped his cargo shorts ... holy mother of the gods, what if he was commando?

Please, please be commando—damn. Plain black trunks. But even so, his thighs were muscled like the rest of him, and the bulge in the front ... Every bit of moisture that had whisked from her mouth pooled in her core.

"Looked enough yet?" Rohan asked.

Busted.

Cyn yanked her gaze to his face, but only curiosity filled his expression, and she answered honestly. "No."

"You're welcome to look all you like, you know." He stepped into the foaming water. "Now?"

She looked him up and down, found herself in the *perfect* position to appreciate that bulge, the freckles—everywhere!—and the long lines of muscles.

"Yep," she lied and settled deeper into the water.

"Liar," he said with a chuckle.

Considering he was right, she didn't bother disagreeing, but she did keep her gaze firmly on the other spectacular view until she was less likely to jump his bones.

"So what was that movement you were doing?" Rohan asked as he sank into the water too.

Shit. He was asking about her workout. She rolled her tongue back up. "Tai chi. Normally I do a session at sunrise, but it's good for any time I feel the need to … center myself."

"And you needed that tonight?"

"Rohan, I get that you're still 'getting to know me,' but never in my life have I lounged all day by a pool and done nothing but eat and talk shit. So yeah, I needed to relax and clear my mind."

Rohan burst out laughing.

"What?"

"You're the only human—half or otherwise—I know who needs to relax after a day of lounging and eating and talking."

Cyn flicked a splash of water at him and then settled back into the hollow of the tub's headrest.

"Farewell sun and welcome moon," she murmured. She felt rather than saw Rohan turn to her, but then his gaze shifted back to the sky and he murmured the same words.

And much later, after they'd eaten—again—Cyn lay in her bed staring out through the window into the now true night sky, and the daemon's words replayed in her mind. Exactly who was Rohan the Red? And who was his father?

The next morning, thank the mother of the gods, the perfect opportunity to search the compound arrived when Simion invited Cyn and Rohan to join him in the township to sightsee and visit a local open-air market.

Aleesha and Sonja took off in one ATV, and Simion insisted Cyn and Rohan ride with him. But as soon as Rohan had slid into the front seat beside Simion, Cyn faked a headache and swore she'd rest while they shopped.

Rohan looked like he saw right through her lie, so she didn't give him a chance to say anything and ducked back inside.

Finally. She had the place to herself. Well, apart from the staff. So far she'd counted Maurice, the chef, Sienna, the waiter who'd served them by the heated pool, and at least one housekeeper who'd brought out towels when Simion decided to have a swim.

But how many more were there?

As soon as she couldn't hear the ATV's engine anymore, Cyn took a long, meandering walk through the gardens, and hopefully well away from any listening devices that Simion might have ... just in case. You could never be too careful.

Time to check in with the boss.

"Gray, fast update," she said as soon as he answered her call. "Might have a breakthrough here."

"Cyn, why the fuck does your geotag have you in Australia?"

"Because I am."

"Well, that's good. I am too. Apparently, I'm a few hours' drive from you. Do you need backup?"

"Not yet. But Simion has a property we didn't know about—that's where I am now. Can you get Marcella to use the geotag from my location and find out everything possible, including schematics, builders—the lot—on this property and send it all through to my cell? I've got security on the device, so it can't be hacked. This might be it, Gray."

"I fucking hope so."

"Same. It's only been three frigging years getting to this point. How's Isa?"

"She's ... well, I'll get to that later. Right now, we have a few problems."

"What?" Cyn stilled, tuned out everything else. "What's wrong?"

"Isa had a vision. She saw Forneous get one seed from R-104B."

"Holy fuck." Cyn's breath stalled. "The myrrh? How? When?"

"No fucking clue. Could've been when Isa had the vision, or be about to happen, or will happen some day far fucking off in the future."

"When was the vision?"

"Just yesterday."

"Can she divine for the seed again? Last time we spoke you said she was gaining more control—"

"Yeah, that's problem number two. Isa tried again immediately but couldn't see anything. In fact, she hasn't been able to bring a vision on since then. It's looking more and more like she might not have another vision for another nine months or so."

"Nine months—hold on ... are you saying Isa's pregnant? Holy, *holy* fuck. Congratulations, Gray, to you and Isa. That's wonderful news. How is she?"

"Tired and nauseous or tired and hungry. And she keeps getting the urge to head to Cheshire, which is giving me the creeps. Listen, with her daemon heritage, we're looking for information on similar pregnancies. Anything you can do to help me out here?"

"I'll check in with Mother. See what she says. If you can swing your way to Cheshire, the library at the Watcher's castle has some good texts I used for research on *my* heritage so that might be an option."

"Good call. I'll put the word out discreetly."

"What's the discretion for?" Cyn asked.

"I'm ... wary of people who want Isa for their own agendas. Normally she has her visions for protection, but right now, she's defenseless in that regard. Plus, she's not feeling well—we guess standard pregnancy stuff, but she's been wiped out after the vision of the myrrh."

"Got it. Hey, if you're worried about Isa, are there any witches Isa's comfortable seeing?"

"She gets on well with Evangeline—"

"You mean Eve from the Watchers? She's warded some of our Templar relics, right?"

"That's her. Eve's been working with the Watchers to modernize their operation, but it's a slow process."

"I bet. The Watchers might have some of the strongest witches in the world, but man, last time I visited their castle in Cheshire, it felt like we'd travelled back in time to the Middle Ages."

"Tell me about it," Gray muttered. "But in good news, Eve's in Brisbane right now, about an hour and half from here."

"Wait, the Watchers have an office in Brisbane? When did that happen?"

"It's not an official office. Eve and Isa's brother, Raph, are together, and she's just moved into his place—in Brisbane."

"Well, great to have her so close. And I can come up as well if Eve gets called away. Do you have the jet nearby?"

"Yeah."

"And the property building plans?"

"Shit," Gray said. "Yeah, will have them over soon."

"Thanks, and wow. No wonder you said problems plural."

"Actually, that's not all of them. Not that the next thing is my problem."

"In that case, it must be mine. What's up?"

"I'm guessing you don't know about your mother's petition to the council?"

"Shit. What's she done now?"

"She's asked the council to formally move you out from the US ops division and into a special operations division."

"What the fuck? I've never even heard of that. And when did she do this?"

"Two days ago," Gray replied. "I found out today when the council told me it had been approved. And the reason you haven't heard of special ops before is because it's just been created. Congratulations, Cyn, you no longer report to me. You're now your own Special Ops entity reporting only to the council."

Blood thrashed through her veins so hard it drowned out every other sound, and she gripped her cell so tightly she had to unclench her hand for risk of breaking the damned thing.

"Cyn? You there?"

"Yeah." She swallowed the knot that lodged in her throat. "I'm really sorry she went around your back, Grayson."

"I don't care about that—and I happen to believe you are more than capable of running a division—special operations or otherwise."

"Fuck," Cyn said. "That means dealing with politics and all that BS, right?"

"Yep, congratulations."

"Pfft. You should be offering me commiserations."

"Plenty of people would be thrilled to be in charge of their own division."

"Then my mom should've offered them the chance. This is pure nepotism—you know that, right? And no wonder she didn't tell me; she knows I would've said no."

"Not sure you could, it's a council order."

"Damn her. And sorry, I know I sound ungrateful." Which she was. "Do you have time for one question?"

"Sure."

"Do you recall the daemon you were with at Fathom LA last year?"

"Rohan? Of course. Why?"

"Do you trust him?"

There was a moment's silence before Gray sighed. "In some ways, yes. We had a mutual agreement to help each other, and he upheld his end of the bargain and then disappeared before we could do much from ours. I also trust him with Isa—she told me he was trying to look out for her when all that shit went down with Forneous and the bounty hunters. And you already know he's Isa's cousin—although we don't know the exact tie. So what's he got to do with your investigation?"

"His ... involvement in my case is a requirement right now. I'm trying to work out how much I can trust him."

"As in, can you trust him with the secret of R-104C?"

"Yeah. That."

"Sorry, I can't say one way or the other there. But I'll say this—I didn't trust Isa with some sensitive information last year, and I sure as hell regretted it later. But at the end of the day, it's your call, Cyn."

Well, hell. Apparently, now it was. And damn her mother for not telling Cyn first. That had to be why her mother had visited Cyn in LA. No doubt trying to smooth over the change in command without making it obvious she'd been the one to petition the council.

But the change of command was nothing compared to the rest of Gray's news.

Forneous with a seed of R-104B and Isa pregnant.

And then it hit Cyn. She was officially the leader of this op now. No more reporting to Gray outside of official channels.

Mother of the gods. Like Gray said—everything was her call now. To trust Rohan or not. To make a decision in one direction over another ...

Anticipation warred with doubt in her belly all the way to her room. Then her cell pinged with an incoming message from Marcella with the property schematics.

Now all she had to do was evade the staff, get into the owner's suite ... which, according to the building plans, was at the opposite end of the compound, and get out of there before Simion and everyone returned.

No time like the present.

In the corridors, Cyn searched for surveillance but found hardly any, unless Simion had a concealed system— possible—but her gut said he just didn't care for that kind of thing, and all the way to the owner's suite, no one popped out of hidden doorways or demanded she turn around.

Double doors opened soundlessly into a palatial space with soaring ceilings, a floating palace of a bed, and yet another deck with stunning ocean views.

Holy shit, this was some bedroom.

An actual waterfall spilled down rocks amid ferns and other plants; talk about shitting all over any other water feature she'd seen, and beside it, two doors led to— according to the plans—an ensuite and a walk-in closet.

The love whisperer's business clearly did very well.

Shit. Snap out of it, not the time to gawk at the room *or* the view. This was about R-104C.

Cyn brought the plans up on her cell screen and made her way around every inch of the bedroom. Nothing.

Next up, the walk-in closet. She opened the door and pulled up short. What the hell? This wasn't a closet. The room was easily as big as her suite and filled with gorgeous clothes and shoes and bags. A glass-topped timber island cabinet in the middle held an array of jewelry and belts and wallets—how many wallets did you need in a seaside town? —and a mint-green studded-leather couch looked like the perfect place to recline and try on all your gorgeous clothes.

Not bad, Simion. Not bad at all.

And on any other day, Cyn would have loved to indulge in the colors and fabrics—something she'd never enjoyed until she'd gone undercover and started expressing herself as a high priestess.

She knelt and started feeling along the back of the walls. Maybe he had a secret—

"Good to see the headache's feeling better." Rohan's voice flowed into the room like a roll of silk.

Cyn jumped. Her head hit the underside of the wardrobe shelf with a solid thwack. "Shit!"

7

"Ouch. You okay?" Rohan gazed around the space. Exactly how much clothing did one being need?

"No thanks to you." Cyn rubbed her head and checked her fingers. As she did, the ring on her right hand glinted in the light. His gut tightened. That ring had to go—and now might be the perfect opportunity.

"Bleeding?" He kept his voice mild.

"No." She scowled at him. "What are you doing here?"

"That was my question to you. You look like you're sneaking around our host's dressing room searching for something to steal." He shifted to block the way out of the closet.

"I'm not a thief."

"But you're sneaking around."

"And what are you doing here, then?"

"Simion sent me to check on my possible future soul mate and see what she needed—he said to let my senses guide me or something like that. So I followed my sense of smell and look where I ended up." He tapped the side of his nose. "Also, Simion found a friend in the village, and I get the feeling they'll be heading up this way soon, so I suggest you wrap up whatever you're doing fast and come with me."

Backing up his claim, voices echoed from the entry to the suite.

Cyn's eyes widened, and she grabbed Rohan's arm and pulled him to the floor behind a big timber chest of drawers.

Now this Rohan was okay with, but exactly what was the intriguing high priestess up to now?

"Shh."

"What are we doing?" he whispered.

"Hiding! At least the cabinet's big enough; we're hidden unless someone walks around this side. Now seriously —shh!"

Out in the bedroom, the voices grew louder.

In the closet, the heat turned up. No surprise there. He'd been in a constant state of arousal since meeting the high priestess, but right now, he had more important matters to handle. "Hey, can you squeeze over? Think they can see me," he lied.

"Shit. Really? I don't have any room on this side either. Fine. Come closer."

Rohan did and then picked up her hand.

She yanked it away. "Stop that," she whispered.

"What? I'm trying to hold myself still here—is there something else I can hold?"

He'd said the words as a way to get her hand back, but then her gaze dipped to his lap, and, of course, he rose to the occasion as if that look had been a physical caress. And then the sweet scent of her arousal hit the air.

"Cyn," he breathed her name. Inhaled more of her delicious scent. Would she—?

She kissed him.

Not gently, not searching. Just a full-on mating of their mouths.

A groan rumbled through him, and damn but he wanted to strip Cyn naked and taste every single inch of her—

But fuck, the knockout ring. He interlinked his fingers with hers and tightened his grip even as he thrust his tongue into the sweetness of her mouth.

His balls tightened. His cock went spike hard—

The ring. The *frigging* ring.

He ran his interlinked fingers up and down hers in a tight caress over and over, then shifted his thumb, and on the next upward slide, pulled the ring off and made a fist to hide it in his hand.

He held his breath—had she noticed?—but then her tongue stroked his, and with her free hand, she clenched the material of his shirt as if she was going to yank it from him, which he was totally onboard with.

Then she froze, her breath shuddered, and her eyes glowed electric blue right before she wrenched back—and the gods damn him, but all he wanted was to dive back into her. He tightened his grip around the ring.

"They're going," she whispered. Which Rohan hadn't noticed. But at least they could get out of there now. "Why don't you head out and I'll meet you soon?"

"Leave you alone in our host's bedroom with all these valuables?" He smiled. "No can do."

Cyn rose to her feet, and he got to his too. He might have her ring, but who knew what other tricks the high priestess had up her sleeve?

"I told you, I'm not a thief." She looked down that long straight nose at him, which was impressive given he had her easily by half a foot in height.

"Since I don't really know you, who's to say?" Rohan

shrugged as if they were having a casual chat about the weather.

Cyn went to twirl the ring on her third finger—

"Looking for this?" Rohan opened his hand and showed her what she was missing.

"What the? Give it back." She lunged, but he ducked back fast.

"What? This ring?" Rohan pretended to think. "The ring you used to knock me out on the plane?"

Cyn sighed and folded her arms. "When did you guess?"

"You could at least pretend to look guilty. And as soon as I woke up. One minute I thought we were about to get to know each other *really well,* and the next, I was waking up with a headache strong enough to send me Hellside and a mouth full of cotton wool. And I saw you take down the trichorn, remember? So either you drugged my coffee or you used the ring."

"Fine. It was me." Cyn flicked the ends of her hair. "So sue me. You were up in my face and we had hours to go. I didn't feel like talking."

"You can put on that 'don't give a damn' attitude for everyone else, but I've seen you at work now, *High Priestess,* the real you—with that woman back in LA, with the people the night of the trichorn attack. So I know you do care."

"Who's to say that wasn't the act?"

"Guess I'll have to find out for myself."

That evening, Rohan drove the ATV back into town and took Cyn to a small place overlooking the water that he'd noticed was popular with the locals when he'd been there earlier with Simion.

They ordered drinks at the bar and then, without speaking, made their way to a free table nearest the water.

Cyn took a seat and, for a moment, stared at the ocean.

Rohan's gut tightened. How could one creature be so perfect? But perfect-looking meant jack shit.

What was she up to? In the short time he'd known Cynane, she'd taken on and defeated a trichorn and had a Templar councilor visiting her shop—not to mention she'd helped Grayson, another Templar, six months ago. She'd also knocked Rohan out on the plane, and now he'd caught her sneaking around Simion's rooms.

Although, technically, as long as whatever was going on here didn't interfere with his finding the hellgate key, none of that mattered. Rohan just needed to make sure that was the case. And now he had two pieces of leverage—Cyn's ring and the knowledge she was up to something.

Which would get him further here?

"So what do you want?" Cyn murmured. She stared him straight in the eyes as if he didn't hold the upper hand.

"I want my hellgate key, which means you need to do your spell now. I want to know that whatever else you're working on here—and don't try to tell me the Templars aren't a client—isn't going to interfere with my job. And then I want to know that you'll never use this on me again." He held up the ring.

"Wow. There's a fair bit to unpack there." Cyn's mouth curved. And damn if his pants didn't grow tighter. But he'd focus on pleasure later. Right now, Rohan had a high priestess to wrangle. "Let's see. Your spell. I'm going to need very specific equipment—as well as a sacrifice—to make that happen."

"Let me know what you need, and I'll make it happen."

"Fine. Then the Templars?"

"I know the councilor who was in your shop yesterday," Rohan said. "And Grayson has you on speed dial. Why?"

Cyn pursed her lips and stared at him for a long moment before leaning forward, her expression serious, and then lowered her voice. "*If* the Templars were a client, then hypothetically, I'd have signed a nondisclosure agreement, so I wouldn't be able to tell you."

"You could tell me if any hypothetical client's job would impact my search for the key, though."

"Technically, yes, that could be divulged. And the ring? Would you even trust me if I said I wouldn't use it on you again?"

"If you make a binding contract," Rohan said.

"I can't make that promise." Cyn folded her arms, and her chin lifted.

"Why not?"

"Because who knows what circumstance might arise in the future where I need to knock you out? Promising you this vow might come back to bite me."

"Then I'm keeping the ring." Rohan slipped it onto his pinky finger. Yikes, but it was tight. At least she wouldn't get it off him easily.

"That ring belonged to an important relative of mine, and believe me, Rohan the Red, I'll get it back."

Anticipation tightened in his gut. "I look forward to you trying."

She smiled a grin as sharp as the fire in her eyes. "I wouldn't if I were you."

And damn if that didn't make his body tighten even further. "Fine. We agree to disagree on the ring. What about the spell and the Templars?"

"So you're promising to guarantee your silence with Simion?"

"I'll even make a binding contract," Rohan said, "once you make the same to agree to find my key. And then provide assurance your job on behalf of the Templars isn't interfering with my search for the key."

Cyn eyed him for so long that he found himself holding his breath—although why this was so important, aside from the hellgate key, he had no frigging clue—and then she nodded. "Deal. Hold out your hand."

"What, you want to do this here?"

"Why not? Let's get this shit show going."

"What's the spell?" Rohan asked.

"It's simple, but it does require a sacrifice—from both of us. That's how I make magic."

"A sacrifice?"

"Hair, blood, a nail, skin even. Or something precious you would truly miss if it were gone forever."

"I can do a strand of hair."

"Done." Cyn reached out whip fast and yanked a hair from behind his ear and placed it in her palm.

"Ouch."

"Don't be a baby. My turn." She took the pin that held her hair up—the silky strands tumbled around her face—and stuck the pointed end into the tip of her middle finger. A single bead of blood welled. "Here, hold my hand."

Shit. The slide of Cyn's skin against his had a lick of heat curl through him. Hell. If he ever got to touch more than just her palm, he'd go up in flames.

"How will I know it's worked?" Rohan said.

"Standard way. We'll both get marks on our bodies to confirm the vow."

He eyed the designs wrapping up Cyn's arm. Every one

of them was a work of art and, he was sure, held a wealth of symbolic meaning. Were any of those binding contract vows?

"No, none of those," Cyn said.

"Mind reading too. You're one powerful high priestess."

Her lips tilted up. "You have no idea. Now, spell time. And shh, I need to concentrate. No matter what happens, don't let go. This is my vow. Rohan the Red, I'll undertake a spell to find your hellgate key—although I will not vow to the success of that spell or how long it'll take to work."

She squeezed his hand. Guess it was his turn now. Shit. He had to get this right. Binding contracts weren't to be made lightly.

"Cynane, High Priestess, I will not divulge to our host Simion that I found you in his dressing room—for at least six days."

She tensed against him, and her eyes narrowed, but after a moment, she lowered her lashes, and with her thumb and forefinger, she traced a triangle around his palm where her blood and his hair lay. "Bind the vow and secure the word. Deny by deed or will inviolate, and with this power, make it so."

His skin tingled beneath her touch, and as she retraced the shape over and over, the sensation grew stronger, hotter, like someone had placed a sparkler in his palm. He tensed and glanced up, colliding with Cyn's gaze. Her beautiful eyes glowed like an electric charge—and suddenly, that electricity surged where their grip connected them. Exploded through his body.

His heart took off. His cock went ramrod hard. What was going on?

Shivers gathered at the base of his spine and pressure gathered in his balls like he was about to come.

Oh fuck. Fuck, fuck, fuck.

Across the table, a flush tinged Cyn's exquisite cheek-bones. Her hand clenched around his, and she let out a low moan. The addictive, delicious scent of arousal bloomed in the air.

Stars teased at the edge of his vision as he teetered on the verge of orgasm, and then the stars crashed, tension released and the rest of the world blanked out as utter pleasure shot through him.

And Cyn. Her eyes squeezed shut, her lips parted before she gasped. Her body quivered, and then she dropped forward onto the table, still clasping his hand.

Frigging hell, that had to be the most erotic sight ever.

8

THE NEXT MORNING, sunrays streaming through the sliding glass doors made the darkness behind Cyn's eyelids turn bright. Ugh, who said it was a good idea to have an ocean view on the Eastern Seaboard?

Couldn't it stay dark for one more hour? She jammed a pillow over her head. Come on, mind. *Back to sleep ... back to sleep.* Considering she'd had all of two hours' shuteye last night because she couldn't stop thinking about what happened at the beach bar, sleep was exactly what she needed.

As if just thinking about the spell triggered it, the new tattoo high on her inner thigh tingled.

Fuck. Fuck, fuck, *fuck*.

Cyn threw the pillow aside and sat up, staring at the new tattoo inked into her skin. A frigging arrow—an *arrow!*—like something Cupid would fire from a cutesy bow, pointing at her vagina.

Seriously? Like what, the universe hated her or something?

That type of sensation had never happened before with a binding contract. Was it linked to Rohan being a daemon? Or was there something else at play here? And it wasn't like she had a heap of people she could ask, and Cyn hated to rely on anyone else anyway.

Someone banged on the suite door. No magic to know who that was. And damn it all, her belly tightened just knowing he was there. Because while she hadn't asked for that orgasm last night, holy shit, it had been amazing. And she wanted more.

Well, time to face Rohan—and they did need to talk about the spell last night. At least now she could speak and not sit opposite him with her entire body clenched and on fire like he was fucking her right at the table by the ocean.

Maybe it had been the full moon?

Maybe it had been ... fuck. She just didn't know. And that was a problem. A thirty-year-old high priestess should know enough about her heritage to figure this shit out.

Well, she'd work through the problem. And who knew, maybe Rohan had some clue?

"I know you're in here," he called through the door.

"Fine. I'm coming." Shit. No, no, she wasn't coming. Freaking hell, one orgasm last night and sex thoughts about the delicious daemon dominated her mind. Except, who was she kidding? She'd been having get-naked-and-dirty thoughts about Rohan from first time she'd seen him.

"Hurry up," Rohan said. "Simion's driving me nuts. Something about love needing to find a garden to thrive in? Come on. Apparently, since the sun's up, we're meant to be up. Seriously, I'm not going back down there on my own."

Shit. Cyn gave the bathroom a long glance. So much for that idea. Maybe when she went looking for her ritual supplies, she could find a sex toy shop as well.

And since she was up, she was going to do a tai chi routine. She'd get at least one good thing out of the morning. Cyn pulled on black leggings and a sports bra, with a burned orange loose tee—Simion did have good taste with clothing—then grabbed her cell and over-the-shoulder purse.

She yanked the door open, and her mouth dried up. Rohan wore a tight, long-sleeve tee that hugged the curves of his biceps and the breadth of his chest, with his hair tied back in another of those messy, sexy, buns. All round freaking delicious.

He let out a long whistle. "And good morning. You look stunning."

A shot of pure pleasure raced to her belly. But Cyn shut it down and instead tried to surreptitiously check out his skin—what she could see anyway.

Where had his binding mark gone? Nowhere visible. So it had to be somewhere beneath his clothing—like hers.

Huh, was it … really like where hers was? Heat pooled in her core at the thought of investigating that delicious body to find out.

And damn if the color of Rohan's eyes didn't deepen as he stared at her before reaching out and tucking a strand of hair behind her ear.

Her nipples tightened. Fuck. She was in trouble. "Let's go," Cyn muttered and strode past Rohan without another look.

"Good morning, dearest ones," Simion called as they entered the pool deck. "And what a beautiful day it is."

"It's also early." Cyn couldn't help from pointing it out.

"I don't want you to miss out on a single second of this beautiful getaway. I hear you do nothing but work, work, work, my dear High Priestess."

"Well, there are a surprising number of people who need spells. What's a witch to do?" Cyn gave a playful shrug and ignored the tingle that Simion's words caused inside her.

Work was a good thing. It had purpose. She had purpose. The Templar Knights had a purpose greater than anyone here could know. But even if she was truly only a high priestess, the fact was, surprisingly, she was also speaking the truth about people needing her help. Just look at Jaz and her creepy stalker ex.

Simion had had his chef set up a light breakfast—thank the mother of the gods because no way could Cyn eat anything heavy at that time of day—then declared it was time for Cyn and Rohan to get to know each other 'more.'

Cyn held back a groan. This lead had better pan out. "Okay, Simion. What do you have in mind?"

"Well, you share a lovely Jacuzzi on your deck—"

Oh no. No freaking way. She'd barely restrained herself from leaping at Rohan that first night in the hot tub, she'd jump the guy for sure now. She didn't even look at Rohan before she leaned forward. "Actually," Cyn said with the brightest smile she could muster, "I didn't get a chance to see the town yesterday, so after I do a workout, I might go down today." And get the ritual supplies for the hellgate key spell she was now bound to undertake. "We can get to know each other there."

Twenty minutes later, with her hair twisted into a high knot and her favorite dagger earrings in place, Cyn chucked her purse in the backseat of the ATV. "I'm driving."

"Really?" Rohan said. "I saw how you drove in LA."

"Please, this ATV is nothing compared to my 'stang. And what—is the big daemon scared of a little drive?"

"Scared for your neck if you crash, yeah."

"Worry about your own neck." She flashed him a grin, pulled her sunglasses on, jumped over the side of the ATV and slid into the driver's seat. "Well? Are you coming?"

Rohan said something under his breath, but when she looked back, he was shaking his head and hopping in beside her.

The drive down the hill was fun, but they reached the town way too soon. Maybe one day she'd come back here and drive the ATV along the coastal roads—except no. Once this mission was over, she'd be back to driving safe, sturdy black SUVs and not racing around in ATVs ... or flashy Mustangs.

"You okay?" Rohan's voice took Cyn out of her thoughts as she parked the vehicle in a small parking lot.

"Absolutely." She forced a smile.

"I think I saw a witchy-looking place," Rohan said. "But it didn't look open."

Crap. "Let's check it out anyway—it's still early, and it's a Sunday. Maybe they open later."

Rohan crossed the road, and she followed him to a small row of stores, and sure enough, a sign stating Arcane Treasures hung in front of a pretty white shopfront with beautiful wood trim.

"Yep, they're closed. But the sign on the door says they're open Tuesday." Cyn peered through the window. "And good news, they carry a lot of what I'll need."

"Can we break in?"

"Rohan, I'm not stealing from a fellow witch. You'll just have to wait for your spell. Come on—what will two more days hurt?"

His jaw clenched, but then he nodded, and his tension dropped away. Huh. What was that about?

"So, since we're here, I need coffee." Cyn turned around

—but instead of coffee, a discreet door up the street caught her eye.

Thank you, mother of the gods.

"Hey, Rohan, see that café at the end of the street? Let's head there for a coffee, but on the way, I need to make a stop. You can come with or not."

Three stores down, Cyn pushed through the door of the Bewitching Adult Entertainment shop and didn't wait to see if Rohan followed ...

Which he did.

"Interesting business," he murmured. "You needed to come here?"

"Absolutely. Sex is a need, after all."

"Can't argue with that." Rohan glanced at the display of butt plugs. "Is that the best they've got?"

"What, the butt plugs are bigger in Hell?"

"Cyn, everything is bigger in Hell."

"And I bet you tell that to all the girls," she smirked. "Well, Red, I'm not here for something big. I'm after one of these." She led the way to a display of oval-shaped devices.

"Now those I haven't seen before," Rohan said.

"When was the last time you were in an adult entertainment shop?"

"They were called sex shops at the time—does that give you an idea?"

"Wow, okay, lots to share with you here. So these are clitoral stimulators—you put that end over your clit, and wham, big O time. You know what I mean by that, right?"

"Yeah." Rohan's voice dropped. "I know what an orgasm is."

Yikes ... given how hot last night's beach-side orgasm had been, just how much more amazing would one be with him actually touching her?

"Now these I recognize." His gaze shifted behind, and she turned to see what he was talking about.

The BDSM section. Of course. Everything about Rohan shouted *hot, wild, delicious sex right here! Come and get your orgasms 24-7!*

"I think the chains in my shop are superior to these," Cyn said. "And my whip is definitely better." She tapped one fingernail against her lower lip and pretended to think. "But the silks ... these are nice."

"Are you buying these, too?"

"Nope, just the stimulator for me today. Silks take two or more to play, and I'm all about looking after myself right now." Cyn went back to the clit stimulator display, grabbed what she wanted and went to pay.

Rohan joined her and leaned back against the counter while she completed her transaction.

"Why are you looking at me funny?" Cyn asked.

He tapped the tip of the dagger in her ear. "Why do you always wear something pointy?"

"I prefer the term stabby. As someone who makes magic from sacrifice, sharp implements are tools of my trade."

Outside the shop, Rohan stopped midstride and clicked his fingers.

"What?" Cyn said.

"Just realized I wanted something from inside. You go on, I'll meet you at the café."

The urge to demand what he wanted to buy surged through her, but she bit the words back. His taste in sex toys was his business.

She'd just ordered their coffees when he joined her, holding a black shopping bag. Damn. No way to see inside what he'd purchased. "That was fast."

"I knew what I wanted," was all he said.

Ugh. Now she really wanted to know.

9

Two days later, Cyn woke before sunrise and got in her morning tai chi on the deck in blissful privacy. And she was *not* disappointed that Rohan hadn't joined her.

Keep telling yourself that, beeatch.

Damn, she hated her inner voice sometimes.

But at least she was centered and ready to continue her hunt for R-104C. She found Simion sitting by the pool, wearing a beautifully embroidered kimono, Aleesha and Sonja at his side as always.

"Aren't you cold?" Cyn asked. "The days get warm enough, but the mornings are chilly."

"Not really." Simion beamed at her and held out a hand. "Come and sit, dearest one. Today, I wish you to do something for me." He sat forward like an excited child. Then he glanced over her shoulder and his eyes lit up. "Rohan, our hero, perfect timing. Come and join us."

Cyn traded looks with Red. The daemon looked as wary as she felt.

"And that is?" Cyn said after a beat.

"I wish for you to get to know each other ... properly. So,

I've set up a little picnic at the beach for you. Champagne. The most delicious lobster and fresh local fruits. You'll be totally spoiled. And I must insist you go—since I'm leaving you to your own devices and all."

Shit. This wasn't on the plan. She'd just make the picnic part superfast. "Of course we will," Cyn said quickly. "I need to head down into the village anyway, to the witchcraft shop —Arcane Treasures."

Simion's eyes widened, and he leaned closer. "Do you know Tanya?"

"Uh, Tanya?"

"She runs the witchcraft shop."

"No, not at all. We passed by on Sunday morning, and I found it intriguing, that's all."

"Well, Tanya is a wonderful witch and a special friend. I'll let her know you're coming—I have no doubt she'll make sure you have everything you need."

"That's not necessary—"

"Worry not, dearest heart. This is what we do for our friends."

After breakfast, Simion regaled them with more love whisperer antics—couples he'd set up, and there were some eye-openers among the names. Finally, Simion declared it was picnic time and sent them off back into town—and Cyn couldn't wait. Not for the picnic but for the chance to delve into Arcane Treasures.

This was the longest she'd been away from her witchcraft shop since going undercover, and it was surprising how much she had already missed the connection with ritual and the parts of her life associated with magic.

She grabbed the ATV keys and pulled up short when she found Rohan already sitting in the passenger seat, his satchel on his lap. "Don't tell you me you've brought your you-know-whats?"

"Like I'd leave them behind."

"Thought they were spelled?"

"That's to remove them from their scabbard—they could still be stolen. Plus, I like to be prepared for anything."

Cyn rolled her eyes. "We're in a small seaside town, don't think you have to worry about hellbeasts." But Rohan just folded his arms and settled back into the seat. "Fine. But keep them hidden."

Fifteen minutes later, they walked through the doors to Arcane Treasures. Small chimes rang out, and sage and sandalwood tingled in her nose. Cyn's shoulders dropped. And she took a deep, even breath for the first time all day.

Home.

This shop might differ from hers in layout, but in essence, it was exactly what she loved about her place. Herbs, timber, stone, cotton and flax. Crystals. Candles.

"Blessings." A woman—surely this was the Tanya who Simion had mentioned?—with long dark hair emerged through the doorway; she had beautiful dark brown eyes and skin to match, and it was almost impossible to put an age on her.

Tanya's gaze locked on Cyn's forehead—like most practitioners—and a generous smile broke over her face as she glanced between Cyn and Rohan. "Simion's friends."

"Blessings," Cyn murmured back. "And Simion said he might call, but please don't feel the need to do anything special for us."

"Well, how lovely to meet you both, especially another of the craft. And not just any craft ... This is a rare treat. I should've known I'd be meeting a high priestess today—the moon gave me that feeling last night."

"The moon does tricky things sometimes," Cyn muttered.

"That she does. Now, what can I do for you?"

"I'm looking for a few things for a ritual. I'm making a potion to find an item for someone." Cyn went through all the ingredients she needed.

"I can help you with most of that, except the sweet cicely root. Although I can source that overnight," Tanya said.

Rohan stiffened at her side, and she elbowed him to stop him from saying anything. "That would be great, thanks." She ushered him outside before his negative energy affected the shop. "What's wrong?"

"Another day?" Rohan's jaw clenched.

"Yes, you gave me six days—we've still got three left."

"I didn't think you'd need all that time. Listen, Cyn, I need this key."

"Clearly. You blackmailed me into doing a spell for it."

"No, you don't understand. This key is crucial."

Rohan led the way to the beach where Simion had set up the picnic, but he had zero interest in food. He had a decision to make—did he tell Cyn about the real reason he needed to find the hellgate key? Would that help her prioritize finding it for him?

"So, are you going to fill me in?" She folded her arms and held his gaze.

"Man, you have a good death stare."

"It's a skill," she said without missing a beat.

"Okay, I'll explain, but let's walk and talk. This isn't

something I want overheard. I take it you're good to skip the picnic?"

"Please, yes."

Rohan cut her a glance. "You really don't like sitting around and eating, do you?"

"Not all day."

"Yeah, neither do I. Let's head toward the lighthouse. Okay. Truth time. I'm a representative of the Daemon Congress, and technically, I've been searching for the hell-gate key for the last six months. I know it's somewhere here in the human world, just not where—or with who."

"Wait—you've been looking for this key all this time?"

"No, I started six months ago. I've spent almost every moment since then fighting off hellbeast after hellbeast. I finally got some ... help at the gate that's unlocked."

"The unlocked gate—that's in LA? That's why the trichorn came through."

"Correct."

"Oh shit. But isn't there a gate lord who controls who comes and goes?"

"Because the key is humanside, Lord Deimus—the Lord of the Tenth Gate—can't keep it closed."

"Rohan, that's bad. Very bad."

"Why do you think I'm here? The Templars agreed to work with me to find the key, but I haven't been back to them to follow up. And then I thought of you."

"Shit. You should've said something sooner—I would've helped ... well, as soon as I could. So who's stopping the hellbeasts from coming through right now?"

"My uncle sent one of his dark daemons—they're a supernatural force that helps him manage the ebb and flow of Hell—which is a big deal because while he's at the gate, part of Hell isn't being managed, but Uncle will have to figure that—"

"Uncle? Why do you keep saying that?"

"Okay, next truth. My uncle is ... Shit. How do I say this? Okay, don't freak out, but he's the devil."

"Oh." Cyn stopped.

"You don't look too ... shocked."

"Surprisingly, I'm not. So the Templar trust you enough to agree to work with you?"

"I'm a rep for the Daemon Congress—"

"You told me that already. So what do the congress do, exactly?"

"They run Hell—each of the gate lords, my uncle, and his inner circle all sit on the council."

"Wow. You're one well-connected daemon."

"I looked you up. You're not too badly connected your-self. Lord Balfour, huh? Lord of the Seventh Gate."

"He's my father, yes. Apparently, I'm his tenth halfling in about a thousand years, although none crossed over, so I don't have any siblings alive. But I've had zero to do with him since birth, so I don't exactly go around calling him Dad."

"Family can be tough," Rohan said eventually. "What about your mother? Any half siblings?"

"Nope. She did her job with me—one child is the goal in my family." Cyn's lip curled. "So what's with all the questions?"

"Just trying to get to know my partner."

"We're not partners."

"Fine. Getting to know my ... fellow key hunter."

"Well," Cyn said, "at least we'll be able to prove to Simion we've actually gotten to know each other. And thanks for telling me about the key. I'll spell for it as soon as

I can, but here's the thing, I really do need the ingredient from Tanya. Then I have to make a potion."

"Why a potion?"

"That's where my strongest magic is." She shrugged. "I'm not bad with standard spells like stuns, and to be honest, I'm even weaker with spells for divination—and I did tell you that, remember? So yes, your spell needs a potion, and that will take time. But the good news is I'll do your spell tomorrow, no matter what."

"Really?"

"Yep. You'll need to make a sacrifice, though."

"No problem. So, we're making this look good for Simion, right?"

"What do you mean?"

"You and me," Rohan said, "seeing if we're a love match. That's what you want Simion to think while you do your thing for the Templars that you can't tell me. Don't worry, I'm not looking for your secret. Just a thought, though. Let's make this look good here, and then we'll get you back to the compound so you can do your search for whatever, and I'll help keep the staff out of your hair."

"Wait. You'd do that for me?"

"Sure. You're helping me, remember?"

"Because you blackmailed me."

"Doesn't really matter now, does it? We have a binding contract to work together."

"Speaking of ... Where did you get your tat?" Cyn clenched her fists to avoid touching hers.

"Inner thigh. What about you?"

"Thigh as well. Never had one there before."

"Me either," Rohan said.

"Any ... shape in particular?"

"Just a line. Why—what did you get?"

"Something like that, too."

They'd reached the headland, and without pause, they rounded the rocks to the other side. This stretch of beach went on forever, just with fewer people around. Two adults and three young children splashed in the waves near the shore, and several surfers were farther out. None were close enough to overhear this conversation.

"So do I get to ask questions?" she said. "To make it look like we're really getting to know each other?"

"Of course."

"How old are you?"

"I've been alive for roughly three hundred years."

"You're shitting me."

"Nope. That's part of being a daemon—long lives."

No wonder he was such a good kisser; he'd had plenty of years to practice. What else would he be good at? Heat licked through her veins, and damn if her nipples didn't pebble. And damn it to hell and back because Rohan noticed. His nostrils flared. A red tinge hit high on his cheeks.

"Do you know one more daemon trait I have?" he said in that smooth, rich voice. She stilled, her feet somehow welded to the ground. "My senses are sharp. And that includes my sense of smell. Which is how I know you're turned on right now. You can't hide that sweet scent."

Mother of the gods—he could smell when she was turned on? Damn. How was she meant to hide her reaction? Although ... maybe the time for hiding was truly over. "And I never said I didn't find you attractive. You know what— maybe you and I should just bang and get this ... this ... tension out of the way."

"Sex so we don't get distracted?"

"Works for me." Cyn forced a casual shrug. Because

casual was the total opposite of the blood zinging through her body at just the thought of having sex with all this gorgeousness. "You have a problem with that?" She lifted her chin. And he stepped closer. His gaze dropped to her lips.

Suddenly, Rohan tensed and spun around. Cyn followed his gaze.

"Help! Help me—please, help us all!" One woman from the group of five splashing in the waves shouted as she held two children to her. The other woman was farther out with one child, waves pounding over their heads.

Rohan took off. "Help her," he yelled over his shoulder, pointing to the nearest woman and children. "I'm going for the other two."

Cyn dumped her purse in the sand, then sprinted as fast as she could through the crashing waves to the nearest woman who clutched two children against the pull of the water.

"Let me help—" Cyn took the hand of one child and put all her strength into her legs to keep upright. "I've got her."

"Thank you, but Chrissy, she's out with—"

"My friend got to them. Come on, let's get the kids to the beach."

On the beach, Cyn knelt in front of the children and checked them out. "Did any of you swallow water?"

They all seemed okay, so Cyn went back and helped Rohan.

"Thank you so much," the second woman gasped to Rohan as she flopped to the sand. "We were fine one minute —just splashing up to the knees—and then Jada got caught in the rip. It pulled her out so fast. If you hadn't come for us —I don't even know how you got us both back in; the current was so strong."

"Just glad we were able to help." Rohan knelt in front of the oldest girl and held her hands. "You're okay now. That was scary, though, hey?"

The girl nodded, and the two women took their children and headed back to the foreshore.

"That was close," Rohan murmured as he watched them go.

Cyn rubbed his back—she almost stopped, but the tension running through his shoulders was a real thing. "You were onto it before I even heard them cry out."

"I heard the child make a gasping sound and then the woman splash. But by the time I got to them, they were both going under—that happened so fast."

"Guess those supersenses are good for more than just figuring out if I'm turned on, huh?"

Rohan smiled, and the tension in his shoulders eased.

"Hey, you don't feel the cold either, do you?" Cyn said.

"This isn't cold. Why?"

"Since we're already wet, why don't we go for an actual swim?" She yanked her dress over her head and dropped it beside her purse.

If all the hellbeasts from every realm that had, did, or would exist charged the beach right now, then Rohan still wouldn't have been able to move.

Toned muscles. Delicious curves. Ink that made him want to uncover every secret of her skin, including an arrow high on her inner thigh, pointing right at ... well, well, well. So now they had matching tattoos?

"So, where's yours?" Cyn lifted her chin.

"You really want to see?" One of her perfect brows rose. "Okay." He unbuttoned his shorts and kicked them away. Cyn's gaze locked on his actions as he rolled up one leg of his trunks.

"Oh." Her eyes darkened, and her lips curved in a way that made the blood rush to this cock. But then she smirked. "Cute." Then she spun and ran into the water.

Cynane. High Priestess. Kick-ass spell crafter, potion maker and hellbeast wrangler. Tough. Brave. And so damned hot she was like every sexual fantasy he'd ever had brought to life.

Half human. Fragile.

Shit.

Did she even want to cross over and become fully daemon? Was she happy as a halfling? And if she did cross over, she'd have to answer to Lord Forneous—like everyone did except the High Lord and his inner circle daemons. Rohan blanched. Shit. Cyn, with such close ties to the Templars, would suffer under his sire's control.

Rohan blanched. He wouldn't wish that on anyone—and for Cyn? Never.

"Are you coming?" she called over her shoulder.

He blinked, and once again his focus snapped back to the lush curves of Cyn's butt.

The black one-piece swimwear she wore dipped low in the back and gave him the perfect view of the phases of the moon tattooed up her spine.

Everything inside him stopped for a split second—and then returned to life with a roar.

"Well?" Cyn was up to her knees and spun around to frown at him. And gods but she was everything he could ever dream of. Her smile. That glint in her eyes. The glorious tattoos adorning her long arms and legs.

Strong. Wild. Capable.

Mine.

The thought was in his mind before he could stop it. And fuck, he shouldn't want her. A half-human high priestess, for hell's sake. But damn if he could do anything other than follow her into the ocean.

By the time he caught up to her, the waves, as they crossed farther out, bathed her up to the shoulders in white water.

"Are you a good swimmer?" Rohan asked.

"Yep."

"Why am I not surprised—is there anything you can't do?"

"Still finding that answer out," Cyn said. "What about you?"

"I can swim for a long time." He didn't say he'd had to swim across an entire sea in Hell once to track an aquatic hellbeast.

"So, as a daemon, can you drown? Is that the same for all daemons?"

"Technically daemons can drown. But I'm strong and have stamina."

"What about a shark? Could that bite you and kill you?"

"If it ate me—yep. But if it just bit an arm or a leg, provided I didn't bleed out from a major hemorrhage, I should regenerate."

"What about—?"

"What about if I do this?" Rohan held her gaze as he yanked her into his chest. Cyn wrapped her arms around his neck. Her breasts rubbed against him, and he swooped down and captured her mouth.

His growl echoed in his ears, as loud as the waves crashing around them, at her lush, sweet taste. Rohan wasn't after soft. And thank the gods neither was Cyn.

She nipped his lip, and then her tongue stroked into his mouth. She retreated, and he followed, licked into her like she had to him.

Over and over they dueled and stroked—each demanding the other's taste. And with every caress, his cock grew stiffer. He reared back. "I want to tongue fuck you so badly, princess."

"Is that a promise?" Cyn ran a hand down his stomach, and he sucked in a breath when she found him through his trunks.

"Yes." He grabbed her hand. "You really want to touch me here?"

Cyn looked around; then, a wicked grin tilted her lips. "No one's close by. Why? You got a problem with public displays of affection?"

"No, as long as I can go first." Rohan traced his fingers along the fabric of Cyn's swimsuit, along her inner thigh, then up into her slit.

Hot. Silk. Wet.

His cock went ramrod hard. And when he brushed the tight bud of her clit, she gave out a little mew that made his blood fire. Fuck, he *needed* to make her come. Right here. Right now. "Put your arms around me."

"Mother of the gods, yes. But wait. This is banging only. We get this ... craving out of our system, and then we focus on work—the spell, I mean."

"Fine. Banging it out works for me. But I need more than just once. My cock has been hard for you for frigging six months. I can't see this as a one-orgasm deal."

"How about three?" Cyn said.

"How about ten? We review after ten orgasms."

She tilted that gorgeous throat back and laughed, and before he could stop himself, he latched onto the skin at the base of her throat and sucked hard. Her legs curled around him, and damn if her pussy heat didn't scorch him through her swimwear and his. He found her clit again and, this time, rubbed harder.

"Red," she gasped, "I'm all for hot and heavy right here and now. But we need to get somewhere. I'm allowed to see you naked."

"Where's closest?"

"Shit. Not the ATV—how about the toilet block?"

"Cyn, I'm not fucking you for the first time in a public urinal." He nipped at the skin he'd sucked; his mark right here alongside all the other art adorning her skin, and primal satisfaction surged through him.

"Then, as much as I'm happy to ride your finger right here, I'd prefer to have more of you than that. Let's get back to the compound."

10

CYN PUSHED Rohan ahead of her and dragged in a breath. Holy mother, he was hot. He turned around as she reached the beach, his gaze raking over every inch of her as she walked out of the water. And damn if that look didn't make her feel more powerful than all the sacrificial magic in all the world.

And shit. Look at him. His dick filling out his swimwear was so freaking fine she had the batshit urge to grab it—him—and tumble him to the sand right here.

In fact, if they'd been alone, she would've.

The heat flaring in Rohan's eyes told her he wouldn't have minded one little bit.

He grabbed her hand—maybe to keep her from grabbing his dick, good call there—but didn't tug her into his side. Probably another good call. Too much skin rubbing and she'd be dragging him off into the bushes after all.

Cyn pulled her dress back on, and he his cargo shorts—though happily, not his shirt.

By the time they'd made it back to the parking lot and

the ATV, even the rubbing of her thighs with each step had her body thrumming with heat and need.

Rohan's nostrils flared, and his lips pulled tight as he all but shoved her into the ATV's driver's seat.

Cyn would've teased him about his hurry, but she had the same craving to get—

Rubber screeched behind them in the parking lot. Cyn scowled. What now?

A huge black SUV screeched to a stop behind the ATV, and three men piled out from the back seat—they wore military-style pants with tight-fitting polo shirts. First out had short black hair. Second out had a truly huge nose. Third out was the largest of the group and had an icy-blond buzz cut.

The driver and another man in the front passenger seat stayed in the SUV. But all their gazes locked on Cyn.

Well, fuck. With other vehicles parked on each side, and bollards at the front of the parking lot, the ATV was boxed in.

She glanced at Rohan and found him watching the men with exactly the right level of caution before he turned to her, one eyebrow raised.

"Sorry, Red," Cyn said. "Looks like it's pause time on our 'bang it out' plan. But hold that thought—this won't take me long."

She grabbed her hairpin from her purse, twirled her hair into a knot on top of her head, and jammed the pin through the strands to hold it steady before turning to face whatever bullshit was coming next.

"Hello, boys. Someone looking for a high priestess? Let me guess—you need a spell to keep your muscles inflated? No? Oh, I know. Your dicks have shrunk and you want some grow juice."

Black Hair growled and lunged forward, but Buzz Cut shot out an arm and held him back. "That wasn't very nice, Miss ..."

"I wasn't trying to be. And you can call me High Priestess. That's my title."

"Perfect. So, High Priestess, we hear you might be able to help our boss with a problem he's having."

Cyn didn't have to move to know Rohan had walked around to take up position behind her, and funny, it was nice to know her back was covered.

Buzz Cut's eyes shot behind her, and his sidekicks spread out as if they wanted to flank her. At least Buzz Cut brought his attention back to her—the other two clearly lacked smarts because they'd dismissed her as a threat and focused on Rohan.

"Is that your boss in the car?" Cyn asked. "Perhaps he could come out and ask me himself."

"He's asked me to handle this," Buzz Cut said. "So, I'm going to give you the chance to do the right thing and tell us where you stashed her."

"Her?" Cyn tweaked her chin. "Hmm, let me think. Her ... her ... your last girlfriend? No? Maybe the cat? Wait—I know, I stashed all the gummy bears—yep. I love those candies."

"Jasmine Inverloch. Seen entering your LA premises last week but hasn't been seen since."

Jaz. Shit—these men were here for her client? Well, no freaking way these pricks were getting anything from Cyn. And she mentally cheered—the potion had worked. Good for Jaz. And wait—Jaz had mentioned something about her ex-fiancé's men following her to Cyn's. They must've followed Cyn all the way here.

"Jasmine ... Jasmine ... Nope, still can't say I've stashed

any Jasmines anywhere lately. So, since we've got that out of the way, think you can ask your boss to move the car? I have a date that I really want to keep. Now."

Buzz Cut shook his head. "Thought you might make it hard. And the boss said if she makes it hard, it's her own fault. And whoever the fuckhead is with you—don't matter how big you are—you're one man against three. And those numbers mean the two of you are coming with us until we get the information the boss needs."

Adrenaline surged through her, and Cyn rolled her neck and shoulders. Gods, it had been too long since she'd got to really use her skills.

"Boys." She widened her stance. "Bring it on."

"What do you need from me?" Rohan called from behind her. "You don't have what you used with the trichorn."

"You think? And it's fine. These twats aren't even close to an upper hellbeast. Just stay out of my way. I'll let you know if I need a hand."

"Get her. And him if he interferers," Buzz Cut ordered.

Black Hair and Big Nose came at her from the side, and Cyn let them close in on her ... closer ... closer ... She grabbed Black Hair's arm, pivoted, grabbed Big Nose and pivoted again, locking their arms together. Then she pricked her thumb on the hairpin point and whispered, "Sleep well, sleep long. Wake for none."

Instantly they fell together into a heap to the ground, arms still linked, softly snoring.

"Sleep spell. Short term, should wear off in about ten minutes." She winked at Buzz Cut. "I can knock them out for longer—but I really do have to get out of here. So, you're next. What'll it be?"

Buzz Cut's eyes widened as he looked from her to his errand boys. Then he reached behind him and drew a handgun from his back. Looked like a 9 mm semi-auto Ruger P95. One of Cyn's favorite weapons. He flicked the safety off and pointed it at her chest. "Don't fucking move. One whisper, one jolt—"

"Keep her alive. She's no good to me dead," the man from the front passenger seat yelled.

She smiled. *Oh sweetie, so good of you to give yourself away. Boss Man, aka Jaz's asshole ex, was going down.*

"Ah, High Priestess—need that hand yet?" Rohan's voice held a note of tension she hadn't heard before. But then, he didn't know handguns like she did.

"Nope," Cyn replied. "Not yet."

Buzz Cut shifted the gun to Rohan. "Fine. What about him?"

"Him, you can do what you like," Boss Man said.

"Rohan, keep your satchel closed." She didn't need the headache of explaining hellblades to the local authorities, thank you very much.

"Really? I can end this now if you want."

"Nope. All good."

"So you've still got this?" Rohan said.

"Aw, you're getting to know me after all."

"Shut the fuck up, you two," Buzz Cut said. "Now, High Priestess, come this way, and I won't have to shoot your boyfriend here."

"I prefer the term fuckbuddy, thank you. He's not my boyfriend. Do you know we met at a mansion in LA? We worked together to handle a small trichorn problem. He told me how to act, and I did, and it came off perfectly." Hope to hell Red picked up on the reference. All she needed was to get close enough to the Ruger ...

"I remember the trichorn well," Rohan replied. "And fuckbuddy? Is that what you're calling me?"

"Well, I could call you my fuck-enemy, but that sounds mean. And we're not enemies right now, are we?"

"Seriously. Over here." Buzz Cut waved the gun. "Keep your hands up where I can see them and your mouth closed. It opens—and whoever the fuck this dude is, he's either hurt or dead."

Cyn made a show of putting her hands up and pursed her lips tight even as she regarded Buzz. The flat, cold look in his eyes screamed he'd pull the trigger without hesitation.

Right now, the boss needed Cyn, but Rohan could end up collateral damage in a second, except he was a daemon ... not truly immortal, but it would take a lot more than a bullet to kill him. Although it would hurt him.

Cyn's stomach tightened. That was not happening.

She waited until she was close to Buzz Cut, then held her arms out as if offering herself over to him. He watched her carefully, but he had to hold her hands with one of his, and then she moved.

She spun around, broke his grasp, covered his grip on the Ruger, and depressed the button to drop the magazine. It clattered to the ground.

"Fuck!" Buzz Cut yanked the gun, but Cyn went with him. No way was she letting go. But she knew what was coming—readied herself for the blow she needed. Then he yanked his hand back and punched her in the jaw. "Take that, bitch."

Pain slammed into her. Stars shot across her vision. But even as the metallic tang of blood filled her mouth, she smiled. *Thank you very fucking much, motherfucker.*

Power trembled in her palm, and she called her stun

spell and flung her hand toward Buzz Cut. He froze, midsnarl.

Yes. This was power. This was how she was meant to use this bubbling, rolling energy that built inside her. And not just on Buzz Cut. She'd freeze all their asses—

Crack. A shot rang through the parking lot.

"Not her!" the boss yelled. "Get us out of here. We'll get the bitch later. We need to go now before the cops arrive."

"Oh, really?" Cyn readied another spell. Her palms hummed.

"Let them ... go," Rohan said from behind her.

The power crested. Go? No, these assholes deserved to—

Rohan groaned. She drew in a sharp breath and whirled. Blood stained the middle of his shirt and seeped between the fingers he pressed into his stomach.

"Fuck, Red." She darted to him. "They shot you?"

"Yeah. You okay?" Rohan ran a hand over her cheek and his thumb passed over her lip in the softest sweep. "You're bleeding."

"Just where he hit me." She moved her jaw, winced. "Yeah, hurts like a bitch. But nothing's broken. What about you?"

"Hurts too." Rohan hissed as he lifted the end of his shirt. A small dark hole bore into his stomach. "The frigging driver got me. Think he was aiming for you, but the boss clearly didn't like that, so he grabbed his arm, and I got hit instead."

"Well, shit," Cyn said. "You took a bullet meant for me?"

"Looks like it. Are they gone?"

"Yeah, I got their plate number, though, so they can't get too far. Listen, I can do a healing spell, but how do your daemon genes work?"

"I'll heal eventually, but if you can spell me, it might go faster."

"So, do we get the paramedics or not?"

"Not."

"Okay, let's go. I'll do the spell in your suite. Just try not to bleed all over the seat. Simion's going to think we're more trouble than we're worth."

As Cyn sped out of the parking lot, and with his gut hurting worse than a trichorn's gouge, Rohan still couldn't take his eyes off Cyn. Fuck but she was something else. If Rohan was going to fall for someone ever again, the high priestess would be that being in a heartbeat. How the hell did someone so perfect exist?

Not even the pain radiating like a fire through him could stop that knowledge.

"How did you do that thing with the gun?" Rohan said. "And can you teach me?"

"Should you be talking? Aren't you meant to conserve your strength or something?" Cyn took the turn for the hilltop road so fast he slammed into the side of the ATV.

"Fuck," he hissed. "You're driving is doing more damage than me talking."

"I don't want to hang around in case they decide to come back. I've got power, but that'll run out fast—my energy can't last that long without more and more sacrifice. And if they bring a ton of guns, I don't like our odds."

"Think they know where we're staying?"

"If they don't," Cyn said, "it won't take long to find out. Simion's not exactly low profile."

"Shit."

"Don't worry. I'll get rid of them."

"What, just like that?" Rohan clicked his fingers. "That's some magic."

"No magic needed here. I'll call my Templar ... contacts. Get their help."

"You must do a lot of work for them to respond to your requests so fast."

"You could say that."

Something in Cyn's voice made him stop and assess her, but then she took the turn into Simion's driveway even faster and skidded to a halt at the gates. Rohan rammed into the dash. Pain tore through his stomach all over again.

"Shit, Cyn. Can you at least ease into the corners?"

"Oh, hush. I'll get you right soon. And what happens— will your body expel the bullet or something? Finally, they're opening the gates. Not long now."

"Never been shot before, but I'm guessing so," Rohan said. "We heal faster than humans, that's all. Superfast. Just like you'd heal a cut on your hand, I heal the same way, but the damage will begin to repair immediately."

"So, I don't need to worry about you?" Cyn shot him a look. "Still think I'm going to park as close as possible to the doorway near our suites—in case you fall down or something."

"Don't think that's going to happen, but like I said, first time being shot." Guess the adrenaline was wearing off now because as Rohan twisted to lever over the side roll-bar of the ATV, pain grabbed at his gut. His breath caught.

"Frigging hell," he whispered when he could breathe.

Cyn was at his side fast, and he had no choice but to lean

on her to get himself onto the ground. "Some day, huh?" She wedged herself under his arm and took part of his weight. Even so, pain cut through him.

"You're good with understatements," Rohan ground out.

"It's a skill. Come on, let's get you somewhere I can do some healing magic."

"Trust me, I've been injured worse than this."

"Well, the bleeding might've stopped, but you're still covered. And since you're not dying—you told me that, right?—I'm taking you to the bathroom first."

"And then we can have sex?"

"You know you're shot, right?"

"Trust me, one part of me will work around you no matter what."

"Ew. Gross. Keep your shorts zipped, thanks."

"You weren't saying that before."

"You weren't coated in blood before. Here, we're at your suite."

Rohan propped himself against the wall as Cyn opened his door, letting her help him into the ensuite.

"Okay, stay here," she muttered. "I'll get my things and be right back."

Using the sink to steady himself, Rohan surveyed the damage. A dark and jagged-edged hole—maybe the size of his fingertip—drilled into his stomach beside his belly button. Cyn had been right about the bleeding, but when he moved, pain cut through him all over again. Rohan sucked a breath through his teeth and, with one finger, pressed into the wound.

Fuuuuck. Fuck, fuck, fuck.

"What are you doing?" Cyn's voice cut through the silence. But he didn't stop.

"Getting the bullet out."

"Good timing. When can I do the healing spell?"

"After I'm finished here. Every time I move, it hurts like a trichorn's gouging my gut—and trust me, that is not something I want to experience over and over."

"Fine. Do you need a hand?"

"No, think I've ..." He probed deeper, and sure enough, his fingertip brushed something hard. "Shit. Got you, you little bugger. Hell, there's another bit."

"Shrapnel. Happens sometimes. Do you need to get every piece?"

"Got this bit; hope there's not too many more." Rohan gritted his teeth and pulled the bullet free. "Done." He sagged for a moment, then dropped the squashed bullet into the porcelain sink. The clatter echoed around the bathroom.

"You're bleeding again." Cyn grabbed a towel and pressed it against the wound. "And you already lost a fair bit earlier."

"It'll stop soon. And I just need time to mend, that's all. Your spell should kick it off fast."

"Okay, stay there. I need to set up."

Through the mirror, Rohan watched Cyn's reflection as she opened up her satchel and removed a candle, a bunch of herbs, a small bowl and a knife.

"You going to cut me?" Rohan asked.

"Usually I would, but you've lost enough." Cyn took her hairpin, and instead of pricking her thumb, she pierced the skin of her inner elbow.

"Hey! What are you doing?" Shit—she was cutting herself for *him*?

"Told you, you've lost enough blood already. Hand me the bowl."

"Shit, Cyn, you didn't need to do that."

"Well, I just did; now shush and let me go to work." She flexed her arm, and then a bright red trickle splashed into the bowl before she grabbed a towel and held it to her elbow.

Her brows pulled tight as she mixed her blood with the herbs and held the candle over them. Then she took her athame and used the tip to mix everything in the bowl, then dabbed the mix on the wound.

Standing this close, Cyn's lashes were inky arcs hiding the brilliance of her eyes as she focused on his stomach.

"Don't move as I say the spell," she murmured. "Mend and heal, rout the pain. Bind the damage with spell and flame. With these words, make it right, with my will, bind it tight."

Heat and energy flashed into him. Tingles started at his stomach, worked out and out and out until they covered every part of him, then they intensified, turning him into a human sparkler, and in another flash, they were gone.

Cyn hissed, then wobbled back.

"Hey, you okay?" Rohan said.

"Sure. Just used a lot of energy today."

"No, no, I've seen you wiped before. You're in pain. Fuck. Did you take my pain?"

"It's part of the healing process," Cyn said. "And I'll be okay. Any reason you can't have a wash?" Her nose wrinkled.

"What, do I smell?"

"I'd say more like stink."

"And do you want to ... wash with me?"

"No, I need to talk to my Templar contact and make sure the motherfuckers who shot you don't come at us again, and hopefully get the Templars to run interference with local law enforcement. You wash. I'll go into my room and take a shower and meet you back here and check the wound."

He dropped his swim trunks and headed for the shower. And was it his imagination, or did her breath catch? He inhaled deeply—the metallic tang of blood lay heavy in the air, but beneath it all … one more scent that made his mouth water. Hell, but he wanted that taste against his tongue. Down his throat. Wanted to dive into her and not come up for air for a month.

And that removed any doubt that his body was in perfect working order for what Rohan really wanted.

He washed fast—made sure he didn't stink—and wrapped a towel around his waist and joined Cyn in his bedroom.

Huh. No sign of Cyn. Was she still in the shower? An image of water streaming down that strong, toned body—of him kneeling at her feet, palming her thighs and spreading them, then diving in to taste her pussy made his blood surge, and he bit back a growl.

To avoid running into anyone unwanted, he left his room through the balcony doors, rounded the hot tub on their shared deck, and parted the curtains leading into her suite.

Well, hell.

His high priestess was sound asleep, like some fierce sleeping beauty from his wildest fairytale imaginings.

Who could've died today. Rohan might heal from a bullet wound, but Cyn was human where it counted—her life. A chill settled through him. Shit. And he'd taken away one of her best defenses—her knockout ring. He could've been part of the reason she'd died today.

11

WHEN CYN WOKE UP, the sky outside her suite was pitch black. She fumbled for her cell—oh shit. It wasn't night; it was the next morning. The sun would be up in minutes. She'd slept for twelve hours?

Damn. So much for her and Rohan banging it out. And double damn—how was the daemon?

She rolled over and then stopped. Her ring lay on the pillow.

Well, that was unexpected.

A soft rain had settled in overnight, and Cyn did her morning workout inside the bedroom. Afterward, she found Rohan and Simion in the enormous living room.

She met Rohan's gaze right away, and while Simion said good morning and something about how rested she looked, she brushed one hand over her jaw—made sure Rohan saw the ring—and gave him a small smile.

He seemed to get her thanks because his lips curved too, and then he nodded.

She dipped her gaze to his stomach. He nodded again.

Relief flashed through her.

"So," Simion said, "dearest ones, I have to leave you for the day, and I wanted to see you before I go."

"What? Why?" Cyn dragged her focus back to Simion. Was this about R-104C? But also ... this was the perfect chance to fully check out the compound.

"Don't be distressed, dear heart. I'm continuing your search for love. However, I am getting the feeling that you two are forming some kind of attachment?" Simion looked between them. "No? Ah well, perhaps my love sense was mistaken. And that makes my mission today even more vital. Tonight, I'm bringing guests back with me! Yes, my dearest, you're looking for love, and so love I shall procure, one way or another."

Oh shit—more people? Cyn had to search the property today.

Simion left as soon as they'd had breakfast, and Aleesha and Sonja went with him. Before Cyn could speak to Rohan, Tanya from Arcane Treasures wandered into the lounge, carrying a wicker basket filled with herbs and ritual implements.

"Hello," the witch said. "Hope you don't mind me intruding—Simion said to come through. I ran into him and his assistants as they were leaving."

"Sure." Except that Cyn had been about to launch her biggest search of this monstrosity of a compound yet. "But please tell me you didn't come up here because of my order? I could've come to you."

"No, no, all good." Tanya waved a hand through the air. "I'm heading to the shop, so it was easy to drop these off on my way in." She eyed Rohan and then Cyn. "And I also wanted to see for myself if the two of you are okay."

"News travels fast around here, I guess?" Cyn murmured.

"When it involves guns and shootings. We don't have trouble like that here often."

"Trouble's one word for it," Rohan muttered. "How did you know it was us?"

"When I heard that a giant of a redhead and a stunning blonde were involved in some kind of alteration, I had a good idea who it was." Tanya shrugged. "Not that I said anything about your identities."

"Thank you," Cyn said. And she meant it—the fewer people who knew of her involvement here, the better. "Can we look at the supplies?"

"Of course." Tanya picked up the basket at her feet. "Everything you asked for. So where will you do the spell?"

"Somewhere quiet, ideally, and private."

"Are you up to it?" Rohan interrupted.

"Of course." Cyn didn't bother to hide her scowl.

"Well, I thank you for your business, and it's been my pleasure to bring these to you." Tanya cut Rohan a disapproving glance. "And as I said, we'd be honored if you'd like to join us while you're staying here. And I have a place I can suggest for your ritual. I'll tell you on my way out."

"Did I do something wrong?" Rohan asked when Cyn rejoined him by the pool.

"You questioned my capability in front of another of the craft. Big no no."

"How was I supposed to know?"

"She assumed you're aware of our customs—as did I, to be honest. How do you not know about dealing with high priestesses and witches?"

"It's been a while," Rohan muttered. "Right. Well, I promise not to do that again. Thought she was gonna hex me or something."

"Good. Because I was going to be right behind her with a spell of my own."

He stared down at her, green fire glowing in his eyes.

"Why are you looking at me like that?" Cyn asked.

"What?" His grin grew wider.

"That right there. I just threatened you and you're smiling. Do you get off on pain? Is that it?"

"Nope. But you ... I have a feeling I could get off on you very easily." Rohan stepped so close she had to tilt her head to hold his gaze. "And the look? Pure appreciation, princess. Because every time you kick ass or take someone down with that sharp tongue or threaten to use your wicked power, I swear my chest seizes up, and I do this dance between melting like those s'mores you humans like and erupting like a volcano and devouring you."

"Wow. Devour. S'mores. You're talking my language, Red. But it's High Priestess, remember?"

"Actually, I think you're both. And around others, fine—you're High Priestess. But when it's just you and me ..." He leaned into her neck. His breath washed over her ear. "You're *princess*. What do you think of that?"

Talk about volcano ... a pool of lava swirled low in Cyn's belly, and her nipples pebbled ... at his words. Mother of the gods, what was it going to be like when she actually got him inside her?

Her lady parts clenched as if cheering that thought. *Settle, girl.* She still had a job to do, and the window for that was narrowing fast.

And judging by the intensifying gleam in Rohan's eyes and the way his nostrils flared—oh mother of the gods he was hot when he did that—Rohan knew just how turned on she was.

"Red, I think it's time you and I did this thing—but first,

I need to search this place. Second, I can do your spell, although we need quiet and privacy. We do those two things ... then you and I are on."

"Why don't we bang first?" Rohan said.

"Fuck, you're tempting, but no—I'm here on a job. And my ... client is important. And what about your hellbeasts? Don't you need the key fast?"

"Hell, but I hate it when you're all practical. Give me hot-headed, rash Cyn any day."

"That Cyn will more than likely get you gut shot, remember? And right now, you're stuck with this Cyn." Which was a good thing. Job. Job. Job.

Yes, she was going to bang Rohan the Red. But *after* she'd seen to her duty.

"So, am I helping with the search?"

Cyn stopped. Shit. Trust him with something as impor-tant as the R-104C? Images flew through her mind ... Rohan rescuing the girl and her mother from the water ... then leaping onto the back of the trichorn.

Well, it was her call now. And the fact was, she did trust him. "Come on, we'll talk while we walk. Don't want to waste any more time. And one more thing. I don't do fuck-ups. Not from me, not from others. So don't mess this up."

"We're searching for a bowl of resin?" Rohan scowled as he trailed Cyn to Simion's suite. The windows along the back of the house were filled with the view of the subtropical rain-forest leading up to the crest of the hill. "What's so impor-tant about a bowl?"

"A bowl of resin," Cyn said. "And that part I can't tell you."

"Why? Don't the Templars tell you?"

"It's got nothing to do with that."

"Huh. So what, they just pay you to find it? And why not just do the spell and then let them do the retrieval? They seem damn good at doing that in other areas."

"Long story."

"You know, I'm here to help you—legit—but you're making it very tough to think you're being honest with me, princess."

"And you need to trust that I don't give a fuck what you think, and I'm not telling you anything more. Now, you either come and help or stay here and pout. Up to you."

"It's not pouting," Rohan said. "It's called trying to have a conversation—something you're remarkably good at avoiding."

"You want to talk? Fine, we can talk … later."

Hell. Swallowing a sigh, he followed Cyn into the suite at the far end, and together they made fast work of searching the entire room.

Three hours later, Cyn jammed her hands on her hips. "Nothing. Where would he hide it?"

"Does a safe need a reinforced wall or anything like that?"

"Shit, of course." Cyn took out her cell and brought up images of … floor plans?

"How did you get those—no, of course, your client. They have their hands in every frigging thing."

"Why do I get the sense you don't like the Templars?" Cyn asked.

"It's more I don't … trust them."

"Which sounds very personal. What did they do to you?"

"Not to me. But to someone I knew once. The Templars have this motto—do you know it?"

"Once a Templar, always a Templar." Cyn's face tightened.

"Yeah, you've had run-ins with them too, don't deny it. That vow comes before everything and everyone else."

"So are you ... anti-Templar?"

"Not anti, exactly. You don't have to worry; I won't get in the way of their job. But I like my dealings with them to be tightly bound so I know they're not going to backstab me." Cyn visibly recoiled. "Hey, I doubt they'd do that to you—you're obviously working for them on more than one job. But just don't trust them with everything you've got. That's all I'm saying."

Cyn stared up at him, speechless, and he was going to reassure her again when she ducked her head back to the cell screen and cleared her throat. "Right. Reinforced walls. Nothing ... nothing ... nothing on any of these plans. Doesn't mean it's not here, though."

"What about magic? Could it be spelled? Your witch with the basket of goodies said she's known Simion a long time."

"Good call. It's possible that it's glamoured and we just can't see it for what it is."

"Okay, so potion time. Finally!" Rohan said.

"Yep, you got it," Cyn replied. "I'll mix it in my bathroom, and you keep guard. Okay?"

Cyn took her basket into the bathroom and started to pull items out and line them up on the vanity. A frown tugged at her forehead, her gaze locked on her ritual.

That absolute concentration was both sexy and annoying—because he had the loco urge to drag that focus back to him.

Which was a no. Cyn was about to do his spell. And none too soon—solstice was on Friday. Two days to find the key and return it Hellside.

Stay close to the high priestess.

His cousin's words replayed in his mind. Damn, but she better be right about this.

12

CYN HANDED ROHAN THE BASKET, then led the way past the pool and up into the bushland.

"You sure about this?" Rohan said. "There's not even a trail."

"That's how the witches keep their sacred space hidden, apparently. Okay, almost there."

A subtle buzzing brushed her skin as they reached a small rise, and then the trees cleared to give way to a pool of water, surrounded by mossy rocks and fed by a cascading waterfall.

Rohan stopped and rubbed the back of his neck. Was he feeling the power here too? Then he let out a long whistle. "This country just keeps getting more spectacular."

"It's special, isn't it?"

He nodded instead of replying, and as they both stood in silence, the world of the forest came to life. Bird calls whipped out. The thrum of the water on the rocks. Rustles and scrapes as small creatures scuttled through the leaf litter.

"Should we be here?" Rohan whispered.

"We have permission; otherwise, Tanya wouldn't have told me." Cyn pointed to a tree close to them. "See that blessing attached to the trunk? This is where Tanya and her coven come to practice their magic. And why it's perfect for us. Although I'll leave a blessing for this land and the spirits here, too, they deserve that."

Cyn gave Rohan one last glance as she knelt opposite him on the pebbles by the pool. The last rays of sun flickering through the treetops cast that fiery glow all over him again, and damn if everything inside her didn't scream *this was exactly where she was meant to be. With this man. Making magic.*

Except, he didn't trust Templars. Which meant he didn't trust her. Shit. To hear him say that so blatantly had made her chest freeze. If he knew who she really was, what would he do? Well, there was no way she was telling him now. She needed him to keep up the deception with Simion.

Love. What a joke. Now lust ... the fiery halo glinted around Rohan. Her heart picked up pace.

Shit. Not here. Not here. She had a spell to do. Two spells to do.

And given she was dealing with a daemon who didn't trust Templars, she was damn well doing it right.

"Cyn, you okay?"

"Yep. All good. You stay there. Don't move for anything."

"How long does it take?" Rohan asked.

"If it's still dark and I haven't had an image come through, we're in trouble."

"Has that happened before?"

Given how many times she'd used her magic to find R-104C over the years—following in the footsteps of many others—yes. But she just gave Rohan a tight smile and continued unpacking her ritual tools from the basket. "Blood, hair or nail. What do you prefer?"

"Here." Rohan pulled out two strands of hair and laid them in her palm.

She placed his sacrifice in the bowl, added the herbs, lit the candle and dropped a splash of wax into the mix. From the basket, she took out the twine and a tower of clear quartz. "I'll make a loop around my wrist, then a loop around yours to bind us together. There you go. And now we're set. I'll go first, and then you."

Cyn calmed her mind and dipped a finger into the bowl.

The energy of the sacrifice and budding magic hummed through her, rich, intoxicating, like bubbles from the finest champagne laced with an electric charge. She took a deep breath, then traced a backward seven onto Rohan's hand, then repeated the ritual on hers.

"What's that?"

"It's an ancient mark for sight. Now, no more talking."

Cyn waited till he nodded, then she closed her eyes and let the bubbles of power travel through her, and pictured the hellgate key as Rohan had shown it to her. "Where lies that this being seeks, reveal the place or being who keeps."

As the spell unspooled through her, Cyn focused on the magic. She'd expected the tug from where their twine linked them. What she hadn't expected was the throb of the tattoo on her thigh.

She'd opened her eyes before she could stop herself— and her gaze smashed into Rohan's, his filled with burning green light.

Shit, shit, shit. Why was this connection happening? And why Rohan?

But the magic was working—the magic rippling through

her—and she wasn't messing this up. So with their gazes locked, Cyn let Rohan's spell fly.

And she held his stare—let the magic run and run and run—as the sun disappeared over the trees behind the pool, and the cool early winter air settled around them.

And finally, rays from the rising moon touched the waters of the pool.

Cyn sighed and let the twine fall from her wrist.

"Anything?" Rohan whispered.

"No," she murmured back. "Stay here." She rose to her feet and stretched muscles kinked after staying still for so long.

She picked up several twigs, leaves and three pebbles from the edge of the pool, laid them at the base of the tree with the witches' offering and whispered her own words of thanks and blessing.

On the way back down, Rohan didn't talk—which she got. This place was spiritual, and speaking out loud—especially now, at night—felt wrong.

Within minutes, they were at the boundary of Simion's property, and once again, the murmur of voices—this time, many of them—echoed from the house.

Cyn shared a look with Rohan.

"Simion's back," Rohan said.

"You can make that out this far away?"

"Supersenses, remember?"

"Who else?"

"I don't recognize the others, but there's quite a few."

"Shit. Okay, let's go over your spell before we join the party. I didn't get any information back, but the thing with a location spell is that they can take time—sometimes a lot. Now I've run the magic, I'd also like to try my tarot deck. Let's do that next. Between the spell and the tarot, I might be able to speed up your results. And I don't need privacy for the reading—although, a party isn't ideal either."

"Can we skip the party?" Rohan asked.

"I promised Simion I'd see him—so let me make an appearance, and then we can get out of there." She turned around and walked to the gap in the foliage.

"And then ..." Rohan grasped her hand—right where the twine had bound them together. Warmth licked through her and she froze.

Damn. She'd been all for burning off this sexual tension with Rohan—but now she knew he didn't trust the Templars, it made her ... wary of going there with him. Would he be so keen if he knew who she really was?

"Are we still on for ... how did you put it? 'Banging this out'?"

"Rohan, you don't know me—not really. Are you sure you want to have sex?"

"Cyn, after seeing you help that woman in LA, and the family at the beach, and watching you handle the assholes yesterday, and doing that spell at the pool, I don't see how I could need to know one more frigging thing about you to know exactly what I want."

Shit. Well, he'd said it. And the mother knew Cyn wanted him too.

"Let's get this party done—then you and I can have our own party. But this is strictly sex, right? No emotions. No expectations apart from getting rid of this ..." The tattoo on her thigh throbbed. An answering beat pulsed in her core.

"Yeah." Rohan's voice deepened. His gaze dipped to her mouth. "Do you know your perfume is the most scintillating turn-on I've ever known?"

"I'm not wearing perfume."

"That's not the scent I'm talking about." He stepped

closer and whispered into her ear, "Your arousal makes my mouth water."

Her body flooded. Instantly. Shit. And by his smile, he knew that too, damn it.

Fine. Maybe sex was still the best answer.

"Come on, Red. Let's get this party over with."

"Princess, when I get inside you, the party will be the last thing on your mind." And then his lips pulled back in a shark's grin that made her heart thump.

With his cock stiffer than it had ever been, Rohan had to adjust himself before he followed Cyn and emerged at the back of the pool area.

And then their host strolled out onto the deck. "Cyn," Simion called out. "My dearest heart, what *are* you doing over there?"

Cyn sent Rohan a fast look, which he read as *don't say a word about the spell*—like he would—and they joined Simion and his guests.

"Rohan and I were enjoying your grounds."

"Well, after what happened at the beach with those awful men, no wonder you're staying close to the house. But I promise you, behavior like that is a total rarity. I'm assuming those terrible people didn't cause any harm?"

"Harm?" Cyn's brows drew tight. "They—"

"We're absolutely fine," Rohan cut in. He jostled Cyn's shoulder. She scowled up at him, but he flashed a look at the rest of the party—they had no idea who these people were, after all.

"Yes, fine," she agreed. The cool smile resurfaced in her expression, and this time, Rohan felt something click inside his chest—that cool smile was a facade. Finally, a tell he was finding out about his princess. He filed that little piece of information away, though, because Simion linked his arm with Cyn's in a move that made Rohan's gut tense.

"Now, dearest heart, tonight I have brought the finest specimen options just for you."

Why did this sound like they were talking about purchasing a fancy gem or something?

"You were serious? Then why did I need Red here?" Cyn nodded at Rohan.

Wow. Way to make him feel special.

"These are backups, in case after your day together, you've found our wonderful hero not the right fit." Simion waved at his assistant. "Please bring them in. Cyn, dearest one, have a seat with me." He sank in a graceful dip to the same poolside couch he'd been sitting on when they'd arrived and pulled Cyn down with him. "This is going to be a night to remember."

Cyn shot Rohan an amused smile as if this was all a bunch of laughs—but he caught the hint of a query in her eyes—before she turned back to Simion. "Bring on the show."

Aleesha pulled the doors open and five males, ranging from human to witch to daemon to fey, ambled into the pool area.

As one, their gazes locked on Cyn.

"High Priestess, may I present to you my curation—in fact, I think this might be the finest array of possible love matches I have ever assembled. Powerful. Looking for love. Attractive. Exactly like you."

Oh, hell no.

Cyn coughed. Rohan tried to catch her eyes, but she was facing the house and the males, and he'd have to literally walk around to stand between her and the—what did Simion say?—the array of possibilities.

"My new friends," Simion said, "please come and meet the high priestess, Cynane. My dearest, may I present Azin; he has been visiting this world for other purposes but has found himself with time on his hands."

A seven-foot, muscle-bound male at the back of the group came forward.

Azin, a third-gate daemon.

Rohan stared hard until the other daemon met his gaze —recognition flared in Azin's eyes—but he didn't say anything before he looked back to Cyn. "The pleasure is all mine," Azin said smoothly before leaning in and giving Cyn a kiss on the cheek. Rohan's hackles rose, and he had to bite back a growl.

Simion said, "Next we have—"

"I'll introduce myself." A human stepped forward, jostling shoulders with Azin—which was saying something —and picked up Cyn's hand. "Alexi. Lovely to meet you, High Priestess."

Cyn murmured hello back, but Rohan didn't take his gaze off the human.

"Alexi, remember I'm to do the introductions." Simion sighed. "All this testosterone, I guess. Well, next we have Sebastian, a witch of great renown, I'm told. Very good with his hands or something. Then beside him is Theson with the curls, and last is Aeron, one of our fey cousins—he's only visiting the human world, but I'm told he's interested in spending more time here. His English is rather limited, but apparently, he's a quick study."

The males surrounded Cyn where she sat, and Rohan lost sight of her between their hulking forms.

Rohan scowled at Simion—what was the love whisperer thinking?—and then Simion spun around, beaming like a cat who'd just swallowed the juiciest canary ever, winked and clapped his hands.

"Friends, please don't monopolize our wonderful high priestess just yet. I suggest we all relax, maybe have a swim in the heated pool—you'll love it—and then you can get to know each other one at a time. In fact, I've even set up little nooks for you to ... acquaint yourselves better ... around the pool."

Great. These dicks were getting half-naked now? Although, at least they all moved back and let Cyn get some air.

Not that she seemed to need it—her attention was locked on the males as they stripped off their shirts and—

"Oh, you swim naked, Aeron?" Simion all but purred. "Well, this night keeps getting better, doesn't it?"

13
_____

THIS NIGHT WAS *NOT* GOING to plan. Cyn plastered a smile on her face when inside, all she wanted was to scream *clear the fucking room and let her get to the real business at hand.*

The only issue was the blurring of her business: finding the relic and banging Rohan. Except—banging Rohan was the plan to get him out of her system so she could focus on the relic.

Simion's curated array—pfft, what was Simion on there? —swam in the pool, hovered over her on the lounge and fetched her endless sparkling mango juice and food. The fey had even tried to rub sunscreen lotion on her. Seriously, that guy needed to up his research on the human world, unless maybe moonlight burned the fey? His skin *was* pale ... The complete opposite of the witch, Sebastian, who had the most deliciously dark skin she'd ever seen.

Man, this bunch were enough to tempt a saint, and Cyn was nowhere near that good.

But ... for all the buffet of options Simion had presented, she was fully aware of one set of eyes on her. Rohan alone hadn't changed into his swimwear—still wore the same cargo shorts and shirt from earlier. He appeared relaxed. Casual. At home even.

But every time his gaze touched her, a tingle grew along the back of her neck. And those tingles had traveled to lots of other body parts. Looked like only one man was going to scratch this itch right now.

"So, dearest one, what do you think of my selection?" Simion asked.

"You've ... outdone yourself. No question."

"I rather thought I had." He smiled lazily.

"You're looking very impressed with yourself right now."

"And why shouldn't I be? Do you know how much work it took to assemble such a group?" He leaned closer. "Now, I suggest you start with the witch. You're both very powerful, and I have no doubt your magic will make you wonderfully compatible. And if you look over beyond the pool—behind the strategically placed potted palm?—there's a high table and chairs away from prying eyes. Why don't you start there and spend some time with Sebastian? I'll give him five minutes to speak with you alone and then send the next one over. With the palm tree, you have a ... small measure of privacy if you want to get to know them more." He waggled his eyebrows, and Cyn couldn't stop herself from laughing.

"You're incorrigible."

"Why, yes, I am."

"Is this really necessary?" Not that she minded the men, but she had a job to do and a daemon to bang who wasn't among the five-person buffet Simion had laid out.

"Dearest heart, but of course! You came to me, remember? And in this, you have to trust the professional. Here tonight, I can guarantee you have your match."

"Fine," Cyn said. "Five minutes each."

"There's no hurry—and remember, you can't rush love."

"Maybe this location is too pretty for love—after all, it's hard to focus on the wonderful, err, array you've provided when the surrounds are so gorgeous."

"Oh." Simion's smile dropped. "You think so?"

"Possibly." Cyn feigned a casual shrug. While she hadn't found anything in her search of the property so far, now that she knew the compound belonged to Simion, she'd order a full search, which meant getting Simion and his peeps out of there. Plus, if he had this mansion stashed up his beautiful bohemian sleeve, what other places was he hiding?

"Well, I guess we can try somewhere else." Simion nibbled on his lip. "Let me think on it. In the meantime, off with you—I insist!"

Cyn withheld an eye roll and rose from the couch as elegantly as possible.

At least with all these people around distracting Simion, she might get a chance for further reconnaissance inside the compound. She just needed to occupy her *array*. Time to call in a distraction for this party ... She grabbed her cell and sent a fast text message to Tanya. Please let this work!

Then Sebastian appeared, and she pretended to be pleased as they walked to the dimly lit, as-private-as-it-could-get, little cocoon of space Simion had created on the other side of the pool.

She took a seat and forced a smile as Sebastian slid his chair so close their shoulders brushed and only let herself glance around once more to check for any threats—not to see where Rohan was—before she pretended to let the witch take all her attention.

Half an hour later, the last of Simion's options left the little table.

No, Cyn, do not stab, stun or punch anyone. Her left eye

started to twitch, and she had to hold her breath until the urge to cause mayhem had passed.

She finally let herself exhale, and as she did, the tattoo on her thigh throbbed.

Huh? She almost rubbed it—but kept her hands on the table—although she did look around. No sign of any threats still ... or Rohan.

Damn. Rohan better not have gone off and started things on his own—

A warm, deliciously spicy scent at her back had her freeze. Nope. He hadn't. She didn't have to turn around to know Rohan stood among the trees behind her.

"What are you doing back there?" Cyn asked.

"Watching the show."

"'Show' is right." Cyn snorted. Thankfully, the *array* were all now engrossed in a conversation with Simion. "Mother of the gods—am I really speed dating shirtless men around a pool in a tropical oasis?"

"Seems so."

"Why do they look like they're negotiating who's coming back next?" She clenched her jaw. No way was she putting up with another round of speed dating.

"Maybe because I suggested to Simion that you needed a break?"

"Thank fuck you did. I was ready to stab them—or myself—with my hairpin for a moment. Do you know the fey is a prince from his realm looking for humans to bring back to his people? Apparently, they need reseeding or some shit. I swear the gods are testing me here, Rohan. This isn't normal—you know that, right? And I don't have time for this."

"The things you do," he murmured.

Cyn said, "I'm serious. I've got—"

"A job to do. You know, you take your work pretty seriously for a high priestess."

"And how would you know what a high priestess takes seriously or not?"

"Don't get snappy," Rohan said. "I've met one or two before—a long time ago, but still."

"Well, you don't know all high priestesses, clearly. Now stop standing there and sit with me—maybe you'll keep them from coming back."

"Your order is my wish."

Cyn snorted as he took the seat beside her. His expression might be calm and his tone smooth, but the rigid jaw and hard glow in his eyes were anything but.

Damn, he was fine. No, not fine. Utterly delicious and so gorgeous he made her want to fly close to the flames, and who the fuck cared if she got singed? No, she *wanted* to get singed—to burn up with him.

Her heart picked up pace. Warmth pooled low in her belly. And the longer he looked at her, the brighter those green flames grew. His lips pulled tight and his nostrils flared.

"I scented you," he whispered. "You might find those males attractive—but not one of them does to your body what I do. Do you know how that makes me feel? How much I want to own your lips—from your mouth to your pussy—how much I want to lick over every single part of you and eat you out, and dive in and empty myself into you? How much I crave showing these pricks, who think they can have you, that you're never going to be theirs? That even if you did, their dicks would never do to you what I could?"

Oh fuck.

Gush. Now.

Rohan picked up Cyn's hand, traced a circle over her

palm, slid his fingers between hers. A surge of heat shot to her core. Her blood thrummed.

He shifted closer. His breath warmed her neck.

"I'd start here." Rohan bit down on her skin, then laved the point with his tongue before sucking hard. She bit back a moan. "Uh-oh. Looks like they're finished. I'd better disappear."

Wait—what? Cyn lifted her head to look over to Simion, and Rohan dropped to his knees beneath the table, his body hidden from everyone across the pool by the giant pot.

Rohan gripped her thighs beneath the table. Heat radiated from his palms up to her core.

Oh. *Oh.*

"Dearest heart, how are you doing?" Simion called out, then took a sip from his flute. "Are you ready for round two?"

Rohan's hands inched up her thighs.

"Just need a couple more minutes—"

"A couple?" Rohan hissed from beneath the table.

"I'm so horny right now you could flick my clit and I'll come," Cyn muttered.

"Good to know." His dark laugh echoed softly up around her. Goosebumps rippled over her skin. "So, princess, I take it that's an invitation?"

"To make me orgasm? Hell, yes."

"Well, then." His hands pushed up under her skirt and to the hem of her panties. "Let me in, princess."

-((●))-

Rohan inhaled the scent of Cyn's arousal all the way to the bottom of his lungs.

A growl vibrated through him before he could catch it, and she stiffened beneath his hands.

"Shh," she whispered.

Rohan didn't bother answering. She'd given permission for this—and nothing mattered more than the beguiling, intoxicating scent of her pussy, and making her come from his touch.

"I'm not the one who should worry about making noise." He slipped his fingers beneath her panties. "Now sit on the edge of the chair, princess, and spread your legs. You're gonna ride my face."

"Fuck yes. But I'm not sweet. And you'd better hurry; Simion's *possibilities* are getting restless," she muttered. "Three more minutes," she added in a falsely loud voice. "Just finishing my drink here."

"And I'm about to have a drink, too," Rohan said.

He tore the material covering her pussy off, stuffed it into his back pocket, then wedged his shoulders between the glory of her silky, strong thighs. The scent of her arousal made his head spin, his mouth water even more. And thank the gods for night vision. Right now, the glint of her opening, dewy with desire for him, was a sight he'd remember forever.

Rohan lifted one thigh and wrapped it around his neck, then blew over Cyn's pink, glistening flesh. "Baby, I'm going to feast on you. Are you holding onto the table?"

She made a choked cough.

"Are you ready to ride my face?"

Cyn made another sound ... more of a whimper, really.

"I'll take that as a yes." He parted her folds, and then he licked up her seam.

Oh. Bloody. Gods.

The most exotic, erotic, delicious taste bloomed on his tongue.

"More," Rohan snarled. Another swipe. Another taste. He licked his lips. Desire pumped through his blood. "Fuck," he growled against her. Then he licked her high again, tongued his way to her clit and drew the nub of flesh into his mouth.

She gasped. Her muscles went taut.

Huh. Cyn was on a hair trigger, but he had a whole two more minutes to drink her down and no way was he wasting one second.

He squared his shoulders, spread her farther, and this time he tongued her opening and stroked inside.

She clamped around him, and his balls went so frigging tight sparks shot up the base of his spine. Bloody gods, but Cyn was going to be so fine when he got his cock inside her.

Cyn's thighs tightened around his head, and the blood thrashing through his veins synced to the beat of her pulse in his ears, echoed by the tattoo throbbing on his thigh. And then she ground down on his face, and her demand shoved every thought away except to heed the call of her body and make her climax.

Rohan replaced his tongue with one finger, then two, pumping into her, and he licked his way back to her clit; this time when he sucked the bud into his mouth, he lashed his tongue around the sweet flesh, over and over and over.

Her whispered gasp sent an electric shock wave of energy through him. She stiffened. Her body tensed. Around his fingers, her body clenched, and the perfume of her orgasm flowed over him. Her juices drenched his fingers, and he shifted to lick them up, drink them down. It took every ounce of his willpower not to leap to his feet, throw the table off his back, and dive into his princess right frigging there.

As if she knew how close he was, one of her hands reached for his and held onto him just as tightly; maybe ... maybe she felt the same sense of urgency?

"Princess," he growled, unable to modulate his voice one frigging iota. "One orgasm—ten orgasms—will never be enough. We might need to change the terms—let's go for a hundred for you ... then, maybe, I'll have had enough hearing your breath catch and inhaling the perfume of your cum." Maybe.

Her low voice rumbled over him, "Then meet me in your room. Five minutes."

"So, dearest heart, have you had enough time?" Simion's frigging happy voice echoed from the other side of the pool. Hell. The *array* were all still there.

Her trembling leg fell away from his shoulder. "Ah—one last sip."

Her fast breathing was replaced with the sound of ice clinking against glass, and then Cyn dropped his hand and stood back from him, far enough he could look up and see her.

A red tint highlighted her cheeks and lips, and a wonderful slumberous sexiness filled her heavy-lidded eyes.

He'd done that.

"Sebastian," she called out. "I need to get another drink —no, no, this one I insist on getting for myself. I'll join you again soon." She didn't even look at Rohan as she made her way around the pool, disappearing from his view on the other side of the potted palm.

Shit. Five minutes? He'd be in her room in one. Now all he had to do was stand up somehow with the biggest raging erection of his existence. By the gods, he'd never been turned on this much.

And he still had to walk past the *array of possibilities* to follow Cyn inside.

Frick. Down you damn thing.

Maybe he should swim across instead. He dropped his shirt and shorts into the bushes and dove into the pool in his trunks. A moment later, he was in the water and stroking to the other side.

"Ah, there you are, Rohan. I wondered where you'd gotten to." Simion appeared out of nowhere at the edge of the pool, right where Rohan had determined the fastest point to follow Cyn into their rooms.

"So I forgot to bring a towel," Rohan said as soon as he reached Simion. "I'll head inside and grab one—"

"No need." Simion waved a hand at his nearest assistant. "Aleesha—please bring a towel for our hero. And you, Rohan dear heart, you come with me. Let's chat about love." Simion linked his arm through Rohan's and steered him in the opposite direction.

14

Cʏɴ's ʙᴏᴅʏ still hummed as she made her way into the luxe lounge and poured herself a drink at the bar, waving away the server. Leaning against the counter, she casually glanced over her shoulder.

Was Rohan following?

She hadn't looked at him after that amazing orgasm because the moment she looked into Rohan's face, she might ruin everything and dive for him.

An orgasm was one thing—a pop of pleasure. A release of tension. But holy mother of the gods—what had just detonated inside her body was beyond anything she'd experienced before. And that was with his freaking tongue and hands.

And as hot as that orgasm had been, Cyn wanted more.

Oh crap. Simion was dragging her about-to-be lover to the daybed. No, no, no. And as they sat down, whatever Simion was talking about had Rohan tensing.

She bit back a sigh. Well, looked like she was going to rescue her daemon from a love whisperer's clutches. But she took one moment to send a follow-up text to her earlier message to Tanya, and moments later, her cell pinged with a reply message. Yes! Her distraction wasn't far off.

"Boys," Cyn purred in her sexiest voice when she joined Rohan and Simion a few moments later. "Room for one more?"

"Always room for you, dearest one," Simion said. "But wouldn't you rather spend more time with your matches?"

"Not just yet. I'd much rather talk to you two; you're looking so cozy over here. What's up?"

"We're talking about love," Rohan murmured.

"I asked our hero if he'd ever experienced the tender emotion before," Simion said with a serene smile. "And then you arrived."

Cyn went to trade grins with Rohan, but his expression made her falter.

"So?" Simion asked. "Have you? Have you ever been in love, my dearest hero?"

Rohan glanced at her before looking back to Simion. "Yes. A long time ago now—I was little more than a youth." He smiled, but it was only a tilt of his lips, not engaging any part of his face.

What the fuck? Rohan had been *in love* before? And who was this in-lovee? Were they still alive? What had happened?

Cyn clamped her mouth shut tight to stop herself from demanding more information.

Not your business, Cyn. Not your business ... You and Red are all about banging out the sexual tension. Nothing more.

"Ah, first love ..." Simion smiled too, but an unexpected sadness tinged his. "Is there anything so tender, so romantic, so full of possibilities as that first brush?"

"Guess not," Rohan replied.

Simion's expression brightened. "And for good reason—

who we are in our youth is so rarely who we are in adulthood. No, you don't need gentle. You need a robust love as strong and powerful as you." Simion pressed a hand to his chest. "As strong as the beat of this muscle right here." He stopped and stared at his drink.

"You're good at this shit," Cyn said into the silence, forcing a casual tone that was the opposite of the tension gathering in her belly. "No wonder you're a love whisperer."

"Thank you, dearest heart. Now—" Simion stopped as Aleesha came over and gestured to the doorway. "Well, it looks like we have more guests."

"Actually," Cyn said, "they might be my friends—some locals I met today. I understand you know at least one of them, so when I heard about the party, I thought I'd invite them. Hope that's okay?"

"Friends are always welcome," Simion said with such delight she almost wanted to pat him on the head. Man, how was anyone so sweet?

Cyn sat back and enjoyed the show as Tanya, along with her coven, poured onto the pool deck.

Tanya got Cyn alone for a moment. "You won't know this yet; however, the family you saved yesterday—Star and Krystal and their children are family members of one of our covens. They're visiting from down south and weren't prepared for the ocean."

"It was really Rohan who did it. How are they all?"

"Alive, thanks to you and Rohan. When they told us what happened and the figures who helped them, I knew it was you. You have our blessing."

"Well," Cyn said, "if you want to really say thanks—do you think you and your coven can run interference for us? I've been wanting to get some ... alone time with that daemon all night."

"You want us to keep the rest of your party distracted? High Priestess, that would be you doing us a favor. But fine, I'll add it to my tab." Tanya let out a fabulous laugh.

Cyn laughed right back. "Oh, I think you're going to have a blast tonight. Come on, let's get this party really started."

She led Tanya straight to Sebastian and introduced them. Everyone was talking to someone ... perfect. Except— where had Rohan gone now?

"Dearest heart," Simion said, "what are you looking for?"

"Wow, you move fast. And quietly."

"All part of being a love whisperer. Seeing as how our party has expanded, I wonder if I might ask you for a favor?"

"Of course. Ask away."

"Excellent. My suite is all the way at the end of this house—"

House? Cyn withheld a snort.

"—and I want a jacket as it's cooling down, but with Aleesha and Sonja looking after our new guests and me as host, I really don't want to leave."

"No, of course not," Cyn said. "You go be the host with the most. I'll grab your jacket and be back soon."

"You're such a darling. Bless you. I left it on the deck off my room—you won't be able to miss it. There's also the most delightfully secluded daybed where no one can see you, so if you feel the need for some privacy, then take a few minutes. Enjoy the stunning stars."

"Don't you want your jacket right away?"

"No rush, whenever you're ready to come on back."

Well, that idea held merit. "Thanks." On impulse, Cyn leaned over and kissed Simion's cheek. "Be back soon."

"No rush. No rush at all."

Cyn searched for Rohan as she walked the length of the compound. Rohan's room—nothing. Her room. The library. The indoor pool. Nothing, nothing, nothing. The games room—just the fey prince and one of the coven members making out on the billiard table. Hope Aeron had told the witch what he was looking for in the human world. Cyn made a mental note to fill Tanya in about that later on.

Come on, where was Rohan? She'd checked every common area in the mansion and still no sign of the orgasm-inducing daemon.

Fine. She'd get the jacket for Simion, then do another search. Her soon-to-be-lover had to be here somewhere.

Darkness blanketed Simion's suite, except for the little lights illuminating the pool of the waterfall.

As soon as Cyn reached the deck, she pulled up short. She wasn't alone. Rohan stood at the railing, looking out over the view to the ocean. He turned around, moonlight gilding his profile.

"So this is why Simion asked me to come here," he murmured.

Cyn didn't bother to hide her smile. "That wily love whisperer. He got me up here to get him a jacket. What was his story for you?"

"Same here."

"Somehow, I don't think there's any missing jacket. Looks like we weren't fooling him at all. Did he tell you about the daybed?"

"That he did." Rohan's eyes locked on her with total focus. The charged moonlight cast deep shadows over the carved planes of his jaw.

"Princess, are you ready for the next round?" Rohan radiated danger. Power. And an energy so intense everything inside Cyn clenched.

Heat pooled to her core, and his nostrils flared. "I'll take that as a yes," Rohan whispered. Then he swooped in and lifted her into his arms.

"What are you doing?"

"Ravishing you. With your permission."

"Can I ravish you right back?"

"I hope so."

Cyn laughed and wrapped her arms around his neck. The muscles of his shoulders and arms bunched as he strode to the daybed.

"You know," Cyn said, "no one's ever carried me before."

"Then I'm thrilled I get to be your first carrier."

The blazing green fire in his eyes took her breath away, and she drew him down to her and met his lips.

Heat. Spice. Rohan. A taste like no other—and she licked along his lower lip, hummed when he matched her touch.

Rohan shifted the angle of their kiss, and his tongue surged into her mouth, stroked, filled, withdrew and surged again until her core clenched in response. Holy mother of the gods, Cyn needed that plunge to be in her lady parts right now.

As if he read her mind, Rohan knelt on the daybed and lowered her to the mattress.

Refusing to be separated from that intoxicating kiss, Cyn scrambled to her knees, pulled him with her and stroked down the ridges of his abs.

Rohan tensed. She slid her hand lower. Gods, but he was hard. And hot. And huge.

She tore her mouth from his. "Rohan, I need to see you. All of you." She tugged and yanked at his trunks until he was naked and pushed him back to his knees.

Moonlight gilded the length and breadth of his body, turning him into a classic work of sculptured art—like an ancient Roman statue—all sinuous lines and strong ridges. Those shoulders that obliterated the view of the town and ocean beyond, the indent at his waist, the thick column of his dick standing high and long.

Cyn let out a whimper. "Mother of the gods, Rohan."

He palmed his dick, and her body was drenched.

"Like what you see?" he growled.

"Like? No. Love, yes."

Rohan's eyes flared, and that devilish grin curved his lips. "Then you need to get rid of that dress and show me yours. Fair's fair, right?"

"You had your face in my pussy—pretty sure you've seen me already."

"Ah, but I want it all," he purred. "Come on, princess. Share the view." He ran his fist back up the shaft.

Goosebumps pebbled over Cyn's skin at the combination of the velvety flow of his words and the freaking hot way he stroked himself. She yanked her dress over her head and then followed with her bra until she was naked as him. Lifted her chin and let him look.

"Cyn," he finally whispered. "You're ..." He shook his head. "Magnificent isn't even close. It's as if you were made for the moon to dance over your gleaming skin like a lover's hands." He reached out and traced from her shoulders to her neck—down to her breasts, to her stomach, to her hips. To her thighs.

Molten lava pooled in Cyn's core with each pass of his fingertips.

Rohan said, "Every part of your body—each curve, each line of muscle—as fierce and strong and wickedly delicious as your mind. How did I get so lucky?"

Her chest tightened, his words like a match to kindling, and she grabbed him and yanked him to her. "I can't wait any longer. Shit—condom." Cyn snarled at the delay but rummaged through her purse until she found one.

"You've had one in your bag?"

"One? Try a roll. But we can start with this." Cyn pushed until he laid back, then rolled the condom over him—he moaned when she gripped him hard, and his hips lifted under her touch.

"Mother of the gods, you are hot. And I can*not* wait for this." She straddled his hips and took him inside her. Pleasure with a razor edge sang through her as he stretched her to the fullest, but beyond that, a sense of joining, of having him right where he was meant to be—and she rocked her hips until she'd taken him in all the way.

Finally, with her body impaled by his length, she rocked back on her knees and could do nothing more than savor the exquisite sensation of moonlight cascading over her and his hot, hard length inside her.

Pure. Fucking. Perfection.

"Princess," Rohan growled.

She lifted her head and almost whimpered again.

Rohan's teeth were clenched. The muscles at his neck corded as he stared at her through slitted eyes. His chest heaved in a deep, shuddering breath.

"You feel so frigging sweet," he ground out.

"Sweet?" Cyn wanted to tease him about being anything but, except the craving to move and experience more of that breathtaking friction overtook everything else.

She rocked her hips. He hissed.

"Cyn, princess, I'm holding on by a thread here—"

"Good. Because so am I."

She lifted, and her body clenched. She slammed down. The pressure inside her coiled. She rose again, ground back down on him. The tension tightened. Almost crested.

"Just. Need ..." Cyn lifted again.

Rohan pressed his thumb to her clit. Sensation shot through her. Added a shimmering layer to the coils twisting inside her.

"Again," he grunted. "Hard."

She lifted, slammed.

"Fuck, princess—yes, yes. *Yes.*"

The coils sprung free, and her world narrowed to the detonation of her body as she flew apart and her orgasm exploded.

Long ... long minutes later, Cyn took in a shuddering breath. *Work, lungs.*

Rohan's harsh breathing filled her ears, and the glittering fire in his gaze locked on her. And even though she'd come—he'd come—the surrounding energy ignited again.

Even the air seemed charged—was it the moon? This man? Something else entirely?

"Cyn," he hissed. "I need you again."

15

The need for more of Cynane roared through Rohan, along with the craving to prove no one else would ever make her body sing like he could.

He dragged the throw blanket over Cyn to keep her warm and leaped to his feet.

"Where—?"

"Stay there," he growled. "Round two. That stimulator you brought in town—where is it?"

"The clit vibrator? In my suite—wait, you want to use that?"

"Hell, yes. Any reason why not?"

Delight twinkled in her eyes. "Rohan, you just made me come without any extra help, but if you want to give the stimulator a go ..."

"I've been wanting to use that on you from the moment you told me what it does."

"In that case, be my guest." She laughed and made a sweeping arm gesture.

He got rid of the condom, then wrapped a towel around his waist, raced past the waterfall—seriously, who had a water feature in their bedroom?—and ran all the way to his suite. Thankfully, he avoided encountering anyone else, although going by the sounds coming from outside, the party was still in full swing. He grabbed what he needed from both their rooms and raced back to Cyn.

She'd kicked off the blanket and lay naked on the daybed, bathed in moonlight, so utterly at ease with herself, so utterly magnificent with her proud jaw and that mysterious gleam in her eyes. His chest seized up.

"You should only ever wear moonlight," Rohan whispered.

She arched her back, and a wicked smile tilted her mouth. "You promised me round two, so I promise not to wear anything until after that. Deal?"

"Deal."

He dropped the stimulator onto the daybed and held out a hand. "Trust me?"

"I think so." She let him draw her to her feet. "Why?"

"How do you feel about a little bondage?" Rohan took the lengths of red silk from behind his back and held them up.

"That's what you when back for at the adult shop?"

"Yep. You did say you liked them, right?"

"Hell, yes." Cyn's eyes lit up. "Who's tying who here?"

"I've got this idea ..." Rohan snagged the throw and folded it into a square, then pulled her to the deck's edge and turned her to face the ocean. "Does it worry you if someone looked up and saw us?"

She glanced around. "With the lights off up here, it's close to impossible, right?"

"Close, but technically someone might see us. Does that bother you?"

"If I say yes?"

"Then we stop." Not that it would worry him. The frigging opposite—it would satisfy the loco urge he had to scream to the world she was his. But he shoved that urge deep down. "You're in control here, Cyn."

"Tell me what you're thinking," she whispered.

"I want to tie you here." Rohan placed one of her hands on the railing to her right and the other on her left, then slipped the throw between her body and the railing. "You're going to press your breasts to the throw and lift your butt into the air. Then you're going to have the moon and the stars bathing you while I take you from behind." He nuzzled the hair at the back of her neck and trailed kisses down the phases of the moon inked to her skin. "And I'm going to take you hard. I'm going to make you scream. And then I'm going to use that stimulator to make you come all over again. But you will not cry out—you're going to stay silent as your body comes apart."

Her arousal drenched the air, and her legs parted as if she was already seeking him out. He pressed his cock into the curve of her back. "Feel that? I'm rock-hard for you again, Cynane." Fuck, he'd be rock-hard around Cyn for the rest of his life at this rate.

She arched her back and pushed into him. "Deal—on two conditions. I get to have my turn with you at a later date."

"Hell yes. And two?"

"You fuck me fast because we need to get back to the party."

"Damn, but I like your style, princess."

Rohan expertly tied up Cyn and grinned when she complained she couldn't move. He spread her legs farther apart, then couldn't help himself from admiring the round curves of her ass, the exposed pink folds below, so tempting and inviting.

"Ready?" he whispered.

"Hell, yes."

"Thank fuck, because I can't wait anymore." With one hand, he guided her down to the railing. She lifted her butt, spread her legs farther. "Princess, you have no idea how hot I am for you right now."

The scent of her arousal deepened, and Rohan drew it into his lungs, held his breath and captured it there. Gods, he'd love to keep it there forever. He ran his hands down the line of her spine—she arched beneath his touch—palmed the firm flesh of her butt—

Rohan grabbed the stimulator, rolled a condom on, then thrust deep into the snug, wet silk of her body. She gloved him in the hottest grip, and shivers of pleasure gathered at the base of his cock.

"You feel so frigging good." He gritted his teeth against the urge to pound into her. "I could come again right now."

"Don't you dare! At least not until I have."

"Remember, silent—unless you want an audience." He ran his hand over her hip, down her belly, and parted her curls. "This stimulator have different settings?"

"Go for high. But pull it on and off." Tension vibrated along Cyn's back as he did what she'd said, and within moments her gasps filled his ears, her body went taut, and then her body clenched around his cock so hard he had to hold back his own groan.

"Fuck, Cyn," he gritted out. "Can't hold back. Fuck, fuck, fuck." He dropped the stimulator and thrust into her with everything he had, slamming in rhythm to his words, lost in the wonder and velvet-searing clasp of her body around his cock.

"Oh shit, I'm coming again." Her pussy clenched even harder, and she let out a long, low groan as she convulsed. The clamping of her inner muscles on his cock did him in, and he followed her into orgasm, bending over and muffling his hoarse shout in her hair.

And when he could finally suck air into his lungs, he eased back, kissed her neck, then untied her wrists and kissed them too.

"Holy shit, Rohan. Don't think I can walk." But Cyn was smiling, and an adorable flush tinged her cheeks.

"Yeah, me neither." Still, he picked her up, carried her back to the daybed, then collapsed beside her.

"I know we need to get back—but can we just lie here for one more minute? Don't want to fall on my ass in front of everyone."

He chuckled and pulled her into his chest. He took her wrists and peppered soft kisses where the silk had marked her. "These will fade, I guess?"

"Yeah," Cyn said, "but it's gonna make for an interesting story back at the party."

Possessiveness flew through him again. *Yes, it would, fuckers.*

"I saw that look, Rohan. You like the idea of them all knowing, don't you?"

"Won't lie and say no." He forced a casual shrug. "Tell me about these." Still holding her wrist, he traced the ink design that cuffed her wrist and ran all the way to a similar ring around her biceps.

"Binding spell—for myself, to myself. I'll always be true."

"Deep. I haven't seen the design before."

"It's a tenant of being a high priestess. I designed this art, but all high priestesses have a mark or an object with a similar pattern somewhere that means the same thing to them."

"And this?" He stroked the phases of the moon up her spine. "I like this one."

"To remember that life is a phase."

"Ah. And this?"

"Are you going to look at every single one of my tats?"

"You—" He almost said you're the one being I want to learn every part of—inside, outside. What you think. What you like.

But no, he didn't want to know the high priestess like that. *Head in the game, Rohan.* This was sex—a need and a chance to get this craving for Cyn out of his system. Time to lighten the mood.

"You what?" she asked.

"You know you're one up on me, right?" Rohan forced a teasing smile.

"Oh, we're counting orgasms now?"

"Aren't we aiming for ten to get over this ..."

"Didn't you change it to a hundred?"

"Well, if you're game ..."

"Think we need longer than a quickie on someone else's daybed for that. And it's time we got back to the party. I'm looking for a particular bowl of resin, remember?"

"Like I could forget," Rohan said. "Always about the job."

"What about you? Don't you want to know about your key?"

"Well, see, that's the good thing for me. Right now, *you* are the key to my key—wow, that has a ring to it, huh?—so staying close to you means I'm working. Lucky me."

She laughed, and the sound made a bubble of warmth squeeze through his chest.

"Fine, you're the lucky one. Now, come on. I want a

shower, and then we need to get dressed. Not that you have much to put on other than your trunks."

"Yeah, I'll stop by my room and grab a shirt."

"No need on my account." Cyn waggled her eyebrows.

He shook his head. "You're a terror, aren't you? And look at you—so frigging stunning. All I want is to dive back into you and change your mind about rejoining the party."

Rohan forced himself to look away from her lush, moon-gilded body and raced back to his room. He pulled on a shirt and shorts from the wardrobe, then made his way back to the pool deck via the kitchen.

"Can I grab two coffees?" he asked one of Simion's many staff members.

The server offered to bring them out, but Rohan declined and waited for the tray. He liked the idea of bringing a drink to Cyn himself. Except when he arrived in the lounge, she wasn't there.

Huh. Maybe she liked long showers? Damn, he could've gone with her—

"Hey, I'm here," Cyn said from behind him. "Aw, you got me coffee. Multiple orgasms *and* caffeine. Rohan, you're the bomb. But first, sit down. I've got news about your key."

"What? From the shower?"

She took the coffee. "I swear, nothing beats a strong hot coffee."

"Cyn, the spell?"

"Yes. Right—the shower. That's how magic works some-times." She shrugged, and the dropped shoulder from her dress dipped even lower and her smooth skin caught his eyes. Hell, but he wanted to lean over and kiss that gleaming skin, pull the dress all the way down and feast on the tips of her lush breasts.

He cleared his throat. "So, what was it?"

"You okay?" Cyn's brows pulled tight as she checked him over.

"Yes. Just tell me. What was it?"

"Sheesh, touchy much? In the shower, the steam drew into the shape of an old-fashioned key. That means the spell is working. I'll be on the lookout for other signs now."

"By the gods, you did it—"

"No, to be clear, the spell could just be showing me it has identified what you're searching for, not actually giving me the location yet."

"Still." The urge to jump up, grab her, kiss the ever-lasting hell out of her surged through him, and it took everything he had to pick up the coffee instead and take a sip.

Cyn seemed to read his emotions, though, because she mirrored his move, and as their eyes met over the rich brew, the gleam in hers screamed she wanted to dive into him right back.

For a moment, Rohan found himself lost in her eyes—like falling into another world, one he'd never dreamed existed.

This night must be the best ever—sex with Cyn, and he was on the way to finding the key.

"Well, well, where did you two get to?" Simion's voice purred from the doorway. Behind him, his assistants stood shoulder to shoulder. Anticipation sharpened their features, though, and the hairs on the back of Rohan's neck prickled.

"Exactly where you placed us," Rohan said easily. And frankly, he had zero issue with the love whisperer's plan. Finally, Simion was making sense—as if Cyn would choose any of the *array of possibilities.*

"Oh, about time, my dear hearts." Simion clapped and beamed at them like a proud parent. "Didn't I tell you?

Tonight was the night. Now, I have the final part of your love match. The love oil."

"The what?" Cyn stood and stared at Simion. Rohan tried to catch her attention, but she kept her gaze locked on Simion.

"I need to anoint your love match, and then your bond will be truly blessed, and nothing—no one—will sunder the connection holding your hearts entwined."

"You know, I still have no clue what you're talking about?" Cyn replied.

"Never mind. Here, come to me." Simion held up his arms, and the billowing sleeves on his robe fell back. "Aleesha, Sonja, the box."

The assistants nodded and left the room and were back within the minute, carrying a timber box covered in ornately carved scenes.

Aleesha held the box in both hands, and Sonja lifted the lid. Simion leaned in and drew out a small glass jug with a cork stopper, filled a quarter of the way with an amber liquid. He held the jug with reverence and an intensity that only made the hairs on the back of Rohan's neck raise farther.

"Simion," Cyn whispered, "what is that?"

"The elixir of love." He unstopped the bottle and handed the cork to Sonja.

"Is this some kind of ritual?" Rohan planted his hands on his hips. "You all look like you've done this before. Should I be worried here?"

"Of course, you don't need to worry," Simion said. "And yes, this is a ritual. The ritual of love. Now, please both come forward."

"What's your elixir made of?" Cyn asked in that same whisper voice.

The tension in her tone made Rohan freeze and turn to her. "Cyn, what's going on?"

But she ignored him and stalked over to Simion. "What is in there?"

"Stay still, High Priestess. I'll rub this along your fore-head—there, done. You are anointed. And now, Rohan, please join me for your turn. You, too, are now anointed. The oil of a plant that will combine with the love in your souls—"

"Simion!" Cyn snapped.

Everyone stopped and stared at Cyn. Shit. She'd gone from all soft and deadly to loud and deadly. What the frig was going on?

"What's the oil?" she shouted.

"Frankincense. A sacred ... Why does that matter?" Simion's brow furrowed, then his eyes widened. "Oh no. No, no, no. You're here for that?" His face went slack.

"Yes." She stepped closer and held out one hand. "Where is it?"

"But you're a high priestess."

"That I am. I'm also here for the resin you used to make that oil. This is serious, Simion. You don't know what you're dealing with."

"But why—?"

A soft shuffle and scrape—like many boots on tiles, trying to walk quietly—echoed from the front of the property.

Rohan stopped. Whirled around. No one else had noticed yet, but he focused on the sound. Multiple people trying to quietly make their way to the pool area. "Ah, High Priestess?" he said. "Hate to break up the party here and all, but we've got company."

Cyn whirled to face him. "How many?"

"At least seven. Almost here."

"Simion, lock that away." Cyn nodded to the oil-filled jug. "And get behind me."

"What's going on?" Tanya called out from where she and Sebastian sat very close together on the pool ledge.

"Simion's got visitors," Cyn snapped. "Uninvited."

Tanya and Sebastian stood, but before they could leave the pool, the men who'd tried to take Cyn the day before—plus two new faces—erupted into the room, all holding guns and looking totally ready to use them. And as one, their focus went to Cyn.

"No one move," the asshole with the blond buzz cut shouted.

Then the boss man from the passenger seat, a slim human with perfect black hair, stepped forward and said, "If you'd come with my men when they told you, High Priestess, none of this would've been necessary."

"Seriously?" Cyn shook her head. "You really should've learned your lesson from yesterday." She twisted her ring.

Shit, she was taking them on again. Rohan eased forward to stand at Cyn's back.

"And who are you?" Simion asked in a soft voice. Rohan cut the love whisperer a glance; Simion was doing a great job of looking innocent and harmless, but given he was a frigging deity, no doubt the male had moves if he wanted to use them.

"Who doesn't matter," the boss said. "What does is that we're here for the witch—so all she has to do is come along with us, no tricks, and no one else needs to get hurt. My men will stay here to make sure everyone stays put, and then once we have confirmation the witch has given us what we need, we'll return her to the party and let you all go unharmed."

"What, like how you shot my friend here?" Cyn said.

Rohan rolled his eyes. Friend?

"Lads, why don't you put the guns down." Rohan raised his hands as he shifted to stand beside Cyn. One more step, and he'd be able to protect her from their bullets. She could get her magic spells off while he acted as her shield.

But she moved out from behind him.

Damn fool high priestess. Didn't she see what he was doing?

Nope. Clearly not. Cyn glanced around the pool deck—he could see her calculating the people present. But all it would take was one stray bullet and any of the humans here would be dead. Although ... there were also a lot of nonhumans present. Maybe that would even the odds?

"Last warning." The boss pointed his gun at Rohan. "You were shot earlier, so good to know we're not dealing with a human."

"What—you were shot?" Simion gasped.

"Yeah, he was." The boss's expression soured, and he shifted the gun to Simion. "So, you're up next, hey? The witch goes with us, or you get it."

"Wait," Cyn said. "I'll come with you."

"No tricks this time. My boys will place a bullet between fancy-sleeves' eyes."

A rumble echoed from outside the house. Then more and more—as if a dozen powerful vehicles or motorbikes had arrived.

"Who the fuck is that?" The boss jerked his chin at a male with long dark hair. "Check it out." The boss turned back to the room. "Now, no one move."

Rohan eased forward yet again. "I'm sure we can work—"

A scream echoed from the direction the male had gone.

"What did you do?" The boss shouted at Rohan.

"Nothing. Yet." He spun to Simion. "Do you have more guests coming?"

A snapping screech echoed up through the doorway.

Was that a ... surely not? But Rohan knew that sound, had been dealing with similar growls and cries for the last six months. A shiver rushed up his spine.

But only the Tenth Gate was unlocked.

"Cyn!" Rohan grabbed her arm. "That's another hell-beast." He strained his hearing. "Only one—but other beings with it. Sounds like they're herding it this way."

Shit. This was when he needed his hellblades. As if she had the same thought, Cyn whirled around. "Where are your—?"

"Room. Locked away."

"Get them. We'll hold them off here."

"No one's going fucking anywhere." The boss tried to grab Cyn's arm.

"You're not the deadliest threat tonight, asshole." Cyn shook him off and palmed her hairpin. "So either you're against us or with us. Your choice."

"Hey, fuckhead." Rohan loomed over the boss. "Your bullet didn't stop me yesterday, and it won't now either. But what's coming will eat you up and spit you out. And since I'm the only one who can stop that, as the high priestess said, you either run away or fight it out with us. But if you hurt one hair on the high priestess's head—or anyone else here—forget whatever's coming through that door. I will fucking tear you apart myself. Got it?"

The boss's face went pale.

"I said *got it*?" Rohan waited until the boss nodded, then spun to Cyn. "You're still human where it counts," he whispered. "Remember that. Don't get dead." He grabbed her and kissed her hard.

"As if." She snorted.

Hell but he liked her attitude. If only she'd treat her *life* with a bit more caution.

16

ANOTHER SCREECH PUNCTUATED the sudden silence, and Cyn yelled at Tanya, "Can you or your coven fight?"

The witch nodded. "Of course."

"We can too," Sebastian added.

Great. A bunch of witches and otherworlders—and a love whisperer—in their swimwear and party clothes, without a single physical weapon in sight.

"Whose magic is offensive?" Cyn called out. Three of the witches, plus the fey, lifted their hands.

"Defensive magic to the rear—Simion, you and your assistants with them. Do not let go of that box. Offensive magic at the front. Work in pairs—one fire a spell while the other primes their magic, then swap over—that will give us continuous firepower. Keep it going until we have whatever is coming at us cleared or you run out of magic, then fall back. If you have to run—head up the hill behind the pool. The forest is dark, so you should be able to hide."

Another screech—this one closer, louder, followed by a hideous crunching—reverberated through the room. Everyone blanched.

Boss Man's peeps were whipping around and casting worried looks between them—one of them even skittered back with the witches. Smart guy.

"Get back here." Boss Man waved his gun at the defecting minion. "I said—"

Crash.

The smoky-glass wall separating the lounge from the rest of the house exploded, and a giant ... hellbeast ... with six spindly legs, pincers coming out of its mouth, and a huge freaking tail—like a giant scorpion—clattered into the room. Four figures stayed in the shadows behind it. Had to be the beings Rohan had mentioned.

The hellbeast skittered forward and chomped down on Boss Man. Blood splattered. He dropped to the ground—minus his head.

Everyone screamed. Some ran. Some opened fire.

But the hellbeast whirled, and its tail whipped out and cracked into one of them. Bullets sprayed widely.

Shit. If the damned hellbeast didn't kill them all, the bullets would. And then R-104C would be in the wind again.

Not on her watch.

"Hey, Buzz Cut," Cyn shouted. The big man whirled to her. "Get your people back to the pool deck and only fire from that side or I'll stun your asses myself. Tanya—I'll stay here and occupy the hellbeast until Rohan returns. Get your coven to the other side of the pool deck and focus your magic on whoever the fuck is hiding at the back!"

As Tanya and Buzz Cut rounded up their crews, Cyn pricked her palm and threw her magic at the hellbeast, but its tail whipped toward her. Cyn jumped, narrowly avoiding getting impaled by the barb. Her magic went wide.

Shit. She twisted her ring open—although, how did she

get close enough to use the knockout rub without getting chomped on or tail-struck?

To her side, streams of magic rippled through the air as the witches held back the shadowy beings.

Crack. Crack. Crack. Shot after shot rang out as Buzz Cut and his remaining peeps laid down rapid gunfire on the hellbeast. Then the hellbeast swiveled toward the gunfire and launched forward.

Within moments, Buzz Cut and his men were all ... sliced and chomped into bits and pieces ... and then the hellbeast spun back to Cyn.

No way, motherfucker, she wasn't ending up dinner tonight. Cyn tracked to its side, but the hellbeast spun too, and instead of its tail, its pincers were right at her head. She threw herself backward. Something hot and fiery raked down her arm, and she gasped. Her hairpin fell to the ground.

"Fuck!" She scooped it up with her good hand and threw another spell.

Then the hellbeast roared—why did these beasts all make that awful sound?—and clicked its pincers before running at Cyn.

Oh crap. She called another spell—but her power was sluggish to respond. Her heart thrashed in her ears. How many spells had she called?

Then Rohan ran into the room with a curdling cry, both blades out. He slid on his knees beneath the massive pincers, ducked the swipe of the barbed tail, and sliced his hellblades beneath the hellbeast's neck.

-((◉))-

As the skorpi above him shuddered its last breath, Rohan hauled in one of his own right before its scaled head landed on his shoulders. Gods, but that had been close. The skorpi had locked onto Cyn as if she was the most dangerous being there—and perhaps she was.

He heaved the severed head off his shoulders and lowered it to the ground.

"What, by the mother of the gods, is that?" Cyn swiped at the cut running from her wrist to her elbow. "And damn that hurts."

"Skorpi. Midlands hellbeast." Rohan leaped to his feet and supported her arm. "Let me look." Rohan probed the edges of the wound, and when she winced, his gut clenched. "It's not too deep but could've been a lot worse—you're lucky. Did the skorpi sting you too?"

"Are the pincers poisonous?" she said through gritted teeth. "They're what got me."

"Just the tail." Rohan eased her arm to her side. "Can you do a healing spell on yourself?"

She shook her head. "I'm almost out of energy—better to reserve what I've got in case we get another hellbeast attack. How is everyone else—Tanya? Any bad injuries?"

"Dearest heart, how bad it is?" Rohan bit back a growl when Simion joined them, picking his way between bodies and body parts. Where had the bloody love whisper-come-deity been when Cyn had been getting attacked?

"I'm fine," Cyn muttered and looked over her shoulder. "What about everyone else—"

"Broken bones, nasty cuts like yours." Simion frowned at Cyn's arm. "Not life threatening, thankfully."

"Thank the mother of the gods," she whispered, and her shoulders dropped.

"Cyn needs a healing spell." Rohan jerked his chin at

Tanya, who had rounded up her coven. "Simion, ask Tanya who she can spare to help."

As soon as Tanya and three other witches started a healing spell for Cyn, Rohan checked the skorpi from head to tail.

Cyn joined him a few minutes later, her arm tucked to her side, just as he placed the skorpi's head by its body.

"How long will it take to heal?" He nodded at her arm.

"It's just a cut, so a couple of hours given how many witches just combined their magic for me."

"Good to know. But why so do you look so surprised?"

"I'm ... used to working alone, that's all." Cyn knelt beside him, still holding her arm to her side. "What are you looking for?"

"Trying to figure out why a skorpi is here in Byron Bay." He placed a hand over the hellbeasts's eyes. "It didn't deserve to die."

"What? It ate people, Rohan!"

"If it had been left alone in Hell, in the midlands where it belongs, this would never have happened. The skorpi isn't at fault here, Cyn. Whoever let it loose here is. They're the ones who I'm going to kill."

"What do you mean?"

"Hellbeasts don't just appear in the human world ... unless the gate is unlocked—otherwise, they'd have been here snacking on humans a long time ago. Someone brought the skorpi through, and did you see the daemons with it? They ran as soon as I killed the skorpi, and I didn't get a close enough look at them to know who they were. But they were controlling it somehow—not even I can do that— which means someone with a lot of power is behind this."

"Is Forneous strong enough?" Cyn asked.

"Lord Forneous?" Rohan stilled. Why the hell had she

said *him*? "Yes. Of course—any of the lords, or the High Lord himself, could control it. Why?"

"I think he's here—looking for the same thing as me."

"Wait. Lord Forneous is after the same thing the Templars have you searching for?"

She nodded.

Frigging Templars, always sending others to do their dirty work. He grabbed Cyn's good arm. "Listen to me; Lord Forneous is the devil's right hand—and he's more powerful than anyone here in the human world. You might be formidable as a high priestess, but even you can't take him on. The Templars you're working for should be the ones searching here, Cyn. They've got the firepower and the magic on contract, and they'll need a hell of a lot of both if you're really dealing with Lord Forneous."

Cyn's chin went up. "I'll stand my ground against anyone or anything, Rohan. Don't doubt that."

Gods, but she was bullheaded. Underestimating Lord Forneous—or overestimating her own ability against him—would be deadly.

A chill flew through Rohan, but oblivious to his thoughts, Cyn turned to everyone else.

"Any serious injuries in the still living?" Cyn called out. "No? Okay, time for you all to go in case there are more hell-beasts coming." She paused and leaned closer to Rohan. "I need to get Simion out of here. Twice now he's had hell-beasts in his houses—mansions—which can't be a coincidence. Where's the nearest gate?"

"The Seventh Gate is in Brisbane. You know that's Lord Balfour, right?" He waited as Cyn stiffened. Did she even want to see her sire?

"Brisbane is a four-hour drive," Cyn said coolly. Had she purposefully ignored his question? "So I'm guessing they didn't walk it. Okay, so somehow, they got the hellbeast through a gate and transported it here. What are the chances there'll be more?"

"I need to get to that gate and see for myself," Rohan said. Which was an understatement. If a hellbeast *had* come through the Seventh Gate ... something was very, very wrong. He opened his mouth to raise Cyn's sire once more, but her flat expression made him stop. And hell, if she didn't want to talk to—or about—Lord Balfour, who was Rohan to say otherwise? Look at Rohan—he'd prefer not to talk to his sire ever again if he could get away with it. But Cyn's parent wasn't like Lord Forneous. In fact, Lord Balfour was responsible and effective in his role.

"Perfect, you and I are heading in the same direction. I'm going to head north past Brisbane shortly," Cyn said in that same tone, then she turned back around and raised her voice. "Okay, Simion, you're with me. Everyone else, this is what's going to happen."

Hell, but Cyn was every inch the warrior princess now—calling out order after order. Marshaling the troops. And every one of them—him included—followed her orders.

What an extraordinary being.

She finished her instructions, and everyone left until it was only him, Cyn, Simion and his assistants.

"Okay, Simion. It's time." Cyn lifted her chin. "Take me to the bowl with the rest of the resin. We can't afford to wait."

"Who are you to—"

"I'm here on behalf of the custodians of R—of that resin."

"The Templars?" Simion winced. Behind the love whisper-deity, Aleesha and Sonja stiffened.

"Good, you're aware of the organization. So you know

they have the authority here. I also need to take that oil and hand it to them."

Rohan bit back a snort. Bloody Templars—always thinking they were in control of everything and everyone that wasn't entirely human.

Aleesha and Sonja stepped forward, side by side, and Simion frowned at them before turning back to Cyn. "They —*I*—want to know, how can we trust you're really here on behalf of the Templars?"

"Simion, there's no time for this shit," Cyn snapped. Tension vibrated through her. "Your love oil, and the resin you used to make it, is too important. If another of those creatures comes, and someone gets the oil or the resin, you don't know the deadly—disastrous—ramifications that could lead to. So let me be totally clear. You *will* take me to the bowl of resin you used to make that oil. Now."

"Ah, Cyn ..." Rohan shifted so Aleesha's and Sonja's hands were visible. Simion's assistants had their gazes locked on Cyn, and by their expressions, they weren't happy with his high priestess.

"I know," Simion whispered. Then he bowed his head. "This way."

Aleesha and Sonja followed after Cyn, and Rohan held back so he was last in the procession.

By the time they'd reached the owner's suite, tension poured off Cyn. She'd clenched her jaw, and her eyes held a gleam unlike anything he'd seen before. Over a bowl of resin. Clearly, more was going on here than a simple oil.

Simion went up to the waterfall feature and stepped right in, robe and all.

Rohan glanced at Cyn to catch her eye—what was their love whisperer-deity up to now?—but her attention was laser targeted on Simion, and with Aleesha and Sonja acting oddly, and Cyn one-eyed about the bloody frankincense, Rohan wasn't taking his gaze off the assistants for long, so he shifted to stand between them and Cyn. At least he'd protect her back since she wasn't.

Then Simion delved into the ferns and plants along the side of the waterfall and took out a small plant—shit, no, a bonsai tree—in a shallow clay pot.

Power pulsed through the room, pricking the hairs at the back of Rohan's neck, raising goosebumps along his arms.

Carrying the tree with both hands, Simion turned and, with his robe dragging in the small pool, held it out to Cyn.

"What—" Cyn cleared her throat. "Simion, what is this?"

"The frankincense."

"I thought it was a resin." Cyn's voice was barely audible.

"It was ..." Simion smiled gently. "And now it's this."

"But how?" Cyn held her breath—Rohan knew because he registered the absence of her breathing—and then reached out with trembling hands. She stopped, clenched and unclenched her fists, and this time took the pot with her uninjured arm, and held the bonsai to her side.

"*La relique. Ma relique,*" Cyn whispered in such a hushed tone that only through his extra ability to hear did he make out the words.

Rohan easily translated the French, but why had Cyn just said *her* relic?

He stilled. Fuck. Fuck, fuck, *fuck*. His breath halted.

Proficient with guns and strategy ... Templar Councilor in her shop ... Templar Knight Grayson on speed dial ... ah, hell. No, he had to be wrong.

Then Cyn turned; her gaze flashed over his shoulder, and she froze. As did Simion.

Rohan pivoted.

Aleesha and Sonja each held two short blades, their stances evenly set. Ready to fight.

"Weapons down, ladies," Cyn said in a voice void of emotion, expression cool and collected.

But these two looked like they knew how to handle their knives, and as amazing as Cyn's moves had been, even a knife could kill. He knew that all too well. He lunged, slammed Aleesha's arms down, then spun her and threw her into Sonja.

They both hit the floor but sprung back to their feet lightning fast. Then Aleesha executed a fancy backflip, smashing her foot into his jaw.

Pain exploded in his face. Darkness crowded at the edge of his vision. Rohan dropped to the ground, but he shook his head and lurched back to his feet as Aleesha completed her flip and positioned herself behind Cyn, and pressed her knife into Cyn's side.

"Ouch!" Cyn went to pivot, but Aleesha had to be stronger than she looked because she locked an arm around Cyn's neck as Sonja sped at Rohan.

Fuck! He moved as fast as he could and snagged Sonja's arm, spun her round, and yanked her against his chest in a choke-hold. She struggled hard, and he put all his effort into holding her still as with his free hand, he unsheathed one hellblade and held it to her neck.

"Stop the fuck right now." The metallic taint of blood filled his mouth from where his teeth had cut through the inside of his mouth. "Whoever the hell you two are, you need to put your knives—and frigging feet—away right now; otherwise, Sonja here is going to be saying hello to her maker a lot sooner than planned. And you'll be next, Aleesha. And in case you don't have the full picture here, I'm holding a hellblade—this will cleave your soul from your body with one teeny tiny cut."

"Wait," Simion gasped, "Rohan, don't hurt them."

"Hurt *them*? Your assistant's holding a knife to Cyn's side, and this one frigging almost knocked me out. And be careful with Cyn's arm, Aleesha—she's still healing."

"You don't understand," Simion whispered. "They're protecting the frankincense, too. They have been its caretakers for a very long time."

"No." Cyn scowled. She still held the bloody bonsai tree like it was more important than her life, and she seemed unfazed by the knife Aleesha had at her side. "The *Templars* are the caretakers."

Rohan's gut churned. Could Cyn really be ... a frigging Templar? But hell, he couldn't focus on that. Yet.

"I mean that Aleesha and Sonja have looked after the frankincense for two hundred years," Simion said.

"What?" Cyn's scowl deepened. "I thought it went to your family in London after it left the French ship."

"Hey, you two," Rohan yelled. "Enough talk about where the frigging frankincense came or went. We have another issue here." He jerked his chin at Aleesha.

"Aleesha, Sonja, listen to me." Cyn held up the bonsai tree. "Most importantly, whatever any of us do, we cannot jeopardize this frankincense. So I'm going to tell you the truth. I'm more than just a high priestess." Her chest rose as she took a deep breath, and though she spoke to Aleesha and Sonja, her eyes locked on Rohan with that punch-in-the-gut gaze that screamed of fierce determination.

The tightening in his chest turned to lead, dropping to the bottom of his belly. "You're a Templar."

Come on, be wrong. Deny it, damn it.

Cyn held his gaze—jaw set. Eyes flat.

"Frigging hell, Cyn. You lied—"

"For a damned good reason," she shot back and glared at him.

"Dearest ones," Simion's voice slid into the sudden silence. "Perhaps this isn't the time—"

"You know what, you're right." Cyn lifted her chin, but her glare stayed on Rohan. Which was totally fucked up; he wasn't the wrong one here. "So how about everyone puts their knives—and feet—away, and we give the frankincense to Simion to hold while we figure this out?"

Rohan snorted. "I'm not putting my blade away as long as they're holding a knife to your lying ass."

"I told you—I lied for a reason!"

"Oh yeah, that makes it all right."

"Aleesha. Sonja. I believe we can trust our two love-birds," Simion murmured.

"Not lovebirds!" Cyn hissed.

"At least there you're right." Rohan didn't hold back his glare either, even as inside, the lead weight melted into a bubbling pool of hot, furious lava.

"Here, I'll hold the frankincense just like Cyn suggested." Simion inched forward. "Now, Aleesha, Rohan ... your weapons?"

Simion held Aleesha's gaze, but then she nodded and stepped back from Cyn. Shit. Rohan's turn.

"Fine." He let Sonja go but didn't sheath his blade. Yet.

"Okay." Cyn took a visible breath, then jammed her hands on her hips and turned to Simion's assistants—her glare dropping away for them. "Why did you attack us?"

"Aleesha and Sonja just want to protect the frankincense," Simone said gently. "They've hidden in the shadows for centuries, ensuring the frankincense's continuation. They were in Portugal when the monastery where the ancient resin had been housed was ransacked. They saved the frankincense and booked passage on a French ship. And after their ship was captured, they made sure that the bowl of resin went to someone who understood its nature. Who would also ensure its safety. To me. That's always been their only aim—to keep it safe."

"Wait—you mean Aleesha and Sonja gave the frankincense to your family?"

"No, I mean to me. I am my family."

"Who are you, Simion? And how did the resin turn into ... a freaking bonsai tree? Actually, hold that thought. Right now, all that matters is that I'm also here to protect the tree. In fact, my organization has protected the frankincense for over a thousand years, but we lost it two hundred years ago after the monastery was ransacked. We've been searching for it ever since, and we just want to see it safe too. So do we all agree not to kill each other? Excellent. Then we need to get out of here. Because I don't trust that we won't see more hellbeasts soon."

She finally cut Rohan a look, and although her lips pursed, she didn't say anything.

He opened his mouth to demand to know why she'd lied to him—hell, even a '*sorry* I lied'—but the burning in his chest ballooned to his throat, and he couldn't get a word out.

"I need to make some calls. Everyone to the lounge room," Cyn ordered. Rohan rolled his eyes. Of course, still with the commands.

But Aleesha and Sonja just nodded and followed Cyn like they hadn't held a knife at her minutes earlier, and Simion followed them all cradling the frankincense bonsai.

Frigging hell.

Cyn disappeared into her suite and returned with her purse and cell. "Pick up is organized."

"Pick up?" Simion frowned.

"A chopper is inbound now to get the frankincense, and us, out of here. Now, who are you really, Simion? And does it have anything to do with why we haven't been able to divine the location of the ... frankincense ... for two hundred years?"

"I may have used my supernatural influence to keep it hidden. But that was to keep it safe. Do you know how powerful love is? If everyone knew what the bonsai tree could do, they would want it for themselves."

"Wait, what are you talking about?" Cyn looked at Simion like he'd grown another head.

"I did actually think you knew." Simion's cheeks reddened, and he dropped his gaze to his feet. "It's embarrassing, I know, but my special skill is love."

Cyn asked, "You mean the love whisperer thing is for real?"

"Of course. Love is the most important force in this world—"

"Simion. Stay on track."

"Love. Love is my power."

Cyn frowned, and Rohan sighed. She still didn't get it. "Cyn, Simion is the deity—a minor one albeit—of love. He's Eros."

"You knew?" Cyn whirled to him. "Now who's telling lies?"

"Oh no. You don't get to go there." Rohan clenched his jaw to stop shouting. "He's the love whisperer—who else did you think he was with the ability to 'anoint love and find someone's perfect match'?"

Cyn's jaw locked too, then she spun back to Simion. "But if you're really Eros, why do you need the frankincense?"

"My ability to influence love has been ... waning ... for

centuries. When I came across the frankincense resin, its affinity for love called to me. I used what little power I had left to grow a plant from the resin and spent years working it into a bonsai—with Aleesha and Sonja helping. It produces a minuscule amount of resin, and I make sure that the oil of love is only used for true, true love."

"Well hell," Cyn said. "No wonder you weren't hysterical with all the otherworld attacks. And shit—twice now, you've been followed by a hellbeast. I suggest you go somewhere they can't follow ... Maybe the Watcher's castle in Cheshire, England? They've got the strongest security I know of."

"Would they let us in?" Simion glanced at his assistants. "Aleesha and Sonja are at risk, too."

"I'll find out." Cyn stepped away and made a fast call, and within minutes, nodded to Simion. "They'll take you. Okay, let's hustle. We're leaving in ten minutes. Simion, you're going to the UK."

"That was fast." Rohan glanced from Cyn's cell to her face. "How are you making this all happen so quickly?"

"I've had the chopper on standby since we arrived. Just in case. Simion, the rooftop's cleared for a helipad, right? Good. I'll drop you, Aleesha and Sonja at your airfield— don't worry, we'll stay until you take off in case of more hell-beasts. You need to call your pilot now, though, and get them prepping your jet."

"What about you?" Simion asked.

"I'll meet you in Cheshire at the Watcher castle. You all grab your things now—I'll hold the frankincense."

And they were alone. Rohan eyed Cyn again. *Debrief?* *She'd* had the chopper on standby? Every frigging inch the Templar. Fuck.

But he had a job to do—and that meant sticking close to the lying *Templar*.

"You still want to see the hellgate in Brisbane?" Cyn said.

"I need to," he bit out. "Hellbeasts can't be allowed to enter this world."

The distinctive *whomp whomp whomp* of human-world helicopters echoed from the direction of the hill. Too faint for everyone to hear, no doubt. "Your chopper is here."

"Okay, time to go." Cyn didn't even look at him as she cradled the bonsai tree to her chest with her good arm and led the way to the roof. And Rohan followed her up. The lava in his chest turning more and more acidic with every step.

17

AFTER THE PRIVATE jet with Simion, Aleesha and Sonja took off, Cyn strapped into the jump seat of the Templar chopper, checked Rohan was ready to go in the rear seat—his expression remained stony—and gave the okay for her pilot to take off too.

They lifted into the air, and she tightened her arm around R-104C. A Tree. Her priority responsibility was a freaking *plant*, with olive-green leaves and a deep, rich bark interspersed with knots and gnarls.

Cyn's cell pinged with an incoming message from Gray, and she typed back a fast confirmation that she'd be at Isadora's property within ninety minutes.

Isadora's sister-in-law Eve was there, which was perfect. Between Eve and Cyn, they should have enough magic to set strong wards to keep R-104C secure while Cyn worked out the details for its ongoing protection.

Because right now, R-104C's safety—and therefore mitigating the danger posed if it fell into the wrong hands—was all that mattered.

The fact that a hellbeast had gotten so close made her

blood ice over. Why had they gone after Simion twice? And if it was Forneous, which seemed the most likely option, how had he found them?

Rohan tapped on Cyn's shoulder, and his clipped voice came through the headset, icy enough to freeze hellfire. "How long to Brisbane?"

"One hour. We can't land in the CBD, but can get you close. I'll organize transport for you to get to the gate. Car or motorbike?"

"Bike."

"Can do." Cyn tapped out another instruction on her cell. "Done. A contact will meet you when we land with the keys."

"Wow. You Templars snap your fingers, and bam, everyone does as you order."

"When we're saving humankind's asses, yes."

"Keep telling yourself that, princess—sorry, High Priestess. What's one more lie?"

She ground her teeth to keep from snapping back. Yes, she'd lied, and the fact was, she'd do it all over again. But right now, there was zero usefulness in fighting with Rohan —she had plans to put in place.

"After we drop you off, I'm heading to a farm outside a country town called Maleny," Cyn said. "It's a ninety-minute drive north of Brisbane. I'll keep you posted if I have to move."

"I'll message you when I know what's going on."

"Just make sure nothing follows you. The frankincense can't be at risk."

"Anything coming through for my key?" Rohan asked.

"Not yet, but that's not surprising given everything that's happened."

"Frigging hell."

"I know your key's important. And I'll continue searching for it once I've made sure the frankincense is safe."

"Fine. Look after your bonsai tree; I'm not stopping you. But if I don't get that key, your frankincense—hell, everything in your world—is at risk because those hellbeasts will keep coming through. And what you've seen is just a speck of dust in the number of beasts that exist outside your world."

"Then I'll try a spell now while we're en-route to Brisbane."

"And if you can't find it?"

"Rohan, I made a binding contract, and I'll continue to search for your key—but this frankincense comes first."

"Why? What's so bloody important about that bonsai tree?"

"You wouldn't understand."

"Maybe I'll surprise you."

She clenched her jaw and tightened her grip on R-104C. Only the Templars knew the true secret of the frankincense.

"Nope," she bit out.

An icy silence filled the chopper, and she didn't have to see Rohan's face to know she'd just pissed him off even further. And even when she did another reading for his key, he barely said a word, and it stayed that way for the next fifty minutes.

They were coming to land when Rohan's voice came back through her headset, "Do you want Lord Balfour to pass through to humanside? If you stop with me, I can get him through long enough for you to meet."

Cyn's gut tightened. Meet Balfour? "No." And shit, she'd never thought to meet her father—still didn't even know if she wanted to. Because meeting him, acknowledging him, would make her daemon heritage all the more real. And she was already walking a fine line between letting her daemon instinct take over. The risk was just too high for the vow she'd made as a Templar. "So I have to make a call," she lied. "I'll talk to you when you get to Maleny."

Rohan didn't say anything else, thankfully, and she switched comms channels to another secure line—this one to the research and development division of the Templars.

Because how the fuck were they going to protect a living relic?

-((●))-

Standing alone on the helipad south of the Brisbane CBD, Rohan forced himself not to watch as the lights of Cyn's helicopter dissolved into the city night sky.

His high priestess had been lying through her gorgeous teeth all along. And the burn of that wasn't lessening.

And now she was withholding what the hell made the frankincense so frigging important.

But frigging hell, finding the hellgate key, making sure no hellbeasts crossed humanside, had to be his focus. So he met the ground contact, got the keys to a road bike, and took off into the city.

The Carlisle Hotel stood at the corner of a park, and as Rohan drove up, scaffolding became visible, surrounding the lower floors with hoarding blocking off the street level.

He found a place to park, then made his way back to the hotel along with the continuous flow of humans walking the city sidewalks.

A quick check of the perimeter revealed the only way

through the hoarding and into the lobby was a locked door, so he waited until a lull in the foot traffic and then took a running jump, grabbed hold of the top rails, and hoisted himself over and into the dark on the other side.

As his night vision kicked in, he ran up marble steps to a front door, and used his shoulder to force it open.

Muted light filtered through the double-story height windows, revealing an empty cavernous lobby with a counter running the length of one wall. And not another being in sight.

Curved stairs led to a lower level, but halfway down, as the sepulchral arches of the basement ceiling became clear, so did shallow, shuddering breathing.

As Rohan eased around the final bend, the hairs on the back of his neck prickled. What now?

In the pitch black, it took every bit of his night vision to see a figure crawling over the floor at the base of the amethyst gates, something dark staining half of his face, his legs mangled, and most of one arm missing.

"Lord Balfour!" Rohan leaped the remaining steps and skidded to his knees beside the daemon. "Here, let me help."

"Rohan the Red? Thank fuck. Need to tell you. Two hell-beasts got past me. They had help."

"All right, slow down. I'm putting one arm under your good side, going to get you to your feet. Can you stand?"

"Not yet. Regeneration still progressing."

"Let's get you Hellside so you can—"

"No. We need to warn someone here. The hellbeasts are tracking something that's fucking important to them."

A chill bit through Rohan. "Wait here." He propped Lord Balfour up against the stairs. "I have to call someone."

He grabbed his cell and punched in Cyn's contact. *Come*

on. Come on. Come on. Nothing. Why not? She had to still be in the air. Unless she was on another call. He bit back another curse and sent a message instead. She needed to know what was coming.

"Who are you calling?" Lord Balfour asked.

"The Templar with the item I think they're tracking." Shit. Did he tell Lord Balfour everything? "She's your offspring—"

"Cynane?" He pronounced her name 'kee-nah-nay,' but Rohan still nodded. "Why does my offspring have—shit. We have to warn her."

"So you do have a care for her, then?"

"Of course—"

"Then why the hell did you give her no instruction in our world?"

"Katherine, her mother, insisted she control the child's upbringing and schooling in the ways of Hellside."

"Then you should've insisted right back—"

Lord Balfour held up this good arm. A tattooed band wrapped around his biceps. "Binding contract. I couldn't interfere. The only way I can ever speak to my offspring is if she comes to me."

"Then why have a child at all?"

"The witch came to me wanting to strengthen her bloodlines; I had the opportunity to continue mine. Of course I said yes. But why do you care?" Lord Balfour's eyes narrowed.

Good fucking question. Why did he care?

Rohan's stomach clenched. Oh hell, he had an idea about that, but it wasn't one he wanted to even think about. Because would he really fall for another half human? And not just human, but a high priestess and a frigging Templar?

He shut that thought down. "Well, right now, your

offspring is being tracked by hellbeasts and daemons. How many came through?"

"Two beasts and eight daemons, and they were being ordered by someone above me in the hierarchy because they resisted my order to desist."

"So your gate isn't unlocked?" Rohan asked.

"No, a daemon from the Eighth Realm—I didn't recognize him—requested passage through the gate, but when I let them cross, the rest rushed me, then came the beasts. All my guards fell."

"So can any more get through?"

"Not without me there to open the gate," Lord Balfour said.

"Okay, come on. I'll get you through the gate, then I'll follow where they went."

"Why you?"

"Didn't you hear?" Rohan said. "That's my new job. Hellgate key finder and human-world-side liaison."

"Seriously? What are you liaising?"

"So far, it's been more like killing, but I've only been on the job a little while. Still getting the hang of it."

"And how do you know Cynane?"

"She's helping me find the hellgate key." Which he was still no closer to finding. Tension knitted in his gut as he left Lord Balfour at the gate, and made his way to the hotel basement.

Dark. Empty. And how the hell would they move two hellbeasts and eight daemons up to the street level and avoid being seen?

He followed the doors at the far end and found the service elevators.

It would be tight, and they'd have to move the beasts one at a time, but they'd fit.

Fuck, fuck, fuck. Now not only did he have a missing hellgate key, but eight daemons and at least one hellbeast—assuming the other was the beast they killed at Simion's—tracking Cyn.

18

As the chopper lifted into the night sky, Cyn forced herself to look away from where Rohan grew smaller and smaller on the ground. Red better be careful at the hellgate—who knew what else he was going to find?

Her chest tightened, and she scrubbed a hand over her sternum before she could stop herself.

"You okay, ma'am?" the pilot asked.

She nodded and dropped her hand. "Fine. Indigestion."

Focus on the job. She had a purpose, and that was all that mattered. With Rohan gone, she opened a line to Gray and filled him on retrieving R-104C, the hellbeast attack, and the started the next part of her plan. "Any chance you know if the Watcher Eve is still in Brisbane?"

"Actually, I do know," Gray said. "She's on her way up here to see Isa as we speak. Why?"

"I heard she's an expert with glamours."

"I can vouch for that."

"Would she cast a glamour spell for R-104C?" Eve tightened her good arm around the bonsai tree.

"Probably, but I'll ask her as soon as she arrives. Should be soon."

"If Eve says yes, she'll need to prep for the spell, and has roughly thirty minutes before I land. Also, I've got Rohan coming up after he checks out the gate."

"Did you tell him everything?" Gray asked.

"Not everything. He knows I'm a Templar but not about what the frankincense is. Also—and you're not going to believe this—but the frankincense has been transformed into a bonsai tree."

"Magic?"

"Not exactly. I'll fill you in on that later. Listen, Rohan's steamed that I lied to him, but I've seen him take on a hell-beast twice now, and since we know there are still daemons after us, it's better to have him and his blades close by until I can secure R-104C."

"It's your call."

Shit. Yes, it was. The weight of that responsibility made her gut tighten.

"You've got this, Cyn," Gray said in his standard, confident tone.

"Thanks for the confidence." Her cell pinged an incoming call, but she missed picking it up, and then the screen lit up with an incoming text. "Hold on, getting a message ... oh shit."

"What?"

"Rohan confirmed two hellbeasts came through the gate in Brisbane. He killed one in Byron Bay, so there's still one tracking the relic. And eight daemons working with it."

"What the fuck?"

"Yeah. That's my thought, too. Listen, what other local resources do we have?"

"Isa's brother Raph is on a private job on the West Coast.

Flight back will take four hours, minimum. No one else is close."

"Shit. So how's Isa?"

"Really sick. And she's freaking out because, as well as being physically sick, her visions are drying up. Which is why Eve is coming up."

"Think the baby's okay?"

"That's what I'm trying to find out—without worrying Isa."

"Isa's healthy and we know plenty of women have born part-daemons before—look at Isa and me—but I'll put a call in to Mother and see what info I can find out."

"Can you hold off saying it's Isa? We're still ... processing the information she's even pregnant."

"Of course." And frankly, she would've anyway. Her mother was a Templar first—and Cyn had no doubt that would mean using Isa's pregnancy to the advantage if she thought it was called for.

She ended the call and then went to contact her mother, but the message from Rohan was still on her screen, and she couldn't help but stare at the last part of the text.

Her sire had been at the gate—badly injured but alive. Nothing more than that, but for some reason, she couldn't look away. Injured but alive. Sire.

Well, not her problem. She swiped the message away.

And thirty minutes later, as her chopper landed at Isadora's farm, she had several options from the research and development team, although each required build time.

Gray met her at the door to the chopper, and she carefully handed him R-104C before taking the relic back as soon as her feet were on the ground.

"Not letting it go, huh?" Gray said.

"Not after what I've had to do to get the son of a bitch."

"I get it, believe me. So this means your undercover days are over?"

Cyn stopped midstride. Shit. Her undercover days ... her days as a high priestess ... over. She could glamour the tattoo on her forehead away. Close up her LA shop.

Her stomach tightened.

"Cyn, you okay?" Gray asked.

"Yeah, sure. Undercover days over. How's Isa?"

"Resting. She was sick again just before you got here."

"You know morning sickness is common in a lot of pregnancies, right?" Cyn said.

"Yeah, but the vision shit is freaking me out. What did your mother say?"

"No answer, but she'll call back so I'll find out what I can. I also left a message to update the council about R-104C. I expect to hear back on that point faster. Is Eve inside too?"

"Yep. We're in the barn."

"Why not the house?"

"This is Isa's comfy space. You'll see."

Cyn followed Gray around to the back of the barn, which had been converted into one wall of glass, with sliding doors for access and floor-to-ceiling drapes.

She stepped inside—yikes, this was more like an open-plan apartment, complete with a kitchenette, dining table, lounge, a shit ton of paintings and easels scattered around, and even a staircase leading up to a mezzanine level. Cyn couldn't stop herself from letting out a low whistle. "Gray, this isn't a barn."

"Isa remodeled the old building into an art studio a few years ago. There's a bedroom upstairs—Isa's resting up there now—so let's keep it quiet."

"Where's Evangeline?"

"Up with Isa." Even as Gray said the words, Eve appeared at the top of the stairs and held up a hand in greeting before her gaze locked onto R-104C and her eyes widened.

"Is that the gift of frankincense?" Evangeline whispered once she'd joined them.

Cyn nodded. "Eve, good to see you again."

"You too, Cynane."

"Just Cyn."

"When did you two last see each other?" Gray interjected.

"Three years ago—I was at the Watcher library in Cheshire researching historical texts on R-104C. That's what led me to the UK archives and where I found the ship capture log that led me to Simion."

"Well, thank fuck for the Watcher's library," Gray said.

"I do every day," Cyn added. "And that's only half joking. But right now I need a spell to safely glamour R-104C. This tree is a living, breathing life form, and I can't afford for any spell to risk damaging it. Eve, I know you glamoured R-104A; can you explain that spell to me?"

"Of course," Eve said. "I can help with your spell as well."

"Thanks. But there's more—there's a hellbeast and eight daemons right now searching for this, and we have to assume they'll be tracking it somehow. So we need to set up a perimeter ward."

"Done."

"One last thing—Rohan is on his way here now. So we'll have another set of skilled hands at dealing with hellbeasts. Either of you had that pleasure before?"

"No," Eve said.

"Me either," Gray said. His eyes cut to the mezzanine. "Shit. Is Isa safe?"

"Right now, I don't know if anyone's safe."

"I've got the supplies I need for a ward around the property," Eve said, "but it'll take most of my magic and time. For the glamour, though, I'll need different equipment."

"In that case," Cyn said, "let's focus on warding the property first—that way we can keep Isa and the relic safe. And I'll help you there, so hopefully, that will speed up the spell and reduce the stress load on your power."

"So you're really a high priestess?" Eve's eyes tracked the tattoo on her forehead. "I didn't know. I always thought you were a Templar with a bit of witchcraft."

"I'm both—just with dameon heritage, too. Although I'm a Templar first, so that's where my allegiance is if you're wondering."

"No, not at all. More curious to talk magic with you—I've always wanted to meet a high priestess."

Cyn couldn't contain a short laugh. "Don't think we're all that different—except my magic is made through sacrifice. But sure, let's talk and spell."

"I like that plan."

Cyn blew out a sigh of relief. Finally, she was working with another skilled practitioner who focused on the job at hand. No wonder she'd always liked Evangeline when she'd come across the quiet, studious witch during her trainee days.

-(((●)))-

Night darkened the forest as Rohan steered the motorbike up the winding, tree-lined road with only the glow of edge markers and the rare headlights of oncoming traffic breaking up the darkness all the way to the top of the escarpment leading into Maleny.

As he reached the crest, the land below rolled out in a pitch-black blanket to the Eastern Seaboard, far-off city lights glimmering on the horizon.

Which was all well and good, but how long till he got to Cyn?

At least another fifteen minutes based on her message asking him to stop at a local shop in town and pick up an urgent list of witchcraft supplies.

Cyn's directions led him to a strip of small shops on the outskirts of the main road, and he pulled up at the curb.

The bookstore had a small table lamp lit in the front window, and when he turned his bike off, the shop door opened and a feminine figure emerged.

She had long, straight, dark hair with bangs framing eyes that surveyed him squarely. She reached up, and the snick of a lock unlatching echoed through the night.

"Are you Laura?"

"Well, hello," she said. "You're Isa's special?"

"That's me." Rohan stepped onto the floorboards—their treads creaking beneath his weight—as Laura gestured for him to follow her past wide, dark bookshelves.

"You're good to open so late for a request," he murmured.

"Well, Isa's been a good customer over the years." Laura led him through a door at the rear. "She told me what you need, and I keep my other wares through here."

Sure enough, even more shelves filled the next room—

but these were filled with witchcraft supplies not unlike Cyn's shop in LA.

Ten minutes later, Rohan followed the road out of Maleny, deeper into the Australian countryside toward Cyn. And with every mile passed, his heart picked up speed and his pulse pounded in his ears.

Almost back to Cyn. Almost back to Cyn. Almost back to—

No. No, no, no. He was not falling for a half human—a high priestess—all over again. She was a Templar Knight. She'd lied to him—over and over.

No way could he fall for her.

Ah hell, now he was lying to himself.

Where had this intensity of connection sprung from? Sex couldn't be it—maybe their kiss? Even that didn't make sense. Yes, female daemons were rare but not nonexistent. So what the hell was going on?

Whatever it was, the moment he pulled the motorbike alongside the barn with the blue door and Cyn emerged, his racing heart stopped.

No more hellbeasts had gotten to her. She hadn't been stabbed or shot by loco criminals. Yet.

"Stop," she called out before he'd even switched the engine off. "We've got a ward spell set. You can't cross yet."

"What the hell? That was fast."

"Twice the magics and twice the speed when you have two magic makers. It's protection for Isa and the relic. I need to come to you and get a strand of your hair so you can pass through unharmed. The spell is set approximately two feet from the door all the way round the barn."

"Isa's here?" Gods, no. His cousin was in the worst possible place right now if there were indeed hellbeasts coming for the frankincense tree. "And wait—why does she need protecting?"

"I'll let her fill you in on that," Cyn said as she reached him. She held a hand out. "I need two hairs. And yes, before you ask—I like to cause you pain, but I promise to make up for it ..." Her lips curved in that wicked tilt that even after everything she'd done, made his cock stiff and his chest all warm and tingly.

Why? Why did he react this way around Cyn?

Her smile cooled. "Anyway, I'll be back soon. Wait here."

As Cyn disappeared inside, Rohan's feet stuck to the ground so that even if he'd wanted to move, he couldn't have, and his breath caught.

For a moment, the ground at his feet spun, and he bent over at the waist, finally dragging a breath in.

Oh hell.

He had fallen.

Seriously—love? Why now? Why Cyn? Why not just enjoy their time together and keep his bloody heart to himself?

"You okay there?" Grayson's voice echoed from the side of the barn.

Rohan spun around and restrained a growl. Damned Templars. "Grayson. Long time no see," he bit out.

"Six months or so, right? Thought we'd be hearing from you again sooner about your missing hellgate key."

"I was a bit busy."

"Rohan, I'm sensing a level of hostility here I don't understand, and right now, my priority is to look after Isa—"

"You're damned right you'd better protect Isadora. And do a better job of it than Cynane."

"What the fuck are you talking about?"

"Templars still placing human lives—even their own

people—in danger to progress their agenda."

"First of all, Templars will do everything necessary to safeguard humanity. Not sure how that's an *agenda*. And secondly ..."

"What?" Rohan said.

"Cyn can look after herself."

"Do you know how many times she's been close to having her life ended since I met her? Let's see, two hellbeast fights, a shooting, another potential shooting. And where were the Templars while she was on her own? Nowhere."

"And just why do you care so much?" Grayson's eyes narrowed.

"None of your business."

"Well, I'd say it is—I'm her oldest friend."

"And I'm her client." Rohan crossed his arms and held the Templar's stare. "And you don't see me leaving her to find my missing item on her own, do you?"

"Just what's going on here?" Cyn's voice rolled over him like a caress, and damn if that didn't make him even angrier with Grayson.

"We're chatting," Rohan said evenly. "So I take it I can come in?"

"Yes, spell's adjusted. And Gray, Isa just woke up—she said to let you know not to stress and keep walking outside to chill out. Whatever that means."

"It means she thinks I'm hovering," Gray said.

"Which is," Rohan said, "exactly what you should be doing. As well as getting her—and all of you—the hell out of here before the hellbeast finds us."

"Hellbeast?" Isadora appeared at the door beside Cynane and beamed at Rohan. "Rohan! What are you doing outside? Get over here."

19

As Isadora dragged Red into the barn with the ease of familiarity, Cyn caught herself staring at the two of them with an open mouth. What the frick was going on here?

And how did Grayson feel about his pregnant human wife getting so close to a daemon? Apparently fine, given the fact he was scowling at Cyn instead of Rohan.

"What?" Cyn said when he kept staring. He squinted like he wanted to talk in private, so she raised her voice and called out to Isa and Rohan, "I'm taking a look at the perimeter with Grayson. Be inside in a minute." She pushed Gray outside and closed the door behind her. "What's going on?"

"What's up with Rohan? He got up in my face before about the Templars."

"Rohan is ..." A walking smorgasbord? "Good in a fight, but he's got some kind of issue with the Templars."

"What issue?"

"I'm still working on finding that out."

"Right. So you're pretending to take him on as a client for the hellgate key?" Gray said.

"It wasn't pretend. We have a binding contract for me to find the key."

"That's actually good. We promised him we'd help with his search—never promised an outcome—"

"Neither did I."

"Then the Templars are meeting their obligations."

"Glad I can help out," Cyn said dryly enough to start a grassfire. "So this is what you wanted to talk about?"

"Actually, one more thing." His jaw tightened, and he dropped his eyes from hers for a moment.

"Gray? Whatever it is, spit it out."

"Cyn, I'm saying this as your oldest friend—"

"Pfft. My only friend." And she refused to acknowledge the pang of regret that struck in her belly at that thought. You couldn't miss what you'd never had. And considering her entire life had been about becoming the best possible Templar and then going undercover, true friends hadn't been an option. Except for Gray—and that was only because they'd grown up together after he'd joined the Templar ranks as a trainee.

"Either way," Gray said, "you don't report to me anymore, and even if you did, I'd still say this—is there something going on between you and Rohan?"

"That's what the look was about? Not the relic or the job?"

"Well, if there is something going on between you two, I just want to say—be careful, that's all."

"Gray, I can take care of myself."

"I'm not talking about physically. I know you've got that under control."

"So you're worried about my emotional well-being? Wait—who are you and what have you done with real Grayson?"

"Haha. I'm serious. Come on, Cyn, we're allowed to care about you, you know."

"Well, don't bother. I'm not looking for love here. Red —*Rohan*—and I agreed this is just sex to reduce the tension while we're working together. Nothing more.

"If you're sure ..."

"I'm sure. Stop worrying, Gray; sounds like you've got enough on your plate already."

"Tell me about it." He ran a hand through his hair. "Any news from your mother yet?"

"No. And if I follow her up, she's going to be curious why I'm persisting with the question. You don't want her to know about Isa's pregnancy, right?"

"Correct. We're keeping this locked down until we understand what impact the pregnancy will have on Isa and the baby."

"Okay, so we wait. Although, I think there'll be information in the Watcher library if we need to know more. They have a good section on daemonology. In fact, there's probably more there than even Mother knows."

"Okay, that's a possibility."

"You know, the Watcher castle is the best option for us all right now. Even once R-104C is glamoured, I need to protect it behind the strongest wards possible until I can find permanent storage—it's not like I was expecting to be safeguarding a living, breathing plant."

"That's actually a good plan."

"Okay, then, as soon as Eve's finished the glamour spell, that's where I'll go. And the sooner, the better. We still have a hellbeast somewhere on the loose."

"I think Isa and I should come with you. As you say, the Watchers have the information we need, and the wards there are the strongest place right now for Isa too. Forneous wanted Isa, Cyn, as much as he wanted the myrrh. I need to keep her safe."

"Okay, we can't move R-104C until Eve's spell is done, but get the jet on standby, and we have the chopper here, so all we need to do is stay safe for another two and a half hours."

Cyn headed inside, where Isa and Rohan sat on the couch; their knees were turned toward each other, their voices low, their eye contact direct.

"You two look awfully comfortable." Shit. She snapped her mouth shut and squashed the jealousy brewing in her chest. They were cousins, of course they'd be comfortable with each other. "Actually, Isa, can I steal you away? Gray asked me to use my craft to see how you and the baby are doing."

"Eve already did that."

"Well, I'll just take a look, too. Gray's insisting. Back in a minute, Red. And just a heads up—I'm going to call a sound barrier spell for my chat with Isa—privacy and all that, you know?" She didn't wait for Rohan to agree or disagree before she tugged Isa up the stairs to the loft-style bedroom.

"Cyn, want are you doing?" Isa asked.

"Shh." She yanked a strand of hair and quickly ran the spell for a sound barrier. "Okay, we can talk now. Rohan can't hear."

"What are you talking about? What's going on?"

Cyn quickly explained what she'd kept hidden from Rohan—he knew Cyn was a Templar Knight, and that she'd been searching for the frankincense, but he didn't know about the true power of R-104C.

"Uh, Isa, why are you chewing your lip like that? Come on, this is Templar business."

"I just told Rohan everything that's happened since I last

saw him—Forneous trapped, then getting free, the myrrh vision. Everything."

"Hey, I'm sure none of that's going to cause an issue." She hoped. But stressing Isa out now wasn't on the cards.

"Plus ..." Isa did that lip-chewing thing again.

"What?"

"You know Rohan's my cousin, right?"

"Yeah, what's that got to do with anything?"

"I feel ... I guess, a little protective of him, that's all. He's very close to my mother, and I think that bleeds over into how he feels about me. Protective, like a big-brother thing." Isa shrugged. "But don't worry, I know what you and Gray do is important, so I won't say anything about what the frankincense—all the gifts together I mean—can do."

"Thank you." Cyn dropped to the bed beside Isa. "Do you know where the family connection is between you and Rohan?"

"He's never said, so I can't answer that one, sorry. And I haven't seen him in six months, so I just blurted out everything that's happened since then. Rohan went silent, and then you came in and pulled me up here."

"No need to apologize. Okay, so let's talk about you. What did Eve say?"

"She ran a healing spell and said it pinged back to her instantly as if there was nothing to heal, so she thinks I'm fine."

"Well, that's good. But how do you *feel*?"

"Super tired and either wanting to vomit or eat."

Cyn eased back. "And what are you right now?"

"Don't worry." Isa patted her knee. "Right now, I'm hungry."

"Then let's feed you fast to avoid the other state. But before then, I can help with something for the nausea—I've got a potion I've made for humans before; I'll just need to do some research that it's okay for halflings." She also had to do Rohan's spell and live up to her end of the bargain—her arrow tattoo throbbed on cue—then get rid of the hellbeast threat, and after that, end her time with Rohan and go back to her regular Templar life.

And that was not regret panging her stomach.

She was hungry. That's all.

-(((●)))-

After Cyn dragged Isadora up the stairs, Rohan couldn't have spoken if he'd wanted to. Lord Forneous had been trapped for six months? And now he was humanside—with a seed of myrrh. Why the hell was that so important?

Shit. Why hadn't his uncle or cousin said anything? Had they worried Rohan would leave his job to try a rescue mission? As if.

Tension knotted in his gut again. No sign of the key. Cyn and her lies. Hellbeasts. And now Lord Forneous. What else could get fucked up here?

"Hey, you there," the witch, Eve, called out as she stayed perfectly still inside the salt circle she'd made in the middle of Isa's art area.

You there. So eloquent. He held in a sigh as he stood. "I take it you mean me?"

"This spell is taking longer than I expected and I need another candle."

"And you're asking me to get you one? Sure." He placed the candle exactly where the witch wanted, then backed away.

"Testy much?" she said without looking up at him.

"Yes." But his anger and frustration weren't *this* witch's fault, so he forced himself to speak calmly. "It's Eve, right? You were in the middle of an incantation when I came in—I take it you're warding or glamouring the frankincense?"

"Glamour. Going to make our bonsai tree here look like an urn to anyone who doesn't know of the spell. Can't afford for this to fall into the wrong hands. And you're Rohan?"

"Rohan the Red. Daemon. Current humanside liaison on behalf of Hell."

"Wow. Some title."

"Yeah. Not nearly as fun as it sounds." Except for the part about having sex with the most amazing being he'd ever imagined existed, even in his wildest dreams. Shame she'd turned out to be a lier and a *Templar*.

"Cynane told us you were coming. You're the guy with the hellblades—and Isa's cousin, right? Ever worked for Forneous?"

He couldn't stop himself from stiffening at his sire's mention. "Yes, and ... no. It's complicated. What do you know about daemon hierarchy?"

"Probably not everything. But I know that whichever gate you come from, daemons from a higher gate can basically order your butt around."

"That's right."

Eve rubbed her chest for a moment, then resumed her position of hands over the frankincense tree. "So, which gate are you from?"

"Thirteenth."

The witch whistled. "Wow. You really are related to Isadora?"

"Yeah. You seem to know a lot."

"Do you know Isa's brother?"

"Not yet, though I'd like to meet him one day if the opportunity comes up. We were always ordered to stay away from both Raphael and Isa until now."

"I'll pass that along." She took a deep breath and did something else with the spell before looking back to Rohan. "Raph and I are together, in case you didn't know."

"No, that hadn't been mentioned. Together as in mated?" Well, this was interesting. Power radiated from Eve—not unlike Cyn, and there was a touch of something familiar about her ... "Are you a high priestess too?"

"Nope. Ordinary witch—just powerful. Although there is some daemon heritage if you go way, way back. Now, I have to concentrate on this spell for Cyn. So stay back and don't interrupt me anymore." With that, Eve closed her eyes, and the air around her shimmered as she poured more energy into the spell.

Seriously, what was it with all the bossy witches? But Eve was just doing her job, and Rohan had more critical matters to worry about, like exactly what fuckery Lord Forneous was up to now? Knowing his sire, there wasn't a chance in hell it was good.

"Rohan, did you hear me?" Cyn's voice had him turn around, and he faked a calm expression as Cyn and Isa descended the stairs from the mezzanine level.

"No." Talking of bossy witches.

"I said I want to check something out for Isa's nausea and then get onto your tarot reading."

"Fine." He had to talk to his uncle. Exactly what did the High Lord of Hell know about Lord Forneous and the myrrh?

"I thought you'd be more interested in the tarot reading?" Cyn said. "You still want your missing item, right?"

"Of course I do," he snapped. Then Isa looked at him

oddly, and he had to hold in a sigh. "I'm just okay with Isa getting seen to first."

"Hey, Rohan? I'm hungry—want to help me make food?" Isa said, giving him another of those odd glances.

Not really. But this was Isa, and he'd do what he could to help her, so he sighed and joined her at the kitchenette. "What are we making?"

"Toasties and coffee. Tea for me."

"Toastie?" Cyn asked from the little dining table.

"Toasted sandwiches," Isa replied over her shoulder.

As they made enough toasties to feed an army—just as well because he was hungry—Isa talked about her art and the farm, sounding genuinely happy, which he found oddly comforting. Then she piled a few of their creations onto a plate. "Okay, I'm taking these outside to Gray. You hand out the others."

Cyn looked up from her spell book when he dropped a plate in front of her. "Still pissed off, I see."

"Yes." He put another plate over near Eve and, with nowhere else to sit, joined Cyn at the table to eat. "That a problem?"

"If I said yes, would you get over it?"

"Not likely."

Cyn rolled her eyes. "Well then, back to work. Good news and bad news. I can make the potion for Isa, but I'll need specialist ingredients."

This time he didn't hold back the sigh. "Am I going back to the bookstore?"

Cyn's face scrunched, but then she shook her head. "No, I think having you and your hellblades here right now is more important than Isa's nausea." She grimaced.

"What's wrong?"

She shot him an odd look. "Why do you think something's wrong?"

"Getting to know your expressions, that's all. So? What is it?"

"I have this feeling that we shouldn't stay here too long. Even with the wards around the barn, I wouldn't want to come under any kind of attack with R—I mean, with the frankincense and Isa here."

"What kind of feeling?" Rohan asked. The hairs on the back of his neck prickled and he couldn't stop himself from looking around. Nothing out of the ordinary.

"It's hard to explain, but my gut is uneasy. And I always listen to my gut."

Shit. "How soon can we leave?"

"Hey, Eve? How soon till your spell's done?"

"If you're done chatting up the sexy daemon and help me out, maybe an hour. But hey, your call on priorities." Eve shrugged but kept her eyes closed and her hands over the bonsai tree.

Rohan regarded Cyn for a long moment. "How come it's your call? Isn't Grayson in charge here?"

"It's more of a mutual decision-making situation right now."

Rohan let Cyn go, because if Cyn's gut said something was wrong, he'd listen. But he didn't miss that she'd evaded his question. Why did everyone here, bar him, know what made the frankincense so special? Why was Cyn holding back that level of power that looked like sapphire flames burning in her eyes? What more was going on here that he didn't know? Frigging hell. More and more questions. But he was going to get his answers, one way or another.

Once they got the hell to somewhere safe.

20

————

CYN WAITED until Eve gave the okay, then poured her own salt circle overlapping Eve's and stepped beside the Watcher.

The barn was starting to fill up with all the energy sources gathered under one roof, the air holding a charged intensity.

Maybe that's why the hairs on the back of her neck were prickling.

With one last surge of power, Eve and Cyn completed the spell.

Cyn opened her eyes to Eve's frown—a look she knew was mirrored on her own expression.

Eve glanced around. "Something's—"

"Not right," Cyn finished. All the drapes were pulled, so no one could see in. But ... "Rohan, check on Gray. Fast."

As Rohan raced out of the barn, Cyn turned back to Eve. "How much power have you got left?"

"Enough for three stuns—maybe four. Thank the goddess you helped with the glamour spell; otherwise, I'd be out. You?"

"With enough sacrifice, I could stun half a dozen; plus, I've got this." She flashed her ring. "I just have to get close to make it work."

The door to the barn crashed open, and Rohan and Gray rushed inside.

"Company?" Cyn called out.

"Yeah," Gray replied as he ran to a duffel bag in the corner.

"Two black vans coming up the driveway." Rohan grabbed his satchel. "Lights off, but you can hear them, and I can hear something else out there—can't make out what exactly yet. Coming up through the front paddock."

"Right," Cyn said. "Fast recap of powers. Isa, you've got offensive magic, right?"

"Normally, yes," Isa said. "It pulls me and whoever I'm with into the vision realm, but I haven't done that since finding out about the baby. No clue if—or how—it'll even work right now."

Damn. Isa was out for offense. "All right, Isa—you stay upstairs with the frankincense. Eve, your ward spell will stop the daemons, but what about a hellbeast?"

The Watcher frowned. "Never had to spell against one, so no clue."

Double damn.

"What are you thinking?" Rohan lifted his satchel onto the table.

"I think you and I go out the back door and sneak around to flank them and we focus on the hellbeast. Gray—I need your spare set."

"Spare what?" Rohan asked.

"SIG Sauer handguns. Gray always carries a spare set in his car duffel. Eve, you take the front door of the barn and use your remaining power to stun any daemons going for

Rohan and me. Once you're out, head upstairs to Isa. Gray, you cover Eve while she's out front, then monitor the back door to the barn. And remember, no matter what, stay clear of Rohan's hellblades. Okay, weapons check."

Cyn took the SIG, slid the rail back, checked the rounds, then the weight, then tucked it into the waistband at the back of her jeans. She went to ask if Rohan could hear how close the vehicles were, but then the rumble of their engines echoed through the barn.

"Let's go," she said to Rohan. "Gray, Eve, you good?"

"Go. We've got inside covered." Gray placed two knives from his duffel on the table, then picked up two handguns.

Eve was wolfing down a toasted sandwich. "I'm good too, energy loading now."

Cyn led Rohan out through the sliding glass doors at the back of the barn. Crickets chirped. A gentle breeze brushed over her skin. Stars lit up the sky. A freaking too-perfect night for what was coming their way.

She'd just gotten the R-104C back. She wasn't losing it now.

They skirted around the side toward the front of the barn. The crunch of multiple tires creeping up the gravel driveway grew louder, and Cyn eased to the corner—

Rohan grabbed her and pulled her back.

"What?" Cyn whispered as she tugged her arm loose. "I know what I'm doing."

"Really?" His eyes narrowed. "So you know a karcha's out there?"

Shit. She suppressed the urge to look for herself. "What kind of hellbeast is that?"

"It's got three heads—I can hear them all panting." He scowled down at her. "You were going to run out there, Cyn, completely unprepared."

"You're not in charge here, and I was scoping out—"

"You should've checked with me first. Right now, we're downwind, but if that changes, it will scent us straight away."

Cyn ground her teeth. Damn it, Rohan was right. Ugh. "I know you're pissed off—"

"Try furious."

"Fine, *furious*. But can we not do this now?"

"I—fine. Truce. For now. And Cyn, I know you're capable, but you're still—"

"Shh, the cars have stopped. I need to see how many daemons we're dealing with." She eased around the corner as the sliding doors on the vans opened, and four figures disgorged from each vehicle. Shit. All eight daemons here, now. And all armed with long-bladed knives. At least they weren't hellblades. Thank the mother of the gods for small mercies.

Then a ghostly-hued hellbeast with three grotesque heads—each with a jaw of needle-sharp teeth—and a long-barbed tail, lumbered past them, then stopped at the closest daemon and let out a growling howl.

That was a karcha? Cyn swallowed hard.

The daemon hissed something, and the karcha shook all three heads like it was in pain before turning a circle, all three noses sniffing the air, and lurching toward the barn.

Oh shit.

Cyn eased back to Rohan.

"Eight daemons. And the karcha is coming for the barn. How do we kill it?"

"Let me look." They traded places, and when he turned back to her, Rohan's jaw was locked tight. "It's mature, so it will be slower, but with three heads—and that tail—it's deadly from all angles. I've taken on two before and got injured both times. Badly. I can't believe it's not eating the daemons with it now. Someone damn powerful is behind all this."

"Do you recognize any of the daemons?"

"No, none of them. So there's still someone else out there. Listen, I can take on the karcha, but you'll need to keep the daemons distracted because as soon as I go for the karcha, they'll come for me."

"Done. Karcha takedown time. Ready to go? I've got you covered,"

"Frigging hell, I should be covering you." Rohan unsheathed his hellblades.

"Next time, I promise."

"There better not be a next time." His lips tightened.

Cyn clenched her jaw. "Agreed on that. Let's go."

They raced around the side of the barn together as the karcha reached the ward around the building. It stopped, let out another howl and all three heads turned back to the daemons who'd formed a semicircle behind the hellbeast.

Rohan ran for the karcha.

Cyn pricked her finger, called a stun spell and threw it at the first daemon closest to Rohan. But Daemon One ducked, and Rohan raced past him, only for another daemon to break away from the karcha and charge at Rohan.

Beyond them, the karcha let out another howl, and all three heads snapped to Rohan.

Oh shit.

Cyn sent another stream of magic at Daemon Two— then dropped and rolled as the first daemon she'd gone for threw a knife at her chest.

Shit, that was close.

Heart pounding, she leaped to her feet and threw

another spell at Daemon One. Got him.

Then more streams of magic shimmered through the air from the house—thank the mother, Eve was sending her spells into the fray, too.

Cyn primed another spell—shit, she was blowing through energy fast—and yelled at Rohan, "Red, duck!" He didn't even look back but went low, and she sent a stream of her magic over Rohan's head.

Daemon Three froze. Rohan slashed with his blades.

Rohan ran in for the karcha, then dropped to the ground as the barbed tail sliced through the air right where Rohan's head had been.

Oh mother of the gods, this was bad.

Daemon Four left the karcha and ran at Rohan, but Rohan's attention was on the hellbeast as its tail spun in another arc, and those three heads went low, medium and high. Dameon Four got close and lunged. Rohan hissed. Blood stained his side. But he leaped back as Dameon Four lunged again, and then he had to jump over the karcha's tail.

Cyn's heart froze. She went to call out—but snapped her mouth shut. Not the time to distract him.

Instead, she drew the pin through her palm for a greater blood sacrifice, but even as she called her next spell, all she got was a sluggish tickle of power.

Shit. Shit, shit, *shit*. Tapped out.

Plan B time. She grabbed the SIG Sauer from her waist-band and started firing at Daemon Four, who dropped to the ground.

Rohan finished Dameon Four with two fast slices, then did one of those batshit leaps onto the back of the karcha and jammed his hellblade through the highest head.

The karcha's howl stopped midscreech, and then the hellbeast fell to the ground.

Finally. But there was no time to celebrate. Another daemon holding two knives launched at Rohan's back. Oh shit. Rohan couldn't see—

She emptied her weapon into Daemon Five. The asshole dropped to the ground, writhing and clutching his gut, and Rohan whirled to her.

"Thanks—" His gaze shifted over her shoulder. His eyes widened. "Watch out!"

Pain exploded in the back of her head, and something shoved her to the ground, but she rolled at the last moment and landed on her back in the gravel.

Another figure loomed over her, and then she blinked, and Rohan leaped above her head, his blades outstretched.

She twisted to follow his movement, but her head swam, and although she tried to keep her eyes open, everything went dark. Rohan's guttural cry echoed in her ears, and then strong hands cradled her to a hard chest before she lost touch with all sensation.

The Templar's fancy jet had been in the air for over two hours when Eve came out of the back cabin where Cyn was sleeping and gave everyone a thumbs up. Rohan's breath whooshed out. Thank fuck.

Grayson was on his cell—he'd been on it nonstop since they'd taken off—but he nodded from where he sat beside Isa, one hand on her thigh, and Isa pressed a hand to her chest and mumbled a thanks.

"How is she?" Rohan sat forward.

"Resting easier," Eve said with a sigh as she dropped into

a seat opposite Isa. "I exhausted my magic on a healing spell, so she should wake up without any headache, and the bruising is already mending. But now I need to crash. Someone needs to sit with Cyn, though, just to be safe." Eve's eyes closed.

"I'll do it." Rohan stood up.

"Red, she needs rest, no funny business," Eve muttered, eyes still shut.

"She got bashed unconscious. Trust me, I'm just there to watch her." And right now, he was so angry with Cyn, sex was the last thing on his mind. Except, hell, that wasn't right either. He had a sinking feeling he'd be hot for Cyn for the rest of his existence. But it *was* the last thing he'd act on.

"I can go if you want?" Isa gave him a wan smile.

"You look as tired as Eve. You rest, I'll sit with Cyn." He was in the rear cabin before Isa or Gray could come up with a reason for him to stay with them. And he refused to examine why it was so frigging important to be the one with Cyn.

Talk about fancy. A wall-mounted television, a bathroom at the end, and a bed with Cyn lying in the middle, her hair fanning out over the black cover like a spray of white gold. Her cheeks had finally lost the ghostly hue they'd been when they'd boarded.

Asleep, she was ... softer, deprickled from her usual state of extreme awareness and ever-present fire. And then her eyes opened. And the breath he hadn't known he was holding whooshed out.

"Hey, Red."

"Hey. Welcome back to the world of the awake."

"What did I miss?" Cyn sat up and frowned as she touched her head.

"Let's see. Eight dead daemons. One dead hellbeast. Me

carrying you to the helicopter, then to the plane. Eve did a healing spell. We've been on the plane for two hours, heading to the UK. And that's about it."

"Where's R-104C?"

"You mean the frankincense? Strapped into its own seat up with Grayson and Isadora. Hold on, what are you doing?"

"Going to see it."

"Take it easy. Trust me, the bonsai tree is safe. Wait here and I'll go get your bloody frankincense."

But Grayson insisted on bringing it down to Cyn—the icy Templar wouldn't budge there—and only when Grayson stepped into the cabin and held it up did Cyn's shoulders sag and she dropped back to the bed.

"Thanks," she whispered when Grayson left.

"Okay," Rohan said, "so apparently, you need to rest for at least an hour, and I'm here to keep an eye on you."

"I've rested enough."

"Witch's orders—let the healing spell do its thing. So, how are you feeling? Any pain? Exactly how good is this Watcher?"

"She's the best of her kind. Why do you think the Templars contract the Watchers to do most of our wards and spells? And actually, I'm not in pain. Just tired."

"Well, good to know about the pain issue. Want a water or something? The fridges here are stocked even better than Simion's jet. Guess the Templars like their luxury, huh?"

"Why are you being so nice? Where's 'furious' Rohan? Are we still ... trucing?"

Good frigging question. The anger was still there—it had just ... simmered after Cyn had almost died. Again.

"Do you want the water or not?" was all he said.

"Think I'll stick to water ... and coffee?"

"Of course."

The Templar's cabin crew were as efficient as any butler service Rohan had ever seen, and in no time, he was back in the sleeping cabin with Cyn.

"So you got stuck with babysitting duties?" She took a sip of the coffee and sighed. "Man, I need this."

"Someone had to."

"How is everyone else?"

"Eve's wiped out and currently sleeping. Grayson's been attached to his cell phone since we took off—he wants the cleanup at the barn done fast and quiet. Isa is a combination of tired, hungry, and ill—not sure which she's up to right now. Don't get between her and the restroom, is all I'm saying."

"What about you? You got stabbed in the side."

"Just a prick."

"So you're mended?"

"Yeah. I still can't believe how many daemons you took out." He swallowed as the memory of Cyn's face on his lap, cheeks pallid, eyes closed, struck him again.

"Hey, Red, you okay?"

"Yeah. Just remembering how you look when you're bashed unconscious. I want to kill that asshole all over again."

"Shh, it's okay. I'm here. Alive."

"Just. It could've gone the other way tonight, Cyn. So very, very easily." His gut tightened all over again. Because even as furious as he still was with her, the thought of the world without Cyn was a million times worse. And what did that mean for him and Cyn being together?

He turned away and stared through the window.

How much of Cyn's time with him had been a lie, after all?

21

After landing to refuel, Cyn and Rohan had also picked up a change of clothes, and thank the mother, the Templar jet was finally on the last leg of the flight to Cheshire. Cyn wore a comfortable pair of tight-fit black jeans, a plain, long-sleeve black tee and black heeled boots, and sitting at one of the tables in the forward cabin, she was feeling refreshed enough to try another spread for Rohan.

If he wanted her to. He'd barely spoken two words since his time to sit with her had ended.

With the sun shining so brightly through the private jet windows that she'd drawn the sunshade, Cyn riffled through the tarot deck.

But the moment her hands were occupied, her mind went to one place.

Rohan sat beside Isa again, and their closeness both made Cyn smile and the back of her neck itch. Which was batshit. So what if he was close to another woman? They were cousins.

And damn. She still needed the ingredients for Isa's morning sickness.

Cyn made her way into the middle cabin outfitted with a full comms center. Gray occupied one of the desks and didn't even look up from the call he was on. But with Eve sleeping in the back cabin and Rohan and his super-hearing up front, she called a sound bubble spell to cover the comms cabin as she put a call in to the Watchers and asked for the list of ingredients she needed when they landed.

"Asking the Watchers for help now?" Gray said from behind her.

She turned around. "Wow, off your cell finally?"

"That was a real clusterfuck back at the barn. You wouldn't believe how many international—inter-divisional—agencies wanted in on that case. The council have asked me for a full report; did they ask you, too?"

"Yeah, first time. You've always filed the reports in the past."

"Welcome to the life of a division leader."

"I never wanted that, you know?" The words were out before Cyn could catch them. "I mean, I just hate the political BS, that's all."

"Then why did you take the job?"

"Good question ..." She sighed. Shit, she knew the truth, even if she wasn't ready to admit it to anyone else. Her mother. Because the expectation from birth had been that Cyn would one day become a councilor like every other Montbard. Which meant first becoming a leader in one of the Templar divisions. "Anyway, doesn't matter now. I'm here, so I'll learn to deal with it."

"Cyn, this is your call—and I'll support you however you need but consider bringing Rohan fully into your confidence. I trust him, and with his connection to Isa, I think he has a reason to work with us. Now, I'm going to try to get a couple of hours sleep. Wake me if you need me."

As Gray left the cabin, Cyn picked the cards back up and riffled through the deck.

Could she trust Rohan with the entire truth?

Her chest tightened. No, the better question was, should she?

As leader of this op, what if, because of Cyn's trust in Rohan, something went wrong? And she still needed to know what his issues were with the Templars. Well, that was one thing she could tackle.

As soon as the Watchers confirmed her list of ingredients would be made available on their arrival, Cyn returned to the forward cabin. The back duo of chairs had been turned around and set up into a double sky bed, and she gave Gray and Isa their privacy by not looking in their direction.

But that left Rohan alone at the forward set of chairs.

Was their truce still holding?

"Time I tried another spread for you," she murmured.

"I'm all yours," he bit out.

And damn if her heart didn't pick up the pace at those words. Shame his tone was icier than a frost spell. But he was talking to her; that was all that mattered if she was going to get his spell done and then broach the other matter.

"Okay, let's do this." She took the chair opposite him. "And then—can I ask a question? It's not to do with the key, but it's something I'm curious about."

"If you're curious, by all means." He folded his arms, and a mocking light filled his eyes.

She ground her teeth and bit back the urge to tell him to shove it. This was something she needed to know, damn it. And that was an understatement. Cyn craved information about this man—second only to how much she craved more of those amazing orgasms he induced. She cleared her throat. "The Templars—why don't you trust them?"

"Is it important to know?"

By the mother, yes. But all she did was give a tight nod.

Rohan glanced to the window—something deep and dark shifted in his expression, and his brow furrowed. Shit, maybe he wasn't—

"Fine." He pivoted back to her. "Can't believe I'm telling you this."

"If it's too hard—"

"No, in fact, I think it's good for you to know." He glanced toward Gray and Isa's bed, then leaned forward. "Maybe then you'll understand why I don't trust the Templars. Do you remember what I told Simion—about how I'd been in love before, in my youth?"

"Of course." Cyn's gut burned, but she feigned a calmness opposite to what was going on in her belly. "Go on."

"Late nineteenth century—"

"As in the eighteen hundreds?"

"Yes. I was studying humankind at Oxford—"

"Wait, you went to university?"

"Are you going to interrupt the entire way?"

"Sorry, continue." Holy shit. Who was this man? Scholar? Badass killer? Lover? All the above?

"That's when I met Eleanor. She was ... beautiful. Ethereal, somehow—with this long golden hair and delicate blue eyes. She was a high priestess."

Holy shit.

"She was gentle, kind, used her magic to help others, and we just hit it off."

Ethereal? Gentle? Shit. The total opposite of Cyn. Her stomach tightened.

"We were talking about a future together when a

Templar Knight approached her to work with them on a case. Ele wouldn't tell me everything about the job because they swore her to secrecy, although I gleaned enough to work out she was to pretend to be a buyer for a particular item so the Templars wouldn't be directly associated with the purchase. But when she went to the house to make the buy, the seller got spooked and killed her. And where were the Templars? Nowhere—not even watching out for her. She died because they wouldn't risk themselves."

"Oh shit." Cyn's mouth went dry, and she had to lick her lips before she could get a word out. "Who—who was the Templar?"

"She was from the Montbard family."

Fuck.

"So that's why I don't trust the Templars to put anything or anyone else above their duty. I mean it, Cyn. You need to look after yourself—hell, I'll look out for you too. But don't put all your faith in them. And shit, I know that's not what you think of them, but it's the truth."

"Rohan, I don't think a Templar would knowingly put a civilian at risk—"

"I was there, Cyn. I found Eleanor—and I was there when the Templar came to see what had happened with their purchase—they didn't even stop to see if Eleanor was alive."

Cyn's gut seesawed. Surely, he had it wrong.

Mother of the gods, Rohan was going to be furious when she told him the truth about R-104C.

But Gray was right. Rohan was an asset, and this op needed all the help it could get—not to mention no one else was taking out hellbeasts here.

But if she was keeping him with her, it was going to be impossible to lock down the truth about her identity. Too many people would be there who knew her, even if they hadn't seen her in years.

Time for the truth. Shit. Shit, shit, shit.

"Why are you looking at me like that?"

"I need to tell you something."

"What, something worse than you're a Templar?"

What more could there really frigging be here? Rohan's blood iced over. Cyn clearly hadn't liked what he'd said about Eleanor—her jaw had stiffened, and her chin had lifted in that way of hers that said she was going to run roughshod over whatever the hell anyone else had to say or wanted. But he'd told only her the truth—he couldn't make her like it or accept it.

Hell.

And now she clenched her jaw so hard she was going to break a tooth.

Then she glanced over her shoulder. He followed her gaze to where Gray and Isa slept on the chair-bed. Another fancy Templar offering.

"Looks like they're asleep if that's what you're worried about," he whispered.

"Yeah. Don't want to wake them up." She chewed on her lip for a moment—and while normally thinking about those lush curves would have his body tight with desire, the only thing tense right now was his chest.

"Cyn, what's going on?"

"Keep your voice down," she whispered, glancing back again over her shoulder.

"Why? Because you don't want anyone else to know you lied to me?"

"They already know—"

"Of course, they do. And the only reason I'm not yelling at you right now is because Isadora needs her sleep."

"Listen, I know I lied, but there was a reason."

"There always is. Like the Templar who lied to Eleanor about keeping her safe, right? The greater good outweighs the lie."

"Yes. Yes, it does, sometimes. Because the greater good here is millions of lives if the shit hits the fan and the things we're tasked with safeguarding fall into the wrong hands. You do know that, right?"

"So, one life for a million—a billion?"

"Yes, exactly."

"You're just like her." Rohan's stomach churned, and he could barely look at Cyn until something flashed in her eyes. "Wait—what's that look for?"

She took a visibly deep breath, and her words tumbled out. "I'm also a Montbard."

His entire being crashed like he'd smashed into a glacier and the entire river of ice had shattered over him, crushing the breath from the breath from his lungs. What. The. Hell?

"No," Rohan squeezed past the constriction in his chest. But her gaze didn't waver.

Cynane ... High Priestess. Human. Templar Knight. *Montbard*. And the woman who his damned idiot heart had somehow fallen for.

"Rohan, three years ago, I found a lead on R-104C which indicated Simion's—well, I thought his family at the time—had come into contact with the relic. We tried being up-front about our search for R-104C, but he wanted nothing to do with the Templars—"

"Yeah, no doubt he's had enough shit from them, too."

Cyn's eyes flashed, but she kept going. "We couldn't get close enough to Simion to determine if the lead was the real deal or not. So I went undercover and embraced my daemon heritage to become a high priestess and build his trust. I couldn't break cover after you and I met in the club back in LA before Christmas, and back then, I had no clue if I could even trust you. Then you disappeared for six months."

"Because I was fighting hellbeast incursions at the Tenth Gate. And after I came back and we were working together? Having sex together? Do you lie to everyone you fuck?"

Cyn winced, and he balled his fists to restrain the loco urge to comfort the frigging lying, beautiful high priestess *Templar Knight*.

"I don't fuck everyone. And anyone I met as a high priestess met me in that guise—so yes, I did lie to others. And, Rohan, I'm not going to apologize for lying to you."

"Of course not, because that would mean you care, right?"

"This isn't about caring. This is about me doing my job and retrieving R-104C."

Somehow a punch of pain made it through the ice encasing his body and smashed into his chest.

Of course, Cyn didn't care about him. "Why the hell does one frankincense tree matter so much to you?"

"Because Montbards have been Templars for hundreds of years, and my family were the ones who lost it in Portugal. So yes, it matters to me. Restoring my family name matters to me. But the main reason—more important than anything else—is the entire human world is at stake for as long as R-104C can be claimed by anyone." Her jaw tightened.

"Cynane, what do you mean?" He leaned forward. "Cyn. Tell me what the hell is going on."

"Just chill," she snapped. "This isn't easy. In fact, I've never told this to anyone outside the Templars." She drew a breath and then her glittering gaze caught his. "The frankincense tree is one of the three gifts of legend—along with the gifts of gold and myrrh."

Rohan couldn't stop twisting around to face the bonsai tree currently strapped into the chair behind him. "That's *the* relic of frankincense?"

"Yes."

"Bloody hell." He racked his memory for everything he knew about the three gifts. "They each have a unique power, right? And now it makes sense why Simion used the frankincense for his love oil—that gift was all about love. But what's the huge danger they present—is it any worse than an open hellgate?"

"You don't know the true nature of the gifts?"

"Clearly not."

"Fine. Yes, each gift has its own innate value, even power, but the danger is that together, the power of the three gifts is amplified. So much so that anyone who holds all three can control the hearts, bodies and minds of humankind. That's their true power. And that's why the Templars were tasked with keeping them separated for two thousand years. And I'm not about to stuff up that fucking promise we made for the good of all our world."

"Shit."

"Yeah."

Someone—some *being*—could control all humankind? That was bad. So very, very bad.

And damn Cyn, she held his gaze as if she totally

believed everything she'd said. And, oh hell—Lord Forneous had a seed from one of those gifts?

"Okay, so you told him everything. Can we pretend to wake up now?" Isa's dry tone cut the silence. Cyn scowled and stood up.

But Rohan couldn't move if he tried. "Why now?" he whispered. "Why did you tell me the Templar's secret?"

"Listen, can we do this later? Everyone's here—"

"No, I don't give a fuck who's here. Why now? Why did you tell me now?"

"Because, as it was pointed out to me, you're a useful asset given the danger with the hellbeasts. And others trust you." She nodded at Gray.

"What about you? Do you trust me?" Cyn's lips twisted, and he knew the answer before she could speak. "Don't bother lying. I see exactly how much you trust me."

And the ice in his gut splintered, the shards cutting deep.

All this time he'd been falling for Cynane, and she didn't even trust him.

22

THE AIR in the Templar jet had been icy for the last five hours, but finally, they were on approach into Cheshire, and maybe once they landed and Cyn left the pressurized cabin, she'd be able to draw an easy breath.

Eve had woken up an hour ago and was talking to Gray in the middle cabin—something about Watcher business. Isa had gone back to sleep in the sky bed, and Rohan and Cyn had slept in the forward chairs facing each other. Or at least Cyn had tried to shut her mind off for the last two hours.

But instead of the oblivion of sleep, all she saw was Rohan's clenched jaw and the hurt ... like, actual hurt ... in his eyes when she'd inferred she didn't trust him.

Damn stupid brain. She stopped trying to sleep and instead picked her tarot deck back up.

Damn it, why did Rohan's anger feel so freaking bad? He'd agreed to work as an asset for the op, which was exactly what she'd wanted.

She snuck a glance at Rohan. Again. But instead of sleeping, he stared right at her.

"Let's try another reading," she blurted. "For your key."

"A guilt reading?"

"We have a binding contract, remember? You're awake. I'm awake"—unfortunately—"so let's just be professional and use the time to get this thing done."

"Fine." Rohan shifted forward. "But I need coffee."

Damn, caffeine would be good right now. But she bit her lip to stop asking him to get her one too.

And when he returned, he only had one cup. An odd emptiness panged in her chest.

"Right." Cyn cleared the knot in her throat. "I'll do a spread." She shuffled the minor arcana and laid seven cards face down on the table. Then she took the major arcana and spread them all face down closer to Rohan. "Okay, I'll do the spell next. What would you like to sacrifice?"

A wave of emotional ice blasted through her. She tensed and stared at Rohan. "Was that you?"

"What?" Rohan said.

Shit. He wasn't a witch, so either she was picking up his energy wavelength on her own—no magic called on—or she was imagining things. But she wasn't an empath, and this type of connection had never happened before. Maybe she was projecting?

"Nothing," she muttered. She held out a hand. "Hair?"

"No." He reached out and tugged the hairpin from her bun, then pricked his thumb and pressed it into her palm. "Blood this time."

She held in a sigh and called the divination spell; then, she hovered her hands over the minor arcana. "All right, we're ready. Pick one."

Rohan's hand was a blur as he leaned in and tapped one card.

"You didn't have to think about that?"

"No. You said pick. I picked."

Cyn didn't bother hiding her sigh this time. This wasn't going to be fun. She turned the card over.

The Moon.

"Why are you frowning? Did I do something wrong?"

"No, but this is interesting. The Moon represents, among other things, illusion, deception, or confusion. Strife even."

One of Rohan's brows rose. "Well, I think we can all get what the deception means."

"This is your card, Rohan, searching for your item. So how about you think what deception might be involved there? Now hush and choose one from the minor arcana."

Once again, he reached in picked without hesitation.

"Really?"

"Yes."

"Well, now you've picked the ... Nine of Cups. Upright. Huh. This is normally a good card—one of the best cards to get in a reading. It means that your goal is close by. Or that you'll achieve your goal soon."

"But what does that mean for my key?" Rohan said.

"That's what I'm doing the spell for—to take this reading and use it to find your blasted key. Now hush and let me concentrate." Damn it. Cyn opened her eyes. "Listen, I can't get a thing from the spell right now."

"What? Why not?"

"Because, right now, there's too much interference," she snapped. "And to be clear, that's icy, angry, negative energy." She glared at him and stood up.

"Hey, you okay, Cyn?" Isa's voice had her stop scowling and turn around.

"Yep, sorry, didn't mean to wake you up."

"All good," Isa said. "Not you—I'm hungry. And seriously, you look ... err ... not your normal self."

"Just a headache," Cyn lied through her teeth.

She gave in to the urge and scrubbed a fist over her chest, the real ache, as she made her way to the bathroom and locked herself inside. She stared at her reflection in the mirror.

The mark of a high priestess. Something she'd taken for the job. Always the job. Although the moment she'd gotten the tattoo—at the time, confident she'd glamour it away after the mission—something had snicked in her chest, like a key finding the perfect lock.

And it had been the same sensation as when she'd kissed Rohan at Simion's LA mansion. A key finding its one and true lock.

Fuck. Fuck, fuck, *fuck*. Cyn didn't want to feel bad about Rohan. Being together had been about sex—clearing the tension and nothing more.

No stupid feelings, she shouldn't even be having, getting in the way.

Now Rohan had become a drug, and somehow, she just wanted more of it—of him.

Knock, knock, knock. "Sorry! Need the loo," Isa called through the door.

Cyn took a deep breath and forced a calm expression. "All yours," she said when she was done.

"Thanks."

Back in the main cabin, Eve and Gray had joined Rohan, and the makeshift bed had been reconfigured into table and chairs, so Cyn grabbed a coffee and, this time, sat opposite Eve, who leaned forward as soon as Cyn sat down.

"Can we talk about the relic of frankincense?" Eve sat forward. "I'm curious about its history."

"Sure. But why?"

"I'm thinking of a way to keep it secure—and you

mentioned it had been shrouded from sight. I just want to get the whole picture. Can you tell me everything you know about the relic?"

"Can do," Cyn said. She quickly recapped how the relic of frankincense had originally been the resin of an ancient species—sadly extinct—and how Simion had transformed the last of the resin into a living tree.

"So the relic in its resin form was at the monastery for how long?" Eve opened a small book and started making notes.

"Templar inventory records show R-104C at the monastery in 1795." Cyn opened her cell and brought up the photo she'd taken from the Templar archives. "You can see here—the date, the relic and the location."

"Wow. Okay. And then what?"

"In 1814, toward the end of the Napoleonic Wars, the monastery was sacked—the Templars got word of the potential issue, but by the time they got there, they found the frankincense gone. This is the next record in the ledger —the date, location—and the note '*la relique a disparu.*' It translates to the relic has disappeared."

"What about before it went missing? Could you trace it then?" Eve asked.

"No clue—we never logged any attempts. And I looked. And then, about three years ago, I was in the Watcher library and found the mention of a ship capture log that alluded to a resin of power. So I went to The National Archives of England and looked through all their records— you have to go in person as they're not online."

"Ah, what's a ship capture log?" Isa put her hand up, and Cyn looked around. Isa, Gray and even Rohan were watching and clearly listening in.

"You all want to know this, too?" Cyn asked.

"You're kidding, right? This is intense." Isa took a bite of her meal and waved. "Go on."

"Fine. Not so sure this is the intense part. Okay, so it was standard practice for the English to stop and board ships operating under enemy flags. The ships were often confiscated and added to the Royal Navy fleet, and their contents —things and people—were meticulously logged, and then sold off at auction. Hence the term, ship capture log. So at The National Archives, after weeks of reviewing these documents, I found the log of a privateer—basically an English pirate-hunting ship—that captured a French vessel in the year 1814. That log recorded, along with two civilian women and numerous ship's crew, a shallow clay pot containing a small amount of fragrant resin."

"So you had a starting place," Eve said.

"Yep. The captain of that ship belonged to a prominent family, and when I started researching them, I came across records of sale of several items captured from various ships —although there was no mention of the bowl of resin—to a private collector to pay off gambling debts. I traced that connection to Simion."

Cyn went on to explain how she'd gone on to become an undercover—albeit real—high priestess. She didn't say how much she'd enjoyed the opportunity to … cautiously explore her powers. The first time since they'd manifested that she'd done so without fear of repercussion.

"And Simion shrouded it all this time without a spell?" Eve leaned forward.

"Simion is a minor deity," Rohan said from where he sat. "His power goes beyond magic, and don't forget his assistants. Aleesha and Sonja are from a race of people I don't think I've ever seen before—although I have read about them—and they were seriously invested in protecting the bonsai tree."

"I think they're descendants of the original beings who presented the gifts," Cyn murmured. "They seemed to be fine with Simion having R-104C—they just didn't want it unprotected. I think their goal is to see to the physical safety of the frankincense rather than who holds it." Cyn's gut tightened, and she twisted the ring around her finger. "So the next step is transferring R-104C to the castle." Cyn turned to Eve. "What security protocols are in place?"

"A lot," Eve said. "The wards at the castle wall are the most powerful of anything we have, so once the relic's past the gates, no one is getting to it who isn't allowed into the castle in the first place. And we have the glamour spell."

"Are there any counterspells to glamours?" Cyn asked.

"Yes, but you'd have to have a strong witch or a high priestess." Eve raised one brow.

"Okay, so possible, but not that many beings out there who fit the bill."

"What about a hellwitch?" Rohan murmured.

"A what?" Cyn asked. "I don't recall reading anything about them."

"Hellside resident with magic. They don't usually leave Hell, though, as they're bound to the Lords of Hell—either a gate lord or one of the congress—and *they* don't let the witches out of sight in case they find a way to break their bonds, which can only happen humanside."

"You keep slaves?" Cyn's stomach dropped.

"Not me. But yes, some do. There are rules, though— which you'd know if you spent time with your sire to learn them."

Cyn shot Rohan her iciest look and then turned back to Eve. "Okay, so we have hellwitches—possibly—to worry about. So we need to consider an attack between landing and getting to the castle."

"Really?" Rohan looked around. "Who knows where you're going?"

"Templars only. And they'd never speak."

"Of course not. The high and mighty Templars."

"Hey—you're talking to two Templars right here and two more on contract. Remember that."

"Like I could forget. Because you all lied to me." Rohan glared at them all. His gaze softened a little for Isa before coldly settling back on Cyn. "Anyway, what about Simion and his assistants? They know you're meeting them, don't they? Could they have told anyone?"

"Shit," Cyn said. "Possibly. What about hellbeasts—how do we know if any more have come through?"

"I'd have to cross Hellside to find out. The nearest gate is in Glastonbury. Can you get your people on the ground to see if there have been any reports of unusual killings or attacks?"

Cyn looked at Gray. "Can you contact our people in the south?" She didn't wait for Gray to nod before she turned to Eve. "You and I need to be at full power. Let's refuel and then rest until we land."

Cyn forced herself to eat, then tried again to sleep, but even with the cabin lights dimmed and the shades down, all she saw was Rohan's grim, icy eyes—the utter opposite of the devilish gleam she loved.

Damn it.

She checked the time. Thirty minutes to go. Maybe a reading would help—for herself.

She took a deep breath and, saving her magic, let the cards lead the way and dealt the major arcana face down in front of herself.

She stared at the relic, calmed her mind, then chose one card.

The Two of Wands. If she was doing a reading for a client's career, she'd have advised that person that a change was coming—either in profession, rank or duties. And soon. The tightness in Cyn's gut intensified.

"Shit," she whispered. What was coming next?

23

THICK FOG DRIFTED out from the trees and blanketed the ground all the way to the runway on either side of the Templar's fancy jet when it landed.

"Is the mist always so thick here? I can't see anything but the runway," Rohan said.

"Standard Watcher wards," Cyn murmured. She was sitting up and alert, glancing outside as if she could see through the fog. Maybe she could?

Moments after they'd landed, Cyn and Gray stood up and moved around each other as efficiently as if they'd done this a hundred times—they took silver cases from the overhead lockers and placed them on the nearest table. Gray took two out handguns, checked them over, and slid them into his shoulder holster.

Cyn pulled out a duffel from another compartment and withdrew a leather holster similar to Gray's, and two leg sheaths.

"Thought you'd be back in a black suit or something," Rohan muttered. And he was not getting turned on as she strapped the holster over her top and a sheath around her jeans on each thigh.

"Don't have one handy." She flicked open her silver case, withdrew two short-bladed knives and slipped them into her thigh sheaths.

"Do you know how to use those?" Rohan asked.

"Of course," she replied without pause as she took two guns and checked them over the same as Gray had done. "I might not be up to speed on hellblades, but I know my way around other knives."

Frigging hell.

Do not get hard. Do not ... Shit. No hope there.

"So, is this standard Templar getup?"

"When we're transferring precious cargo, yes. Gray has this motto—"

"Prior preparation prevents piss-poor performance," Isa added with a roll of her eyes. "Although, I have to say, his five Ps have helped us out."

"See?" Gray muttered. "Don't know why you all give me shit for doing my job."

"I'm perfectly fine with the five Ps." Cyn smiled.

And for a moment, the easy comradery between Cyn, Gray, Isa and Eve made Rohan's stomach pang. Damn, but he'd like that. Except, no. He was the daemon here. Not to be trusted.

And hell, maybe they were right.

He hadn't told them who his sire was. But ... Rohan had zero to do with Lord Forneous anymore and would continue not to for as long as Rohan reported to the High Lord of Hell rather than his sire.

"Okay, entering the hangar now," Cyn called out. "Disembarking in three minutes."

As the plane stopped, Cyn ordered the cabin crew to

lower the stairs, and she pulled one handgun from her holster and held her hairpin in her other.

She and Gray did a check of the hangar, and Rohan assumed everything was okay because while they didn't put their guns away, they did lower them.

"Time to go," Cyn called. "Gray, you drive. I'll keep lookout until everyone's in."

She descended the steps, and Rohan waited until last.

As he passed Cyn, she suddenly froze.

"What is it?"

"Look over there, through the hangar door on the ground."

"The birds?"

"There are nine sparrows in a row. Like the nine cups on the card that you drew. I think ... I think this has something to do with your key. I think it's close."

"What, close, as in nearby?"

"Close in some form. The card can also mean achieving your goal soon."

"Okay. Good to know. So what, do I go looking around the hangar for the key?"

"You can do whatever the fuck you want, Red. I'm saying it's close."

"What am I meant to do with 'close'?" He threw his satchel over his shoulder.

"Don't push me, Red."

"Of course not."

"Hey, you two?" Isa chafed her hands. "Can we please get going? It might be summer here, but it's still frigging cold. I take it that's another Watcher thing?"

"Yep." Eve nodded. "But it's worse in winter, so there is that."

"Believe me," Isa said, "I remember."

"Okay," Cyn said. "Isa, you and the relic are in the back middle seat. I'll sit up front with Gray. Eve and Rohan, you're in the backseat with Isa. Remember, protect the relic—"

"And Isa," Gray growled.

"—at all costs."

Rohan didn't bother hiding an eye roll. "Like we wouldn't."

Cyn pursed her lips but didn't say anything as they all piled into the car.

"Can't they get bigger SUVs?" Isa wriggled her hips.

"I'll put your formal request in, shall I?" Eve said dryly.

"Yes, please."

"Okay, okay, enough chatter," Cyn said. "Eyes open, everyone."

And bossy Cyn was in charge. Funny—whether she'd been high priestess or Templar Knight, that was one thing she hadn't been able to hide. But who really was Cynane Montbard?

Rohan found himself studying the back of her head as they exited the hangar. The tattooed runes winding up the back of her neck were familiar—a pattern he recognized from his mother's people. One for strength, another for protection. Did she realize that's what they meant?

Knowing Cyn, yes. She wouldn't do anything without purpose.

"Eyes sharp," she ordered.

"I can barely see anything," Rohan muttered. "Is this fog really from the Watchers?"

"Yes, it should ease back a little in town, then thicken again as we go up the hill."

"What's the town?"

"Ashforton. It's named for the castle on the hill."

"It looks old."

"It is. Fifteen hundred years old, to be precise."

"Wow, older than me. I never came this way when I was last in England." As one, almost everyone turned to stare at him—even Grayson looked at him through the rearview mirror. "What? I'm several hundred years old. I'm not allowed to talk about it?"

"Not surprising you didn't come this way," Eve said. "The Watchers have—had—issues with otherworlders in the past."

"Even half daemons?" Rohan said.

"Not if they're human." Eve cleared her throat. "But if they cross over and become fully daemon, then again in the past, yes. So when we get there—"

"Shit. Two silver motorbikes coming up fast behind us." Cyn twisted to look out the back window. "And another. Gray, they're coming fast."

"I see them. Going to try and lose them in the village."

"Eve," Cyn said, "can you put a call in to the castle and let them know we're coming in hot? Do they have offensive witches who can meet us?"

"Can do and will ask."

"Rohan, support Isa," Gray barked. "These turns will be hard and fast."

"Got her and the tree." He locked an arm around Isa to stop her from flying side to side—and within moments, Gray sent their SUV into hard turn after hard turn over the cobblestone streets.

Shit. The village looked like something straight out of a realm of Hell, except the shop names were much tamer.

The Wheel and Barrow instead of the Skull and Sword.

"You've lost them," Rohan called out as he checked again.

"Not for long, though," Cyn muttered. "They'll have to

know where we're going. Gray, how fast can you push the drive up the mountain?"

"Without driving us off the edge?"

"That'd be good."

"Fast. Just hold on, everyone. We're five minutes out."

"Watchers are heading to the gatehouse now," Eve said.

"Gatehouse?" What the hell was this now?

"The castle is surrounded by a warded wall—nothing is getting past or over that except via the gatehouse—and you can only get through if you're with a Watcher."

Rohan checked again behind them. "Shit. Motorbikes have caught up." But at least these were only daemons—those they could handle. "Will the wall keep out hellbeasts?"

"Eve?" Cyn called. "Do you know the answer to Rohan's question?"

"Not with certainty, and I really hope today isn't the day we find out."

Gray steered the car in a hard turn and pressed the gas as they headed up a steep incline.

Rohan kept his gaze on the motorbikes. "And is the fog getting thicker?"

"I'd say the Watchers have upped their wards," Cyn said.

"Good." Rohan shifted to check out the terrain. "Except, if there are hellbeasts out there, the fog will keep them hidden until they're right on us. I can get my blades out, but we're jammed so tight in here it'd be dangerous."

Cyn glanced over her shoulder. "What are you thinking?"

"I'll jump out around the next bend and run parallel to you. That way, I can hear if there's anything hunting the SUV and take it out before it gets to you. If a hellbeast rams us right now, we're all going over that edge. You concentrate on getting into the castle."

"What about motorbikes?" Cyn bit out.

"I'll take them on, too."

"Shit. You sure?"

"I can survive a tumble down that drop-off—can anyone else here?" He didn't wait for a reply because they all knew it. He gauged the bend coming up. The motorbikes behind them. "Okay, jumping out in three ... two ... one ..." Rohan flung the door open and, with his duffel under one arm, threw himself clear.

He hit the gravel hard and his breath punched from him. Shit! But he let the pain roll through him even as he leaped to his feet and disappeared into the fog.

As soon as he was hidden enough, Rohan took off after the SUV's taillights, and while he ran, he unzipped his bag and took out his blades.

They settled into his grip perfectly, and he ditched the bag and took off in his longest, fastest strides.

To his left, multiple vehicle engines rumbled, their tires crunched over gravel. To his right ... noth—

Thump, thump—thump, thump.

Something big ran in the forest. Had to be a hellbeast. The earth vibrated beneath whatever the creature was. Rohan held his breath, tuned out the vehicles.

The thuds tracked at an angle to intercept ... him. Hell. He must've alerted the hellbeast. Ah well, better it came for him than the SUV.

Those rhythmic thumps ... had to be four feet. No swooshing of wings. But it also made no snarls or growls. That might just be worse.

Ahead, the SUV's brake lights glowed through the fog, and the engine stopped.

Yes. Relief flooded his chest—

The thump, thump—thump, thump grew louder. Rohan froze.

Back down the road, the rumble of the motorbikes drew closer. But a deep, long growl had the hairs on the back of his neck shoot up. Through the fog, an outline of something dark and feline in form, slinking low to the ground, caught his eye. Standing still, he held his breath.

There.

A santarka. No wonder it had got here so fast. It could leap high and far—like a tiger in the human world, but with enhanced sight, smell and hearing. Fuck.

Then the click and clunk of four doors opening echoed through the fog. The santarka hissed, then leaped.

Sailed right over Rohan's head.

Shit. Shit, shit, shit. He spun and took off as it landed between Cyn's group and the gatehouse, gravel spitting into the air around the santarka's feet as it skidded, then righted itself.

"Cyn, Eve!" Rohan shouted. "Stun it. It's not armored. One go high, one go low—stop it from leaping!"

On cue, Cyn drew her hairpin across her thumb and shot her hand out. Eve followed, and twin streams of energy made the fog shimmer. But the santarka leaped to the side, away from Rohan, and closer to the drop-off.

Rohan did his own leap down the embankment, hit the gravel running and took off after the hellbeast. "Don't hit me!" he yelled.

Rohan raced past Cyn and Eve as Isa—still carrying the bonsai tree—and Gray ran for the gatehouse.

But the santarka twisted on its hind legs and leaped back over Rohan, landing between Isa and Gray, and the gatehouse.

Isa screamed; she and Gray skidded to a stop.

And then the motorbikes shot around the bend, screeching to a stop. A black Mercedes sedan followed and stopped behind them. The rear passenger door opened.

The hairs on the back of Rohan's neck pricked.

"Eve," Cyn yelled. "Where are your Watchers?"

"Coming!"

"Better be soon," Cyn hissed back. "Everyone, back to me. Rohan, you face the hellbeast. Isa, keep the relic in the middle of us. Gray, Eve, you're with me and these pricks."

"Cyn," Rohan said, "the santarka can jump high and long. Right now, it's not pouncing—there must be a reason why. Someone is controlling it." And when he found out who, they were going to pay.

"Some*one*?" A familiar voice called out from the sedan just before a figure emerged. A male in a perfectly cut navy suit, ageless in appearance, with icy disdain and arrogance dripping from his expression.

Rohan's blood roared in his ears. Fuck. Fuck, fuck, fuck. "Lord Forneous," Rohan spat the name out.

Cyn hissed behind him; a collective snarl went through the group. Guess they'd dealt with him before.

"Why, Son, how good to see you again. Thank you for rounding them up all so neatly."

"Like fuck you get to call me *Son*." Rohan leaped at his sire, but then the santarka rammed into him, propelling him toward the drop-off. Rohan sliced his blades—Lord Forneous had signed the santarka's death warrant the moment he'd sent it in such a poor move—but all he could see was the horror on Cyn's face as she watched him fly over the edge.

Well, hell. Was that horror for him—or at him?

24

Son.

Son.

Son.

What. The. Fuck?

Cyn's heart froze—as did the rest of the world for a split second as Forneous's words echoed over and over in her head. Then her surroundings roared back to life in a blur of sound and movement.

Forneous screaming for the frankincense.

Rohan tumbling over the cliff.

Cyn jammed her hairpin into her thumb, gathered her waning power, and screamed a stun spell. She threw the magic, but whether it worked or not, she had no idea as over the hellbeast's shoulder, Rohan's gaze locked on her, and something blazed in the depths of his green eyes, visible even from across the gravel road—before he and the hell-beast disappeared out of sight.

Rohan.

"No!" The urge to run to the edge slammed through Cyn —but shit. They had other problems. And Rohan had said he could withstand the fall. Fuck, he'd better be telling the truth.

"Oh, I wouldn't worry about him," Forneous said. "Although I do find it curious you would care what happens to my son. But I'll deal with that later. Finally, I have two pieces of my property. Hand them over, and I'll let you all live."

"Like fuck," Gray growled.

"Pieces of property?" Cyn spat. "You fucker."

Forneous gazed at Gray for a moment, then turned to Cyn. Interest sharpened in his eyes, and he cocked his head to one side. "Now, now, no need to speak like that, little daemon. And while I need the diviner, I think I'll take you, too. And Evangeline—how sad I was to see you slip through my fingers. But, good news, we can all have a nice reunion soon. My soldiers have you surrounded, so I'll take the daemon, the diviner and the frankincense. What have you done with it? Ah—let me guess? Another glamour? And, yes, there is my diviner, carrying a vase."

Oh no. No fucking way.

"I'm not yours," Isa called out.

"Enough of this shit. Take him down," Cyn yelled. She drew more blood, called more magic and sent her stun spell at Forneous, then she took out her SIG Sauer.

Forneous zipped to the side, and her stun spell missed him, but her bullets didn't, although he kept going. Freaking daemons. But with the hellbeast gone, the way to the castle was open.

"Everyone inside!" Cyn whirled and faced the coming hostile daemons. Then Isa stumbled, and R-104C fell to the ground.

"Get them!" Forneous cried out. But Gray grabbed Isa, picked her up and ran.

"R-104C—" Cyn ran for it, but two daemons came at her, both holding short-bladed knives. She shot her sixteenth round—the last—and gathered a new spell. Sent it at the daemon still running for her. She hit him square in the chest, but the second daemon threw his knife.

Pain sliced through her shoulder, and her arm went dead. She gasped, her gun fell to the ground, not that it mattered, she was out of bullets. With her good hand, she took her second gun and covered Gray, Isa and Eve as they ran for the gatehouse.

Then stream after stream of magic-charged air shot past Cyn's shoulders. The Watchers had arrived. Thank you, mother of the gods.

But Forneous ducked and snatched R-104C from the ground.

No. No, no, *no*. She lunged at him, but the daemon who'd stabbed her threw his other weapon. She ducked—the blade spun over her head—and she kept running.

She wasn't losing R-104C, not after finally getting it back.

Cyn stretched her arm and shot at Forneous, but if she hit him, he didn't even pause as he reached the sedan and threw himself inside.

The vehicle came careening at her, and she stood her ground; and with one arm hanging limp at her side, she emptied the last of her bullets from her second gun into the windscreen.

No way was she moving. They'd have to run her over—

Something slammed into Cyn and shoved her out of the way right as the sedan ran over where she'd been standing. She landed hard; small stones bit into her cheek and forehead. The air punched from her lungs.

Then the sedan's wheels spun in the gravel as it took off

back down the hill, the motorbikes disappearing into the fog behind it.

Cyn sprung back to her feet, shoved at the hands pulling at her arm.

Rohan? Who—what—?

"Where did you come from?" she snarled. Relief eased something in her chest—the fucker wasn't dead after all— but she didn't stop to hear his answer. R-104C was gone again. Speeding down the hill at this very moment, and she had to go after it.

"What the hell were you doing?" Rohan got up in her face. "You just stood there while they almost ran over you!"

"My job—stopping the sedan, which I would've done if you hadn't shoved me out of the way." She ran around him to the SUV.

"Where are you going?"

"Where do you think? After them—"

"Cyn, you're bleeding. Just stop!"

"No!" She shoved him away again, ignoring the pain punching through her shoulder. "You stop. You can go the fuck anywhere else—I don't care—but I'm going after that car."

"How?" Rohan shouted. "You can't move your arm— again. And you look like you're about to pass out. Probably both, right? You pass out down the hill—drive off the edge —kill yourself, and then what happens to your precious frankincense?"

"My op. My responsibility. First fucking time as a leader and I lose the very relic I'm responsible for."

"Who the fuck cares? If you lose your life ... Damn it to hell, Cyn, twice in one day you've almost died. What the hell is going on here? You can't put your life above these relics."

"Yes, yes, I can. That is my job. And I believe totally in

the cause I'm fighting for. I'm willing to die if it means saving a bunch of humans. But I guess you wouldn't understand since you're a freaking immortal daemon."

"Oh, I understand the length you go to save something you care for. And just stop. You're a Templar; don't you have other resources? You wouldn't even find Lord Forneous right now in this fog."

"Fuck. Fuck, fuck, *fuck*."

"Listen, instead of chasing him, let's figure out why the hell Lord Forneous wants—"

"You mean your father—" The burning in her chest grew even stronger. "Oh, mother of the gods, your *father*. He's your father.

"Don't call him that."

"Are you working together?" Cyn said. "Is that what this is?"

"Cyn!" Rohan shook her good shoulder—but pain still ricocheted through her injured arm. Other aches and pains made themselves known too. Her face. Her hip. But she just clenched her jaw and stood her ground.

"Let go of me right now. I might be out of bullets, but I'll still take you down." Except suddenly, the tiny patch of gravel she could see through the gate began to swirl around her.

"Hey, take a breath. We can get the relic back."

Breathe? How could she? She just got R-104C after all these years! And now she'd lost it again. The knot in her throat expanded to her chest. The ground spun—

Suddenly Rohan pushed between her shoulder blades, and she found her head between her knees, and his warm hand stayed right there.

"Inhale, princess. Come on, you're human, you need air to live, remember?"

Sure enough, the spinning stopped, and she forced a breath past the constriction in her chest.

"Cyn! Rohan, what the hell happened to you—?" Eve skidded to a halt in the gravel beside them. "Are you okay?"

"Don't you dare touch me." She shrugged Rohan away and whirled to Eve. "Where's everyone?"

"Gray's with Isa up at the castle. She's got some stomach pains after the fall—"

"What?"

"The baby?" Rohan whirled to Eve, too, and his cheeks paled.

"Our medical team are checking her over now. But the frankincense ..."

"Gone."

"Oh shit." Eve's cheeks paled too.

Forneous would be out of the village by now and who knew which motorway he'd—damn. That was it.

Cyn whirled around and searched for her cell. Where was it, where—there! She grabbed the device and punched in a message to Templar HQ.

"What are you doing now?" Rohan grabbed her when she wobbled. Shit. Maybe she needed to take care of the shoulder wound.

Cyn yanked a hair and called her magic—but her energy was as weak as the last dregs of a pot of coffee—damn it all. But she used what she had and sent it into a healing spell. It would have to do.

Fainting from blood loss was not on the cards.

"Cyn." Rohan shoved his hands on his hips. "I said—"

"Nothing." Nothing that she could tell *him* anyway. "Just reporting in on what's happened." And requesting surveillance on all local roads out of the village. Human tech could follow Forneous from surveillance feeds in town and then onto the motorway.

"Finally," Rohan said. "You're making sense, but seriously, you're wobbling on your feet. We need to get you inside—"

"Rohan, you don't need to get me anywhere ever again. In fact, if I never see you again—" The tattoo on her thigh stung like someone had stabbed her with a hot poker, and she gasped a breath past the new pain. "Shit."

"Bad luck. You've still got one on the contract to look for my key, remember?"

Fuck, yes, she did. "Fine." As soon as she said it, the pain in her tattoo subsided.

"And there's more. Listen to me, Cyn—just listen. Isn't the gold relic locked securely away?"

"Yes, no one's getting through my ward," Eve said.

"Then why is Lord Forneous still going after the three gifts? There's something else we're missing here—you need to find out what it is. Do two together have some other power we don't know about?"

Shit. Cyn glanced at Eve who shrugged. "We're not aware of anything, no."

"Bit of an issue there ... you're not aware of anything," Rohan said. "Not that there *isn't* anything. So what *do* you know?"

Cyn said, "That I shouldn't have gotten involved with a daemon. I knew that."

"Too late for recriminations, isn't it?"

"Isn't there a saying about sex in haste, repent in leisure?" Cyn bit back a hiss when she went to cross her arms—fuck, but that hurt. She made do with holding it to her side and tried to hide the fact it was freaking on fire and useless.

"No, not familiar with that one."

"Too bad." She pasted on a smile. Fool fucking her for getting involved with the son of their enemy.

Well, that was one thing she could fix right away. Cyn might have to do his spell, but as of now, sex with the lying, traitorous, walking orgasm of a daemon was not ever fucking happening again.

And if Rohan *was* in on Forneous's plan ... She exhaled long and slow. Well, she'd do what she'd done to every other minion of Forneous who'd stood in her way.

Dispatch him with prejudice.

-((●))-

"Cyn, you're hurt!" Rohan tried to gentle his voice, although hell knew the urge to shout and snarl was frigging hard to resist. "At least let me help you into the gatehouse."

"No—"

"Cyn, come on," Eve said gently. "You need that shoulder looked at. And I just went through so much magic I can't heal more than a paper cut right now. And I'm guessing you're the same."

Cyn scowled at Rohan as if he'd been the one to point out the obvious, but he just held back a sigh of relief when she didn't argue any further.

Energy buzzed over his skin as he entered the small, sparsely furnished, windowless stone-walled room.

"You don't like visitors in your gatehouse, huh?" Rohan said.

"What do you mean?" Eve glanced around as if the room wasn't bare but for an unlit fireplace, one table and a chair.

"It's not exactly ... inviting."

"It's not meant to be," Cyn snapped.

"Fine. So what now? We just prop you up in this cold, weird room?"

"You and I wait here. Eve—don't let him through until he's submitted to a truth spell. Can you get everything we need?"

"Really?" Eve said. "You want to spell him?"

"Seconding Eve, here. You want to spell me after I just saved your ass?"

"He's Forneous's son. Damned right I'm spelling him. He's lucky *his* ass isn't stunned right now."

"All right, you two, be back soon. Don't kill each other while I'm gone." Eve headed out through the door on the other side of the room.

"Right here, High Priestess. You can look at me when you threaten me, you know." But Cyn didn't even glance his way. "At least sit before you fall."

Rohan didn't wait for her answer before he eased her onto the chair, restraining the urge to drop her butt-first onto the hard timber.

He stood for a moment and waited for her to actually look his way, but she just stayed stony in her silence, her body rigid.

Fine. If she didn't want to talk—and clearly, she didn't trust him—then he wasn't going to say anything either. Plus, he had to figure out what the hell his sire was up to.

Damn, but he wished he had access to the library in Hell City. Chamber after chamber held scrolls and tomes no one had probably laid eyes on for a thousand years, if not more. Surely in there he'd find the answer about the three gifts.

But going Hellside wasn't happening for ... he checked the time ... shit, just over twenty-four hours to return the hellkey. His uncle better be right about sticking close to Cyn to get the bloody key back. Time was running out fast.

"Your cell won't work on the other side of the gate-house," Cyn's voice had him look around.

"Deigning to talk to me now?" Rohan asked.

"Just passing the time." But a shiver shook Cyn.

"Fuck, you're cold. Why didn't you say something? Is there a blanket or something here or a way to light the fire?" He stalked around the room. Nothing. "Can you light the fire with magic?"

"Used the last of my energy to do a healing spell on this." She nodded at her shoulder, and another shiver shook her.

Concern tightened in his chest. Why was she so cold? What if she'd lost too much blood before she'd done the spell? What if it hadn't worked?

So *human* for all her magic and weapons skills. "You might not like it, but you could be going into shock."

"I'm not."

"Well, it's not *that* cold and you're shivering. Bloody hell, are you that stubborn you refuse to acknowledge going into shock?"

Fuck. And why did that even matter? Except, it did.

Then the door to the gatehouse from the castle side opened, and Eve and an unfamiliar man—maybe in his late forties—stepped inside.

"About time," Rohan said. "Listen, Cyn's shivering—can you do something for her? She might be going into shock."

"I'm fine." Cyn glared at him. "Ignore the idiot daemon over there."

"Idiot? Because I'm worried about the fact you were stabbed in the shoulder and then just avoided getting run over? Sure, *that's* idiotic." He glared back at her before turning to Eve and the male. "Can you do something with her, Eve?"

"I'll light the fire, and yes, we can look at the Templar," the male said.

"And you are?"

"Warrick, Watcher and castle bailiff. I'm in charge here. I'm told you intend on staying with us?"

"This one owes me a spell," Rohan bit out and nodded at Cyn. "Plus, right now, I'm the only thing standing between this crew and the hellbeasts that keep finding them."

"You're also an otherworlder—we don't usually let your ... kind beyond our walls."

"Well, my *kind* has been responsibly saving these kinds' butts. But up to you."

"Warrick, calm down," Eve said from where she was checking out Cyn's shoulder. At least someone was looking at the wound. "We're here to truth spell Rohan, so we can find out what he's really after and then decide what to do."

"Seriously, you people need to learn a bit of trust. I've literally helped get you all, and your precious *R-104C,* here."

"Hey, I'm fine for you to come in, but I'm not the one you need to convince." Eve probed the wound on Cyn's shoulder again. "This is barely healing, and I'm no medic, but you might've broken it."

"You're too trusting of otherworlders," Cyn muttered. "And ouch, that hurts."

"Surprise, surprise," Rohan said at the same time. "Can you treat Cyn at the castle while we do the truth spell?"

"Red," Cyn said, "you *are* an idiot if you think I'm not going to be part of your interrogation."

"Truth spell," Eve said quickly.

"Call it what it is." Rohan held Cyn's gaze. "Fine. The sooner we get this done, the sooner you can get seen to, I get my key spell, and maybe we can uncover what the hell Lord Forneous is up to."

And an idiot? He had to be. Because, for all her distrust and icy disdain, he still couldn't stop worrying about Cyn.

"Be right back." Eve ducked outside and returned in a few minutes with a basket full of implements. "Okay, let's get this done." Eve set a candle, a crystal, and a bowl filled with herbs and a little bundle of bark—similar to what Cyn had done with some of her spells. "Rohan, it's truth spell time."

"How?"

"If the candle flame turns green, you're telling us a lie. Simple as that. But I will warn you, we've set up a trap here in the gatehouse—you won't be able to leave either door unless Warrick or I willingly take you through."

"You what?" Rohan's hackles rose.

"Calm down," Eve said, "this is for our protection against the son of the bastard trying to get Isa. We're not fucking around with this."

"Shit. You're as bad as Cyn."

"Thank you. I take that as a compliment."

"Yeah, not surprised." Fact was, he meant it as one. "But I really am over this distrust thing. So come on. Ask your questions. Do this spell."

Eve and Warrick set up their ritual equipment, and then Warrick called the spell.

"Do you wish any residents—temporary or permanent —of this castle harm?" Eve asked.

"No."

"Will you enter a binding contract saying you will not use your hellblades on anyone in this castle?" Warrick asked.

"That's impossible—what if someone gets in and attacks us? Then I couldn't use the blades. But I'll make a binding promise not to use the blades in any other way than to directly protect and defend those I care about. How does that sound?"

Eve and Warrick exchanged a look with Cyn.

"My turn," Cyn said. "Rohan the Red, are you in any way working for Forneous?"

Everything in him rebelled at that thought, and he didn't bother to hide his distaste. "I'm not working with, for or on behalf of Lord Forneous—my sire—in any way. Lord Forneous has not imparted to me any information regarding his interest in any of the three gifts nor regarding his great-niece. So, what other questions do you have?"

"Do you have any interest in the three gifts?"

"Yes, in as much as ensuring they don't fall into Lord Forneous's hands. I can only imagine that if he's after them, the reason is frigging bad."

"Why are you so against your own father?" Cyn said.

"Not my father. My *sire* was responsible for my mother's death when he withheld the care she needed to survive. And an endless parade of pain and suffering for many more." Rohan's stomach soured as memories of those awful days flashed through his mind, but he forced himself to sit still. The sooner these questions were done, the better.

Cyn's eyes widened, but she didn't say anything. What was she thinking? Did she even care about him enough to want to know his history? He certainly wanted to know hers.

"Shit," Eve breathed. "No wonder you hate him. But daemons observe a hierarchy, don't they? Even if you hate your fa—sire, you have to do what he tells you, right?"

"Yes, the hierarchy exists. But I don't—temporarily—fall under Lord Forneous's control."

"How is that possible?"

"Just over six months ago, the Daemon Congress, they're

our version of your Templar Knight Council, assigned me to be responsible for managing issues on the humanside of our hellgates. The High Lord pressured Lord Forneous into ceding his control over me until I'm no longer in this role. So right now, Lord Forneous can't compel me to do anything."

And thank fuck for that.

"So that's why you're here? 'Managing an issue'?" Warrick asked.

"Yes."

"And Cynane?" Eve said. "What do you want with her?"

"Is this really necessary?" Cyn blurted out.

He turned to her. Was this a good idea? But he didn't have to wonder; he knew he cared for the frustrating, independent, mesmerizing high priestess—maybe this was the time, now, while he was under a truth spell so she'd know he wasn't lying, to be honest about that, too. Which meant also coming clean about why he'd sought her out in the first place.

Rohan folded his arms and held her gaze. "Cyn and I? We have a binding contract in place for one more day for her to help me find the missing hellgate key."

"Why one day?" Eve frowned.

"Because if the hellgate key isn't returned to Hell by the end of summer solstice, the Tenth Gate will be permanently open. My cousin Nicasia—Isadora's mother—is a powerful diviner, and while she hasn't been able to trace the key, every time she has divined for its location, she saw Cyn."

"What?" Cyn stiffened.

"So that's why I came to you specifically."

"And this isn't something you thought you should tell me?"

"I did tell you I needed you to find me the key. From the

first moment I came back, if you recall."

"But not everything." She sighed and then winced.

"Hello, pot." Rohan shrugged. "Anyway, you need to get that arm taken care of. And look—the candle stayed yellow, so I'm telling the truth."

Cyn rolled her eyes. "Fine. You've—"

"There's more." His heart started to pound. Fuck it, now or never. "I've omitted to explain the other reason I'm invested in Cyn. And that's because I care about her." Cyn's eyes widened, and her cheeks paled, but Rohan willed her to hold his gaze. "There's this part of me right here"—he scrubbed a fist over his chest—"that fills up every time I'm near her. She's fierce and strong and full of fire." He stared at her for one more moment. "So, now you know how I feel."

How do you feel about me? He almost asked the words, but Cyn wasn't smiling. In fact, her expression closed up, and she turned away from him.

Well, hell. Was that his answer? Not that she *had* to have feelings for him. She'd been up-front about her intentions from the start; even the sex had been about banging out the sexual tension.

But he'd told the truth about caring for Cyn, and there was no going back now. Except, *care*? Care was like calling a stampeding trichorn a negligible concern.

And hell, he'd loved a high priestess once before, but he'd lost her through a Templar Knight's disregard for anything other than the greater good. Now here he was again—another high priestess. Another human. And the Templar Knights were once again destroying any chance at a future—but this time from within.

"Any other questions?" Rohan growled. "I want to get the fuck out of here as quickly as possible. Are you letting me in or not?"

25

THE CAVERNOUS, drafty hall of the Watcher castle looked like it hadn't changed much since the place had been built in the Middle Ages, complete with tapestries, medieval weapons, and even suits of armor lining the walls.

And unfortunately, the castle *was* still in the Dark Ages when it came to technology, so three hours after they'd arrived, Cyn drummed her fingers on the trestle table where she sat alone in front of the huge fireplace. Pfft. The fireplace was big enough that they could roast an entire boar in the thing if they wanted—and wouldn't that be the icing on the medieval cake?

Her injured shoulder and arm were in a sling, courtesy of Eve, while the healing spell performed its magic. Cyn rolled her shoulder to test it out. Pain flared through her upper arm, but she could move the joint now. At least the spell was working. Just needed to work faster.

"You still look pissed off." Rohan's voice echoed from the top of the stairs before he made his way down.

Cyn stopped drumming her fingers. "Because I am." She scowled and adjusted her hairpin with her good hand as Rohan came to stand near the fire. "I'm waiting on an update from HQ regarding any surveillance footage. But because there's no damned cell reception, I can either wait in the cold gatehouse or up here." She eyed the daemon for a moment. "How's Isa?"

"Resting. The Watcher medical team seem to know what they're doing, and they think she might've pulled a muscle rather than the baby being hurt when she fell. They're taking any healing magic with her cautiously, though."

He shoved his hands in his pockets, looking like he fit in this old-world setting. An image of him like a knight out of one of the tapestries, only this time shirtless, riding a massive warhorse and carrying a sword and shield played through her mind. Yeah, Rohan totally suited the medieval time period.

"Cyn, are you okay?"

"Yes." She scowled at him and went back to drumming her fingers. "Why?"

"I asked how your arm is, and you just stared at me."

"The arm's fine." Well, it would be. And she ignored his look that said he saw straight through her deception. "Is Gray with Isa?"

Rohan nodded. "Although he's as edgy as you are right now."

"Not surprising. What about Eve? I'm going to ask her to help me with a spell to find your key."

"She's asleep in one of the rooms somewhere."

"After all the magic she used, she'll be out for several hours. Okay, so no Eve for now. I guess I can use that time to track down spell options in the library."

"What about you—your magic must be exhausted too, right?" Rohan said.

"I'll be fine." Except yes, Cyn still needed rest and food

to get her energy levels back to full capacity. Which she'd need to find R-104C and Forneous. Except ... "Rohan, can Forneous cross through a hellgate?"

"He can, but I don't think he will. After what happened with Isadora last year, he's persona non grata Hellside right now."

"So he's staying in the human realm. One piece of good news." She stood up, ignoring the pain that came with the motion.

"Where are you going?"

"None of your business."

"Actually, it is. Warrick asked me to watch you while the healing spell does its thing, since apparently, you refused to stay in the infirmary."

"Fuck that. I don't need a babysitter."

Rohan put up his hands. "Hey, don't shoot the messenger. I'd be just as happy to leave you alone, but since the Watchers have let me in, I'm doing what they say. And Warrick was clear—you're still under a spell right now, which means you have to be careful. Plus, you can't use your arm yet; I know it and you know it. So let me help you get what you need in the library."

Cyn mentally gnashed her teeth. Damn it. She needed space from Rohan, not to stay close to him.

"Do you want Warrick to send you back to the infirmary?" Rohan said.

"Fine. But don't get in my way."

"You remember the truth spell did confirm I'm not working with Lord Forneous?" He trailed her out of the hall, close enough that his damned delicious scent warmed her chest.

"Yes—which is the only reason you're here right now."

"Then why the cold attitude? I'm not the one who lied here."

"But you did hold back damned important information, and what was that shit in the gatehouse?"

"You mean where I said I cared for you? That shit?"

"Yes! You and I aren't living in a fairytale, Rohan. And you don't need to walk that close."

"So that's why you're shitty? Fuck me, Cyn, yes, I care for you. What's so wrong with that?"

"Because I'm a Templar Knight. First and always. I don't do relationships. I don't do friends. I do my job. And I'm perfectly fine with that. And having you come up here and try to make me want things outside of that is not happening. No, no, no way."

They reached the library door, and she whirled around. "We're here. So this conversation ends now. And don't go wandering away unless the librarian gives you the okay, unless you want your ass frozen by a stun spell in a warded aisle."

She pivoted and pushed the thick doors open. Normally she'd stop and take in a breath of the welcoming book-scented air and soak in the view of the forest and sky through the enormous arched window at the far end of the library. But not today.

"You sound like me getting my ass stunned is exactly what you want," Rohan muttered.

She smirked at him over her shoulder as she led the way to the aisle on divination. "Not gonna deny it."

Now, which spell book ... which—there. Damn. It had to be on the top of the double-height shelves. Shit—now she had to ask him for help.

She turned to Rohan. "See the book up there? Top shelf in the blue leather."

"Wow, never thought I'd feel happy at being used." Rohan drew the library ladder over and climbed up—and damn, the view was fine. It was as if his cargo pants were the perfect fit to emphasize the tight curve of his ass. And she hadn't really done much exploring there—

Oops. Do *not* notice how hot Rohan's butt is. "Right, I'll be over here." Cyn sat at a table where the only other chair was far across on the other side.

He placed the book in front of her. "Need anything else?"

His low voice rolled over her in a decadent wave that made her want to strip naked and curl up in his lap.

Shit.

No, no, *no* to curling up anywhere with this man. And certainly, no, to getting naked.

"Cyn, you all right there?"

"Yep, just need some quiet while I read." Cyn didn't even meet his gaze—which she could feel boring into her—as she slunk down in the seat and focused on the book.

Spell time ... spell time ... spell time ...

Except, damn her, she peeked over the book, found Rohan staring at her right back.

Something passed between them—and something hot tugged low in her belly. As if her lady parts knew exactly how much Rohan the Red made her body hum, and now they wanted more.

"Cyn ..." His eyes darkened. His nostrils flared. Oh shit —he could scent her arousal. He shifted in his seat as if his pants had suddenly become uncomfortable.

Imagine ... she could shove the spell book aside, crawl over the table, help him yank his pants off, and then she'd either push his seat back and go down on him right here— or she'd drag him back onto the table with her, and they could make love surrounded by books and with the glorious summer sun streaming through the window—

The scent of Cyn's arousal was both the most intoxicating and the most fucking painful thing Rohan had ever experienced—because it didn't matter how attracted she was to him, Cyn had made it clear she didn't want that attraction.

So he forced himself to sit back and not call her out about her reaction to him. But damned if he wouldn't call her out on her hypocrisy.

"You know, your sire is a decent being. He acts with integrity and the good of his realm as his first priority. But you wouldn't know that because you've never—not once—met him. Talked to him. But even so, I don't judge you by his actions. So what gives you the right to judge me by mine?"

"I'm judging you by your actions. Your lie—"

"I've never lied about who my sire is."

"It was a lie of omission, and don't try to spin it any other way."

"Well, what about you? You outright lied to me—on multiple occasions when I was telling you the issues I had with the Templars—with one of your own family, and you never said a word. That pissed me off, but I listened to your reason, and though I disagree, I'm still here, aren't I?"

"A bit different, Red. Your father—"

"My sire. He's no father to me. Don't get confused by those words—and you'll notice I never call him that, so don't you either."

"Okay ... why not?"

"Let's see ... the fact he refused to let my mother back through any gate of Hell—nor let me leave Hell for my first hundred years? Or, how about the fact he keeps slaves—yes, including witches—or is just a fucked asshole of a being, or that he kept me powerless until my uncle stepped in? Any of those good enough?"

"Why?"

"Because he gets off on control and pain. No other reason."

"Why did he even a have a child if he treated you so ... shittily?"

"*Shittily.*" Rohan snorted as years of being at his sire's beck and call echoed through his memory. The destruction because his *sire* decreed it to be so. But that was over. Rohan had a chance to make a new life outside of his sire's control with his role of looking after the hellgates. And Rohan was taking it, come hell or high water.

"Shit—sorry," Cyn said. "I can see the subject isn't funny."

"I don't think Lord Forneous meant to have me at all is the short answer, for what it's worth. And I don't even know if my mother was with him willingly."

"Oh." Cyn paled.

"Yeah. So no, he's not my father. Let's get that straight."

"This will sound awful, but if he didn't want you, why didn't he pass you off to your mother's family ... or ... get rid of you?"

"Lord Forneous is the second most powerful creature in Hell—that meant that as a babe, I was fully daemon. I have nothing of my mother other than my coloring. So my mother's family weren't the right place for me. And the other—he can't get rid of me."

"But you said he's the second most powerful being in Hell."

"My mother was a minor Norse deity, and *her* father a higher Norse god. Apparently, he laid down the law after my birth to say that if Lord Forneous ever laid a hand on me, the Norse realm would take on Hell. That's when my uncle stepped in and had Lord Forneous agree in blood to the demand."

"Your uncle saved you?"

"Yeah. He's been more of a father figure than my *sire* ever was."

"I'm glad you had him." Cyn paused, and then a huge yawn rolled through her.

"Cyn, I know you don't want to stop and that you hold yourself accountable for the relic, but I can see how tired you are. Once you've confirmed the spell you want, why don't you at least shut your eyes until the Templars get back to you or whatever they're going to do?"

"No—"

"I'm being honest. You need to sleep. We don't know what else is coming for us, but I'm damned sure having you at your physical and mental peak will be crucial."

26

THE LONGER CYN sat in the library reading that spell book, the more the words began to swim on the page. Rohan still sat opposite her, but Cecelie, the librarian, had let out a whoop of delight when she'd discovered Rohan could read several lesser-known daemonish dialects—apparently, there was an entire section of untranslated works—and he was currently translating his second book.

Cyn squeezed her eyes to get some moisture into them and finished transcribing the spell she wanted into her personal grimoire.

One problem at a time—and right now, that meant seeing out this divination spell for the key—then she'd figure out what to do next.

Well, duh. A divination spell for Forneous. She slapped herself on the forehead.

Rohan glanced up. "What?"

"Is it possible to divine for a daemon?"

Recognition flared in Rohan's eyes. "You want to look for Lord Forneous?"

"Why not?"

"I don't know, Cyn. He's powerful—divining for him might not be such a good idea."

"It might be my only one, depending on what our tech team can find with the surveillance feeds." She closed the book and pushed it away. "I'm going to hand this back to Cecelie, then see if there's any update from HQ."

But when she got back to the hall, and of course Rohan had followed her there, still no Templar updates.

"Shit." So the divination spell might be her best option.

"You're thinking of divining for him, aren't you?" Rohan said from behind her.

"Yes, but not now, obviously." Her eyelids were so heavy they wanted to drag on the ground, and she doubted she could even light a candle with magic right now. "I'm going to wait here until Eve is awake."

Cyn glanced between the two overstuffed armchairs perfectly positioned near the giant hearth and the long timber trestle tables with their bench seats.

What a choice ... comfort and warmth versus butt pain-inducing hard and cold.

As she sank into the seat, the fire crackled with relaxing pops and hisses and the mesmerizing flames flickered ...

She shut her eyes. Just for a minute.

Hushed voices, the soft clank of plates and cups and the aroma of coffee beans teased at the edge of Cyn's consciousness, and she snuggled into the thick blanket—

Wait. Blanket?

She shot to full wakefulness and twisted around.

Still in the hall by the fire. Simion, Aleesha and Sonja sitting behind her. No sign of Rohan or anyone else. Hell—how long had she slept?

"Dearest heart, you're awake." Simion beamed and waved her over.

"Uh, yeah." Cyn wiped her face and stopped, looked at her arm. "Wow, that feels better."

"Now, I'm under strict instructions from Rohan the Red to inform you of the following: you've been asleep for"— Simion checked his watch—"four hours. There has been no word on the matter you're waiting on an update for. And our hero is in the library. I'm also to stay here until Warrick, the very lovely bailiff, confirms the spell to heal your arm has finished. Which judging by your comments, must be soon."

"Thanks."

"You're welcome. Now, how goes the love match with our hero?"

"Simion, not sure if you're aware, but we're in a crisis here. This isn't the time for shi—stuff like that."

Simion sighed and exchanged looks with Aleesha and Sonja before turning back to her. "Dearest heart, there is always time for love. Perhaps you need more time in the ... moonlight?"

"The what—wait, back in Byron Bay, I knew the moonlight felt charged. Was that you?"

"It's a small element of my power—to use the moon and the sun to strengthen the bonds of love."

"You really do believe in love, don't you? No, no need to answer. That was rhetorical." She sat on the bench. "I need to ask you something else. How did you shroud the frankincense from all magical sight?"

"As a deity, I can increase or decrease humankind's awareness of certain things. So when I found the frankincense helped me continue spreading true love throughout the world, I used my power to decrease awareness of the frankincense. And yes, I know that was selfish, but humans need love, dearest heart. And through the tree, I've been able to deliver that connection."

Cyn sighed and patted Simion's hand. How did you stay angry with someone so ... naively dedicated to love? "Well, at least we know why we couldn't divine R-104C's location. So does your mojo over awareness of the frankincense tree still exist?"

"Yes, and I can relinquish my hold, but it'll take time for that power to leave this world. It could be months or years even."

"Maybe don't relinquish your mojo just yet."

"Why not?"

"It's not going to help in the short term, but it may aid in keeping R-104C safe in the long term. I'll come back to you."

"Of course, if you think that's the best. Now, about your love—"

"Sorry, Simion, no time." Cyn got to her feet, but then the door at the end of the hall opened, and Gray, Eve and Isa came into the room.

Thank the mother, Eve was awake. But Gray's expression was tighter than usual, and when Eve and Isa sat down with Simion, Gray gave a short jerk of his head, and Cyn's stomach knotted.

"What's going on?" she whispered as she joined him at the other end of the room.

"Word's in from Glastonbury. Not good there—the hell-beast did a lot of damage in the city."

"What the fuck?" Rohan's voice echoed from the doorway on the other side of the hall.

Shit. When did he arrive? She made a shushing gesture and then waved him over.

"Keep it down," she ordered. "There are people present who aren't in the know here."

"Fine." Rohan's jaw clenched, but he nodded. "Tell me everything."

"Local law enforcement isn't naming the creature, but reports are that a lion attacked multiple people—and ate two—in the city before disappearing. Everyone's scrambling to find where it is."

"It ate two people?" Mother of the gods, no.

Gray leaned in. "I'm about to jump on a call with Will, the European ops division leader, re the attack. Rohan, is there anything you can give us to go on here?"

"The Third Gate—Glastonbury—isn't unlocked, so that means something got past the lord of the gate like they did at the Seventh Gate in Brisbane. At the very least, increase security around every humanside hellgate. And these creatures will be close to impossible to take down with human weapons, so get whatever witches you have with offensive power and have them on standby. If you can incapacitate the hellbeasts with magic, then your human weapons might have a hope of killing them."

"Fuck. Got it."

Gray left, and Cyn turned to Rohan. "Why?" she whispered. "Why is Forneous doing this?"

"He's always craved power." Rohan's eyes went flat. "It's as if because he's not ultimately in charge of Hell, he's always had to be meaner, harder, faster than the High Lord. I think he wants to run Hell himself. And he doesn't care who he has to sacrifice along the way."

"Why doesn't the High Lord fight back?"

"If my uncle fought Lord Forneous directly, their power would destroy Hell—and that imbalance would potentially ripple through every realm that exists—so he has to work around him. Believe me, my uncle is trying to handle the situation."

"Looks like he needs to try harder."

Then the door at the top of the staircase opened, and Warrick stepped through. His gaze went to Cyn, and yet again, her stomach knotted.

"What's up?" she said as she met the bailiff at the bottom stairs.

"Your council has requested that we pass on a message. They wish to speak to you."

"Thank you, Warrick. I'll contact them from the gatehouse." Hell, just how much trouble was she in?

Warrick insisted on a fast check of the healing magic on her arm, and then he nodded and confirmed the spell had been completed, and she was good to go.

"Cyn," Rohan said her name quietly, "do you want—?"

"No. I've got this. Stay here."

She gave him a tight smile and squared her shoulders. Whatever was coming next, she'd face it.

-((●))-

Rohan couldn't stop staring at the door swinging shut with a hard clunk behind Cyn as she left the hall alone, into the cold, to face some fucked-up Council of Templar Knights.

"Hey, you want a coffee?" Isadora's bright voice had him turning around.

"Hell, yes. But I'll grab it. Tea for you, right?"

"Gray's already got me one, so I'm good. And no, I insist on getting you a coffee. Here, come over and sit with us. You're part of our crew."

And damn but he wished that was the case. "Thanks, but I should get—"

"No. No, I insist. And I'm your cousin, remember? So sit your butt down now and talk with us."

"You might as well give in," Eve said. "She won't give up."

Rohan looked down at the sprite of a diviner and sighed. "Fine. But only because you're my cousin."

"Good." Isa jostled him with her shoulder. "Cousins unite."

"You know, Gray's a lucky bastard to have you."

"Who's lucky?" Gray asked, coming back into the hall.

"You. How did the ... call go?"

"Fast. Everyone agreed this needs to be coordinated, so I've got fifteen minutes before my next call."

"Here, eat mine." Isa pushed her plate over to Gray. "I'll grab a refill when you're gone." Gray gave her a fast kiss, and then tucked her into his side while he ate.

Now there was a connection.

Rohan lowered his voice. "Can I ask a question while you eat?"

"Sure," Gray said.

"How come you can find love, but a certain other Templar can't?"

Gray paused eating. "Cyn is ... complicated. Are you saying you feel that way about her?"

"You didn't hear about my declaration in the gate-house?" Rohan said. "I thought everyone knew."

"I heard you said you cared for her, right?"

Rohan shoved a hand through his hair. "Hell. I'm not saying—fine. Yes. Yes, I feel that way for her, although hell knows why."

"Because she's fierce and wonderful?" Isa piped up.

"Fine. I know why. Not helping me with why she doesn't want love."

"Who said she doesn't?" Gray forked up another mouthful.

"She did. And shit, it doesn't matter. I'm heading Hell-side tomorrow one way or the other."

"Excuse me, but it does matter." Isa leaped to her feet. "All right, everyone, listen up." She was the smallest of them all there, but she had commanded them with every bit of authority, just like her grandfather. Rohan couldn't help but smile at her. "Rohan needs help with Cynane. He loves her, but she says she doesn't want love. And he's leaving the human realm tomorrow, so we don't have long to help him."

"Isa," Gray groaned. "Now's not the time—"

Rohan couldn't stop himself from scowling. "Really? You want to do this here? Now?"

"Yes. We're your friends. And we love Cyn too; therefore, we want to see if this can work out."

Simion's face lit up. "I knew it! I knew it. Okay, as the expert here, can I start off?"

Rohan looked around the group. "Do I have a choice?"

"Not at all." Simion leaned forward. "Tell me what you feel when you're around her."

"Feel? I feel everything." He scrubbed a hand over his sternum.

"You love her. And I don't need to be a love whisperer to know that."

"Clearly. That's not the problem, is it?"

"Well," Simion said, "it might be if you haven't told her how you feel. Have you? And not the 'I care about you' comment. We all care about each other here. I'm talking about laying your heart out for her—"

"No. No, I have not done that."

"Well." Simion sat back and crossed his arms. "That's my advice."

27

AFTER COMPLETING her call with the council, Cyn swallowed the lump burning in her throat and avoided the main entry to the castle—no way could she face everyone right now—and snuck in through a side door.

Recalled. Tribunal. Review of role.

Fuck. She'd known the outcome was likely, but still. This must be what an injured dog felt like when it got kicked again.

But she'd lost the relic, so she had to face the consequences, and there wasn't time to feel sorry for herself, not that it would help the situation anyway. So she sucked in a deep breath, shoved the burning knot in her throat way, way down, and got to organizing everything—and everyone—she needed.

Thirty minutes later, Cyn took her ritual equipment up to the tower where the Watchers liked to undertake their spell craft.

She chose the chamber with a small balcony and opened the door to let the moonlight in. It might be cold, but she needed all the help possible.

She'd just set up her ritual equipment on the stone floor when a knock tapped at the door and Eve and Rohan walked in.

"Warrick said you were after us?" Eve's gaze went to the equipment. "Looks like you're making some serious magic."

"Thank you for coming up, and yes, I am. I have to return to the council; they're meeting in Rome for the summer solstice, so I'll be heading there tonight."

"What? Why?" Rohan crossed his arms.

"Because of my handling of the retrieval of R-104C. It's the right thing to do. But—"

"Bullshit," Rohan said. "You were up against the second strongest daemon in the universe and a hellbeast, so how are you responsible?"

"I'm not going there again with you, Rohan." She ignored his glare. "It just is. Now, before I leave, I need to track Forneous. Eve, normally I work alone; however, with both our magics, I have a better chance of success. Can I ask for your help on the spell?"

"Of course."

"Thank you." Relief sang through her.

"So that's why Eve's here," Rohan said. "Why do you need me?"

"Two reasons—as a direct relative, your blood can provide an express link to track Forneous. Are you okay with that?"

"You know I am—if it's safe. And the second reason?"

"The second reason is our binding contract. I found a spell in the library that looks promising. The council under-stands that a binding contract cannot be severed and so have given me ... permission to complete that task before I leave."

She didn't add that she'd been severely rebuked for undertaking a binding contract while tracking R-104C.

"So, where do you want us?" Eve asked.

"First, let's talk safety. Rohan, could Forneous have any way of detecting a blood-trace spell?"

"Lord Forneous has more than one hellwitch bonded to him," Rohan said. "Could they make a spell to detect the kind of magic you're making?"

"If they're powerful enough, yes."

"Then that's your answer."

"Okay," Cyn said, "we're going to cast a salt circle first to avoid him tracking my magic. Just in case. Rohan, Eve, let's sit down—this spell won't be a quick one. Eve, have you ever joined a sacrificial magic ritual?"

"Never, and I'm intrigued at the chance, to be honest."

So was Cyn, but she shut that reaction down. Magic was a tool to find R-104C. Nothing more. "Okay. Salt circle is cast—no one moves from this point on. Compass. Athame. Candle. Pewter bowl. Eve, you mix in the lemongrass and rosemary for success and insight and hold the quartz crystal in the middle. Rohan, can I prick your finger? I need three drops of blood into the bowl. Okay, that's done. Now, Eve, take my hand. Everyone ready? Blood to call, blood to find, blood locate of its kind. From four to three to two to one, point the way, night or day. Lock the spell and make it so."

Cyn drew Eve's power along with hers into the spell, took the bowl from Eve, then poured one drop of blood into the compass, and asked, "Where is Forneous?"

The compass arm turned to point west.

"Holy shit, it worked. We have him." Cyn placed the bowl on the floor. "Now the compass is locked to Forneous, no matter where he is, we can track him."

"Wow, that's some spell." Eve's eyes were wide on the compass.

"It's a good ritual for sacrificial magic. For the next spell, I'll use the rest of the blood in the bowl to try and see Forneous."

Cyn held the pewter bowl above the candle. "Blood to call, blood to find, blood locate of its kind. View that being who this spell seeks, face, form, surrounds and all. As I call, make it so. Show me Forneous."

As soon as the words left Cyn, smoke rose from the bowl, and like a sepia projection playing on an uneven surface, Forneous's face formed within the smoke. Then he shouted something and his eyes went black.

A roaring funnel of wind shot into the turret, blasting the smoke image to pieces. The candle snuffed out. The bowl smashed into the wall. The compass tore up into the air before crashing back to the stone floor.

The spell cut off.

"Fuck!" Cyn tried to recall it—but there was nothing. Not even a trace of the spell was left. She lunged for the compass—picked up the pieces. "No. No, no, no."

"Shit. Cyn, you okay?" Eve raised trembling hands.

"Yeah, but the spell's dead. Even the compass. What the hell was that?"

"I've only ever heard of them," Eve said. "But I think he must have a magical trace-and-kill spell attached to him. Forneous chased your spell back to you, but thankfully, the circle stopped him from getting to you. This is bad."

"Would he know who cast it?" Cyn threw all the implements into the basket.

"He'll know it came from the Watcher castle—but the salt circle will have stopped him from seeing us."

"Cynane!" Rohan grabbed her arm. "Are you saying Lord Forneous just killed your spell?"

"And tried to kill her." Eve shivered. "That was close."

"Hell," Rohan muttered. "Cyn, are you sure he didn't see you?"

Cyn checked Eve's face. "Eve looks certain. I've never experienced that before, but I trust Eve. Why?"

"Because Lord Forneous was going to kill you today." Rohan's eyes blazed. "He drove straight at you. You cannot— under any circumstances—underestimate him."

"Well, I won't be tracking him again; however, we know the direction he's in. And I swear, did it look like waves behind him? Maybe he's at sea?"

"Okay, so is that it for me?" Eve rubbed her hands. "I don't know how you two aren't even acting like you're cold up here."

"It's not," Rohan said.

"I'm not," Cyn said too.

"Well," Eve said, "now that you're talking in sync, I'm heading back downstairs. And I recommend you burn the entire basket and everything used in the spell. In fact, burn your clothes, too. I'll strip as soon as I'm downstairs, but I think you should light the fire up here and burn yours now, sorry to say. I wouldn't even wait till after you do your next spell for Rohan. But I'll grab you some blankets to wrap up in."

"Good call," Cyn muttered. "And thanks for your help. Really glad to work with you."

"Same. And I'd love to work on spell craft with you again —minus the track-and-kill spell at the end."

Damn, so would Cyn. "Thanks, but you know the Templars. I can't commit to much right now."

"I get it. Be right back with those blankets."

Cyn exhaled hard. Damn, this was not how the spells were meant to go.

"Okay, time to strip." She took off her boots. "Forneous is going to pay for making me burn these."

"So Eve was serious there?" Rohan said.

"Totally. If you're uncomfortable, I'll turn around."

"Cyn, do you think I care if you see me naked after everything we've done?"

"I was being polite. But fine—strip away. I'll still turn around." Plus, seeing Rohan naked right then was more likely to cause her problems than him, with the way she reacted to his body.

"Knock knock. Blanket delivery," Eve said from the other side of the doorway. "And I'm sure between us all, we've got enough clothes to get a change for you when you come downstairs." She held two thick blankets through the door without stepping into the room. "Can I light the fire?"

"We're not naked yet, so you can come in. And, yes, please." Cyn took the blankets and threw one at Rohan.

"I'll still stay out here since you're doing another spell." Eve called a witch-fire spell, and the fireplace lit up. "That should last about an hour."

Staring at the wall, Cyn stripped off fast, and by the swoosh and zip of Rohan removing his clothes, he was hurrying too. Good.

"Are you done?" She tightened the blanket under her arms. At least it covered her from shoulders to feet. "We need to burn these quickly."

"Done."

"Good. Toss everything." She turned around and threw her things into the hearth and stepped back as the flames took hold.

Rohan added his too, and he clearly didn't feel the cold because he'd only wrapped his blanket around his hips.

And every part of her cheered at having one last glance at that view.

"Why can't you commit to doing spells with Eve?" Rohan said softly. "I can see you want to."

Cyn wrenched her gaze back to the fire. "Because I'm a Templar, and we go where the council needs us. And even if they don't put me on desk duty somewhere—which is probable after this mess—I still have a job to do. As of one week ago, I'm in charge of a special operations unit which right now consists of one person—me—doing undercover work. I have no idea where that will take me next."

"Is that what you want? I thought you liked your magic."

"That was for the relic. I'm a Templar Knight first and always."

"But you're also a high priestess—"

"No, that was only for my cover. Now, let's find your key and get this binding contract over and done with, and you can go your way and I can go mine."

"You really want me gone?" Rohan said.

"Forneous has the relic, so he won't come after us again. You can go. I don't need you in the way."

"In the way? You are a piece of work, aren't you?"

"I'm focused, that's what I am."

"No, you're a child of two worlds who might know what she is—but not *who* she is."

"Cut the psychoanalytic bullshit," Cyn snapped. "We're here for the spell. Now let's go."

"You call it bullshit; I call it the truth. Just like I call it that you're holding back with this key spell."

"What do you mean, holding back? I've been spelling for days now."

"Yeah, but I've seen when you really push your magic, like at the barn, and then again here at the castle. But for ritual spells, I can tell—you're holding back."

"I can't do more."

"Why?"

"Because it's a risk, okay? And how can you even tell?"

"Your eyes glow when you use your power, Cyn. But they blaze when the shit hits the fan. That's how I know when your daemon is fully out. And these key spells—not even half of that."

"That's crap. No one's ever said that about my eyes before. And I found a trace of your key, didn't I?"

"How many full daemons have you used your powers in front of? Yeah, didn't think many. I can see your power in your eyes, and if you crossed over and became full daemon, you'd see it in mine too. And yes, you found a trace of my key already, but if you used your full power, who knows what might happen? What you might find?"

"That's what scares me. Who knows what I'll find ..."

"In yourself," Rohan finished quietly. "You're worried if you let your daemon out fully, you'll lose yourself?"

"Yes," Cyn whispered.

"But what if it's the opposite? What if you find yourself?"

"Rohan, I can't risk it. I just can't. I don't want to lose my humanity—myself—if my daemon takes over. And I know that's possible. I was a teenager when my powers started to grow, and I'd get ... lost in the magic."

"That was your witchcraft, right?"

"Yes, but the daemon side of my power only made that stronger. Now seriously, enough of this. I want to get this done and finish—"

"Cyn, stop."

"No, no more talking—"

"I hereby release you from the binding contract."

Her breath froze. The tattoo on her thigh tingled. And the knowledge something vital was now gone rolled through her, leaving her queasy and uneven. "Why? Why release me now?"

"Because you don't want me to be here, Cyn. And you know what? I won't be where I'm not wanted—I've lived that life for centuries."

"Life isn't only about what you *want*, Rohan. Sometimes, it's about what you have to do."

"Which I know all too well," Rohan said.

"Really? When have you ever sacrificed what you want?"

"How can you say that?" he whispered. "The thing I want more than everything—more than anyone—is right here, and I'm releasing her from the spell binding us together. How is that no sacrifice?"

"You can't want me like that—"

"Then how come I'm hard even when I'm pissed off? How come you walk into a room and my heart rate spikes? Not even Eleanor did that to me. How come your wicked smile, your get-out-of-my-way-or-I'll-stomp-over-you walk, your sass and bite, all make my chest go tight in here?" He scrubbed a fist over his sternum. "How come, Cyn?"

Her heart took fight, beat so wildly it might take off from her chest.

He really felt that strongly for her?

Shit, shut this down, Cyn. Rohan had called the contract off. She should leave and get on the jet and face the council. But fuck it. She didn't want that. Because what if, after tonight, she never saw Rohan again?

28

"Yes, I want," Cyn whispered. "Mother of the gods, Rohan, I want you too."

Those whispered words sent blood roaring through Rohan's veins. Beneath the blanket, his cock stiffened so hard it throbbed.

"What do you want, Cyn? Make it clear—is this just sex, or do you want more?"

Her eyes gleamed, but then she dropped her blanket. And damn but she was perfection.

"You want this?" he growled. He cupped her breasts, thumbed her nipple until it was tight and red.

She whimpered and shifted on her feet, and the scent of her desire punched him in the gut, and as his mouth watered, a growl vibrated through him that he couldn't stop. "I'm going to make you come so hard you'll remember me forever, whether the fuck you want to or not."

"Damn you, Rohan."

"Yeah, damn me. Damn us both." He lunged for her, crowded her back to the stone wall and dropped to his knees. He shouldered her legs apart, then put his mouth on her clit, and tongue-lashed her flesh.

Cyn moaned, and she wrapped a leg around his head, surrounding him with her scent and her heat. "More. Harder. I need your fingers in me too."

Fuck, but he loved how she took what she wanted. He pressed a finger into her velvet heat, found her so slick he thrust another in. Then, over and over, he pumped her body and lashed her clit.

"Fuck—" Her body tightened. Shook.

"Yes, come for me, princess." Her thigh tightened around him. "Was this what you wanted, princess?"

"Fuck you."

"Then take it. Let your daemon out, Cyn."

Cyn ground into his face—harder than she had that night by the pool. Her thigh tightened to the point he'd have bruises. But he just rubbed harder.

Her breath caught. Her body convulsed. And the hot, rich spice of her orgasm drenched him. Rohan shifted to drink up her release, snarling against her flesh as more shudders racked her body.

For long moments, only their harsh breaths filled the silence, and then she slid her thigh off his shoulder.

"Now that's coming hard." Rohan licked his lips and stared up at her, then rose to his feet until she was looking up at him. "And for what it's worth, right now, your eyes are blazing blue fire. At me. So yeah, I see your daemon. And I love it." The tension he'd been holding fell away, and he followed Simion's advice. "Like I love you."

"Stop saying that! Why do you have to make this about more than sex?"

"Because it is. For me, anyway." A bitter laugh escaped him. "Cyn, do you think I want to love you? Another high priestess? A *Templar*? I promised myself to never ever fall for a human again. And yet there you were. Nothing like Eleanor. Fierce. Determined. Taking no bullshit. Up in my face. Stunning. Wicked. Absolutely, utterly mesmerizing. And bloody hell, I couldn't do anything but fall for you. You don't have to love me back, and yeah, that might hurt, but I'll survive. In fact, the only problem here, Cyn, is that you don't know who you are."

Rohan backed away.

"Wh—what about you?" She glanced at his spike-hard cock.

"I already know who I am, Cyn." He picked up their blankets, tossed one at Cyn and wrapped himself in the other, then stalked out of the room. But he stopped in the doorway, hung his head. Damn, damn, damn—did he try one more time? "Come find me when you figure out who the hell you are."

Cyn tightened the blanket around her and stumbled out to the balcony. The cool night air whipped across her cheeks and caught her hair. Caught the tears welling in her eyes.

Angry tears. She dashed them away. She was *not* crying over him.

Who was *she*? Who the hell was *Rohan* to have a go at her self-identity? Fucking asshole—she knew exactly who she was.

Templar. High Priestess. Daughter of two worlds. Lover of a freaking sex-machine daemon who, right now, she wanted to punch in the face.

The burning that had lodged in her chest earlier surged back. She had to clear her throat—but the damned thing wouldn't budge.

Who you are ...

Damn you, Rohan. Why did his words have to replay inside her head?

"I know who I am!" she shouted to the stars. And the stars gleamed back—tiny points of power from millions of years away.

Who you are ...

Shit. Shit, shit, shit.

Who the hell was Cynane Montbard?

Knock. Knock. Knock.

Shit. Her heart flew. But when she turned around, a different otherworld male stood in the doorway.

"Simion." Cyn wiped her cheeks, then stood up and turned around.

"Oh, dearest one, I sense the path of love is not running its smoothest course."

A hiccuping laugh escaped her. "Simion, I have to be honest—I was never here for love."

"Ah, you may think that, but the fact is, you did find your love match. The frankincense anointed you, remember?"

"The frankincense anointed some out-of-the-world sex, Simion. Sorry to burst your bubble there."

"No, no. No. I knew it from the moment I met Rohan—he and you are meant to be together, dearest heart."

"So if your souped-up love senses told you all along that Rohan and I were meant to be together, why did you bring all that man-candy to Byron Bay?"

"Sometimes, to know what you want, you have to first see what you don't want. Each of those males were prime specimens—and I really should offer them all my services after this—but you didn't find any of them even remotely interesting."

"What about you—have you ever found your love match? Have you love whispered yourself?"

"Alas, I found ... and lost ... my match some time ago." Simion's eyes darkened with something powerful for a moment before he shook his head and smiled at her. "Are you really leaving us?"

"I have to go, Simion. But thank you for your friendship; I really do like you. And thank you for being part of me retrieving—even if just for a little while—the relic of frankincense."

To know what you want ... Simion's words played over in Cyn's mind as she made her way down the tower. Could she really want to love Rohan? A pang hit her squarely in the chest, but she shoved the emotion away, because it didn't matter what she wanted—she had a job to do. That had to come first.

Rohan knew the moment Cyn left the castle—a shiver whispered through his chest, leaving him empty. Hollow. Damn her to hell and back. Why did he have to know this shit?

He'd been perfectly happy when his uncle had given him an opportunity to take responsibility for the hellgates humanside; he had planned to do everything he could to prove his uncle's faith wasn't misplaced. And then a high priestess with sass and fire and kick-ass heels had stomped into his world, and here he was now, aware of her on such a deep level he physically reacted when she left the castle. She couldn't have left more of an imprint on him than if she'd taken one of those heels and stabbed it permanently into his heart.

And she hadn't said goodbye because that would mean facing him again—facing a living, breathing reminder of the other half of who she was. And damn but he knew she was a strong person. Stubborn. Fierce. Lethal.

Which was why he loved her.

Well, so be it. He'd put his feelings out there, and she'd made it clear that Cynane Montbard, Templar Knight, high priestess, princess, didn't want anything to do with him outside of sex.

Fine. He'd focus on what he needed to do—find the hellgate key and return it Hellside. In one day.

Just how the hell did he do that?

Rohan found himself back at the library; no surprise there, given how much time he'd spent in them growing up. The perfect escape from his prick of a sire.

Cecelie met him at the door. "Rohan the Red, are you sure you want to be working this late at night?"

"Frankly, yes. I still have to find something I'm after. And right now, a library might be the only place I can do that. I need everything you have on the daemon world. And I'll also get back those texts you wanted translated."

"Only if you have the time, but that would be wonderful. There is so much information trapped inside a language none here know." She led him to the same long table he'd sat at with Cyn. "I'm leaving for the night but will see you in the morn."

As the moon had reached the middle of the giant arched window, Rohan picked up the third tome Cecelie had brought over.

By the time he was onto the eighth, Cecelie opened the library doors.

She made her way to his table, and her eyes widened. "Rohan, don't you need to rest?"

"I'm a daemon; I can rest later. Right now, I have ... hours to find what I'm looking for. Actually, what time does the sun rise here?"

"Around five—which is only minutes away, which *also* means you have been at this all night. Are you sure you don't want my help? You know a librarian is good for more than just opening the door and bringing books over; I also know what's in them."

Rohan sighed. Behind Cecelie, the sky had lightened to a pale gray. "I'm looking for references to a key. Wish you read daemonish; you might know."

"Let me see what books I can find with pictures of keys while you keep reading those."

"Thank you," he said hoarsely. "That would be amazing."

Five hours and one coffee break later, Rohan stood up from the last of the books on the table and stretched.

"Rohan the Red, I've found something," Cecelie called out from deep in the aisles on the upper level.

"Coming!" He took off up the spiral staircase and followed her voice to a shelf at the far end of the library. Cecelie held a giant black leather-covered book, the biggest he'd seen yet.

She handed it over. "Be careful; it is heavily damaged."

"It feels like leather, but rough, maybe from the skin of a karcha—a midlands hellbeast."

"Rohan, is there any book you know that records all the hellbeasts? Appearances, strengths, weaknesses, names, regions—references like that?"

"Nothing holistic, although each realm has its own individual records." Rohan rested the book on the shelf and carefully opened it to the page Cecelie had marked.

And his breath whooshed out. The picture showed a brass key with an ornately twisted bow, shaped into the same form as the tattoo on Rohan's arm that denoted the gates he could enter.

A hellgate key.

Beneath the key, rows of text in a rare daemonish dialect —one so old and uncommon Rohan had only come across it a few times in his life. The text ran end to end on the page.

But his understanding was more than enough to make out the words he needed.

Portal, power, unlock any lock ... solstice. That did not sound good.

He turned the page and read the next text. And reread it.

And this time, his breath did freeze.

Shit. If he read this right, twice a year, the hellgate key would have the power to break through any lock. Any lock at all ... and wasn't a ward just another type of lock?

Oh hell.

"Cecelie, you did it—thank you. But I've got to go." He grabbed the book and ran.

"Wait, Rohan the Red. The alarms—"

As soon as he passed through the library doors, a buzzing ran across his hands, and an alarm shrieked. Shit. Well, hopefully, that would get everyone together fast.

Behind him, Cecelie yelled, but he didn't have time to wait and explain, damn it.

He ran into the hall and skidded to a stop. Eve and a man who was both familiar and a stranger were kissing by the hearth. They broke apart, and Eve turned to Rohan with a smile, but the male grabbed Eve and shoved her behind him.

"Raph, this is him. Rohan—your cousin, well, second cousin." Eve yanked the male's arm and stepped around him. "Rohan, this is Raph. Raph, Rohan."

"Rohan the Red!" Cecelie whacked the back of his head. "I don't know what you're doing—"

"What's going on here?" Warrick's clipped voice echoed from the top of the stairs.

"Hey, morning tea time?" Isadora peeked her head through the doorway at the far end. Then her eyes lit up. "Raph! You're here."

Gray ran in past Isa. "What was that alarm?"

"Good. You're all here. We need to talk." Rohan dropped the book onto the nearest table with a thud. But everyone was talking over each other and no one heard. "Everybody, shut the hell up!"

He took a deep breath. "You all need to hear this." He opened the book and held it up. "See this? This is a hellgate key. One that crossed from Hell to Earth through the Tenth Gate roughly six months ago. Since then, the Tenth Gate has been open for anyone or anything to pass through, including hellbeasts. And there are two very important factors you need to know: first, if I don't get this key back Hellside by the end of humanside solstice, the Tenth Gate stays unlocked forever—and hellbeasts will continue to come through. Second, and this is what just discovered, for those same twenty-four hours, the hellgate key can unlock anything ... including wards. Can you think of any wards that someone like, oh, Lord Forneous, might like to get through? Three gifts ring any bells?"

Eve leaped to her feet. "Oh shit." She glanced at Warrick and Cecelie, and they both paled too.

Rohan nodded. "Yeah, you get it."

"What do you get?" Gray stood too. "And why am I getting a real bad feeling about this?"

"Eve, can you explain why this is so bad?" Rohan said. "Everyone will trust this more coming from you."

Eve swallowed visibly. "A ward spell—like the types of wards we practice here for the Templars and other clients—is technically a magical lock."

"Wait." Gray held up a hand. "You're saying that at summer solstice—which is today—that key will be able to break any ward?"

"Yes." Rohan shut the book with a snap. "From the moment summer solstice commences here in the northern hemisphere, and winter solstice commences in the southern until your planet has spun one full elliptical orbit. As in twenty-four hours."

"What time is the zenith?" Gray whispered.

"Eleven minutes past one." All the color in Eve's cheeks drained away.

"Shit. Anyone know the time now?" Rohan looked around at everyone.

"Ten thirty," Gray said. "Rome's an hour ahead of us, so it's eleven thirty there now."

Rohan's gut sank. "That's less than two hours."

"Rohan," Gray said quietly. "Who has the key?"

"I think Lord Forneous."

Everyone erupted again, and once more, he had to yell for them to stop. "The key is shrouded, so we can't divine for it. But when our best diviner Hellside—Isa and Raph's mother—tried to see the key, all she saw was Cyn. So I had Cyn try to spell for the key. And while she didn't find it either, she did get the sense it was 'close' right before Lord Forneous attacked us. And it makes sense he has it because if the key is shrouded like we suspect, it takes a powerful being to do that—like Simion did for the frankincense." Everyone stared at him with deepening horror. "Yeah. Because Lord Forneous has two out of three gifts already, right? This is bad. Like bad on a level no one here ever wants to see."

"What if he's not going for the gold relic?" Gray asked. "What if he comes for Isa instead?"

"Then we need to divide and conquer." Rohan looked at Raph. "You can control the shadows, right?"

"Yes, but they're not something I can pull out anytime, anywhere. They're dangerous to everyone around them."

"But they can kill a hellbeast. I suggest you stay here and guard Isadora—she absolutely cannot fall into Forneous's hands. I'll go to Rome immediately." Rohan turned to Gray. "We need to let Cyn know."

"The council have an initiation today, so she'll be there now. I can get a message through but won't be able to talk to her until they finish."

"Hell. Okay do it. I need to get to the third gate; that's the fastest way I can travel to Rome."

"I'll get the jet ready. We can fly you to Glastonbury in thirty minutes—and then I'll head to Rome by air and meet you there."

Frigging hell. This was bad. So bad.

29

THE CIRCULAR INITIATION chamber of the Templar's Municipio IX headquarters in Rome had three levels, each with an internal balcony overlooking the center. Wearing her official black-and-red robe over the standard Templar suit and shirt, Cyn stood on the second balcony, shoulder to shoulder with her fellow Knights.

Cyn's mother stood on the top balcony along with the other councilors. Cyn didn't exactly want to catch her mother's eye, but she did gauge her expression for an indication of what was to come ... the clenched jaw and flat gaze weren't promising. Especially at the initiation—this was normally a solemn but special moment.

Every time Cyn had been to one of these since her own, a sense of pride had welled inside—to be part of something bigger and aiding the world in a way that most beings would never see, let alone understand. But right now, it was taking all her willpower to stand there and observe instead of turning on her heel and walking out.

Failure.

As soon as the newly initiated Knight took her sword

and made the pledge, Cyn picked up the floor-length hem of her cape to stop tripping over the thing and exited silently through the door at the rear of the balcony.

Her hearing was up next.

Well, time to face the fire.

Cyn held her chin high and headed straight for the open-air walkway that linked the Templar's original tower and the new extension of glass and concrete.

The council's interview chamber had a cool, power-laden corporate feel, the complete opposite of the ancient round tower, with a large boardroom table, seven high-backed leather chairs, comms equipment, and glass walls on one side that could be blocked out at the push of a button for privacy.

Cyn waited in the alcove by the doorway, thankfully out of sight of anyone else, until the *click click click* of extreme heels over the tile floor announced the first councilor to arrive.

"Mother." Cyn nodded once.

"Cynane. Good, you're early. We have three minutes until the other councilors arrive, and I need to speak with you. Have you or have you not been conspiring with a daemon of ill repute—?"

"What? We're here to talk about the R-104C."

"No, that's why the council is here; I'm here to ask if you've been with a daemon. I understand your role required you to take on the form of a high priestess and integrate yourself into that world; however, you cannot cross over. You know that will negate your vow."

"I'm not crossing over," Cyn said. "And if you didn't want the possibility that I could become fully daemon, why the hell did you have a child with one?"

"For the good of our bloodlines, you know that. Now, if

there is no daemon—"

"Yes, there's been a daemon. But he and I are not a thing."

"Are you certain?"

"Do you want me to repeat everything I say?" Cyn crossed her arms and stared at her mother.

"Fine. No more on that; the council will discuss the R-104C."

"Mother—"

"No. The council is coming. You'll wait here and do not speak until we call you in."

"I know how this goes."

"Then behave as befits a Montbard." With a swish of her robes, Katherine entered the chamber. Well, motherly love had never been her strong point.

The rest of the councilors arrived, robes in place, faces stern, if not outright glaring, as they all shuffled past her without a word.

Great. The silent treatment.

Cyn squared her shoulders, checked her cell one last time—one message. She scanned it fast, and her heart stopped. "Oh shit." Forneous had a way of getting to the relic of gold. And if he got that ... he'd have all three gifts. Together.

Her blood iced over, and she whirled and ran into the chamber.

"Cynane." Her mother stood up. "What are—?"

"No time. Forneous might be—is likely—coming here. He has a way of breaching the ward at the Vatican and getting the relic of gold, so I have to go there now. We cannot let him get the gold. You can chew my ass out later for insubordination or losing R-104C or whatever you want. But as of this moment, I have the three gifts to safeguard."

"It's impossible. The Vatican is secure—the Watcher warded the vault."

"No, listen to me; Forneous has found a way in."

"How do you know?"

"Because the daemon we were talking about? He just told me. And yes, I trust him. Now, am I still in charge of this recovery operation for R-104C?"

"What are you—?"

"Am I. Still. In. Charge? Because if so, I have an op to continue—and all three gifts to contain. So you need to tell me right the fuck now—"

"Cynane!"

"Am I still in charge?"

Her mother's jaw clenched, and the councilors traded looks before her mother nodded. "For now. We will reconvene on your handling of this case after this issue is managed."

"Fine." Cyn refused to acknowledge the relief coursing through her veins. "Call our Vatican rep and clear me to enter the vault. Then I need every available Templar to meet me at Saint Anne's Gate."

"We can't just demand entry," her mother spluttered. "There's protocol—"

"Then get ready to have Hell on Earth. Your decision."

Cyn didn't wait for a reply from any of the councilors, just ran from the chamber.

No time to waste. She fired a message back to Rohan—where was the gate? Where would Forneous come through?

Come on, come on, come on.

No response. Shit. Was he still passing through? She put her earpiece in as she ran and contacted Grayson next. Thank the goddess he picked up first ring.

"Where is he?" Cyn said.

"We just flew him to Glastonbury," Gray replied. "He's coming to Rome via the gates, and he'll be arriving hopefully in about forty-five minutes at the grounds of the Castel Sant'Angelo."

"Thank fuck." Her breath whooshed out. "I'm heading to the piazza now via the armory. Mother is sending backup from the Knights here. How many are in Rome right now?"

"Trained? You've got the council plus one field team of six. I'm flying in with Eve, but we're still two hours out."

"Shit. Well, I'm here. Lucky I've got magic and guns."

"Be safe."

"Yeah, you too."

Cyn hit the armory fast, dropped her cape, and grabbed a case of combo tech-and-magic prototype bombs, and slid two handguns into her shoulder holsters. From there she ran to the basement, dove into the nearest Templar vehicle, and sped over the Tiber River into ancient Rome.

From her vehicle window, the old city gleamed in the beautiful midday sun; people strolled everywhere, adults, children, the elderly ... with no clue what was about to transpire.

No. No way was she letting Forneous get his hands on all three gifts.

Her Templar vow might have been given because it had been expected, but everything that made Cyn who she was screamed with absolute dedication to the purpose behind that vow—to make sure that bastards like Forneous didn't hurt innocent beings through the misuse of the three powerful gifts she and the other Templars protected. And nothing would change her pursuit of that.

She turned onto the main thoroughfare leading to the Vatican and stopped her car on the side of the road as close as she could get—ignored the calls from drivers behind her and people around her—and then ran across the piazza, through the ring of colonnades with their towering statues to Saint Anne's Gate.

Standard protocol—drummed into every Templar—do not cross the gates. The Vatican and the Templars had reached an accord on how they would work together, which strictly forbade the Templars from taking one step further.

But fuck. Cyn was beyond that now. If Forneous came here and she had to get inside to protect the gold, so be it.

And mother of the gods—there were still so many people around. Tourists. Vatican employees and residents. This had all the makings of a supersized clusterfuck.

Okay. First things first.

The Templar field team and the head of the Vatican security met her at the gate, and she bit out orders. Evacuate all civilians. Work with local law enforcement to set a perimeter. Station the team in pairs at each entry point to the Vatican.

Shit. Cyn needed way more people. But this was who she had, so she would make do.

As soon as the Templars were briefed, she put a call through to Eve via Grayson. "What's the spell to pass the ward? I'm the last resort right now if we need to physically guard the gold relic."

Eve precisely relayed the spell and then sent it via message as well.

Cyn took a steadying breath. Checked the time. Twenty-one minutes.

More and more Vatican guards in their formal uniforms streamed into the piazza, and she found the head of their security team—and thankfully, she didn't balk at Cyn's instruction for the Vatican guards to protect the building entries and to leave the piazza clear.

Then the guards closest to the gate looked over Cyn's shoulders and raised their rifles.

Cyn eased her jacket open, drew her handgun—

-《《●》》-

After running into the city center, Rohan passed through the moss jasper Third Realm Gate in Glastonbury and emerged Hellside at the rose quartz gates of the Ninth Realm.

He opened his mouth to shout a greeting to Lord Nostrasus—

Rohan spun around.

The gates were vacant. No lord, no sentries, no one even in the distance beyond the steps and down the cobbled street, normally a bustling place of beings coming and going. In fact, no movement at all.

The hairs on the back of his neck prickled.

But he didn't have time to investigate what the hell was going on; he had to get to Cyn.

Rohan emerged humanside through the Ninth Gate, straight into the lush, green grounds of the Castel Sant'Angelo. Between the canopies of giant established trees, a fast check of the sun's position meant he didn't need to bother calculating time zones to work out how far away the solstice was.

Damn it to hell, they didn't have long.

His cell pinged with messages, and he found one from Gray—Cyn was heading to Saint Anne's Gate to set up base there.

Racking his memory of where to go, Rohan took off

through the grounds, across the river, and wove up and across the streets toward the Vatican.

As he ran, he scanned for any signs of hellbeasts already present, but while plenty of people were moving fast away from the Vatican, there were no screams or signs of terror. Yet.

Was he wrong? Was this not the day?

But the prickling on the back of his neck refused to subside.

No, Lord Forneous wasn't waiting another six months and risking having either the key or the relics taken from him.

Rohan pushed hard and raced through larger and larger groups of people, knocking into one group, but he couldn't stop.

As soon as he reached the first entry to the Vatican, a line of Vatican guards rushed at him.

"Stop!" a familiar voice rang out. "He's with me."

He scanned behind the guards—and his breath whooshed out.

Cyn stood in a black suit and white shirt, earpiece in, shoulder holster in place, with a case at her feet, and looking capable, powerful and totally badass.

Her gaze locked on him, and something blazed in her eyes—relief or happiness, who knew?

The guards let him through, and while there were a million things he wanted to say, now wasn't the time. "I'm here. What do you need?"

"You have your blades?"

"Of course. And I have news. Bad." He filled her in on what he'd seen Hellside.

"And you think they're coming here?" Cyn said.

"I think it's way too much of a coincidence that the hellgate Lord Forneous needs access to, if he's bringing a shit ton of hellbeasts into Rome, is deserted. And I didn't wait around to find someone to ask."

"Then get ready to use those blades." She knelt and flicked open the black case. A dozen black round objects with one flat side—the size of billiard balls—mounted in thick molded lining filled the interior. "You're my lookout while I prep these and lay them out in a ring. Got it?"

"Got it. And what are those?"

"Bombs."

"What the hell? Cyn, you're handling them like they're spinning tops. Shit, be careful!"

"Rohan! I know what I'm doing. They're on a trigger that won't go off until I hit it. Trust me, if an army is going to attack us, we need to lead them where we want. The piazza is perfect, and these will give us an advantage, and frankly, by what you just said, we need all the help we can get."

"Good call."

She took off through the colonnades and into the empty piazza.

"Where is everyone?" Rohan spun around.

"Exclusion zone." Cyn placed the bombs in a circle in the middle of the piazza, and Rohan kept an eye on the time, as well as their backs.

"Okay, these are set. Come with me—" Cyn took off, only to stop so fast he ran into her.

"Oomph." Rohan grabbed her arms to keep her upright after the force of his body slam. "Cyn, are you—?" But something in the way she stilled had him stop and follow her line of sight.

"What the fuck?" she whispered. "What's that?"

Ice flew through him—turned his blood to a frozen river. "That is bad. Very, very, frigging bad."

30

CYN GRABBED Rohan to stop herself from stumbling. Rome's perfect azure sky disappeared as hundreds of black aerial creatures lifted into the air above the Vatican, turning day to night with their massive wings overlapping.

"Flying hellbeasts?" Cyn said. "Mother of the gods, I didn't know they existed."

"They do—and it looks like every one of them is here. And they're carrying daemons." Rohan drew his hellblades; his satchel dropped to the ground. "Cyn, Lord Forneous must be close. He's the only one with the power to control this many hellbeasts. But that means his focus will be on them—making sure they don't turn around and eat the daemons with him—instead of us. We have to find him."

"And not get eaten or killed."

"Right."

"Well, shit. Just a leisurely stroll in the park." Cyn grabbed her cell and made one call. "Gray, confirming attack is on R-104A—not Isa. I'm on mic with the team from here on out." She nodded at Rohan. "Ready?"

"Ready."

"Then let's go." She put up a hand and gestured to her earpiece. "All right, teams. Everyone into the colonnades. We've got bogeys coming in from above. Watch for more from the sides. The piazza is rigged and ready to go. Do not cross the square. Repeat. Do not cross the square."

She joined the Templars in the colonnades, and within seconds, the wave of winged hellbeasts landed, their daemons leaping off their backs.

"Bombs away," Cyn whispered into her mic.

She triggered the spelled devices.

Boom! Boom! Boom! Blast after blast after blast. The daemons and hellbeasts who'd landed or were close to the ground were caught in the explosions, bodies flung, crashing into the pavement and the colonnades.

One smashed into the column beside Cyn. "Fuck!" She ducked to the side and chunks of stone flew everywhere. But the explosions had done their job. "Square clear. Go, go, go!" she ordered.

The Templars emerged from their positions and started shooting at the daemons and the remaining hellbeasts, but their strikes were only slowing—not stopping—the attack.

"Rohan! More hellbeasts coming from the other side, twelve o'clock. Has to be a dozen of them."

"Shit. I'll go. Watch your back."

She just nodded and took a shot at the next daemon.

But there were so many. Another ran at Cyn, and she stabbed her thumb into her hairpin and threw a stun spell at him.

The next daemon came in faster, too fast to call a spell. She shot him twice in the chest and he fell, writhing on the ground.

Shit. They couldn't keep this up for long—they'd be out of ammunition in no time. She whirled around. The

Templars were being pushed back into the colonnades by more and more daemons and hellbeasts.

Across the piazza, Rohan took on the new hellbeasts, but the daemons there were now targeting him.

"Templars, back to Saint Anne's Gate," she bit out into the mic. "Rohan!" she screamed. "Behind you!" She pricked her finger, rushed a stun spell just in time to stop the daemon about to stab him.

Rohan spun to her, and she jerked her chin over her shoulder, hoping like hell he got the message.

And he did because he took off toward her.

She backed up against a column and emptied her handgun, covering Rohan until he reached her.

"There's too many." Cyn reloaded and took down another daemon. "Our bullets aren't stopping them, and I'm running out of magic fast."

"And I haven't even seen Lord Forneous. Fuck."

"Plan B. I'm going for the gold. Can you cover me?"

"I've got you."

Another daemon came at them. Cyn ducked his knife but stumbled and fell over a body at her feet. Her hairpin flew from her hand when she landed on all fours, but she didn't have time to grab it before Rohan picked her up.

"Go!" he yelled. Shit, her hairpin. But she had her earrings.

Trusting Rohan to have her back, she ran for Saint Anne's Gate. Vatican guards and Templars held the narrow entry.

"I'm going to the vault," she shouted. "Hold this location for as long as you can."

Cyn ran down the alleyway to the official entrance— took one moment to check on Rohan, but he was at the entry, fighting with the Templars to withstand the incoming tide of hellbeasts.

Mother of the gods, please let this work.

"Halt!" Two guards and a priest stood at a long desk. More and more guards raced out of the building and past them.

"I'm here for the gold. R-104A!" Cyn said. "You will let me pass."

"*Strega*—" The priest's hands shook as he looked from her to the carnage on the other side of the windows.

"Not a witch. Templar Knight and high priestess."

The priest blanched. "Please understand, this is not how we do things."

"And I don't give a fuck. What I do give a fuck about is the threat coming this way. And you know why?"

"The relic of—"

"Yes."

"Our guards—"

"Are getting chewed up and spit out. So unless you have anyone else here who can hold back a thirteenth-gate daemon or a hellbeast, you will let me through."

"Cyn, run!" Rohan shouted from the doorway.

Cyn spun around. A giant armored thing—oh fuck, a trichorn again—rammed into Rohan and sent him hurtling through the air and out of Cyn's view.

Her heart stopped. But then, through the window, she saw a figure step past the fighting, calm and precise. He had a satchel strapped across one shoulder, and a terrible smile curled his mouth.

Forneous.

She whirled to the priest and screamed, "Now!"

Whether it was the hellbeasts or the daemon or her scream, he yelled at the guards, "Take her."

They both took off, and she followed, racing along a long corridor lined with tapestries and paintings with more and more people running toward them instead of away.

But she couldn't worry about them. Right now, the relic of gold was all that mattered.

They ran down and down and down spiral steps that seemed to go on forever until finally they reached the bottom. A long, dark corridor stretched into the dark in both directions, but the guards took a lantern off the wall and headed to the right.

Cell doors came and went, and down here, there were no sounds of terror or attack; somehow, that made it even worse. What was happening up top? Was Rohan—?

Shit. No. Don't think about him. Head in the game.

The guards stopped at a barred door and handed her a set of keys. "The wards—"

"I know. Stand back and dim your lamp as much as you can."

She dealt with the padlock and pushed the heavy gates open—their grinding screech blasting through the brittle silence.

Shit. If anyone was looking for the gold relic, they'd know where to come now.

With no time to wait, Cyn took one earring and stabbed her thumb.

Once she had enough blood, she called the spell Eve had given her. Please, by all the mother's grace, let this work; she held her breath and stepped into the vault.

Magic tingled over her—uncomfortable enough to make her wince—but she didn't freeze, and no alarm bells shrieked.

"I'm in," she whispered to the guards. "Resetting the ward and lock now. Now you two go—head up the other end and leave the lantern up there—make it look like you're far away. Every single bit of help we can get right now counts."

-«(●)»-

Rohan slammed into a stone wall, and pain blasted through him. His breath punched from his chest. Everything went black.

But he came to in time to see the trichorn stampeding toward him. "Fuck." He rolled to his side, dodged the elephant-sized feet before they smashed where his head had been.

And then a familiar figure strode up the street. Two Templars came running at him, firing their weapons—but Lord Forneous hurled knives at them, and they both dropped to the ground.

Oh hell, no.

Rohan rolled to his knees, dragging himself to his feet against the stone wall. "Stop."

"You again?" Lord Forneous said. "Thought the hell-beasts would've ended you by now, Son."

"Nope, not yet." The trichorn behind him snorted and scrambled to right itself. Shit. He eyed his hellblades on the ground. He must've dropped them when he smashed into the wall.

"I may not be able to kill you with my own hands, but I'm sure a hungry hellbeast or ten will do the trick. At the very least, they'll keep you busy while I see to my destiny."

"If you hurt her, I'll kill you."

"Her? You really do care for this one, don't you? Oh, this

is the best news—you've fallen for a high priestess. Again."
Lord Forneous's lip curled. "I killed your last human lover;
it'll be my pleasure to do away with this one, too."

"You?" Rohan froze. A red mist came over his vision.
"You killed Eleanor?"

"Of course. She had what I needed. And it was even
sweeter knowing your involvement. But then, you always
have had a pathetic choice in lovers. Human, Rohan? Even
though your mother was a waste of power, you're still the
son of two gods—"

"You're not a god!"

"But I will be. Very, very soon." Lord Forneous pointed
his finger at Rohan, and the trichorn reared into the air. Its
huge feet crashed down on his head.

In the absolute darkness of the vault, Cyn forced herself to
inhale ... exhale. Even breaths. In, out. Calm and focused.

Then footsteps, measured and even, echoed outside the
vault. And though she couldn't see a thing, she knew who
was at the gate.

"Ah, my little human halfling, there you are." Forneous's
voice rolled out from the dark. The hairs on the back of her
neck prickled.

"I'm not little. And also, not yours."

"You will be—before I kill you anyway."

"So you must have the hellgate key, then?" Shit. How
long till the zenith? It couldn't be far away now.

"Well, looks like my pathetic offspring figured it out. So
sad he won't see the glorious final result."

"Wha—Rohan?" No. No no, *no*. Cyn's chest tingled, and her lips went numb. "You're lying. He was fighting them off."

"And yet, he's not here. Your lover is dead, halfling. Finally. And you shall join him soon enough. You really would've been better off joining your lot with me instead of him."

Nausea cut through her stomach, but she swallowed it down. *Focus, Cyn.* The future of everything she'd dedicated her life to, and everyone she cared for, came down to this. "If by join, you mean kicking your ass and stomping on your remains once you're dead, then I'm still up for it. But if you mean anything else, I doubt you're a good enough fuck to make that prospect worthwhile. Unlike Rohan. Now, he's quite the lover. And man is he big. Must come from his mother's side, huh, motherfucker?"

"Such a way with words." The humor in Forneous's tone disappeared. "Happily for me, they'll be among your last, and then you'll wish you hadn't mocked me."

"Mock you? I don't think you're worth spitting on. And what's going on? Your key not working yet?"

The slide and click of the padlock disengaging echoed through the vault, followed by the screech of the gates as they swung open.

Shit. Only the ward remained.

"Once I have these three gifts, all of humankind will revere me as their god. And I'll have more dominance than my brother—than any other deity in all the worlds, because you, pathetic mortals, you piles of flesh and bones, have that belief in your hearts that gives us our power."

Without any light, Cyn couldn't see Forneous, but suddenly his breath was on her cheek and his voice sounded at her ear.

The ward was unlocked.

"I shall own you all," he whispered against her neck. Her skin crawled, but she made herself hold still. Needed to let him think he had her while she repositioned the knife earring still in her hand. "Your souls," he continued. "Your minds. Your bodies. I shall bathe in your blood. Eat the flesh from your bodies, fuck the—"

Nope. She'd had enough of this fuckery.

"Blah, blah, blah. You know what? I'm more of a show-don't-tell kinda girl." Cyn sensed where Forneous stood, then grabbed his head and pulled him down as she rammed her knee high. As he dropped to the ground, she stabbed the earring into her neck, cut herself deep. Too deep.

But the greatest magic came from the greatest sacrifice. Power roared through her—more than she'd ever called—even as her blood gushed.

She fell to her knees.

"Blood magic, life magic, run deep, run true. Set in stone that which moves, hinder not what must be used. Freeze, motherfucker," she yelled.

The power of her spell crested—soared out of her, flew on the wings of her draining lifeblood.

And Forneous stopped.

"Yes, I'm going to die, but you're not getting the gold, you bastard." Her whisper echoed into the sudden silence.

Cyn smiled, then the icy sensation of her life seeping away expanded through her.

Please, please let one of her team find them. She'd bought them minutes, maybe—depending on how fast Forneous could pull out of the stun.

For a moment, Rohan's beautiful eyes slipped into her mind—and a bubble of warmth heated her chest, even as that terrible cold inched further through her. Damn. Looked like she did want to love the daemon after all.

Then the cold floor of the vault rushed up to meet her, the last thing she saw before everything went dark was the enraged face of her enemy.

-«(●)»-

Rohan waited ... waited ... the trichorn shuffled. Rohan rolled, then stretched high and drove his hellblades straight through the gaping mouth above him.

The trichorn shuddered and fell.

Fuck, where was Cyn? Rohan lunged to his feet and ran into the building where she'd gone, but only bodies and body parts littered the floor. No sign of his high priestess. His chest tightened.

"Down ... go down." The whisper had him whirl around. An elderly male lay on the ground, injured but alive.

"Where did they go?" Rohan dropped to one knee. "Where—?"

"Corridor, tapestries—to the steps. The bottom floor ..." The man's eyes closed.

"Fuck. Fuck, fuck, *fuck*!" Rohan jumped back to his feet and took off. Corridor ... corridor ... but hell, which one? He took a deep breath.

Cyn, where the hell are you?

In the distance, he saw a tapestry hanging on a wall. Yes! He ran for it—passed more and more bodies.

Tension poured into his chest, and his pulse thrashed so hard it filled his ears in sync with her name. *Cyn, Cyn, Cyn.*

He hit the bottom of the steps. Left or right? A pinhole of light shone off on the left, but ... the hairs on the back of his neck prickled, and like he'd known the moment Cyn had left the Watcher castle, he *knew* which way to go.

He ran to the right. His night vision kicked in, and then a metallic smell hit him. In a doorway ahead, something pale lay on the ground. Gods, no. No, no, *no*. He pushed himself faster. Through the doorway—and holy fuck.

Cyn on the floor. Lying in blood. Eyes closed.

Lord Forneous behind her, reaching for something on a table in the center of the room.

"Lord Forneous!" Rohan raised his weapons. Rage and righteousness and determination that this fucker never blight any world again raged through Rohan.

"No! How did you get away from the—" His sire's gaze locked on the hellblades. "My son, wait—"

"Go to hell." Rohan leaped over Cyn and slashed the blades across his sire's neck. Lord Forneous's eyes widened. His mouth dropped. His head dropped. And then his body dropped, too. "I'm *not* your son."

White-hot energy punched into Rohan's chest, blowing him off his feet. Stole his breath. And it didn't stop—the force expanded in all directions until it consumed every part of him. Sight. Sound. Taste. Smell. Feel.

His mind shut down. The welcome oblivion of darkness beckoned—

But hell, he couldn't give in. He had to get to Cyn.

He rolled to his hands and knees. Forced a breath past the inferno still raging inside him.

Cyn. Cyn. Cyn.

He might not be able to see, but he didn't need eyesight to know where she was. He crawled to her body, and with every inch closer, his senses came back.

And then he had her. Cradled her in his arms.

"Fuck, Cynane." His breath seized all over again, and his

hands shook as he moved her head—oh gods, that was her wound. In her neck. He pressed one hand to the wound, tried to stem the flow, then pressed the other to the good side of her neck. *Come on, come on, come on ...*

The shallowest of pulses beat against his fingers, but gods, she'd lost so much blood.

"Hell, Cyn, come on, princess. Come back to me, baby." He lifted her into his arms, her blood coating him. "Cyn, you're dying. I can save you—but you have to cross over. Do you—do you want that?"

Her head lolled against his chest. Shit—had that been her? Had she nodded?

Rohan took off, running two steps at a time back up the main floor. Up the corridor. Out the main doors. People yelled at him to stop. Vatican guards, Templars. He ignored them all. Then a familiar figure ran at him.

"Rohan," Raphael called out. Dirt and blood streaked the other male's face, and more blood ran down his arms.

"Guard the vault," Rohan shouted as he raced past the other male. "No one touches Forneous or the relics."

Keeping one hand on Cyn's neck, trying to preserve whatever blood she had left, Rohan ran faster, harder, through the Castel Sant'Angelo grounds and to the rose quartz gates of Hell.

But had Cyn made the call to cross? She had. He knew it.

So he passed through and kept going and going and going until he reached the Thirteenth Gate's obsidian arches.

"Please, fucking hell, *please* let this work." As soon as he crossed into the Thirteenth Realm, he fell to his knees, laid Cyn on the cool marble, and pressed a hand to Cyn's neck again. Come on, princess ... come on.

Her heart beat. The wound on her neck closed over. But her eyes stayed closed.

Footsteps coming up the steps had him leaping to his feet; then, his cousin Nicasia emerged from the mist. Rohan dropped back to Cyn.

"She's alive," Rohan whispered. He stroked the hair back from Cyn's face.

"Leave her with me," Nicasia said. "Your uncle needs to see you. You did it—you saved the human world and ours. Go on now; I'll look after her."

"I can't."

"You have to. This can't wait, Lord Rohan. You have assumed your sire's power. And there is much to be done at this very moment to ensure those daemons still running riot in the human world do no more harm. They'll respond to you now. They are yours."

"I don't fucking want them."

But Nicasia just shook her head, even as she knelt beside him and ran a hand over Cyn's hair.

He stopped and stared at Cyn's perfect face. Gods. He'd come so close to losing her. And now, here she was—tied to him, to this world—forever. What if she hadn't wanted this? Had he been selfish to make that call on the basis of one motion?

"You did the right thing," Nicasia said.

He hauled in a breath, drank in Cyn's face. "I hope so." The urge to press a kiss to her lips, to inhale her scent, before she opened her eyes and possibly hated him for eternity surged through him.

"Come," a voice he knew better than his deceased sire's ordered directly into his mind. *"Return to the Eighth Realm."*

And as powerful as Rohan now was, he wasn't going to disobey that command.

His last sight of Cyn, as he stepped backward through the obsidian gates, was of her lashes lifting. Her gaze locking on him. Flat. Cold. Hate-filled. Unflinching.

Well fuck. His heart stalled. He may have saved Cyn's life, but that look said everything else—he'd lost her still.

31

When Cyn opened her eyes, a beautiful woman with familiar eyes knelt beside her.

"Where is this?" Cyn sat up and turned around. Holy shit. Two massive black gates rose high, high, high into the sky.

"The Thirteenth Realm of Hell," the woman said.

"And you are?"

"Nicasia."

Cyn pushed the name through her memory. Still nothing. "And am I dead?"

"No, you crossed while your heart still beat—although, I daresay, had you come through a second later, that would not have been the case, and this conversation would be taking place in a different realm."

"So I'm not dead. Then ..." Fuck. Fuck, fuck, fuck. "Did Rohan bring me through?"

"Yes, I thought you saw him—before he left."

"No, the last face I recall seeing is Forneous. Shit! Forneous. We have to go—"

"Shh, calm yourself. The former lord, Forneous, is deceased. Lord Rohan killed him. With your help."

"Holy shit." Cyn reeled for a moment. "Rohan killed his fath—sire?"

"Yes, and then he brought you here to save your life."

"Where is he now?"

"I don't know where exactly, only that he had to go as there are ... urgent matters requiring his attention."

"And how long have I been here?"

"A minute, perhaps two." The woman smiled, and that's when Cyn made the connection.

"You're Isa's mother—right?"

Nicasia's eyes lit up. "Yes, how did you know?"

"You look alike. Even Raph looks like you. Same stunning eyes and dark hair."

"Well, thank you. I think I'm rather happy Lord Rohan the Red brought you to us."

"Um, great, but since I'm not dead—and I've only been here for several minutes—I have to return to where I came from. To Rome, I mean. Is that ... possible?"

"Of course. Are you healed?"

Cyn took a cautious breath. "No pain at all. Not even ..." She rubbed her neck where she'd stabbed herself.

"Excellent. In that case, yes, you can leave. But do you *realize* what you are now?"

Cyn's belly churned, but she lifted her chin and nodded. "I know. And I'll deal with that later. Right now, I'm still a Templar—" Shit. Was she still a Templar? Well, she'd figure that out later too. "And I have a job to do. The three gifts need to be made safe once again."

"Of course. You'll find Rome through the rose quartz gates. And Cynane? I look forward to seeing you again."

"Thank you, and honestly, as out of the world all this is, me too."

Cyn took a breath and stepped between the black arches. Charcoal mist surrounded her, but then a set of green arches appeared. She kept walking, and more arches came out of the mist: black opal, red agate, and then a white crystal with long black shards—they had to be sodalite. And finally, arches in a soft pink.

Rose quartz without question.

She stepped between them, the mist disappeared, and the human world was there.

Green grass. Blue sky. City air. Sirens blaring in the distance.

People were still running away from the Vatican, but Cyn took off and ran against the flow. Everyone gave her a wide berth; some looked at her with horror. One person grabbed her arm—she shook them off—the blood covering her wasn't an issue now.

She got to Saint Anne's Gate and stopped short.

So many bodies. Templars and guards. Daemons and hellbeasts.

But none of those walking appeared to be out to maim or kill. How had such a ferocious battle ended so fast?

She grabbed the nearest Templar. "Status of R-104A and C?"

"In the vault. A contract operative is guarding it after they"—the woman's skin paled—"took out a lot of the daemons."

"Are any councilors on site?"

"No."

"Then I'm assuming operational control."

"Thank you, sir. We're in ... disarray."

At least they still recognized her as one of them. "I want

an update on wounded and a rep from all relevant local law enforcement agencies. Then I need a direct line to the council. I'm retrieving the R-104 relics now and will return in ten minutes."

"Is that safe—?"

"Yes. The individual behind this attack is neutralized. Convey that to the council when you make contact."

Cyn set off, and this time, no one stopped her.

"Raphael," she called as she approached the vault. Last time she'd been here, she couldn't see a thing, but now … what had once been dark was just various shades of light.

"Cynane," Raph said. "I'm in here."

She took a deep breath and went inside. Blood covered the floor, and on the table were R-104A and R-104C. And one tiny seed of myrrh—R-104B.

Her breath whooshed out. Thank you, mother of the gods. "Where's Forneous?"

"Rohan was here only minutes ago, and collected his hellblades and Forneous—both bits of him. He asked me to stay here and guard the relics."

"And since we're both in here, the ward is still down?"

"Yeah, looks like Eve will have to redo them from scratch," Raph said.

"In that case, I'm taking all the relics with me."

"Where?"

Shit. Good question. But there was only one place Cyn could think of right now.

-‹‹‹●›››-

It took two hours of arguments with the Templar Council to get full agreement on the temporary housing of the three gifts at the Watcher castle because while Eve had arrived in Rome and could redo the ward, the consensus was that the Vatican needed to focus on its people and repairs, not any further potential threats.

Even then, the council had refused to let Cyn continue as lead on R-104C and had only agreed to the Watcher castle option when Grayson confirmed he'd assume responsibility for all relics until a permanent home was arranged.

They had also grudgingly agreed for Cyn to remain on to assist Grayson, but she didn't care. Getting out of Rome right now was all that mattered.

Her mother hadn't even met her eyes before she and the council had closed their chamber doors and continued planning their handling of the "incident" as it was now being called.

The flight back to Cheshire was spent planning out options for the three relics' protection, and at least with Eve, Raph and Gray, no one seemed to mind Cyn being part of the team.

But also, none of them asked her about crossing over and becoming fully daemon. And if they had, what would she even say?

She was happy to be alive?

But when Cyn got back to the castle, Isa, Simion, Aleesha and Sonja, Warrick, and even Cecelie were all waiting for them in the hall.

And after the hugs and the tears and making sure everyone was physically unhurt, Isa stood up and demanded they all tell her everything that happened.

"If we're doing this now, can I get coffee first?" Cyn put her hand up.

"No, you cannot get the coffee." Isa slapped her hand on the table. "I'll get the coffee for you as soon as you start talking."

"You know you're awfully tiny to be this bossy." But she smiled at Isa. "Okay, this is what I know ..." She filled the group in on everything and found herself hugging Isa when it came to talking about Isa's mother. "And that's it. When I came back, Raph was in the vault with the three gifts, and then Gray and Eve arrived. Someone else will have to fill you in on what happened while I was gone."

"Wait." Isa put her hand on Cyn's arm. "So you're a full daemon now?"

Cyn nodded, and suddenly her mouth went dry. She'd thought they'd known ... Would they feel differently toward her now, like the council?

"Well, you'll run fast now from any more hellbeast attacks," Eve said dryly.

Cyn couldn't stop a laugh from escaping. "Really? That's what you have to say? What about the rest of you?"

"You're still our Cyn. Don't think going from a halfling to a full daemon is going to change that." Gray smiled at her. "And believe me, the council will figure that out soon. They just need time. Now, Raph? Tell us your part."

"I got to the Vatican as Rohan was bringing Cyn out. She was ... you were ... clearly needing help. He told me to guard the vault. But to get there, I had to get through a fuck-load of daemons and hellbeasts, so I got the Templars to help move all the guards and Knights out of the piazza, and then I called the shadows. It didn't take long," he added in a quiet voice. "Twenty minutes after I got down to the vault, Rohan ran in, picked up the body and head—"

"Wait, body and head?" Isa's eyes went wide.

"Uh, yeah. Rohan decapitated him."

"Oh." Isa went green.

"It was the only way to kill him, Isa. And there's not much more. Rohan ran out, and not long after, Cyn returned."

"Oh wow." Isa suddenly stood up.

"Isa? You okay?" Gray stood too.

"Yes, sit down. I just remembered something. When I trapped Forneous in the vision realm, Grandfather said, 'Only the blood of the blood through great sacrifice can wield that power.' So, Cyn, you gave the greatest sacrifice with your lifeblood. And then Rohan—the only being in the entire universe who was blood of blood—killed Forneous. Holy shit, Cyn. Only you and Rohan, no one else, could've taken Forneous out."

Much later, after they'd gone over and over the details, and Eve had done temp wards for the relics, and everyone was so tired not even coffee was keeping them awake, Cyn looked around the hall.

What an amazing bunch of peeps.

Butterflies started to buzz in her belly, and she pressed a hand to the unfamiliar sensation before she could catch herself. Well, shit. This was her family. This complex mix of individuals who truly didn't care whether Cyn was a high priestess, a Templar, a daemon—or, in her case, all three. They just cared for her like she cared for them.

Somehow, she'd gone from having no friends, no one she'd willingly call family, to a table full.

Although ... there was one member of their family missing.

32

Two months of running Hell—or being responsible for decisions regarding the running of Hell—was almost as bad as facing a stampeding trichorn at full pace.

Well, almost.

Rohan had moved his interviews and audiences from the cold castle in Hell City to the tavern at the Tenth Gate.

At least he could base himself in any of the thirteen realms since he wasn't responsible for a specific gate.

And he felt closer in the Tenth Realm to Cyn—even if it was just in his mind.

But was Cyn even there, still at her LA shop? How had she acclimatized to life as an immortal? How were the Templars treating her now? Had she secured the three gifts somewhere safe?

In what had become a habit, he rubbed the back of his neck—and tried to ease the perpetual burning urge to travel humanside and find her. See her for himself.

"You can go and see her, you know," a warm voice said from behind him.

"Nicasia." Rohan turned around and smiled for the first time in weeks and weeks. "What are you doing here?"

"I'm on my way to see Raphael and Isadora." The hope on her face made his chest contract. "But right now, I'm here for you." She patted his arm, then gestured for him to sit. "I've heard good things from the lords of the gates about your work here."

"I'm just helping with their questions while they right their realms."

"Ah, but without those answers, the lords who aren't so scrupulous will make up the rules as they please. In fact, your predecessor seemed happier that that was the case."

"I'm nothing like him."

"And we're grateful for that," Nicasia said. "Well, I need to get going—are you sure you don't want to come with me?"

"No, you go; I don't have a reason to be there anymore."

"At least walk me to the gates."

Rohan saw Nicasia off and found himself staring at the agate gates. The itch along his neck burned harder than ever. He could pass through and run to LA in no time. And see for himself if Cyn was—

The air between the gates shimmered with an incoming arrival. He stepped back, and Cyn strode through as elegantly as if she was strolling on a sidewalk, not stepping into an entirely new land.

Thigh-high black boots, skintight denim jeans, a stunning gold jacket, and her crescent moon tattoo glowing brightly on her forehead.

His breath whooshed out, and he couldn't move—couldn't speak—

"Well, Red, I came here to find you, but can't say I expected you to be right here."

"Cyn." His words came back to him. "Or is it still High Priestess?"

"Either or." She looked behind him and her eyes widened. "This is Hell?"

"You don't remember from last time?"

"I didn't see anything last time." Cyn took her time looking around. "It looks like a medieval village or something."

"That's about right—for the Tenth Realm, anyway. Is that why you're here? To see Hell?"

She blew out a long breath, then turned back and met his gaze. Gods, but she was beautiful. Still. No, even more so. And of course his cock went hard, and his blood began to heat.

But her gaze didn't leave his eyes, and he forced his attention back to her words.

"So, how does this work? I understand from Raph, that since I went through the Thirteenth Gate, somehow, I'm tied to that gate—likely through you."

"Yeah, you should be limited to the Seventh Gate— where your sire is from—but it turns out I have the power to change daemon hierarchy. I guess subconsciously, I just needed you to be in the Thirteenth Realm—it was the only place I could think of to keep you safe while you healed, so now you're ranked as a Thirteenth Realm daemon."

"But you can still ... control me?" Cyn grimaced, and his heart ached for her at that.

"Yes," Rohan said, "I can't stop that. It's a function of Hell."

"Exactly how does 'controlling me' work?"

"Technically, if you don't do as I ordered, I could compel you."

"So I could either be controlled by you or the devil?"

"Yes, but I would never—"

"Stop." Cyn shook her head. "I get it; sometimes the way things are is the way things are." She swallowed hard like she had something in her throat. A feeling he knew all too well. "So, is there anything you ... need from me right now?"

Need? His body went into hyperdrive. He needed Cyn. But more, he needed her to want him.

"No. Well, yes, I have to know one thing—no, please, if you *want*, tell me one thing. When I took you through the Thirteenth Gate and left you with Nicasia, you looked at me in that moment as if you hated me more than anything. Like you wanted nothing to do with me. I swear, that's why I haven't come to you. I thought you never wanted to see me again. Is that ... is that the case?"

"No. Mother of the gods, no. When I called the lifeblood spell, the last thing I saw before everything went dark was Forneous's face. I came to wanting to punch his teeth out, and at first, I thought he was still there. I didn't even see you."

Rohan's mouth went dry, and the tension that had weighed on his chest for the last two months released so fast he almost wobbled.

"So you don't hate me?" he whispered.

"No! Mother of the gods, no."

He tried to scramble his thoughts together—but this was the last thing he'd expected to hear. "What ... what do you need? Is there anything I can help you with? Are you ... still a Templar?"

"I'm not *not* a Templar. But they're adjusting to the fact that while I took a vow, you now have control over whether or not I stay true to that promise, which they don't like."

"I would *never* use that power on you." Forcing Cyn to do his bidding? Oil slicked through this gut. "I can promise—"

"But you could go back on your promise. I even thought about a binding contract, but you could just order me to cancel the contract on my end. No, it's okay. You saved me, Rohan, and the three gifts."

"What about your ... immortality? Do you hate me for that?"

"No! I wanted to live. Even though I called that lifeblood spell and knew—well, thought—I was going to die, I did that as my last option to save the human world. Of course I wanted to live. And while I don't recall anything between calling my spell and waking up in the Thirteenth Realm, I do know I would've said yes. And maybe that makes me a bad Templar, and I'm sure there are some who'd have preferred me to just die—"

"Bastards."

Cyn smiled, and that tilt of her lips made his heart clench. "Yeah. Bastards. But remember, they have a job to do, too."

"So, if you're not *not* a Templar, what are you?"

"Right now, I'm a high priestess who reports to the council every week to confirm I haven't received any instructions from you." She shot him a look. "Is there anything you would like to relay to the Templar Council?"

"Ah, no—wait, yes. There is, in fact, one thing. But are you saying you could be a liaison between Hellside and humanside?"

"Is that an order?"

"No. Hell, no. I told you I'll never order you to do anything."

"Why? You have the right—according to the laws of Hell, anyway."

Rohan couldn't stop a sigh and had to shove his hands all the way into his pockets to stop from reaching out and hauling her into his arms. "Cyn, I miss you. I miss you so damned much. So I'm doing this for you. Because I love you. Nothing has changed about the depth of my feelings for you in the past two months."

"But I can't be with you, Rohan. You and your uncle have a power over me that I can't accept."

"I can cede my power over to him—"

"And he can give it right back, can't he?" Cyn shook her head. "I'm sorry, more than I realized—I came here, hoping to find there was some kind of option for us, but now ... Love or no love, I can't do that."

His loco heart started to beat a wild dance in his chest. "So you do love me?"

Her cheeks went ghostly—but her eyes blazed that electric blue that told him her emotions were charged.

"Rohan. How could I not? I sold myself this story that I wasn't looking for love. But it's been right in front of me from the moment I saw you at the club back in LA. That night, I felt you the moment I entered the club, and then I saw you—and you scared me then because I think I already knew, you call to me on this level so deep, so integral to who I am, that it would be a risk to my Templar vow. And I didn't think I could allow that. Risk that."

"So what changed?"

"When I was in Rome, before the attack, I realized that the vow I believe in comes first, but that I don't have to be a Templar to live that vow. You were right; I have never embraced who I really am. I hid my sacrificial magic. And then I tried to limit it. But in the end, it was only by embracing that magic that I stunned Forneous. And you helped me see that, Rohan. You pushed and pulled and forced me to confront the truth of who I am. A powerful daemon with sacrificial magic who vows—regardless of the organization I'm affiliated with—to help protect our worlds from dicks like Forneous. And that's why ..." Cyn's cheeks tightened, but she held his gaze.

"You can't be with me."

She nodded, and the misery in her expression made his heart clench all over again.

"Then wait for me," Rohan blurted. "Wait for me to find a way out of this—this binding between you and me. Please?

"I have to—don't I?"

The sadness in her eyes made everything in him hurt.

-◀◀◉▶▶-

Cyn helped Aleesha and Sonja put the final touches of their additions to the fall equinox buffet on Simion's finally remodeled pool deck.

"Looks good, ladies. Want a sneak taste before everyone arrives?" Cyn stepped back and did one last check. "We've got cheese-and-olive bread shaped like witch's hats, spiced pumpkin cakes, and chocolate-rum spiders. Just don't tell Chef—he confiscated the last lot of additions I made to one of his buffets."

But they both just smiled and sat on the daybed, hand in hand, resting against each other.

"I have a feeling I know why you protect the frankincense tree. It helped you find your love, didn't it?" Aleesha beamed, and Sonja smiled. "Wow, can't say I blame you. Seeing your love for each other is a beautiful thing."

A familiar emptiness panged in her chest, but she'd gotten good at ignoring the increasingly regular sensation in the last four months. So she forced a smile for the two women who were now part of the permanent protection of R-104C in the Watcher's castle grounds. "I know you can't stay long in LA, but one day, you're going to let me know how you communicate since you never speak."

"Cynane?" Simion called out from inside. "Someone is here for you, dearest heart."

"Is it Jaz?" Cyn's client hadn't batted an eyelid after finding out about her asshole ex's demise in the jaws of a hellbeast, and when Cyn had introduced Jaz to Simion last month, the love whisperer had made it his mission to find Jaz her true love.

"Nope, not Jaz," Simion called out.

"Someone for the party, then?"

"No, definitely here for you."

"Don't eat all the spiders." She traded looks with Aleesha and Sonja, but they just shrugged. "Coming," she yelled back.

She turned around and her breath jammed in her throat.

Rohan.

He stood beside Simion, still inside the house, wearing jeans and a black polo that revealed the marks running up his arms. Were there more marks than before? And it wasn't just the tats that were different. His eyes were flat, their twinkle extinguished. That pang shot through her.

"Ro ... Rohan." Damn. She cleared her throat. *Do not crack again, voice.* "Good to see you."

Truth. It was so good she wanted to run at him, wrap a silk rope around him and never let him go. She balled her fists at her sides to keep from doing just that.

"Cynane." His cognac voice made goosebumps roll up her arms like it had the night of the trichorn attack.

"Aleesha, Sonja, perhaps you could help me in here?"

Simion jerked his head in the most unsubtle move. "Thank you, lovelies."

"May I join you?" Rohan asked when Simion, Aleesha and Sonja had disappeared to who knew where.

"Sure." Cyn rubbed her suddenly sweaty hands on her black jeans and walked over to the railing overlooking the city lights far off in the distance. "So, how's Hell going? Isa told us you've been working pretty hard and that everyone's happy to have you there."

"There's been a lot to do. A lot of injustices my ... predecessor put in place that needed to be righted."

A jumble of butterfly wings picked up in her belly, and Cyn interlinked her fingers to stop from doing something batshit, like grabbing Rohan and kissing him senseless.

"I heard you met your father?" Rohan said.

"Yeah." She smiled at that memory. "It was good. Odd because I met him here, and my mother came." She shook her head. "I won't say we're a family, that's not the case by any means, but we talked, and I'm happy to have his guidance when it comes to the new side of my life."

"And what about the Templars?"

"Still working through the potential for me to act as a liaison. But I'll never be a full Templar Knight again. And I'm ... coming to terms with that. The one good thing is that I'm fully practicing sacrificial magic now and really learning what it—I—can do. So that's been an unexpected upside. But is that why you're here? I didn't think you were coming to the party—Isa said she'd invited you but that you couldn't make it. I have to say this because you're making me edgy here."

"Me making you nervous? Cyn, I'm freaking out."

"Why? Wait—is something wrong? Did you come to order—?"

"I'm not here for anything to do with a command or an order," Rohan said. "Please, can we just sit?" He gestured to a daybed.

She sat. "Okay, go ahead."

"I know you can't stand the idea of being controlled by me."

"Not just by you. By anyone. I gave a vow to the Knights, at first because it was expected, but it's something I now believe in utterly. What happened at the Vatican made me see even more how important that promise is; only I can't make that vow my first."

"What if you could?"

"What? Not be a daemon?"

"No, that's done now. But ... I spent every moment of my spare time in the last four months looking for a way. And there is one option. I went to my uncle and petitioned him to remove you from the binding placed upon you when I crossed you over."

"How is that possible?"

Rohan held up a necklace with a tiny spinning orb inside. "This is a fragment of the universe when the universe was born. A minute piece, so small that even though it shines so brightly, it's actually smaller than any human could detect. But if you wear this, keep this on you, you'll have the power to say no to me, to anyone in Hell. Even the High Lord."

"What?" She froze, then slowly reached out and touched the pendant. "Are you serious? But why did he give me this?"

"Because I told him the truth—that I love you and want to see you happy. And I know your vow is more vital than anything else you'll ever do. So I suggested that if we did this, we could *ask* you to act as a liaison between the worlds —Hell and Earth. Make it harder for fuckers like Forneous to ever get so close to utter disaster ever again. Uncle was open to that idea. He also agreed on the provision I take control of the hellbeasts—all of them."

"You did this for me?"

"Of course."

"How do I know if this is real?"

"Easy. Kiss me."

"What?"

"I said, kiss me."

The urge to press her lips to him surged through her, and she'd pecked him on the lips before she could stop herself. "Shit. You—I—"

"Yeah. That was a compulsion." He held up the necklace.

"Fine, hand it over. But if you try anything—"

"No tricks, I promise."

Pinpricks of sensation danced over her skin as she rested the pendant against her chest.

"Kiss me again." His eyes glittered.

Cyn took a deep breath and waited for the batshit-ass urge to do as he said ... but none came. Oh shit. He'd done it. He'd found a way.

She launched into his arms and kissed him with everything she had—but crap, Rohan wasn't kissing her in return. She leaned back. "What's wrong?"

"I swear, my uncle told me the pendant would work. Fuck." Rohan ran his hands through his hair. "I will find a way to make this work—"

"Stop, Rohan." A bubble of warmth filled her heart, and damn it all, she had to blink the moisture out of her eyes. "I kissed you because I wanted to."

"Really? It worked?"

The hope in his expression made her throat clog up, and she nodded.

"Thank fuck." A fierce light entered his eyes, so brilliant she couldn't look away. "Because I have to tell you this, Cyn. Four months ago, when you came to the Tenth Realm, you asked what I needed. You, Cynane. I need you. Nothing else even begins to fill me. And if any other fuckers like Lord Forneous, hell, if anyone ever comes for you again, I'll hunt them down and cut their heads from their bodies every single time."

Cyn's breath caught.

"Come on, Cyn, give me a chance to show you how much I love you—how much—"

"Stop." Cyn launched at him, cradling his cheeks. Held his glowing gaze as she found her words. "Rohan the Red, love of my life, I'll happily stand by your side and freeze the butts of any mofo trying to hurt you. And if you need to go corral hellbeasts, I'll be there for that too—although, I'm not riding any bareback."

"Wait. You said the L word. Simion would be so proud of you."

"Yeah, well, don't tell him this, but he may have made me realize that I wasn't dealing with a severe case of heart-burn all this time."

"Cyn. My princess and high priestess. Gods, but I love you. And just saying, it didn't take any fancy-ass love whisperer to know it. So I'm claiming one-up on this occasion. But I love you too. Forever."

"So what next?" Cyn said.

"I think that as the emissary to the Courts of Hell on behalf of the Templars, you'll be spending a bit of time Hell-side, right?"

"Looks like it. What did you have in mind?"

"Well, I need to take you on a tour of our world—it's not all nightmares and darkness like humans have made out.

Although ... there are special places where my uncle does his work. He still has a job to do and all that."

"And what about when I'm working humanside?"

"It would be nice to have somewhere to crash together ..." Rohan paused as Cyn pressed her lips to his. "So, it's you and me, then?" he whispered into the kiss.

Her heart filled to the point it might take off and fly out of her chest. "All the way, Red. All the way."

"Well, I have a favor to ask."

"Already?"

"Can I drive your 'stang?"

"You want to drive my baby?" She broke the kiss and pushed back. "As if."

"I'll let you tie me up in silks."

Warmth immediately pooled low in her belly. "Well, in that case ... but you better be good to her, or I'll hurt you."

"Always."

EPILOGUE

EVEN THOUGH SPRING had well and truly sprung around the Watcher castle when Cyn and Rohan arrived to celebrate the equinox with their family, she couldn't help but chafe her hands as they walked up from the gatehouse.

"I swear these Watchers make it freezing on purpose." Cyn linked her arm in Rohan's. "Here, keep me warm. This is cold even for daemons."

"How about I keep you warm in another way ..." He stopped and pulled her to him. His lips melded over hers, and she forgot all about the temperature—

"Hey, you two. Save it for after the bonfire!" Eve's voice rang out. "Everyone's meeting in the garden at the back of the castle, and we're just waiting ... on you."

"That witch has the worst timing," Rohan muttered against her lips.

Cyn laughed and gave him one last nip. "I'll make it up to you later. Come on, let's go see our family."

Eve and Raphael stood in the doorway to the castle, their arms around each other. Cyn smirked when they joined them.

"Hey, Eve? Is that a hickey on your neck? Looks like we weren't the only ones enjoying a pre-bonfire smooch."

"I swear someone busts us every time we try to sneak away for a few minutes. Raph's been gone for a month. Like four entire weeks. Of course I was kissing him!"

"So, who busted you last time?" Cyn asked as the four of them walked through the hall and out through the conservatory to the garden.

"Isa." Eve rolled her eyes. "She was bossy before Mischa, but now she's a tiny general. Watch out if you're a second late."

"Speaking of, where is the baby?" Cyn glanced around. "I haven't seen Mischa in two weeks."

"You mean my *niece*." Eve said with a smug smile.

"I'm claiming honorary aunt title, just so you know. And have they identified any daemon traits?"

Eve's eyes brightened. "Isa thinks Mischief—"

"Mischief?" Cyn scowled. "Is this a nickname and no-one told me?"

"Apparently Gray's started it. Anyway, Mischief is exhibiting some preternatural awareness already—especially when it comes to milk time or cuddles. Like she'll have her arms already raised when Isa looks over to pick her up."

"Oh wow, we are gonna be able to teach that kid so many cool things." Cyn rubbed her hands together.

"They're going to try and out-crazy each other in the loco-aunt department, aren't they?" Rohan said over Cyn's shoulder to Raph.

"And these loco aunts are right here, Red." Cyn arched one brow. "Watch out or you'll be on the receiving end of some loco-aunt magic."

"Cyn! Rohan—you're here! And you're fifteen minutes

late." Isa sat with Gray, who held Mischa cradled to his chest, with the proudest smile on his face Cyn had ever seen on him.

"Told you," Eve murmured.

But Cyn just laughed; she'd take this loco-ass family any day.

Well after the flames had burned low, the equinox rituals were completed, and everyone had headed inside for what was left of the night, Cyn grabbed Rohan's hand and held him back.

"Come here." She pulled him to the log they'd used to sit around the bonfire.

"Don't have to tell me twice." Rohan sat down and pulled her into his lap. "Any chance you're up for another ... outdoor ... experience?"

"Hell yes!" She laughed. "But not yet."

"We're not having bonfire sex, then?"

"Later, Red. I promise. But right now, I have a gift for you. However, it needs a drop of your blood."

"I have to bleed to get a gift?" Rohan tilted his head and looked around. "Is this a high priestess prank or something?"

"Yes, I need your blood. And no, smartass, no prank. Now, do you want this or not?"

"Sheesh, yes."

"Hold out your hand." Cyn used her hairpin to prick his skin.

Then she opened her knockout ring and held his thumb so the blood dripped into the salve.

"What are you up to, princess?"

"I'm making you immune. You made me an equal with my choices, so I'm making you my equal too. I'll never be able to knock you out again. And ..." Cyn withdrew a new silver ring from her pocket. A pale green crystal in the center gleamed in the firelight, and she swiveled the crystal around to reveal a hidden compartment just like hers. She added a rub of the mix from her ring to the new one. "This is for you. I made it myself—apart from the peridot stone. That came from lava deep within a volcano."

"You made jewelry for me?" Rohan said.

"Yes. Yes, I did. Only fair since you gave me a necklace."

"Cyn. My Cynane. I have no fucking clue what I did to deserve this. To deserve you. Because you have made my entire existence make sense. I love you, Cyn."

"Right back at you, Red. Now, about that outdoor sex ..." Cyn reached into her other pocket and pulled out two lengths of red silk.

The End

ALSO BY HM HODGSON

Relics and Legends

The Three Gifts Trilogy

A Relic Of Magic And Gold

A Relic of Magic And Myrrh

A Relic Of Magic And Frankincense

Novellas

A Wreath Of Thorns

The Immortal Keepers

Book 1 The Last Keeper

Book 2 Keeper Of My Heart

Book 3 Keeper Of My Desire

Anthologies

Mermaid Kisses

THE LAST KEEPER

Looking for more steamy, witchy, paranormal romance? Then read on for a sneak peek for The Last Keeper, Book 1 The Immortal Keepers.

A waning crescent moon disappeared behind storm-fueled clouds as India Jones shut the hotel room door and sagged against it. The bed was right there ... five short steps away. She just had to force her legs to take them.

Mustering the energy to move, she pushed off the door —and her stomach growled. Of course. Because she hadn't eaten since ... she scowled, when *had* she eaten? She forced her fatigue-fogged brain to think.

Huh. She'd stopped for petrol before the border, over four hours earlier, and had grabbed something greasy and quick to eat. She eyed the bed. Her belly growled again.

Food first, then sleep.

Except, right then, all-too-familiar goosebumps prickled over her arms, and the fresh green scent of her magic tingled in her nose. Her stomach dropped. *Oh crap, what next?*

She pushed off the door, darted into the small bathroom and grasped the edge of the chipped cabinet.

A dash of icy water hit the back of her hand. She jolted, automatically looking up for the leak.

A torrent of water smacked into her face.

Adrenaline shoved through her and she yelped, spluttering. What the hell? Shielding her face, she tried to make out what had to be a bloody big gaping hole in the ceiling of the tiny bathroom.

Except—the ceiling was perfectly normal.

India stifled another cry as more water poured down, echoing the driving rain from the storm outside. Holy crap, the storm might as well have been inside, beneath the perfectly fine-looking ceiling.

Shit, shit, shit. *Not again.* She needed a spell—needed something to stop this screwed up magic.

A knock sounded at her hotel room door. Her heart rammed inside her chest. *Oh no, uh-uh.* No way could anyone come in here.

She darted a look around the small room—towels, she needed towels. Lots of them. But first she had to stop the rain. If only she knew the spell for that. But, crap, India didn't even know the spell to make it start.

Then the rain ended as abruptly as it had begun.

The knock sounded again, slightly louder.

"India, this is Simone, the manager here." The muffled words filtered through the door. "I just checked you in."

"Ah, hi," India called out across the room. She swallowed hard, tried to calm her racing pulse. "Just a moment."

"No worries. I've brought you up an extra blanket. And I know the room's small, but I hope you find it okay."

Okay? *Okay?* India's chest rose sharply beneath rapid breaths. She swallowed and turned around.

The bathroom was covered in water, the small square tiles slippery beneath her boots. The once neatly folded and fluffy white towels were now lumpy sodden messes. Water-logged carpet, where the bedroom floor met tile, squelched underfoot as she took a step toward the bed.

No, the room was not okay. *She* was not okay.

Though, thankfully, the water seemed contained—mostly—to the bathroom.

India tiptoed to the door, her dark hair plastered to her neck and shoulders. She slicked the long bangs off her face. With a deep breath, she opened the door a smidge and peeked out from behind it, making sure her drenched shirt and jeans were hidden even as she forced a smile.

Sure enough, the woman who'd checked her in earlier stood there, a thick woolen blanket folded in her arms.

"Hi," Simone said. "Hope you don't mind me coming up, but it gets chilly here at night, even in autumn, so I've brought you an extra blanket. And since the kitchen's closing soon, if you're hungry, I can take your order so you don't miss out on a hot meal."

India blinked. The easy, genuine smile on Simone's face was almost soothing, but India couldn't let her guard down. And she couldn't take the blanket without displaying her wet sleeves. "Thanks for the blanket, but I'll be fine. And I'm happy to come down to order something to eat."

Simone tucked the blanket under her arms and chuck-led. "No way, that's not how we treat visitors in the country. And hey, any chance you're related to Liz Jones? I source some of my produce from her and heard through the local grapevine—it's a reliable source of info here in town—that her granddaughter was visiting."

Butterflies took flight in India's stomach. She shifted her feet and ran a hand over her hair. The damp material of her sleeve brushed against her cheek, and she dropped her arm fast. But Simone's gaze only moved over India's hair.

"Oh, wow, you were having a shower," she said. "I'm so sorry for interrupting you. How about I save you a plate of tonight's special? It's chicken schnitzel with mash. The mash is made from Liz's potatoes."

"Um, that'll be great, thanks. I'll just finish up here and then come down." India managed to keep the smile on her face until Simone left. Closing the door, she sank against it.

Her grandmother—"Nan" to the family—was the reason India had reluctantly returned to her childhood home. Nan was India's only hope of understanding her magic. No way would she have come back otherwise.

Because, holy crap, did she need help with her magic!

Order The Last Keeper now to read more about The
Immortal Keepers and the battle
for the World Tree.

THANK YOU & REVIEWS

Dear Reader, thank you so much for reading A Relic Of Magic And Frankincense.

If you enjoyed Cyn and Rohan's story, can I please ask that you leave a review (even just a rating) on your favorite reading platform? Every review helps me continue my dream career as a writer.

FREE EBOOK GIVEAWAY

Can a cursed Merprince blackmail his way out of a fairytale nightmare?

Read now to enjoy this Beauty and the Beast retelling!

Download your free ebook now by joining my reader group at

www.hmhodgson.com

ACKNOWLEDGMENTS

Bringing A Relic Of Magic And Frankincense to life has been both a pleasure and a challenge, however without question, this book would not be here today without the help, advice and time of many people. And it's to these wonderful peeps I want to say thank you.

Henry, Indi and Chance, my wonderful loves who are there every step of the way, often helping with little (and big) details with my stories.

My sister Julie, one of my earliest and constant sounding boards from the beginning to the end of the story. Mum for reading the first draft before anyone else sees it. Dad for reading the final product with his eye for detail, and in particular with this book his knowledge of all things 1800s naval history (any errors made here are totally my own!). And then my family in general, for the many, many chats about names and places and words and cover images.

And then my writing family ... I am fortunate enough to be surrounded by wonderful writers whom I adore. Lou, Jo, Jacqui, Mel, Jen, Tanya, Samara and Renae. Thank you for your support, encouragement, time, eye for detail, and some of the funniest GIFs a writer could ask for!

In terms of the book you've just read, my utmost thanks, appreciation and love to editors Sarah Calfee and Jo Speirs who both go way, way, way above and beyond the call when I hand over my very rough words to them. And then to Amanda Pillar whose brilliance brought Cyn and Rohan to life on the cover.

ABOUT THE AUTHOR

Award-winning Brisbane author, HM Hodgson writes about wicked romance (steamy scenes a must!), intrigue and magic. Magic that moves worlds and takes her to another place.

In 2021, HM Hodgson won the Romance Writers of Australia First Kiss competition with the first kiss scene from her novel, Keeper Of My Heart, as judged by producer and director, Tosca Musk. Hodgson also won the Australian Romance Readers Association award for Favourite Continuing Romance Series 2022 with The Immortal Keepers.

When not writing or reading or daydreaming about her next literary hero, you can find her sipping coffee and eating chocolate (more often than not at the same time).

Keep in touch with HM Hodgson at: www.hmhodgson.com

THE END

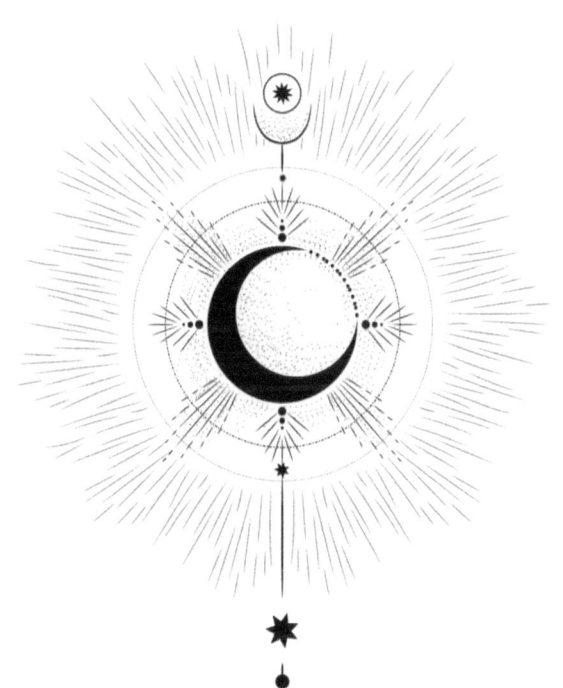